RED
TIDE

IRMA VENTER

Translated by Karin Schimke

CATALYST PRESS
EL PASO, TEXAS, USA

Published by Catalyst Press.
www.catalystpress.org

For further information, write to info@catalystpress.org.

In North America, this book is distributed by
Consortium Book Sales & Distribution, a division of Ingram.
Phone: 612/746-2600
cbsdinfo@ingramcontent.com
www.cbsd.com

Originally published in Afrikaans
by Human & Rousseau in 2015.
First published in English by Tafelberg in 2022.

10 9 8 7 6 5 4 3 2 1

ISBN 9781960803139

Library of Congress Control Number: 2024942086

GLOSSARY

Aga: A coal stove once popular on South African farms

Bakkie: Pickup truck

Biltong: Raw, dried beef

Braai: Barbeque, cooking meat on a fire

Dominee: Reverend

Ja: Afrikaans for yes, but used widely by almost all South Africans as an affirmative

Karoo: Semi-desert located in the southwestern part of South Africa

Karretjiemense: Poor, itinerant farmhands, often found traveling from farm to farm looking for seasonal work in donkey carts, or "karretjies"

Kraal: A pen for holding sheep or other farm animals

Nastergalkonfyt: Black nightshade or sunberry jam

Stoep: Veranda, porch

Tannie: Aunt or auntie, used in Afrikaans culture to refer not only to a family member but also to an older woman, normally as a sign of respect

Oom: The male version of tannie

Tik: The drug methamphetamine, especially in a powdered crystalline form

Veld: Grassland

Velskoene: Rugged lace-up shoes, traditionally brown or tan in color, made from leather

JAAP

1

It had rained before she died. An unprecedented amount for July but, then again, who understands the weather these days? The rain fell incessantly from heavy, dark clouds for three days. At first, the parched earth drank the water gratefully, but it was soon sated.

Water had begun to dam up by the sheep pens, then at the barn where the old light-blue Nissan Diesel truck had stood for years on flat tires and with an equally flat battery. When it had reached the house it pushed through the kitchen, leaving a muddy trail from the back door to the front entrance, over the stoep, and down the stone path to the garden gate.

The rain gathered in the pan—or rather, in the middle of the veld that had become a pan—between the flat-topped hills and the telephone poles, thick with dense nests the sociable weavers had built, pooling around the single big tree on the plain where no one picnics beneath the twittering dun birds anymore.

A cross made from tambotie wood stands there now.

Every year it is newly varnished.

It was quiet on the morning of her death, as though the whole Karoo was holding its breath for the rain to wear itself out. And it was freezing. Lungs burned from the icy air and clouds formed with every breath exhaled. The farmers who'd come to help find her shuffled around on the stoep in their muddy boots in a frozen waltz to try to stay warm, standing with their hands tucked into their armpits, heads bowed, hats off.

Uncomfortable. Worried. Angry with whoever had taken her.

But it was her father who'd discovered her when he'd gone out for some fresh air. The house had been full of women with endless theories about what could have happened, and he'd just walked out into the veld, the morning's third cup of coffee in hand.

He found her alone on the plain. The newly formed pan was still slightly frozen from the night before. It cracked underfoot, making fine spiderwebs as he carefully inched closer to the red bicycle and the figure who lay there on her side, half—exactly half—of her trapped in the muddy ice.

The old post-office bicycle wasn't hers, but he recognized the wedding dress. The white fabric was torn off high up her thighs, but the long lace sleeves were intact. She'd fetched it in town the morning before from Mart Visser, ready for the following Saturday.

No one knew where the red fabric trailing behind the bicycle had come from. The deep-red velvet had been spread about five meters across the pan, like a wedding train.

Or like wings, perhaps.

It is the eyes that reveal that you are dead. That you are gone. The color seeps out, as though the windows have been shut, the front door closed and locked, everything packed up. Abandoned for good.

Her father had dropped his coffee and crouched down beside her, frantically trying to dig her out with his hands.

It almost looked like she'd fallen over while riding the bike—high-heeled black ankle boots still on the pedals—and had stayed there, a dazed look on her face, as though her lack of balance surprised her.

She was wearing old World War I pilot's goggles and the left eye—the one above the ice—was open.

If you'd taken an aerial photograph, it would look as though she were riding the bike, her fingers still clutching the handlebars.

After her father had tried in vain to breathe air into her lungs, he'd taken off his jacket and covered her with the thick sheepskin. Then he scrambled home and shouted for someone to call an ambulance.

The paramedics arrived quickly, but eight, nine hours too late.

Janien Steyn was dead.

Janien Steyn was my godchild.

2

I pour some coffee from a flask and blow on it out of habit even though it's already cooled down. It's been over an hour since I pulled the Corolla over next to the plain with the tambotie wood cross to wait here in the bitter July weather.

Every year I grow more uncertain about what I'm waiting for. Inspiration perhaps, or a new idea about what might have happened to Janien.

"You still here?"

Obie comes and stands next to me, leaning against the car, pipe in his hand. His shoes are wet from the shortcut he's taken from the farmhouse through the veld.

"Vonnie wants you to come and eat," he says when I don't answer.

Obie and Vonnie Steyn of the farm *Lekkerkry*. "Joy."

You'd imagine that meant they'd live here happily ever after with their three children. Here in the Great Karoo semi-desert, just on the other side of Carnarvon in the Northern Cape province of South Africa.

But neither of their two boys wants to farm, and Janien was their only daughter.

Obie draws on the pipe, only to realize that it's dead. "It's been almost three years, and still nothing. What does Isak say?"

His eyes are locked on the horizon, where a pale chanting goshawk circles in the sky.

He looks everywhere except at the cross with its white roses.

Isak. Not Sergeant Slingers from the South African Police Service.

It took a long time for Obie to call Isak by his first name, which is probably understandable when someone imagines you capable of killing your own daughter.

It also takes time to believe that maybe the police did everything they could to track down the killer. But this tends to happen only when the rage has slumped into despondency and then into impotence. An acute, terminal presence you try to make peace with. And then, if you're lucky, you can finally give yourself over to the depressing routine of the everyday and manage for two, three minutes at a time not to think about what happened.

I know this. Being in the police for years teaches you about helplessness.

Obie takes a box of matches from his shirt pocket. Lights one. Struggles to get his pipe going again. "Any new thoughts about what happened?"

As always, he asks me out here, in the open, where Vonnie can't hear.

No idea. None whatsoever. But I don't say that.

I know the facts off by heart. All the facts, not only those that appeared in the newspapers and on the websites, regurgitated for months and then forgotten, overtaken by other acts of violence.

Vonnie called me the morning it happened, crying hysterically. I dropped everything in Pretoria and came here. It came as a shock that the case was only the investigating officer's third murder. I'd hoped for someone with more experience. Isak Slingers and Janien had gone to the same school. Granted, he was four years older than she was, but he was still wet behind the ears. A mere child.

I tried to help, until he chased me away.

I'd probably have done the same. I was a know-it-all, convinced that, with all my experience, I'd be able to solve the case. I'd elbowed in, pushing and shoving where I had no right to interfere. Stepped on Isak's—and everyone else's—toes.

The case was thin on fact. Vonnie and Obie had been braaiing at their prospective in-laws in a big pre-wedding do, like most of the people in the area, and had only got home late that night.

Janien and her brother Leon had stayed home. He'd dropped his girlfriend in town earlier that day and had come back home to watch the Springbok—Australia rugby match with her. He didn't like Janien's fiancé, Henk van Staden.

Leon said he'd gone to sleep early. He and Janien had watched TV until he'd turned in, and he hadn't seen her again after that.

Nothing had been stolen from the house, and there were no signs of a break-in.

The only clue was a few boot prints frozen into the ground of the pan. Size ten, or maybe eleven. According to the depth, probably a man of reasonable bulk. The row of tracks exiting the pan, when he was no longer carrying Janien, reveals this.

Isak suspected Leon. He wears size ten shoes. But so do I, and so does Obie and Obie's neighbor, and Janien's husband-to-be. And all of our shoes would have been caked in mud, because it had rained for days on end.

There was no sign of blood or a struggle on Leon or his clothes, or anywhere in the house. The inside of his left upper arm was bruised, but Janien always pinched him there when he teased her. And he'd been teasing her endlessly before the wedding.

I turn to Obie. "I still don't have a clue what happened. It's driving me mad."

"Are you going to look around her room again?"

"Yes."

"You know Vonnie wants to pack it all up and set it on fire. She's been preparing the site since last month."

"The ditch at Janien's tree? I saw it when I went for a walk yesterday."

Janien tried to climb that tree, about a hundred meters from the house, for the first and last time when she was four years old. She and Vonnie'd had a fight and she'd run away.

My sister was up until late that night cleaning Janien's wounds.

An acacia thorn is a bugger, especially when you've wormed your way up the branches to get away from your seething mother.

Obie nods. "That's the place, yes. I think it's a good idea, so does Dominee Tiaan. Vonnie just can't bear to look at Janien's room every day anymore."

"That means I have one more chance." I finish off the last bit of coffee in my cup. "And then I should probably also let it go."

3

Janien's room looks the same as it did last year and the year before. One wall is painted black and covered with photographs. The remaining walls and bedding and curtains are white. The many scatter cushions are blood red with black birds flying toward the window.

When Janien painted the wall black one Friday night, Vonnie immediately had Dominee Tiaan come over. She was fourteen, and Obie and Vonnie suspected the worst: some kind of devil worship. Janien told them they were being silly. She was going to put up photos—all of them taken with her phone—and black provided the best background, she argued.

The cellphone had been a gift for her thirteenth birthday, though Obie had been dead set against it for ages. But Vonnie's argument —that Janien could call them from boarding school whenever she wanted to, and that she needed the phone for her own safety when she did sport on weekends—won out in the end.

Janien made few calls. Instead, she used her phone to take pictures when she wandered around on the farm. In town, too, where everyone knew her by her skinny legs and long black hair. Carnarvon, the town in the middle of nowhere that had suddenly begun to draw attention from Europe to Australia because of the Square Kilometer Array radio telescope that was being built here.

Janien had been very excited about the SKA project, although quite a number of people in the area were still skeptical about radio telescopes studying the galaxies. It was, Janien had said, technology art: looking into the unknown and trying to define it.

Her very first exhibition was a collection of photographs and conversations with people from the sparsely populated Northern Cape about what it meant to survey the universe.

She'd started with Oom Geel Koos and Tannie Queenie, karretjie-mense she'd got to know when she was still little. All the SKA meant to them was that Geel Koos might find employment there one day. He was forty-four years old, though he looked seventy.

He died two years later. His lungs just gave in, Tannie Queenie had told Janien.

I sit down on Janien's bed, as I did last year and the year before that. The same single bed she'd had as a child, then as a student and, later, as a guest visiting from the city. Even after she and Henk had decided to marry, she'd slept here alone when he stayed late and had to stay over, because that's how Vonnie and Obie preferred it.

But you'd have to be blind not to see the truth.

Janien was twenty-six when she died—one of South Africa's most promising young artists, according to the newspapers.

Pity they'd never said that while she was alive.

I straighten my right leg as much as it is willing to move. My knee hurts like hell. Must be the cold. I'm used to Pretoria and its moderate winters. I rub my leg as I survey the room again.

A lot has changed in here since Janien's death. She could never pack anything away, but Vonnie had always left the messy room as it was. Now she cleans it weekly and makes sure everything is in its place.

The police searched Janien's room several times—first Isak and his team, and then a specialist forensic team from Cape Town.

Obie still refuses to come in here.

I once caught him standing at the door. Doing nothing, just standing there as though he was looking for something. Finally, he'd turned and walked away.

Vonnie is right. Maybe it is time to pack everything up and burn it to ashes.

Almost everything.

I haven't told her yet, but I'm here for Janien's computer and her phones. Isak had given Vonnie everything back from the evidence locker. There was nothing useful on them. He'd made it sound like he hadn't yet given up hope, but I knew he had. You just never say that to victims' parents.

I have a plan for the PC and the phones. It's only the vaguest of possibilities, but after three years, it's better than nothing.

"No."

I know that tone—Vonnie's not going to budge.

"I just want the computer and the phones," I try again. "Including the phone Janien got when she was thirteen. Nothing else."

Vonnie sweeps her hair out of her eyes and plunges her hands into the dishwater again. "Eat up and give me your plate."

I put the last bite of bacon and egg into my mouth. "Vonnie…"

"No."

"Please."

She wipes her hands on her apron, walks over and takes my plate. She's younger than me. Fifty-six. Ma had the three of us nine years apart each. The oldest, Douw, died of a heart attack two years ago. Yvonne—Vonnie—the youngest, had been a surprise.

She tucks her curls, which have been dove-gray for years, behind her ears. I know this gesture too: her patience has run out. But I don't want to let go.

"I met someone last year. She has a friend who can help us. Someone who can search in places the police can't."

Vonnie dumps the plate in the sink, scrubs loudly enough for me to hear.

I drink coffee while she finishes washing up, she doesn't like help when she's doing the dishes. No one does it as thoroughly as she does, and she's the only one who knows where everything goes.

I watch her as she dries and packs away the cutlery, then the crockery.

Janien's death stole every soft curve in her body, hijacked her joy in broad daylight. The cheer has only recently begun to shine through again. Obie Junior's wedding in Johannesburg early next year has brought a fresh smile to her face. And Leon's wife is eight months pregnant.

They've wanted children since the day they got married, not long after Janien's death. It's as though Leon wanted to make his mother happy again by giving her a new little life to focus on.

When the last of the dishes are packed away, Vonnie unties her apron. I can see she's considering my request, although she doesn't want to admit it. She is wary of false hope. The ditch she has dug with so much care is waiting. That, at least, is definite and certain. Materially there. Real.

She frowns and rubs her nose. It's our father's nose, just like mine. Squarish. Slightly too big for a woman, but attractive on a man, if my first school crush was to be believed.

She folds the apron and asks, without looking at me: "Who do you know all of a sudden that might be able to help?"

"Her name is Sarah. I want to take the computer and the phones to Pretoria for her to have a look at."

"No."

"Vonnie…please."

She keeps quiet for a long time, then says: "This Sarah woman can come here."

"I can't…"

"I don't care. It's Monday. You have until Friday. No longer."

"Okay. That's fine. Thank you."

I'll take what I can get. I have no idea how I'm going to get Sarah Fourie here, but I'll make a plan.

"And remember, Jaap, I don't want to know a thing. Until you can give me a name, until you can say it was him or him or him, I don't want to know anything."

SARAH

1

The KTM 690 Enduro is tired. Like me. Five months to the Ngorongoro crater, past the Victoria Falls, Kariba and Lake Malawi. Back again.

I had to get away after my father's death. People either kept talking around what happened, or buried it under an avalanche of promises that it would get better with time.

Talk, talk, talk. It was like no one could shut up.

The long kilometers salvaged my sanity. Your mind switches off when you have to struggle over roads that are hardly more than a faint line on the ground. When you leave behind your tablet and laptop—the internet and its tools so intent on locating you wherever you are.

There is no silence when you close your front door in the noisy center of Pretoria, only less noise. Silence happens when you get into your sleeping bag in the bush and switch off the flashlight and the dark envelops you. When no cars drive past and no bright advertising boards try to sell you anything. When no one speaks or laughs.

Those first few nights under mosquito nets in tents or in simple rooms at cheap lodges, the darkness had parked itself on my chest and I had struggled for breath. It was as though the night had become a sweaty wrestler pinning me to the ground. An hour or two later, after the silence, after the waiting and the listening to the sound of nothing, the night's inhabitants would finally arrive, and I'd hear lion coughs and the hyenas' shrill laughter.

I got used to that too, the way I got used to the silence. Slowly. Eventually.

And now, today, the city's noise is overwhelming. The traffic, the people on the streets, and the sound of text messages, emails, likes, calls, and updates. Ping, ping, ping. More, more, more. Now, now, now.

I last heard from my mother three weeks ago. I somehow lost my phone charger at a campsite in Zambia and never bothered replacing it.

Now I wonder whether she's ever going to talk to me again. My brothers and sister might not either.

My father always called me his favorite, but only late at night, when we were alone and working on the Aston—a silver Aston Martin DB5, like the one James Bond had in *Goldfinger*.

But I was not to tell anyone he'd said that, he'd whisper, as we shared a cigarette in secret.

I suspect he said the same thing to all his children.

We shouldn't have smoked. Emphysema is a bitch.

I haven't smoked for 67 days. I last lit a Marlboro in Arusha. I was staring at the snowy peak of Kilimanjaro and called my father's number to listen to the message on his voicemail.

If it's about a car, send a text. If it's one of my children looking for money, you have the wrong number.

I walked into the night and cried, and then smoked another six cigarettes. Started the return journey to Pretoria the next day.

These days I drink Coke and rooibos tea as if there's nicotine in it.

I leave WF Nkomo Street and turn the KTM into the Acacia Flats driveway.

Take my helmet off and drag my fingers through my hair. I had it cut short in a little roadside shack just outside Musina, because I wanted it off before I traveled further north. That was almost five months ago, and the hair is feathering around my ears again.

I've decided to leave it like that for now. It'd drive my mother insane if I showed up at her house without hair.

Her house. Not their house.

Progress.

I pull my glove off and place my right thumb on the access scanner to get into the gate.

A car door slams behind me.

I look for the source of the sound. Motorbikes are hijacked as often as cars in Pretoria West these days.

I immediately recognize the tall, slim man with the bony, wire-hanger shoulders. The slight paunch. The dicky right knee. The pale-blue eyes and the smile that says you should trust him.

Impossible. What's Jaap Reyneke doing here? He's a friend of a friend—a good friend. A detective who helped her in the past.

I do a quick mental calculation. Do I owe him anything? No, not that I remember.

"Evening, Sarah. Ranna said you'd probably be back this week."

He sounds tired. And his creased clothes, smelling faintly of sweat, look as though he's been sleeping in front of the gate all week.

I switch off the motorbike, swing my leg over the orange machine with its specially lowered suspension. Stuff my gloves into the helmet and look at my watch. It's seven o'clock, Wednesday evening.

Why would Ranna have told him when to expect me? And how does she even know? An educated guess? Or is she tracking me somehow?

"How long have you been sitting here?" I ask.

"Since Monday night. Well, probably Tuesday morning."

"Why?"

He looks down at his brown lace-ups, his hands stuffed deep in the pockets of his green bush jacket. A cold wind is ruffling his straight gray-blond hair.

"I tried calling, but Ranna said you stopped answering three weeks ago, when you were on your way back, near Lusaka...I'm sorry about your father."

Strike one. For the sorry. No, make that two. The police thing counts against him too, even if he is retired. I am, after all, a convicted hacker.

I suppress a yawn. "What are you doing here, Jaap? I'm tired and dirty. I want to shower and go to bed."

"I need your help." He steps closer and then checks himself, as though he remembers that I don't like strangers standing too close to me.

Anyone, in fact.

"What help?"

"Something important. I have R35 000. I can pay you."

That's a lot of money for a retired cop. An honest one, at least, according to the background check I've done on him.

"What if I don't want to help?"

"Then I'll pitch a tent out here and stay until you say yes." He shrugs. "I'm sure your clients will appreciate having the police so close by. You know, to look after their interests."

"That would only piss off the other tenants."

"You own this entire building."

Shit.

"You wouldn't dare."

"I have all the time in the world. More than you can imagine." He smiles, shrugs.

"I'll freeze all your accounts."

"Go ahead. I don't have much more than that R35 000." His eyes take on a steely glint.

I look to the heavens.

Sigh.

Doesn't sound like I have much of a choice. My clients aren't necessarily big fans of the police and, by the looks of it, Jaap Reyneke is willing to sleep in his car for quite a while longer.

I hook the helmet over my arm and gesture for him to follow me through the gate.

Maybe I'm just tired. Or stupid. Maybe the months away in the bush have made me soft. Or maybe my head is scrambled from the fall on the KTM near Mpulungu.

I get back on the bike and switch it on. Feel the reassuring thrum vibrate through my body. I wonder for a second whether I should race off, but then I drive meekly through the gate.

Stupid, I decide.

That's the right answer. That's all I am. Bloody stupid.

2

"Take a seat."

Jaap looks up and down the spacious open-plan apartment before sitting down stiffly.

The place is dusty and airless after being locked up for so long. I go to the kitchen and switch on the water heater and the plugs, open the windows for fresh air. The mid-week evening noise drifts in from the street below.

I put my backpack on the coffee table and take out the milk and tea I bought at Spar on the way home. I've missed milk more than anything this past month.

Ice-cold, fresh, full-cream milk.

I concentrate hard not to look at the row of computers lined up against the wall as I walk to the fridge, look out of the windows instead. At the bright lights of the city center and the other apartment blocks here near Pilditch Stadium in Pretoria West. At the corner shop, whose red Coca-Cola sign you can just make out if you stand on the tips of your toes in the corner of the kitchen.

I missed being online. Too much almost. Missed it like other people miss their lovers and family.

"Make us some tea," I tell Jaap. "I don't have coffee. I'm going to shower."

Twenty minutes later I wrap a rough towel around my body. Bliss. My own bathroom. A strong, steady stream of hot water.

But the walls are too close. And there are too many of them.

I sit down on the bed and look at the woman in the mirror.

Tanned and sinewy after the long months on the road. You have to be strong enough to pick your bike up if it falls over. You can't ride something you can't put back on its wheels on your own. Neither can you pack anything you can't carry yourself. I learned that quickly enough.

I muss my hair, which is sticking up in every direction. Rub my eyes. They always look greener when I'm tanned. I have my father's eyes and my mother's husky voice and unwavering logic, says my dad.

Said my dad.

I should look different after his death, shouldn't I? But I look the same. Short. Red hair. Twenty-five, even though I feel much older.

"Tea's ready," Jaap calls from the kitchen.

I get up and pull on a T-shirt and jeans. It's time to find out what brought the retired policeman to my door.

"Janien was my goddaughter."

Jaap takes a photograph from a yellow file and puts it on the coffee table in front of me.

I look at the image of the woman in the short black dress and boots. Black and red socks to her knees. Red ribbons in her shoulder-length black hair. Her mouth is a deep darker red. She is looking directly at the camera, flirting like Marilyn Monroe years ago, hands on her thighs and her lips in a playful kiss. A densely built-up city forms the backdrop, cars and motorbikes driving by in a street on the left of the image.

"How old was she when she died?" I ask.

"Twenty-six. The photo was taken a few days before her murder, three years ago. She died on the twentieth of July."

I pull the photo closer and drink some of the rooibos tea Jaap has made. Wish it was a Coke.

A cigarette would have been even better.

"So? How am I supposed to help you? You were the policeman. The detective colonel. You probably did everything you could to find her killer. You're pretty obstinate, if I understand correctly."

"Stubbornness doesn't help when you don't have any concrete leads."

"Nothing? No DNA, no suspect?"

Jaap's eyes are bloodshot. Has he really been sleeping out there in the street for so long?

"The last activity on her phone was a call to her fiancé, a few hours before her death," he says. "According to him, she called to talk about her dress and to say that she hoped he enjoyed his evening. There was a big braai on that night. Cellphone records show that he was on or near his parents' farm when Janien called. After that his phone was off. He says the battery was flat."

"So you think he killed her?"

Jaap holds up his hand. "That's not what I'm saying. The best clue we found was a bloodstain on her dress, in a fold on a part of the dress that was buried in the mud. But, as there were no obvious suspects, we couldn't take anyone's DNA to test it against."

He rubs the photograph thoughtfully. "Most people in town think it was some vagrant high on tik. We're pretty sure it was a white man—that's what the DNA suggests, even though we can't use that information in court. The science of DNA and race and ancestry still needs some work. Or that's what the white coats tell us anyway."

"Find a way to get the fiancé's DNA."

"Not that easy. He left town and he doesn't trust me. And, besides, it was the weekend before the wedding. As I said, there was a big braai that evening at his parents' house, which means that everyone has alibis, him included. The only person without an alibi is Leon, Janien's brother."

"Then it must be him."

Jaap shakes his head heftily. "Janien was his little sister. He adored her."

"Then it was a robbery gone wrong. Or a junkie, as you said."

"Not the way Janien was dressed."

"What do you mean?"

Jaap takes out another photo. "She was in her wedding dress, on her side on a bicycle, on a frozen pan, with this blood-red train of fabric, easily five meters long, spread out behind her."

I look at the picture. "Weird. Why? What statement is this supposed to be making?"

Jaap leans back in his chair. "I don't know. No one is sure. I've looked everywhere. The forensic psychologist I spoke to thinks the murderer is a white man of between twenty and forty. Someone who knew Janien. Probably someone who was angry about her imminent wedding. He said it was a strange murder, even for South Africa. The effort. The bike. Everything." He shakes his head. "Not that his information helped me. A good forty men in that age bracket were expected to attend the wedding. Everyone in the district was going to be there, and some of Janien's friends from Cape Town."

I finish the tea. "It sounds like you've done everything you could. What do you want me to do?"

He crosses his arms and looks at me. "Janien was a little like you."

"Me?"

"She was mad about computers."

"Everyone's mad about computers these days."

"No, she wasn't on Facebook and Twitter or whatever all the time. She was a digital curator. She had a fairly successful website where she exhibited new art—work out of Africa that she considered important. And people could buy the art, as I understand it. The site got a lot of attention, especially from German and French galleries and clients. And some big international companies setting up shop in Africa."

"Okay. Interesting," I concede. "But that's miles away from what I do. I write code, do a bit of programming, and data mining. Dig around where I shouldn't. Nothing illegal," I add hastily.

Jaap puts the photographs back in his folder. "That's why I'm here. I need your help because the police say there's nothing on Janien's laptop."

"Impossible. No computer has nothing on it."

"Okay, nothing of importance. One email address with mostly business mail. That's it. But where's all her personal correspondence?"

"She probably had a tablet. And she most definitely had a cellphone."

"There was no tablet, and her phone doesn't reveal much. Just a WhatsApp account where she chatted to her friends and her fiancé. No second email address for personal messages, and almost no text messages. You know, SMSs."

"That's a bit strange, but not at all impossible. Not everyone emails their friends. And who still uses SMS? Did you look properly?"

"Yes."

I get up. It's been a long day and I'm exhausted. "Then it's on the laptop. Look again. Look harder. Maybe it was wiped. The police should know that data can very seldom be completely erased. Even you lot aren't that stupid."

He frowns at the insult.

I don't care.

"We tried to recover the erased data, but Janien knew what she was doing," Jaap says. "There are only fragments left and we... the police can only spend that much time and money on one case. That's why you need to take a look. Search Janien's computer and phones, find what we missed. I'm sure you'll find a lead I could follow. And, as I say, I'm willing to pay."

"Are you sure that's all you want? Or do you want me to do something illegal? Dig around where the police aren't allowed to look? Because I won't."

He rubs his nose, lifts his bony shoulders in a slow, tired motion. "No, that's not what I'm asking. Not at all."

I don't want to give in. "And if there's nothing to find? If your colleagues were right and there's really nothing on that computer?"

"Then it is what it is, and I will have to accept it."

There's a desperation in his voice that suggests otherwise. And I'm not sure I'm in the mood for this mess.

"Jaap…"

"Please, Sarah." He looks up, his pale blue eyes pleading with me.

I shake my head, closing my eyes for a moment. Then I gesture toward the file, his car out on the street. "Leave it here and come back in a week. I'll take a look as soon as I've slept for a few hours."

He shifts around in his seat. "It's a bit more complicated than that. The laptop is at the farm. Janien's mother wants to burn her daughter's stuff this Friday. It's her final goodbye. She wants to get rid of everything that reminds her of what happened in some sort of funeral pyre. And she wants to do it before the anniversary of Janien's death."

"It's Wednesday now. Evening."

"Exactly." He looks at me hopefully. "It's the last chance I will ever have to know what happened. Please, come to the farm."

I curse Jaap.

"Where's this farm?" I ask.

"Other side of Carnarvon."

"Where the fucking hell is that?"

Turns out you head southwest from Pretoria to reach Carnarvon.

I open up the KTM so that the dust of the dirt road fans wide in my wake. I've been riding for hours. First the N1 highway to Kimberley, then toward Douglas, Prieska, and finally down south toward Carnarvon.

The farm *Lekkerkry* is just past the town, on the road to Vanwyksvlei, according to my phone's map app.

It's not bad to be on the open road again. On the contrary, it's quite nice. But I'm smart enough to know that I'm just putting off looking my mother in the eye and apologizing to her for disappearing like I did. And I know I'm simply stalling fetching my dogs from my older brother and having his wife ask me ten times if I'm all right. Really all right.

Lekkerkry's old white farmhouse is on an incline. The stoep in front of the house is long and wide, and a neat stone path winds toward the front door. The day's last light reflects off the row of windows staring out at the plains. A line of high, thin trees buffers the house on the western side.

Where's Jaap? I don't see his Corolla.

If he's not here I'm leaving. I'm not in the mood for strangers. No. I'm not in the mood for people, full stop.

But it's too late to run. Someone's seen the bike's dust trail or heard the engine. Probably the latter. The KTM's roar is loud in these wide-open spaces. A grayhaired woman appears on the stoep, wiping her hands on her white apron.

I park the bike under the line of trees, kick out the stand and get off. I remove the helmet and rub my hair, stand there indecisively.

The woman stuffs her hands in the pockets of her apron. She looks like my mother. Past fifty, hands always busy. Shoulders that have started to stoop from a lifetime of physical work. Nice hair, though. The gray curls are soft around her sharp features. Sharp chin, bevelled cheekbones.

She finds my eyes, but I can only hold her stern gaze for a moment.

Must be Janien's mother. Jaap's sister.

I busy myself with my bags. Where the hell is Jaap? I take off the gloves and unwind the scarf tucked in under my black leather jacket. Hitch the backpack over my shoulder and the helmet over my forearm, take the sports bag in my left hand.

The woman turns toward the front door and calls: "Jaap, she's here!"

I walk to the stoep and put down the sports bag.

"Hi."

Then I remember my manners. "Good afternoon. You must be Mrs. Steyn."

She shakes my hand warily. "You can call me Tannie Vonnie."

"Thank you," I say uncomfortably. I don't like saying tannie. I call my own aunt by her name.

I wonder if it's the motorbike that makes Vonnie's voice so tight, just like my mother's sometimes. Or maybe it's the short hair, or the heavy black knee-high boots. Maybe it's the torn jeans. Take your pick.

Tannies have never really been too fond of me.

Jaap appears in the doorway, a white linen napkin in his hand.

"Come in," he says. He looks from Vonnie to me. "We were just about to sit down for supper."

He drove down last night, immediately after he left my place. I only hit the road early this morning. I don't want him to think I'm just going to jump whenever he snaps his fingers.

We walk into the spacious farmhouse. The furniture looks comfortable and well used. Photographs line the walls, the first images mostly of children in their school clothes and sports kit. Then formal pictures of two sons and a daughter at their graduations, standing next to proud parents.

Vonnie's husband is a little older than she is, or maybe he just looks older. According to the photos, he turned gray early. There are deep lines around his eyes, as though his gaze has always been fixed on the horizon. Sun-browned face and lean, strong body.

The house feels like my mother and father's...no, like my mother's. And one of the people in these photos is also dead.

We walk to a formal dining room where the man from the photos is waiting, a pipe tucked into the pocket of his khaki shirt. He is taller than he seems in the pictures. And he smells like tobacco, just like my father.

He shakes my hand. His is big and warm.

"Welcome, Sarah. You must be tired and hungry. Would you like to go and bath first? We can wait a few minutes before we eat."

He gestures toward the food on the ten-seater table. Pumpkin fritters, potatoes, green beans, and a leg of lamb stand steaming as though they've just come out of the oven.

My dad loved pumpkin fritters.

I catch my breath, realize it has been getting shallower by the minute. What the hell am I doing here?

"No. Go ahead," I say quickly, swallowing at the dry itch in my throat. "I'll have a quick shower and then get cracking with Jan... your daught...with work. I know how little time we have."

Vonnie's eyes, the same pale blue as Jaap's, flutter closed in something like shock.

I can hear my mother's voice in my head. *Do you always have to be so rude?*

"Jaap can bring me some food," I say quickly. "It looks lovely. Thanks. Please, Mrs. St...Tannie."

JAAP

1

"How do you know that girl?"

Vonnie's cross. She's scrubbing the plates as though she's trying to break them. I warned her that Sarah was a little different, but it clearly didn't help. Perhaps I should have also said that Sarah was a little like Janien.

Actually, she's a lot like Janien. Same obstinate, unruly streak, but with an added curtness I still struggle to deal with.

Vonnie probably still thinks that it's people like Sarah who changed Janien into someone she no longer recognized. It had to have been the students Janien met at Stellenbosch University that made her so "weird"—Vonnie's word, which she said as though it were a swear word. As though it explained everything.

But Janien was born that way. Different. She'd always lived like there was no tomorrow. She had no first or second gear. Always running through life at breakneck speed in everything she did, throwing herself against immovable objects time and again with the firm belief that everything would change for the better if she only tried hard enough.

Almost every attempt left a trail of bloody noses and broken hearts...mostly her own, over and over again.

She'd tried to fit in. Tried to keep her mother and, later, Henk, her fiancé, happy, but it was hard. I could see that, but I couldn't say anything. Children are sacrosanct to mothers like Vonnie. No one is allowed to interfere or suggest a different path.

I sit down at the kitchen table.

"Sarah is brilliant at what she does, Vonnie. That's all that matters."

She wipes her chin, the soap a foamy ball on her hand.

"I'm not interested in why she's here. I told you. Tomorrow afternoon I'm burning everything. All of Janien's things. That's all that matters."

"I hear you."

"Do you really?"

"Yes."

"Then why are you laughing?"

"Because it's something Janien would have done—this burning thing. Your wayward child and her strange habits."

It's quiet for such long time that I wonder whether I've crossed a line. If I've reminded Vonnie of the times she was so upset because Janien wasn't like her other children—level-headed and pragmatic.

But she laughs, so fleetingly and softly, I wonder whether I might have imagined it.

"Maybe that's why I'm doing it."

SARAH

Janien Steyn's room feels small after so many hours riding through the open Karoo on the KTM. I open the windows to let the cramped space breathe. To exorcize any ghosts that may linger here.

The cold doesn't bother me. I've always liked winter.

I put on a jersey and sit down at the desk. Push the three cell-phones aside. I'll look at them later. Next I put the framed photo of Janien and her family face down on the desk. It feels like they're all staring at me.

I switch on the laptop. The machine is old by today's standards, but new and sophisticated for three years ago. And expensive. I do a quick search of the desk but find no tablet.

I'd guess it would be unlikely that she would have been able to afford a decent tablet too. And why would she want one? It's still easier to build and run a website on a proper computer.

The screen lights up and I suddenly like Janien a heck of a lot more.

It's a Linux-based system, open-source programming, like the kind I use. No messing around with Windows. Internet browser is Chrome and email is Gmail. Surprisingly so. I would have expected something more private, like ProtonMail, but then again, Gmail is free and easy to use. Everybody understands it.

Why she didn't have a password on her computer is anyone's guess, but at least it saves me time.

I start with the email. I type the first two letters of her email address in the log-in and hold my breath. Yes. The password autofills.

The police, or someone else, must have been in here recently.

I look through the 347 messages in Janien's inbox. Nothing unusual. Mostly confirmations of purchases, requests for exhibitions, and invitations to galleries. I check the trash. Empty, as Jaap said. I quickly look through what Janien might have thought she deleted from the trash.

Nothing of interest there either.

I reach for the Samsung. It's a fairly old phone, overtaken by all kinds of new technology in the past three years. I type in the PIN that Jaap gave me, look around on the device but fail to find anything interesting. Janien used WhatsApp to chat to friends and to her fiancé, just as Jaap said. Not much else.

Back to the laptop. Her business, the name of her digital art gallery, was *So What!* It has its own Facebook page and Twitter, Instagram and TikTok accounts, which Janien updated herself.

Everything looks pretty straightforward. African masks and carvings, landscape paintings and pencil sketches of the Big Five, abstract pieces and videos of performance art that I imagine would only just pass muster with Vonnie. Some digital illustrations that mess with your head, a few nice photographic portraits, and three artists who paint city murals under the brand Urban Zoo Biscuit.

Safe, in other words.

I turn around and look at the room. There are black-and-white landscape photographs and portraits on the walls. Close-ups of people who look like they're from the area, the same faraway look in their eyes as Janien's dad.

I wonder about the website. The photo Jaap showed me. The one of Janien with the short little dress and the red lips. Her fiancé. Her wedding. Jaap said she looked a little like me…

Something doesn't make sense.

Nope, I decide. Not my job. I can't afford to get involved.

I check who visited Janien's site. South Africans, Danes, Swedes. French people and Germans. Some Kenyans and Australians. In the month before her death, she had 3 700 hits. Not bad. Payments were made through PayPal, among others. Her bank account was with First National Bank.

I'll check it out later on my own computer.

I scowl at the thought. Maybe that's what Jaap was hoping I'd do, no matter how sweetly he promised I wouldn't have to do anything illegal.

We'll have to wait and see about that one.

Someone knocks on the door.

"Yes? What is it?" The more often I get interrupted, the longer this is going to take. It's already pitch-black night out there.

Jaap comes in with tea, meaty sandwiches, and a red folder under his arm.

"Here's your supper."

I put the mug down next to the computer, take the plate from him, and start eating.

He sits down on the bed and taps the folder. "Photos of the crime scene, if you're interested."

I shake my head. "No, thanks. You've already told me what happened."

I don't want to see Janien's face again. The photos here, plastered throughout the house, are more than enough.

Jaap takes a stack of photos out of the file, places them on the bed, and holds the folder out to me. "Take the rest then. It's Janien's bank statements, and data and phone records."

He gestures toward the two older cellphones on the desk.

"I put them there in case you want to look at them, but they're mostly photos and texts to school and university friends."

I put the lamb-and-mayo sandwich down and take the folder. "What happens if I don't find anything? Have you ever thought of that? That you didn't find anything because there's nothing to find?"

"You'll uncover something. I know you will. The police can't afford people with your skills. Just get something, however insignificant. I want details of Janien's life on social media. The secret phone. The hidden Facebook page. Whatever she erased. Anything we wouldn't find in a straightforward search. Something the police—I—wouldn't have thought of."

"Why are you so sure she was hiding something? Maybe the stuff she erased was rubbish. Everyone dumps documents and messages all the time."

Jaap pushes a hand through his hair. Shakes his head. "Everyone has something to hide."

"You too?"

His answer is to get up and open Janien's cupboard, his hands urging me to take a look. "See this?"

I look at the floral dresses, jeans, white skirts and T-shirts. "Yes? So?"

He pulls a dress out of the cupboard. It's a delicate piece of clothing, light blue with small white flowers. "This is not Janien—her mother bought it for her. Vonnie's never seen the boots Janien died in, but they're definitely hers. They had the same tread pattern as her other shoes. Lighter on the heels, heavier on the toes."

He points at the sandals on the floor of the cupboard. The straw hat. "Janien wasn't what you see here. She was different."

"Different how?"

"I don't know. Just different. She had a tattoo of a thorn tree on her back—another thing Vonnie didn't know about." He points to the computer, the walls, the cupboard. "Something doesn't feel right, but I just don't know what it is."

He looks at me, the same pleading expression in his eyes as yesterday in my apartment. "Find it please, Sarah. It's here somewhere. It has to be. I'm a hundred percent sure there is something we're not seeing."

I sit back, cross my arms. "And if I find it—if—do you really want to know what that something is?"

"What do you mean?"

"If Janien was so careful about hiding whatever was going on from all of you, do you really want to know her secret?"

"If it got her killed—yes."

I turn back to the computer. "I'll see what I can find. But there's not a lot of time. Don't expect miracles."

"You have sixteen hours."

As if I didn't know. "Can you get me a Coke?" I need the energy.

"Vonnie hates Coke, but I bought you some."

His answer makes me turn around in the chair. "What else does Vonnie hate?"

He smiles as though I finally get it. "Lots of things. She wants to protect her children against everything."

Sounds like my mother. And look at what I did. Next thing she knew her eighteen-year-old daughter was in jail for cybertheft.

Jaap might just be right. Maybe Janien Steyn did have something to hide.

The house is quiet while I work, the only noise the corrugated-iron roof creaking as the night settles down. I'm shivering, but I refuse to close the windows.

I strip the duvet off Janien's bed, wrap it round my shoulders and open the next Coke and the next email—one of the few Janien deleted that I've been able to find so far. It was sent to cheny@chen-wag.com on the day before her death. I couldn't find the original message, just fragments of Janien's reply.

My mother will kill me if she finds out. No, she'll send my father to do it and then never speak to me again. Ha-ha. Maybe that will fix everything. But seriously. I love them. Not always sure why, but that's how it is and probably always will be.

The next email was also written the day before she died, but later that morning.

Can't believe I'm selling so many photos and masks from Côte d'Ivoire these days. I haven't sold one of my own photos in two months.

These people are so frigging old-fashioned. Can't believe Henk comes from a family like this. So narrow-minded. Who still thinks like that? His father drives me nuts!!! I just can't bear it anymore.

What can't her mother find out? And what can't she bear? The engagement? And who is this Cheny?

The small number of personal messages Janien left out in the open in her Gmail inbox are those between her and her parents, Leon, and her younger brother, Obie Junior. Nothing strange or unusual. Wedding plans. Who walks into the church in which order. Who sings, who's doing the flowers. Here I can see both sides of every conversation.

One email has a photo of her and her friends attached. It is the only photo I've found so far. Three women and a man, smiling happily. One of the women has Asian features—fit-looking with a lovely smile. In the left corner of the image is the word *Blink.*

I print the email and the photo using Janien's printer. Luckily it still has ink in it. Maybe one of the people in the picture is cheny@chenwag.com.

As I wait for the printer, the sound of someone snoring rolls through the house. Stops, then starts again.

I get up, the duvet still wrapped around me, and listen for a moment.

There's something reassuring about the sound. Something familiar, like from my childhood. My father used to snore. My mom would battle to get him to turn on his side, but five minutes later the snoring would start up again.

My brothers, sister and I all learned to sleep through the noise.

Funny what you miss when someone's gone. Like RSG, the national broadcaster's Afrikaans radio service. My father always listened to the radio in the garage when we worked on the cars. RSG was on morning, noon and night. From advice about dogs that bark too much, to the late-night confessions of truck drivers.

I walk to the window. The moon is bright and the night air ice cold. I pull the duvet a little tighter, fish the Marlboros out of my jeans pocket, and put one in my mouth. I wish I could light the bloody thing, but I promised my father I'd stop smoking."One of us dying from a smoking-related illness was enough," he said.

It was terrible to watch. The slow, panicky suffocation of emphysema. A giant fist forcing the breath out of him.

I'm mostly able to keep my promise to him about not smoking, but it's so much harder to keep my word about computers. When I got out of jail, I told my mother I would stop hacking, that I'd never look at a computer again.

I sigh angrily, turn around, put the cigarette away and stare at Janien's room.

The black wall. The empty bed. The cheerful floral dresses.

What was Janien hiding from her mother?

I sit down at the desk again and pick up the family photo, look at Janien's black hair, the brown eyes. The dimple in her chin. I look at the picture I printed. She's laughing with her friends around her. Was she a student when it was taken? She left Stellenbosch University four years before her death.

I touch the lively, attractive face in the picture. "What happened to you?"

I'm suddenly curious about how exactly she died. What's on the crime scene photos I didn't want Jaap to show me?

No.

I place the family face down on the desk again and put the photo printout in my backpack. I still don't want to know.

An hour later I find the first big domino. Janien knew how to hide documents and messages on her computer from the people closest to her, but not from someone like me.

I think I know why she didn't use a password. If she did, those same people would probably have wondered what she was hiding.

Vonnie used Janien's computer twice to send emails after she died, and I'm sure she poked around a bit as well. I would guess she probably did so even before Janien's death.

When I was at school, my mother insisted on knowing what I was doing on my computer.

Once I knew where to look, it was easy to find the encrypted information Janien had scattered around on her hard drive and in the cloud.

But it's going to take time to decipher it.

The information does reveal two things, though—Janien was hiding something and guarding something valuable, it seems.

I can see how Jaap and the police around here could have missed her secrets.

You have to be very thorough to find them. And you have to take a leap in your head. You have to think of Janien as an adult woman. You can't look at her life and think this was someone who was just a little bit different, but still young and innocent. You can't think of her as the same little girl who used to crawl onto your lap and whose forehead you kissed at bedtime.

You have to want to know.

JAAP

1

"Is she still asleep?" Obie draws on the pipe and white smoke curls lazily up toward the stoep's ceiling.

"Yes. She worked late last night. Probably more like until this morning."

I steal a glance at my brother-in-law. It's eleven in the morning and usually he would have been gone to the veld by now, but today he's at home. Looking after Vonnie, no doubt. She's at the barn, with Hendrik, her right-hand man, preparing to move the contents of Janien's room to the bonfire site.

"How do you know this girl?"

Obie avoids looking at me, peers into the distance instead.

"I met her a few years ago." I certainly don't want to tell them that Sarah spent almost a year in prison.

"And what exactly does she do?"

"She works with computers."

"She seems very young."

"She's older than she looks."

Obie's cough is like an old man's: dry and long. "Vonnie thinks she's the rudest person she's ever met."

Did Vonnie send him to talk to me? She probably wants Sarah gone as soon as possible.

"She's very good at what she does, but she struggles with people," I say. "The first time we met it took her three days to say two words to me."

"They probably weren't 'good morning.'"

There is a hint of a smile on Obie's lips.

I shake my head. It's another story I'd rather keep to myself. I had, after all, stood on her backpack's shoulder strap by accident as she'd tried to lift it.

Obie gestures toward the orange KTM. The smile becomes a laugh that creases his suntanned face.

"Vonnie says women shouldn't ride beasts like that."

"Sarah can take that bike apart and put it back together again faster than anyone on this farm."

His eyebrows shoot up. "Engine too?"

"She understands machines. What makes them tick."

"Sounds like you and Janien. You understood her. Sometimes you knew better than Vonnie and I did what was going on inside that head of hers."

"You think so?" I'm not sure I agree. "I think we all needed more time. I suspect we would have all done better if we'd been a little older and a little wiser. If we had been a little more patient with one another."

Just like me, Vonnie, and our policeman father.

Like most families, I suppose.

Obie draws on his pipe. "But then there was no more time."

It's quiet for a while before I speak again.

"Tell Vonnie I'll get Sarah away from here as soon as I can. She's only on *Lekkerkry* because I asked her to come. I'm pretty sure she's desperate to get home anyway. She was away for a long time after her father's death."

Obie says nothing, just stares out toward the pan, his lips thin and white around the pipe's bit.

Maybe Vonnie is being spiteful, like when we were children and she messed cereal all over the breakfast table on purpose and told our mother I did it.

She always wanted more attention than I wanted to give her between my boyhood ambition of becoming South Africa's next Springbok rugby fly-half and swimming with my buddies at the municipal pool.

She starts with Janien's computer—not the bed or the desk or her clothes, but the one thing Sarah needs to find Janien's killer.

It's almost noon and Vonnie sends Hendrik for the laptop and the phones. He casts a quick, guilty glance at me from under his floppy white hat as he hurries by and down the stoep stairs. He was the one who taught Janien to drive a truck and to know when the rain would come. He still talks about her now and again, when Obie is in a good mood and doesn't mind.

It's easy to forget that there are other people who miss her too.

I jump to my feet where I am paging through the newspaper in the sitting room. Does Sarah have everything she needs? I haven't heard or seen her yet this morning. Is she still asleep?

I jog up the passage, knock and walk into the guest bedroom. Turn round in my tracks and close the door behind me. It looks like the girl is sleeping naked, with the windows wide open.

No. Woman. Definitely not girl.

And she's definitely asleep. Fast asleep, even though it's an ice box in there.

I take a deep breath and knock again, louder this time.

Eventually I hear movement. I open the door slightly and talk through the crack. "Can I come in?"

"No."

"Hendrik is taking Janien's computer. Are you done?"

She mumbles something and I hear the rustle of bedding. A zip. A swear word I hope she won't ever use in front of Vonnie.

The door swings open. "What is it?"

She's wearing jeans and a tiny, thin T-shirt.

I look away, down the passage. "The computer..."

"I've got what I need."

"Are you sure? What if you missed something?"

"I cloned her hard drive and her phone. The Samsung."

"Is that all? Are you sure that's enough?"

"Yes. What's wrong with your neck?"

"Nothing." Anything not to look at the T-shirt and what's underneath. "So, you're happy with what you've got?"

"Yes. As I said, I've duplicated the insides. All of the insides," she says slowly, as if speaking to a child.

I forget to not look at her. "What if Vonnie finds out?"

"And how would she do that?"

She's probably right.

I turn around. Stop. Sarah said she had what she needed. Needed? "Did you find anything?"

She crosses her arms as though the cold is starting to register. Yawns. "Ja."

"So get dressed and come and tell me."

"Can I have some breakfast first?"

"Breakfast? Lunch is almost ready."

SARAH

1

I've missed another meal, but Vonnie caught on fast. Lunch is in the kitchen, not in the dining room. And we're eating from plain white kitchen plates, not the fancy fine china on the table last night.

I like the kitchen. It's big and warm, with an Aga in the corner. One that still works and in which the bread I'm eating was baked.

Vonnie knows how to bake bread. And make jam. Not to mention the quiche I devoured as a first course.

"What's this again?" I point at the bread. Vonnie and Obie have left me and Jaap alone so we can chat.

"Nastergalkonfyt."

Don't know it. I'll have to google it later.

By the looks of Jaap, it will have to be much later. His body language betrays his impatience. Vonnie wants to light that bonfire and he's worried about Janien's computer.

If he's not going to trust me, why bother bringing me all the way here from Pretoria?

I swallow the last bite of bread, finish my tea and turn my laptop so that he can see the screen. Time to put the man out of his misery.

"Janien had two websites, the one you know about, and another one which she hid very well. She used the name Jane Stone to run that one."

He frowns.

"Jane Stone? The name means nothing to me. It wasn't anywhere in her internet history, and the police and I didn't find anything relating to that identity. Just *News24* and *IOL*, a few galleries in Joburg.

Stuff like that. Vonnie would have said if she found something."

"Vonnie looked through the computer?"

"Yes."

"Thought as much. Did she always snoop around in Janien's stuff?"

Jaap looks unwilling to answer.

"Now and again," he finally admits. "Mostly in the two years before Janien's death. She was suddenly coming home less often and Vonnie was worried about her."

He folds his paper napkin into a neat triangle. "Janien wasn't making things any easier...she could be very difficult. Vonnie wanted to spend time with her when she was here, but Janien preferred to be in the veld taking photos."

"That explains why Janien went to so much trouble hiding everything."

"What do you mean *everything?*"

"One surprise at a time." I nod at the screen. "When you follow the Jane Stone website's money, all of it eventually trickles back to Janien. She had an account in London, which is about R65 000 richer since her death. Looks like some old debt that was finally paid a year after she died, because she cleaned it out quite often."

I wait for Jaap to do the maths about Jane Stone and Janien Steyn.

When he eventually speaks, he asks the same question I asked at two this morning. "Why two websites?"

"Her original website, *So What!*, was mainstream. Safe, average art for the safe, average person. Tourists, Africa-mad Europeans, and people who own safari lodges. *So What Now?* is different."

"Is that the name of the other website? Jane Stone's website? *So What Now?*"

"Ja." I open the site, so he can see. "This one is hardcore. Alternative and explicit, much more sexual and experimental in nature. But bloody good."

Jaap grumbles something I can't quite make out.

I hope he doesn't get cold feet now. I told him to leave well enough alone, but he wouldn't listen. It's not always good to know what's going on in your family's private lives. People keep things secret because they know the truth is going to hurt someone they love.

I point at a video window on the *So What Now?* site. "This one is pretty cool. It's an eighty-year-old woman stripping. She's protesting against the 'social invisibility of the elderly.'"

"That's not art."

"Anything is art if someone says it's art." I move to the bottom of the page. A photo series shows naked black and white men swinging from gallows nooses, all with a yellowish Seventies hue. It's called *Well Hung: A South African Historical Comparison*. And here, a protest at a slaughterhouse, with chicken blood.

Jaap's face reveals his distaste.

"A lot of it is brilliant." I appear to be defending Janien, to my own surprise. "The work she commissioned was also good. Really good. You should all be proud of her. There was a lot of interest in what she was doing, and some of the artists made good money. Two of them took part in exhibitions in New York; one participated in the Paris Biennale. Janien was making a name for herself. There are two requests for interviews in Jane Stone's inbox."

"Why didn't we find all this stuff?"

I close the site. "There are no clear links from *So What Now?* to either Janien or to *So What!* She hid her identity well. It was harder to follow her digital tracks than most people's. She knew that she couldn't risk Jane Stone popping up when people googled Janien Steyn, and she was careful not to leave emails lying around. She also cleared her browser history regularly."

I think about the social media threads I follow. "I also suspect that she didn't necessarily want her global clients to know she was South African. She most definitely didn't want her family to know what she was marketing and selling on *So What Now?*"

What I truly think is that Janien was shit-scared of Vonnie—about what she and Obie would think of Jane Stone and her work

—but I don't say that. We do a lot to hang on to people's love, especially when we perceive it as highly conditional.

Sometimes we're right about the conditions for that love. Sometimes we're wrong.

I watch Jaap carefully, wonder whether I've interpreted Janien's life correctly. Whether, since I got here, I've seen everything as it really is at *Lekkerkry*. I'm not the world's brightest woman when it comes to people, but Vonnie and Obie look and feel conservative and Janien's correspondence seems to support that. And I don't know the town or the district, but I have my suspicions.

Janien never refers to Jaap in her emails, so I don't know how far to go in defending her to her uncle.

Defend.

Since when do I defend people?

Which leads me to my next question. Should I show Jaap everything I found on Janien's computer and phones last night, or is this enough?

Janien also used Snapchat. To send naked pictures like teenagers or stupid adults. The app works because the photos disappear before they can be forwarded or shared on social media. Before mothers and fathers can see them and become hysterical. Snapchat feels temporary, a place where your mistakes won't haunt you forever.

Janien shared beautiful, artistic photographs in which you can't see her face.

If Jaap hadn't told me about the thorn-tree tattoo on her back, I wouldn't have known it was her.

The pics were all sent to the username S&M, which received it on a computer, never on a cellphone.

S&M never sent pictures in return, or rather, nothing I could find. Maybe he was less of an exhibitionist. Or more careful. Or just a little bit smarter.

The bad news for Jaap is that it doesn't seem like S&M was her fiancé.

What would Jaap do if I told him all of this? Would he tell Vonnie?

No, I decide. I should be a hundred percent sure before I put all kinds of images of Janien in his head. Jane Stone and *So What Now?* is enough. I can leave him here to deal with Vonnie's reaction to these little nuggets of information while I go and look for S&M.

Janien and S&M chatted now and again on her second email, her Jane Stone address, but I haven't yet had time to read the mails on there. Their communication is cryptic and abbreviated. Almost unintelligible. Meeting times. A raging argument with lots of exclamation marks.

I've tracked S&M's computer through its IP address and internet service provider. According to these, the messages were sent from a computer nearby, as well as from a second computer somewhere in town. And both computers are still active.

Jaap is still staring at my laptop screen, looking a little dismayed. "Okay, so you found this website. But what does it mean? Does it mean that someone involved with *So What Now?* murdered her?"

"That I don't know. That's your job."

He fishes his reading glasses, a pen, and a tired-looking notebook out of one of the many pockets of his green bush jacket. On the front of the notebook it says *JANIEN* in fat black letters underlined three times.

"What happened on the website on the day she died? On *So What Now?*" he asks. "Before her death? Was there any suspicious activity?"

I turn the computer back toward me and start searching.

"There was a chat about a famous painting. About what makes a painting stand out from the rest. Janien also wrote on her blog about the body as an instrument of art, and she uploaded two rap videos. So, no, nothing suspicious."

He taps the notebook with his pen. "Paintings?"

"Yes."

"Who were the people having this conversation?"

"Why do you ask?"

He fetches a stack of photos from his room and puts them down in front of me. It's the crime scene photos of Janien's murder.

"Don't these also look like some kind of painting?" he asks.

I finally relent and page through the images. The red fabric. The face hidden behind aviator goggles. The bicycle. Janien in her wedding dress, frozen in flight.

"Maybe, yes," I admit.

I think about the hidden emails I've read. The frustration and the rage. Who Janien really was. An art student who was no longer creating art, but curating it. Who was about to marry into a conservative family, moving from one uptight family into another.

Maybe her death was a painting, one she created herself.

But do I really want to know the answer to that question?

I laugh sourly. Too late for that.

Jaap has read me well.

He misinterprets my reaction and grabs the photos out of my hands. "If you don't want to help, you can just say so."

"Wait," I counter. "I'm not laughing at the photos."

"What then?"

"It was more of a personal insight."

He frowns. "About what?"

"Just…nothing. Never mind."

I take the top photo from him, ask him the question that's surfaced in my head.

"Are you sure she didn't…" The words stick in my throat. "Have you considered that she…Is suicide a possibility? You said she studied art. Maybe she was frustrated because she had to stop making art. Because she'd become an art pusher instead."

"Janien was more than that. She was a talented photographer."

I have a feeling there's something he's not telling me. "But?"

"Okay, yes, I know she struggled to make a living from her work," he says reluctantly. "She could photograph weddings, stuff like that, but a photographic installation doesn't put food on the table."

"So maybe…"

"No." He's firm. "I don't care what you say. She enjoyed running her business—the *So What!* website—she couldn't stop talking about it. You don't get that excited about something and then take your own life."

"So suicide is out?"

"Yes. Also because I don't think she injected herself with M99."

"What's that?"

"Vets use it to anesthetize big game, like rhinos and elephants. In its pure form it's fatal to humans. It's not that easy to get hold of legally, but you can buy just about anything on the black market these days."

I don't want to know, but I ask anyway. "Was she injected with this M99 before or after she ended up on the pan?"

"It's hard to say, but it looks like it happened before she died and that she was put on that pan after she was murdered. There's only one set of footprints leading to and from the pan. Size tens, and Janien wore a size six. There were Toyota Hilux bakkie tire tracks around the pan too, but so many people around here have those bakkies, they could have been Obie's, for all we know." He's quick to add: "And no, he didn't kill his daughter."

"If you say so."

He looks at the photo again. "Why do you think it may have been suicide?"

I show him the two emails I found, the ones from cheny@chen-wag.com.

He scans them quickly, shakes his head. "I knew she was unhappy at times, but I didn't know it was that bad."

"Didn't she confide in you?"

"Sometimes. Her relationship with her parents was difficult. They didn't really get her. Hell, I struggled to fully understand her myself, and I had the advantage of being able to look in from the outside. She was just so different to the rest of us. So strange and… bohemian."

"I get it."

He smiles a little. "Is it the same with your mother? What's your relationship like?"

My family is the last thing I want to discuss with Jaap.

I make a U-turn back to my previous question. "Are you a hundred percent certain it wasn't suicide? In spite of these emails?"

Jaap gets the message and drops the subject. "She was getting married the following weekend. Why commit suicide? She and Henk had already bought a house in Somerset West."

I remember Henk's name from her text messages.

"Henk? Is that his full name?" Maybe I'm wrong in assuming that he can't be S&M.

Jaap thinks for a while. "I think it's Henk Joubert van Staden. Why do you ask?"

I'm in two minds for a moment, then I take a deep breath, decide to tell him about Janien's other emails and her Snapchat contact with S&M.

"S&M? That stands for sadomasochism. Pain sex. What the hell was Janien into?"

I shrug.

"Could you track down this S&M? Is it Henk?" he asks.

"I don't have a name yet, just IP addresses for two computers. I'll be able to give you a name once I've cross-referenced that with some other information. I just needed to get some sleep first."

"Is it near here?"

"Yes."

"Finish up and get ready then. I want to see who this S&M is."

2

"Bloody hell. When last did you clean your car?" I ask.

"Sorry."

Jaap sweeps the Wimpy takeaway bag off the Corolla's passenger seat into the footwell, then reconsiders and gets out of the car. He walks around the silver sedan, leans in at the passenger side and picks up the bag, as well as a takeaway coffee cup, two Flake chocolate bar wrappers, and an empty biltong packet.

"It was a long drive from Pretoria," he says as he turns and limps to the house to throw the rubbish away.

I wonder what's wrong with his leg, but I'm not in the mood to ask. I know from Ranna that he was attacked in a street mugging last year, but not much more than that.

When he comes back, he stands at the car door and tucks the bottom of his light-blue shirt, hidden under his bush jacket, into his chinos.

I suddenly wonder whether he was ever married. Whether someone ever told him that a blue shirt really brings out the color of his eyes.

I shake off the thought, get into the car, search for the button to open the window, only to realize I'd have to wind it down by hand.

Jaap gets into the driver's seat.

I shift the seat back and turn the stiff, protesting window crank, my hands sheathed in black fingerless gloves. It's clear Jaap never ferries passengers around. This window hasn't moved an inch in years.

Jaap blows into his cupped hands and pulls away, looking at the open window. "Does that really have to be open?"

"Yes."

I zip up my black leather jacket and pull the checkered scarf a little tighter under my chin, breathe in the fresh air.

As we turn onto the dirt road to the farm gate, I spot a group of people near a thorn tree, one of those beautiful ones with peeling bark like aged gray paper. To the left of them a faded yellow mechanical shovel works away robotically. Above them, the clouds look heavy and low. Two crows fly by, cawing loudly. They land on the nearest telephone pole as if they have bought front-row tickets to a show at the theater.

I turn to watch the scene as we drive by. "Vonnie?"

Jaap sighs. "Ja."

"And that's the bonfire with Janien's stuff?"

"Yup."

"Does she often do things like that? It feels like something Janien would have done."

Jaap looks at me in surprise. The Corolla slows down to walking speed—not that we were ever really going that fast. Then he laughs, long and heartily, a deep belly laugh.

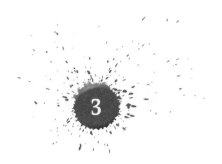

Jaap steers the Corolla through a lane of trees stripped bare by winter. He parks in front of a cream-colored double-story farmhouse. The lawn around the house is as green and lush as the golf courses in the wealthy suburbs in the east of Pretoria, despite the fact that we are in the middle of a semi-desert.

Lankdrink. I like the farm's name. Long drink. There's supposed to be a spring here somewhere, Jaap said on the way here. Must be a valuable commodity in the Karoo. Or on any farm, I suppose.

We get out. An older, heavyset man waits on the stoep as if he's been expecting us. He frowns deeply when we get out of the car, creasing an already heavily lined face.

"Why does he look like someone ate his Rice Krispies?"

Jaap's eyes warn me to shut up. "He and I…things have never been good. I think it's best if you leave the talking to me."

"Okay. Whatever."

He needn't worry. I have no desire to talk to people I don't know—his family has been enough for an entire year.

The man gestures with a wooden walking stick for us to take the stoep stairs. "I struggle to walk," he says. "Torn ligaments. Slipped at the sheep kraal a few days ago."

As I reach the top of the stairs I turn around. From here the veld lies open on all sides. The wintry air smells like freshly cut melon and tastes sweet on my lips. I'll never admit it to Jaap but I'm starting to like this place. This immense expanse, punctuated by low shrubs and the odd acacia tree. The open, endless sky.

I turn back to the men. I hope we don't have to go inside. I've not had time to sit on a Karoo stoep and look at the horizon yet.

The man with the walking stick shakes Jaap's hand, then mine. "Fanus," he introduces himself. "Come. Sit."

He looks roughly the same age as Jaap, but his pale eyes are hinting at the first bleach of old age. He sinks his weight carefully into the nearest wicker chair, then lifts his right leg, encased in a gray plastic ankle brace, to rest on the coffee table in front of him.

Jaap looks longingly at the warmth offered by the big farmhouse before sitting down opposite Fanus, pulling his jacket tighter around his body. I take a seat next to him.

Fanus lights a Camel, which might explain why we're staying outside. His hair is as white as the smoke he releases into the air. He and the Camels must have walked a long road together, judging by his nicotine-stained fingernails and teeth.

He looks at us with watery eyes. "Hope you don't mind."

It's not a question.

I get up and move to the chair furthest from the men, the craving for a cigarette almost overwhelming. Jaap takes out his notebook and pen.

I edge forward in my seat, curious to see how he's going to break the ice about this S&M. Could it be this old guy? Is it possible?

Fanus draws on his cigarette, coughs. "What can I help you...the two of you with?" He glances at me, clearly curious.

Jaap taps the cheap Bic pen on the notebook. "As I said on the phone, we have a new lead in Janien's murder case."

The Camel freezes mid-air. "And it's like I always say: same old shit." He shakes his head, his eyes back on me again. "We, as in you and her?"

"Ja."

"And what new lead do you have?"

"Correspondence—emails, messages—between her and a man. SM." Jaap leaves out the "and."

"Your name is Stephanus Malan. So is your son's."

I try not to look surprised. Jaap never said a thing on the way here. I glance at him and sense the shadow of a smile around his mouth. He enjoyed springing that little surprise on Fanus. No wonder he looked so pleased when I gave him the farm's address.

"Lots of people have those initials." Fanus's voice becomes even more unfriendly.

Jaap looks at his notes again. Pages back, then forward again, taking his time, even though I know he didn't write down a single thing when I told him about S&M. And where are those reading glasses now?

"The IP address indicates that the computer is on your property, Fanus."

"IP address? What the hell is that? Is that all you've got? That and two letters?"

Jaap keeps quiet.

Fanus stubs out his cigarette in an ashtray next to his leg.

"Tell me more about this new...lead of yours." He looks at me. "You probably have something to do with this." His gaze slides down to my jeans and motorbike boots. "You look like those stupid little girls on TV that always dig up this sort of useless crap."

The word sears through me, as it always does. "Girls ar—"

"Just a moment." Jaap's eyes warn me to remember what he said earlier. *Leave the talking to me.*

I look away, toward the veld. Probably would have been better if I'd stayed home. Jaap turns back to Fanus. "All I want to know is whether you or Stefan spoke to Janien before her death. Especially Stefan. It doesn't mean I think you did anything. Janien trusted this SM. She might even have told him things relevant to the investigation."

Jaap doesn't say anything about Snapchat or the nature of Janien and S&M's relationship.

"Look," Jaap tries again, "the kids all studied together. Stefan, Henk, Janien, and Magda. And they were good friends. Someone somewhere knows something that might help us."

Fanus lights another cigarette. "Stefan and Maggie—both my kids—were at the braai when Janien died. Henk too. You know that."

"Then it shouldn't be a problem if we chat to Stefan."

"If I remember correctly, you're no longer in the police."

"Isak Slingers still is. I can call him if you want me to. Then he can go to the butchery and have a talk with Stefan in front of all your customers."

Fanus exhales a puff of angry air. "You had zero luck three years ago. What makes you think you're suddenly going to find the answers now?"

"I called in some help."

Fanus looks at me again and laughs. "Means nothing. You're still a one-trick pony."

"You may be right. But maybe I'm more of a mule."

"Yeah, you're a stubborn bastard all right."

Fanus gives Jaap a penetrating look. "Why can't you let this go? My children were devastated by Janien's death. No one in the district got any sleep for months on end. Everyone suddenly had to do patrol duty, and every stranger was the devil himself. Why do you have to keep on digging? You're just messing things up again for Vonnie. In the end you'll go back to Pretoria empty-handed and she has to stay here and live with everything you've stirred up."

Jaap starts to draw a maze in his notebook, slowly and precisely. "This time it's different. So, tell Stefan to come over, or I'll go find him without your help."

Fanus laughs, but it's a bitter sound. "I'll call the butchery and tell him to come home."

He gestures toward the house. "Maggie can make us coffee while we wait."

JAAP

1

"Stefan says he's on his way." Fanus sinks down in his chair on the stoep again, looks over his shoulder. "Where's Maggie and that girlie of yours with the coffee?"

He shifts his injured leg. "I still don't get why you're here. Why would Stefan have spoken to Janien as SM? They've known each other since they were children. It doesn't make sense. And don't even think that I'm this SM of yours either. I know Stefan was upset because Janien eventually chose Henk, but by the time Janien died, he'd moved on. I'm telling you again: they were all at the braai on the Van Stadens' farm when Janien was murdered. We all were."

I nod patiently. "I hear you, but there were maybe eighty people there that night. Who would know if someone disappeared for an hour or two? And someone killed Janien—someone who knew her."

Fanus crosses his arms. "Says who? It could have been a drifter. Some or other little tikhead who went berserk. I can promise you that everyone around here thinks exactly the same thing."

"There were no signs of a break-in, and a drifter in these parts would have drawn attention."

"Not these days. Shows you how much you know. Anyway, Janien was constantly feeding complete strangers and giving them money. Who's to know she didn't open the door to the wrong guy?"

"Someone had to have brought the red cloth and the bicycle with them, Fanus. And the aviator goggles. Someone who knew what he was doing. Who was trying to make a statement. Who was watching Janien. Who knew she didn't go to the braai that night."

"Maybe," he admits grudgingly. "But it still doesn't mean Stefan had anything to do with it. He's having a hard time, Jaap. Can you not understand that? We all are. Every year, you come back here and you dig around for something you're never going to find. Can't you just let it go?"

"Don't you want to know what happened?"

Fanus snorts. "Does Vonnie know what you're up to?"

"Vonnie has nothing to do with this."

"So, she doesn't, then."

"She knows."

"Let's say I believe you. I can still promise you she feels the same way I do." Fanus takes a fresh cigarette from the pack on the coffee table. "I sometimes wonder how it would have been if you'd left her to make her own decisions. Whether she still would have chosen Obie."

"And not you? Rubbish. There was nothing to decide and you know it. I'm telling you, leave Vonnie out of this."

Suddenly I again feel like I did all those years ago, fighting to get this smooth operator to leave my sister alone. How many years has it been? Twenty-five? More? Vonnie and Obie had been at logger-heads for a while. They were struggling to have children and things were tough. They needed time. What they didn't need was someone like Fanus to sow discord and doubt.

But I could be wrong. Maybe this has everything to do with Vonnie. There's nothing to show that S&M isn't Fanus Malan. Vonnie says he's still a womanizer. It started long before his divorce and it never stopped, and age apparently doesn't matter. What if Fanus wanted another chance with one of the Steyn women?

Half an hour later, Stefan parks his Toyota bakkie in front of the house he shares with his father. He must have hurried to get here this quickly from town. Maybe he's worried. Maybe Fanus is worried, despite the bluster.

Stefan climbs up the stoep, says hello and sits down next to

Fanus. He glances at his father, his shoulders tense. He looks older than I remember. The once athletic boy has become a heavy-footed man with prematurely graying hair and a face that betrays that life has disappointed him one too many times.

"Jaap says you might have had email contact with Janien shortly before she died. He wants to know about someone called SM," Fanus explains before I can say anything.

Stefan doesn't even feign surprise. Fanus probably warned him on the phone about what I was after. No wonder he used the landline to make the call to his son, despite his injury.

I suppose I could have approached this conversation differently. Maybe I should have gone around to the butchery before coming here, although I know Stefan doesn't do anything without his father's permission. He would have just batted away any request to talk to him until he had Fanus by his side.

"Why would Janien and I have emailed each other?" says Stefan. "We saw each other all the time." His size ten boots bounce up and down nervously, just like the last time I interviewed him. "We had coffee together almost every time she came to town."

Fanus draws on his cigarette and stares at me. *See?* his eyes say.

Did he always smoke this much or is he trying to hide his discomfort? I look at my notebook. Draw a spiral. Down, down, down.

I look at Stefan again. "And when she went back to the city? To Cape Town? How did you stay in contact then?"

"We didn't really. She wasn't on social media in her personal capacity and that made it difficult to keep in touch with her. In any case, we weren't that close anymore. Henk was pretty jealous." He runs his hand over his brush-cut hair, wipes his mouth with the back of his hand.

"But you still had coffee every time she came to Carnarvon?"

"Ja, but it was always quick. And at Blikkies Bar, not at home."

"Why not here?"

Stefan blushes a little. "Janien preferred going into town."

Fanus coughs, flicks ash off his cigarette.

I finish the spiral, start a new one. "If I remember correctly, you used to be in love with Janien."

Stefan laughs, but it's thin. "A lot of the guys around here were in love with Janien. She was different. Exotic. If you wanted to get out of here she was…"

His words drift into silence. He glances at his father. His feet start bouncing again. Bounce, bounce, bounce.

"You were saying?" I ask.

"If you wanted to get out of here, she seemed like the ideal escape. Like someone whose car you could get into and drive away without ever looking back." He laughs again, more sincerely this time. "But I wasn't that guy. I'm happy in Carnarvon. Here, on the farm."

"Perhaps, but you could still have felt something for her. This SM she was speaking to loved her. And she loved him."

"Love?" Fanus is angry. "You said nothing about love. Was Janien cheating on Henk with this SM?"

I adjust my stiff leg. "Maybe."

"And you come here with your insinuations? I should have throttled you the moment you set foot on my farm!"

"Wait, Dad, it's fine," says Stefan, his hands urging Fanus to remain calm. "Oom Jaap, it wasn't me. I don't know who SM was. Janien and I dated for a few months while we were at school, yes, but never again after that. It was never much of a relationship anyway. After school, Henk and I went to study BCom at Stellenbosch and Janien and Maggie went to study art there a year later. That was it. Janien wasn't interested in me and I didn't mind. There were lots of other, more willing, girls at varsity." He ducks his head a little and looks at me. "I mean, girls with easier families."

I nod. He sounds honest enough, but I'm not going to give up that easily. The computer that S&M used is in this house.

I draw a new spiral, upwards this time. "And you, Fanus?" I ask without looking at him. "Did you and Janien chat via email?"

I'm not going to say anything about the nude photographs for now. I first need to work out which Malan man is SM, then I'll talk to him on his own. With both men here, on the stoep like this, everyone's bound to lie.

I look up as the silence lingers. Fanus's face is contorted in renewed anger. He glares through the cigarette smoke at the rain that's begun to sift down.

"You're clutching at straws, Jaap," he says. "As always. Here, there. You don't know what the hell is going on and you never will."

I finish the spiral. Smile. That wasn't a no. Interesting.

SARAH

1

"Hi." I wave half-heartedly at the blonde woman filling the kettle as I walk into the kitchen. She is petite and short, like me.

"Maddie?" I try to recall the name of Fanus's daughter. "No. Maggie."

"Maggie, yes." She gives a half-smile. "Hi."

She looks as uncomfortable with a stranger in her space as I feel standing here. It might have been better if I'd stayed on the stoep, although Jaap and Fanus are like two old buffaloes intent on locking horns even if they both know neither's going to win.

Besides, I couldn't stand the intoxicating smell of Fanus's cigarettes any longer.

Maggie switches the kettle on and fetches a tray and a white lace traycloth. Her movements are economical and controlled, as though she's worried about making a noise, about drawing attention to herself.

Her dress says something different entirely. It's long and colorful, and I'm envious of the scuffed red-leather boots.

She tucks her straight, long blonde hair in behind her ears and squats to take three mugs from the cupboard next to the fridge. "I like your earrings," she says, without looking at me.

I touch the six silver rings in my left ear. Dad, Mom, three brothers, one sister.

I haven't done the subtraction yet.

Maggie fills the mugs with boiling water. "Does Oom Jaap take sugar?" The spoon in her hand hovers in the air. There's a delicate gold watch around her left wrist and a gold ring on a chain around her neck. The smooth, pale skin tells me she's wary of the sun.

I think of the chocolate bar wrappers in Jaap's car and guess: "Two? Two and a half."

She puts the sugar in and stirs the instant coffee. "I should probably take the sugar bowl out on the tray like my mother used to do, but, oh wel…" Then she remembers. "I'll make our tea in a minute, if you don't mind waiting."

"I'll take rooibos, if you have." I remember Vonnie's face last night and add: "Thanks, Maggie."

She smiles. "Call me Sparrow. Only my father and the people around here ever call me Maggie." She opens the cupboard nearest her. "Freshpak okay?"

I nod mechanically, my head suddenly on its own mission. It's all Jaap's doing. Colonel Jaap Reyneke and this damn murder investigation.

S&M. Stefan Malan. Fanus Malan. Sparrow Malan?

The IP address says S&M sent various mails to Janien from this house. Could Sparrow have been Janien's other secret?

"How do you and Oom Jaap know each other?" Sparrow asks.

She starts making tea in two blue cups and puts the coffee mugs on the tray.

"He's a friend of a friend," I say.

"And are you also in the police?" She looks up, a little alarmed. "Is thi—"

"I don't work for the cops," I say quickly. "But yes, Jaap asked me to help him with Janien's death…murder."

Sparrow's hands, delicate and ghost white, freeze around the cups. She puts them down hastily, turns around and pulls out a drawer, rummages noisily through cutlery.

I look at the kitchen door, at Sparrow's slender back. Suddenly it's as though the temperature in the big, open kitchen has dropped. Outside the window, the clouds have darkened and the rain is picking up.

Why did I ever agree to come to Carnarvon?

Sparrow turns back, teaspoons in hand.

Where should I begin? Should I begin at all?

"This thing with your father and Jaap," I ask, "has it been going on for long?"

"Ja." She looks relieved that I didn't say more about Janien's death. "Probably from just after I was born, when Tannie Vonnie and Oom Obie moved here. It had something to do with her. With Tannie Vonnie. I'm surprised my father allowed Jaap to even set foot on the farm. He must be bored. I think having to sit still with that leg of his is driving him insane. Usually, he'd have been to town and back three times by now."

She stops speaking, as though she's realized she was babbling.

"But you and Janien didn't get involved in all of that," I say. "You were good friends, right?"

"We were, yes. From the time we learned to walk." She gestures toward her shoes. "We went to London together four years ago. We got these at Camden's punk market." A slight smile. "We saved for ages to buy those plane tickets. We were going to go to New York next."

What else should I ask? How should I ask it? Shouldn't I leave it to Jaap? But would Sparrow even talk to Jaap?

No, not to Jaap. To *Oom* Jaap. The history here is so dense you could trip over it in broad daylight. And who says Jaap's not like Vonnie? I don't really know the man, do I? The internet can't tell you everything about a person.

If Sparrow is S&M it would explain a lot, like why Janien was so careful about deleting the messages.

I tune my ears into what's happening on the stoep. Sounds like Jaap and Fanus are still arguing, with a third voice, softer, probably Stefan's, urging them to calm down.

"Why do people call you Sparrow?" I ask.

She puts the teaspoons down on the gray kitchen counter, the coffee forgotten, lines up the silverware like a row of soldiers.

"It started at university. I was the smallest of the first-years. The littlest sparrow." She reorganizes the teaspoons, putting the first one last, biting down on a full bottom lip.

"Was Stefan also friends with Janien?"

She nods. "We all went to school together. And university. Stefan and Henk are a year older, but we often hung out."

She looks at me, her eyes bright, the memory clearly painful.

I should have left this mess for Jaap, but it's too late now.

"How are you helping Oom Jaap exactly?" asks Sparrow.

"Please just say Jaap, otherwise I have this image in my mind of my uncle and I really don't like him. He kisses me hello with these really wet lips." The words are out before I can stop them.

Sparrow laughs. "Janien also never called Jaap 'Oom.' You remind me a bit of her." She swaps the spoons again, second one first. "What exactly do you do? For Oom...for Jaap, to help him?"

"Computers." I wonder how to make her realize what I'm after. "I'm good at looking for things other people can't find that easily. Hidden things."

Her hands stop momentarily. Then she picks up the spoons and places them on the tray, touches one of the coffee mugs with the back of her hand. "Ice cold. I'm going to have to start again. Will you tell my dad I'm on my way?"

Certainly not. I step closer, press on. "Sparrow, were you S&M?"

She turns to take the coffee tin from the cupboard, puts it down and fills the kettle again. She stands at the kitchen counter with her back to me.

"Sparrow?"

She shakes her head, the blonde hair a curtain. "You don't understand. I didn't...Janien...I can't."

"Can't what?"

"Nothing I know has anything to do with her death. I'm sure it doesn't." She leaves the kettle in the sink, drops her hands slowly till they rest on the countertop. "Besides, it was a lifetime ago."

"Don't you want to know who murdered her?"

She turns around. "Do you think it was me?"

I think of the bicycle. The fact that someone carried Janien and the bicycle through the mud to the pan. The size ten boots. The DNA that indicates it was a man.

"No. But maybe you know more than you're letting on. Maybe you know more than you think you do. Maybe you know something that could help Jaap."

She picks up the mugs, carries them to the sink and empties them.

"There's a blue house in town. You'll find it easily if you ask around. Tonight, six thirty." She avoids my eyes. "We can't talk here."

"I'm no—"

"I have to make this coffee now. Please."

"Okay. I hear you."

I walk back to the stoep where Fanus's voice cuts angrily through the comforting din of the rain. Stefan has already left.

I sit down next to Jaap and stare at my shoes, forgetting to tell them about the coffee being on its way.

A few minutes later Sparrow walks out with the tray. She puts it down on the stoep wall, looks at Jaap and then at her father. "Sorry it took so long. I'm going home. I have to send a package to Mom. Dad, your dinner is in the fridge. Stefan has a date."

I wait for her to go down the stairs, car keys in hand, before I look at Jaap. "Are you done? Can we go?" I point at the tray. "I'll buy you coffee on the way home."

2

"I want to go with you when you talk to Sparrow," Jaap insists.

We're driving back to *Lekkerkry* along a muddy dirt road. The rain has stopped since we left Fanus's farm, but the next shower is already threatening above us.

"She won't talk to you," I say. "And I don't even know if there's anything to talk about."

"Why won't she talk to me?"

"Because you're old. And you're Vonnie's brother."

"Fifty-nine is not old."

"It's old for her."

"And for you."

"Bul—nonsense. My father was fifty-six. I loved his company."

"Did he tell you not to swear?"

"Yes, especially around do-gooders like you. Would you prefer it if I swore? Because I would love to. Trust me."

He mumbles something and turns left at a sign that says Carnarvon is ten kilometers ahead.

We drive in silence for a while.

"Why did you leave SAPS?" I ask. I've been curious for a while now about why Jaap didn't stay in the police until he retired. Why bail at the age of fifty-seven when you've been in the service since you were eighteen?

He gears down to tackle a rutted slope. If he'd picked up more speed on the downhill, he wouldn't have needed to, but I don't say that. By now I've worked out that he uses his time at the wheel to think. And I'm in no hurry to get back to Vonnie and company anyway.

"It was time," he says. "I wanted to go."

He rummages for the notebook in his jacket pocket, takes it out and rests it on his thigh, rustles through the pages with his thumb, one eye on the road. "Can you check something for me? Stefan says he and Janien never chatted via email. Can you see if that's true?"

"How?"

"Well, you know."

"So you want me to hack his account?" I type a silent "I told you so" on an imaginary keyboard on my legs.

He sighs. "If you want to. Only if you want to. I know I promised you wouldn't have to do anything illegal."

I laugh. "Forget black. Gray is always in fashion."

He looks at me sharply.

"Don't worry," I say. "I'll do it. As long as you know you're coming to prison with me if anyone asks."

"I thought you were good at what you do."

"Who found S&M?"

"Ja, ja." He waves my words away. "By the way, I don't care what you say about Maggie, I want to talk to her."

"No."

"I'm the one paying you."

"Keep your money then. I charge R10 000 a day in any case, plus expenses. You can't afford me."

"Says who." He looks at me pointedly, driving so slowly that the Corolla's engine starts to stutter. "Why do you suddenly want to get involved?"

"The car's going to stall."

Even slower.

"I'm driving next time."

He changes gear and speeds up. "Glad to hear there's going to be a next time."

We see it as we get to the top of the hill. Patchy black smoke hiccoughing up into the air like struggling Morse code. Like the SOS of someone lost on an island.

Jaap pulls over. We get out and go and stand under a nearby clump of thorn trees.

A few hundred meters from *Lekkerkry's* farmhouse, where Janien's computer and bed and clothes are burning, Vonnie stands in a sleeveless floral dress with her palms together like someone praying.

She must be freezing. It's late afternoon and the chill is hardening. Dusk is settling in. Above us, the rain starts to fall like ice, hard and audible on the leafy canopy. A single drop trickles into the collar of my jacket and runs down my back.

I pull the leather tight around my body and turn away from the scene across the plain, toward Jaap.

He says nothing, just stands and stares at the bright orange flames. Rubs his eyes tiredly. I watch his breath in the frigid air. The way it billows out, white and unhurried against the black sky, as though he is sighing from a place deep inside. I turn back again, wishing I could tell him that it's okay, but I know that would be a lie.

The rain has stopped. I'm not in the mood for the house and Vonnie and Obie and supper. I fetch my laptop and pack my backpack. There's got to be a restaurant or a pub or something in town where I can work until I have to meet up with Sparrow at the blue house.

I start the bike just as Jaap walks out the back door, clutching a list. "I'm cooking tomorrow. We need peas and cheese. Something strong. Maybe gorgonzola? Can you go and get some if you have time?"

I take the list from him. "You cook?"

"I'm on chapter thirteen of *Cook and Enjoy It*."

"And the other chapters?"

"Mostly done."

"Everything? Done?"

"Almost, yes."

"Why?" I stare at the note in my hand. The writing is practically illegible.

He walks away, says over his shoulder: "I make furniture and I'm learning to cook. So far, it's better than police work. And no one's died yet, if you don't count the neighbor's cat."

3

The blue house in Carnarvon's dusty streets sticks out like me at a Sunday-school picnic. I would know—I had to go to two of them before my mother finally excused me from ever having to attend one again.

I always reckoned that it may have been more for the sake of the other kids than my own.

I park the KTM on the sidewalk, next to an ancient brown Datsun with a red-and-white sticker that says *I ♥ Jesus*. Somewhere nearby someone is watering their garden in spite of the rain earlier.

The gate at the blue house is old-fashioned, like the kind you still sometimes see in Pretoria West—a waist-high wire fence with a metal gate that squeaks on its rusty hinges when I open it. There's a white Toyota bakkie in the short driveway, the back covered with a black tarpaulin.

Whoever owns the blue house doesn't have dogs, only a three-legged cat that bolts to an open window as I walk up the concrete path. There isn't much of a garden, just pots full of herbs dotted around the perimeter. In the corner, a meter-high concrete angel crouches like a mischievous child, her big toe in a fountain filled with muddy water.

The door opens just as I'm about to knock. It's Sparrow, in black rugby socks, wearing a green dress and a thick black cardigan.

An angry Tori Amos is singing from inside the house.

"Come in," she says.

She looks over my shoulder at the motorbike and holds out her hand for my helmet. I take off my gloves, put them in the helmet and pass it to her. She puts it down on a wooden table near the front door, then walks to an outmoded FM transmission radio to turn down the music.

We walk into a warm, homely kitchen, the walls painted purple. Someone in the house clearly loves cooking. Though everything is old, it's well looked after. There is a big, silver stove with a double oven, and a long counter for prepping. The aroma coming from a bubbling pot reminds me that I declined dinner at *Lekkerkry*.

An electric heater in the far corner bathes the room in a faint orange glow.

Sparrow looks over my head at the clock and gestures toward the table.

"Sit."

I take off my backpack and pull out the nearest of four chairs, swallow the discomfort in my throat. Perhaps Jaap should have been the one to speak to Sparrow after all. What do I know about getting information out of people?

Still, somehow I know that Sparrow is unlikely to talk to him, or anyone else in Janien's family. There's too much history there, just like between my mother and me. I prefer speaking to Ranna or to my aunt when something's bugging me. They don't immediately connect every new event in my life to things I did years ago. To those months I spent in prison.

Sparrow rubs her hands together as if to warm them. "Want something to drink? We have beer and iced tea. There's also tea and coffee."

We. Interesting. "I don't suppose you have any Coke?"

She opens the double-door fridge and hands me a tin, followed by a glass from the cupboard behind her. Looks at the clock again, as if she's waiting for someone to come home.

"Are you expecting someone?" I ask.

She nods. "She works at the SKA telescope project. She'll only get home at about eight. There's a meeting tonight with the homeowners' association about the road to the building site. They're worried about the damage the increase in traffic is causing." She holds up her hands. "We're just friends. Nothing more. But I'd still like this to be finished before she gets here. Whatever this is."

She turns toward the stove and busies herself with the pot. Stops stirring and glances at me, worry etched into her face. Should I say something to reassure her? And what exactly should I say?

I pour the Coke into the glass and take off my jacket, hanging it over the back of the chair. "What are you making?"

"Curry. My mom's recipe."

The three-legged cat slinks in and lies down in front of the heater. It gives me a haughty look before curling up to sleep.

"Would you like some?" Sparrow offers. "But I have to warn you, it's quite hot."

"Not a problem. That'll be nice."

She dishes up in two small blue-and-white bowls and passes me one, fishes forks out of a drawer, closes it with her hip, and sits down opposite me. We eat, though she picks at her food more than anything.

"You're S&M," I say, deciding to jump right in. "I saw the Snapchat photos, the ones Janien sent. And I've read the mails."

She looks away. Her pale skin turns pink under the freckles on her nose and cheeks. "I thought the photos were deleted instantly...?"

Her question hangs in the air. I shake my head and take out my laptop, wait in silence for the photos to open. I turn the computer for her to see.

She swallows audibly, presses her napkin to her mouth, and looks at the clock again. "How did you manage that?"

"It's what I do, remember? Computers."

"What else have you found out?"

"I know about *So What Now?*"

"Does Jaap?"

"Yes."

"And about me?"

"Yes."

"And Janien's parents? Do they know?"

"No."

She gets up, walks to the stove, and stirs the rest of the curry. The wooden spoon stops abruptly. She stares at me. Her eyes are green, like mine, I notice for the first time.

"What are you and Jaap looking for?"

"Janien's murderer."

"If you keep on digging, you're going to find much more than that." She watches me candidly. "Are you okay with that? Is Jaap okay with knowing who Janien really was? Because her parents aren't, I can promise you that. They always wanted something she couldn't give. For her to be someone she couldn't be."

I weigh my words carefully before I answer. "I've learned that the people closest to you generally know in any case. That, if they really applied their minds, they would realize that they have always known the most important things about you."

"Do you really think so?"

"Unfortunately, yes."

She smiles wanly. "Janien didn't want her parents to know she might be gay. I say might, because she was still working that out for herself. And the possibility of that actually being the case was hard for her to bear."

She passes a hand over her mouth. The gesture seems thoughtful, sad. "Janien was scared her parents would banish her. From their home. Their love. From that warmth between the Steyn family that every one of us at school was so jealous of. Her family meant everything to her. But she was conflicted. She wanted to marry a nice, decent farm boy and have kids and fit in. She spent her whole life moderating who she was in every way possible."

I put down my fork. "You don't hide who you are."

"That's what you think. My mother doesn't care that I'm gay. She just wants me to be happy. But my father doesn't know. I think he doesn't care to know. And the school can never find out. I teach English at a Christian primary school." I nod again, wonder what to ask next.

Then I remember the photograph I printed earlier. Sparrow is one of the people in it, her hand around Janien's waist, if you look carefully. One of the others might be cheny@chenwag, the person Janien was complaining to about her and her fiancé's parents.

"Did no one suspect anything about you and Janien?" I dig into the curry. "And why would Janien marry Henk van Staden if she thought she might be gay? Would she really go that far to fit in?"

Sparrow puts the spoon down and turns around, leaning against the counter. "I don't have all those answers. All I know is that Janien and I have been friends since we were little. It slowly developed into something more in high school, and not just from my side. At university, away from our families and this place and its small-town churches, we managed to explore exactly what that was."

She sighs. "You don't need the detail, but we were together in the last year of varsity. After varsity, I could only find a job here in Carnarvon, thanks to an old family friend who owed my dad a favor. An art degree means nothing these days and I don't have Janien's head for business. Anyway, when Janien moved to Cape Town, I was there almost every weekend. But it was hard. She started getting scared. Suddenly she wanted to hide me…hide us. She was unwilling to commit and unsure about everything. I asked her what was going on. I begged and pleaded…and one morning she announced that she and Henk were dating. End of story."

Her eyes shine with tears. "Then, one weekend, out of the blue, while she was visiting her parents, she came around and had coffee here. She apologized again. Said she was going to marry Henk. She wanted kids and she didn't want to hurt her family."

Sparrow exhales slowly. She stares at her thick rugby socks, unwilling to meet my gaze.

"I don't get it," I say. "The photos on Snapchat? Those were from just before her death, weren't they?"

I put my fork down. I've suddenly lost my appetite.

"Yes." Sparrow blushes. "Everything was fine until about three weeks before the wedding. It was like Janien suddenly regretted her decision. She was angry. And wild. She came here one evening. We...we slept together. I was still living on my own then. Look, it's not something I'm proud of, but I couldn't let go after that night. And Janien kept sending me photos. She, who had always been so careful. She kept asking whether I would take her back if she and Henk didn't work out. It may have helped that people's attitudes had been changing. Slowly—but still. Even people here were becoming a little bit more tolerant of people who were different."

"Did you want to take her back?"

No answer.

I decide to move on. "What happened next?"

She walks to the back door, opens the top part and leans out as though she's in need of fresh air.

"And then she died," Sparrow says, so softly I have to strain to hear her.

I wait out the heavy, lingering silence, then ask: "Do you have any idea who may have killed her?"

She turns around, wipes her cheeks. "Does Jaap think it's me?"

"Not as far as I can tell. Someone big and strong had to carry Janien's bo—, carry Janien to the pan." I consider the facts. "But it could have been you and Stefan. Or you and someone else."

"Stefan is one hundred percent my father's child. He wouldn't help me...doesn't support me...in anything."

"Jaap thinks Stefan was still in love with Janien."

"Sounds about true. Janien was like life itself. Vibrant, caring. Alive in every sense."

"Did they socialize?"

"Not too often. Janien didn't want to encourage him."

"And Janien's brothers? What would they have made of your relationship?"

She laughs. "Obie Junior would've been okay with it. I think. He was crazy about his little sister. Wouldn't have done a thing to harm her."

"And Leon?"

"He's a different story. He's always been a bit odd."

"Odd?"

"Ja. You know…strange. Difficult to pin down."

Interesting description. "And Henk?"

She considers this for a while, closes the top part of the split kitchen door, sits down opposite me again. Glances up at the clock.

It's twenty past seven.

"I don't think he knew. If he did…But he wouldn't have. No one knew about me and Janien."

I decide to test my theory about Sparrow and Jaap. "Why didn't you tell Jaap back then?"

"Janien made me promise—made me swear—that her parents would never find out, and I wanted to honor that. She was so afraid of disappointing them. And I kept quiet, because Henk had a solid alibi. I mean, I think he's the only person who would have murdered Janien because of her relation—, fling with me. But he was at the braai at the farm that night. Everyone saw him, and there are videos of him drunk and tripping into the swimming pool." Sparrow shakes her head. "No. Her death had nothing to do with us. I'm certain of that."

"Henk isn't the only person who could have killed Janien."

"What do you mean?"

"I mean, wasn't she using you for sex? And weren't you worried about what would happen if the school found out about you and Janien? What if this new Janien tried to come out to everyone?"

"She wasn't using me. And of course I worried. I told you. But that doesn't mean I'd kill her. Why? To keep her quiet about us? Never. I'd never have done that."

"Okay."

"I promise you."

"I said okay."

"Are you and Jaap going to...what are you going to do with the photos? Please don't let Tannie Vonnie...Please don't. That's the one thing I owe Janien."

"Jaap will probably, at the very least, have to talk to Henk. He won't be able to ignore this information."

Sparrow's head drops to her chest.

I reach across the table for her hand, but then withdraw it again.

She looks up, shrugs. "Maybe it's time to look for a new job anyway. A new life somewhere else."

I don't know how to make it better for her. "Is there anyone else you can think of who might have wanted to kill Janien?" I ask.

Sparrow shakes her head. "Maybe. But where do you begin to look? The last while...Janien was really angry. Who knows what she was getting up to? Luckily people thought it was just pre-wedding jitters."

She shifts in her chair and rubs her hands together, points to the clock. "Is there anything else? I've told you everything I know."

I can't think of any other questions. "No, thank you. That's it." I get up and grab my jacket.

We walk to the front door.

Sparrow stops. "Maybe...Maybe it was business."

"Do you mean *So What Now?*"

"Skout, more likely."

I remember seeing the word in one or two mails, but nothing significant enough to nudge me down that particular rabbit hole. Although I haven't got around to all of the encrypted data yet.

"What's Skout?"

"Janien developed it with Yolene Chen. Or rather, they were busy developing it. I think it was still far from finished."

The name sounds familiar. Yolene Chen as in chen@chenwag?

I dig around in my backpack for the photo. Find nothing. Shit. I didn't bring it with me.

"Is Skout a piece of software?" I ask.

"Probably more of an app. We all studied art, but Yollie and

Janien seemed to know that they needed to have a plan B from the get-go. Janien had a head for the internet and for business. She could spot a gap in any market."

"What does this app do?"

"People fill in questionnaires developed by psychologists, and then the program searches the internet for someone who's suited to you. Not someone you think would suit you, but someone who matches your true needs—those you probably aren't even aware of. Once you've filled in the form, Skout evaluates everything you've done on Facebook, Pinterest, Snapchat, Tinder, Google, Instagram and your email—everything—and then tries to find your soul mate. When it finds someone, it pings that person and asks them whether they'd be interested in connecting with you."

I consider the concept. The potholes. The potential. The artificial intelligence behind it.

"What about all the IP involved? The intellectual property. And what about privacy rights?"

"That's why Skout was taking so long. Yolene and Janien had this idea back in our third year. They connected with tons of other people to help fund and develop Skout. And to find out how people would have to give permission for Skout to use their data."

"It sounds like a solid concept."

"It is. It's not a dating site. It doesn't make you look desperate, and it cuts out the chancers. It finds someone who is most likely to understand you. Not someone who likes you the way you think you are, but someone who likes you for who you really are. And if you're no longer interested, or if you find someone, you simply delete Skout."

"What happened to the app when Janien died?"

"It all went to Yollie. Janien always said her half would be mine should anything happen to her, maybe because she felt guilty about what had happened between us. But when she died I gave it all to Yollie. I wouldn't have been able to help finish it anyway, and it was her and Janien's idea, not mine."

"Where's Yolene now?"

"Not sure, actually. I think she's in Gaborone. Her family is from Botswana. Don't let the Chen fool you. Her father is half-Chinese and her mother is Tswana."

Gaborone. That's across the border, north. And if Skout had launched, I probably would have heard about it by now.

I pick up my helmet, take out my gloves and put them on while I look at the series of portraits on the wall in front of me. I missed them when I walked in. They're faces, almost like police identikits.

Strange decoration choice for a living room.

"Are these yours?"

Sparrow nods.

I lean toward them and stare at the lifeless faces behind the glass. They're three-dimensional, more like thin masks than portraits.

"Do you make them?"

"In a way. I create the faces from DNA. Or rather, I did. From cigarette butts I picked up in the street or hair in a hotel basin." She points at the mask of a young woman. "That face comes from a keyboard in an internet café in Lusaka."

Excitement creeps into her voice. "I wanted to show how we leave bits of ourselves all over the place. How we all seep into the same earth. How we're all one, essentially. Branches of the same tree. Black, white, Asian, gay, straight."

A faint smile plays around her mouth. "I won a national art prize for the masks. Second prize, but still. The first and last art prize I'll probably ever win."

I look at the detail in the portrait of the young woman in front of me. It's astonishing. "Did you guess most of the information?"

"I used new-generation DNA tech. It tests for age and race. Susceptibility to certain illnesses. Everything. It's still untested for use in courts and so on, but that'll all change one day. It's called phenotyping." She shakes her head. "It's quite scary, actually. From DNA I can work out where someone's ancestors come from. Their sex, the likely color of their hair, eyes, skin, whether they have freckles, their tendency toward obesity. Among other things. Age I can only guess broadly."

She gently touches the glass over the mask. "Janien helped. She developed software for me that makes certain statistical assumptions."

"How accurate are you?"

"Reasonably. I think. Remember, I literally pick up the DNA. I can never measure it against its donor. The hardest thing is the shape of the face, so the masks show the broad family features, rather than exactly how someone looks. I don't, for instance, know how long someone's nose is."

I'm struggling to take in the scope of what she's telling me. "But if you can glean so much information from DNA, why can't the police?"

"As I said, the science is fairly new. But it's getting better by the day. And yes, you need a proper forensic DNA database. You need money. Trained personnel. And it can be tricky to identify people by race, especially in a country where we were categorized by skin color for so long."

She jumps when the outside light suddenly goes on, looks at her watch.

I read the green hands on mine. "I'm on my way," I put her at ease.

She unlocks the front door and stands aside.

Catches my arm as I walk by.

"Please, whatever you and Jaap do, just call me and let me know. Before everything...before...you know."

She lets go. Walks to the stoep with me and down the stairs. Above us, the stars shimmer behind a thin veil of shifting clouds. A slight breeze blows cold against my skin.

I hear the rumble of a car, look at my watch as I push open the gate. Just before eight. It's going to be a freezing ride to the farm.

My mother calls as I park the bike under the trees at *Lekkerkry*, next to a car I don't recognize. I don't want to answer, but know I must.

"Hi Mom."

I press the phone against my ear with my shoulder while I take my gloves off, open and close my frozen, numb hands, then squeeze them into fists.

"Sarah!" she says, relieved. "At last. I've been worried sick. Where are you? You haven't answered your phone in ages. Ranna said the last time you two spoke, you said you'd be back by now."

"I am. Sorry I haven't called yet. I'm in the Karoo. I'm helping out with an investigation. The police," I add quickly, before she thinks I'm doing something sinister. "It all happened very quickly."

"Are you all right?"

"Ja."

"You're not in any trouble?"

"No."

"Really?"

"Really."

"That's good." Her voice lifts a little. "When are you coming home? I haven't seen you since the funeral."

I push my chin into my scarf and walk toward the stoep, where someone has left a light on. The warmth of the kitchen's coal stove would be so good right now, but I don't want to talk inside.

"I will as soon as I'm done here."

"When will that be?"

"I don't know."

"Sarah, I know I haven't—"

"How are things there? Are you okay?" Suddenly I wonder how she really is. Even though Geo is there, and my other brothers too. And Miekie, my baby sister.

She stays quiet for a beat. "I'm doing fine. Miekie is struggling the most with all of this. She's still so young. Your father's death makes no sense to her."

"How could it make sense to anyone of us?"

"I know."

The line fills with the awkward silence so familiar to both of us.

It has punctuated our conversations for as long as I can remember.

"I actually called to talk to you about Miekie," she says eventually. "Your father's will—"

"We can chat as soon as I get home." I don't want to know. Not yet.

"You can't keep running away, Sarah."

"Soon as I'm home. Promise." I force myself to add more softly: "Night, Ma. Sleep tight."

I chuck the phone into my backpack, hook the helmet over my arm, and hurry in through the front door to the warmth inside. From the kitchen, I hear muted laughter.

I head for my room, then turn back. The cold has made me hungry. Sparrow's curry feels like it was ages ago.

Vonnie puts her hand over her mouth as I walk in, her eyes laughing, the sharp edges of her face softened. She gets up and gestures for me to take her place next to Jaap. Obie waves hello from the other side of the table.

He also seems different. Relieved, almost.

Maybe this afternoon's sacrificial fire was a good idea. The house seems lighter. Relieved of the ghost of Janien. Next to Obie is a chubby young man in jeans, neat black shoes and a white long-sleeved shirt, nursing a cup of cocoa. He rubs his dull brown goatee, gets up and shakes my hand firmly. "Leon. Pleased to meet you."

"Sarah."

He sits down.

Vonnie motions toward the stove. "Are you hungry?"

"Yes. Very." I put my backpack down on the ground, then my jacket and helmet. Remember my manners. "Please. That would be nice." I pick everything up again. "I'm just going to wash my hands and change my clothes."

JAAP

1

"I want to talk to Maggie," I insist, probably for the third time today.

"She prefers Sparrow. And I don't think she wants to talk to you. She's afraid, and she has reason to be."

Sarah finishes her Coke and looks longingly at the pack of Marlboros on the roof of the Corolla. She gives in and takes one but doesn't light it, just twirls it around between her fingers. She lifts her face, hidden under the silver-tinted lenses of her sunglasses, as if seeking the sun's warmth.

It's long past noon and we're parked on the road next to the *Lekkerkry* boundary fence where it stretches into the distance, as far south as the eye can see. Sarah wanted a quiet place to talk where no one would overhear us.

I've waited impatiently for her to wake up so I could hear what happened last night. And now she's adamant that I can't speak to Maggie—Sparrow—about her relationship with Janien.

Relationship. There it is. I knew Janien was different, but not that different. Why didn't I see it? The only comfort I have is that I am not the only one who didn't realize what was going on.

Vonnie should have worked smarter when she dug around on Janien's computer.

"How certain are you that it's not Mag—, Sparrow who killed Janien?" I ask.

Sarah rhythmically taps the butt of the cigarette on the car's roof while she thinks. "You said it was someone with size ten shoes. Sparrow wears a size five, if that."

"She could have had help."

"I thought about that too. Where was she on the night of the murder?"

"At the braai."

She laughs. "Seems like everyone was there."

"Just about, yes."

"With so many people there it must have been easy to slip away for a while, surely?"

"Probably."

I've also thought of that. So have the police. But everyone insists that their children, parents, and friends were all at the braai, and that they remained there until long after dessert was served. And there were numerous cellphone videos and photos to prove it.

But a very long career in the police makes me wonder. It's almost always someone you know. Someone you trust. Someone you invite into your home.

And this thing with the bicycle and the red fabric. It feels personal, as though someone was angry about the wedding. That's what Doc Swarts, the forensic psychologist, thought too.

Isak and I looked at every one of Janien's exes—the ones we knew about—but none of them were near Carnarvon when she died. Henk didn't want to invite any former boyfriends to the wedding. He didn't have a choice with Stefan, since they'd been friends since school. We never considered women, though.

"I need to know what Sparrow thinks," I say. "And what she knows. There may be things you didn't think of asking last night."

"She's terrified." Sarah pushes the cigarette back into the pack. "I think you should rather speak to Henk first. Give Sparrow some time."

"Why Henk? Because maybe he knew about Janien and Sparrow and he was jealous?"

"I would have been."

I've been slouching down against the car, but this nugget of personal information makes me stand up straighter. I stare at the striking redhead who has everyone in town talking. "Why did Sparrow talk to you and not me?" I ask.

"She doesn't trust you. You're Janien's uncle."

"Is that the only reason? I mean...Are you also...?"

She lifts an amused eyebrow behind the sunglasses. "No, I'm not gay, Jaap, but it would make no difference if I was."

"But maybe it mattered here. Between Janien and Sparrow and Henk."

"Exactly. And maybe it mattered to your sister. And to Obie."

"What do you mean?"

"Just what I said. Maybe it mattered to them too."

"Are you suggesting that one of them killed their own daughter?"

"No," she says. "But as a policeman you know better than anyone what families are capable of doing to one another."

It's as though Sarah has read my mind. *It's almost always someone you know.*

"Okay, okay. You've made your point."

I look away, toward the veld. Yesterday's rain is gone and it's a lovely sunny winter's day. "Let's say you understand how Janien's head worked. Where should we look next—with everything we now know?"

She doesn't hesitate.

"I think this Skout app is a good lead. I want to go to Gaborone to talk to Yolene Chen. Maybe the app was at the point where it was going to start making money. And when I say money, I mean millions. That's enough reason to murder someone."

She walks around the car to get in as if she's done talking.

Yolene Chen...The name sounds familiar, but I can't remember why. I'll have to go and look at my old case notes.

I get into the Corolla next to Sarah. "So you think there's a chance Janien's death is not linked to her relationship with Sparrow?"

"That's not what I'm saying, but that particular subject is too messy for me. I'll leave it to you to figure out."

"You know that means that I'll have to go and talk to Sparrow."

I can almost see Sarah rolling her eyes behind her sunglasses. "Ha-ha. Ja, okay. Fine, then. Go talk to her."

"I wasn't asking your permission."

"Whatever."

I switch the car on, pull away. "And you're not going to Gaborone alone. I'm coming with you. Just give me a day or two."

"But you're paying me to help you."

"With the computer stuff, yes."

"So that's what I'm doing. What do you know about apps?"

"More than you think."

"Nothing, in other words," she counters.

"Are you always this difficult?"

"Only on Sundays."

"Today is Saturday. If it was Sunday, you'd be at church with Vonnie now."

She battles the smile forming around her mouth.

"What are you going to do in Gaborone?" I insist. "You'll need some cover story. You can't simply ask Yolene whether she murdered Janien so she could keep Skout for herself."

"I'll think of something. I don't think it was her in any case. Janien would probably have told her she was leaving her half of Skout to Sparrow. What would be the point of murdering Janien then?"

"Maybe, but still. Can you talk to Yolene without making her feel like a criminal?"

"I don't know."

"Exactly. We'll go together. Leave your bike here. We can stop off to chat to Henk on our way to Botswana. He lives in the Free State these days. And when we get back, I'll go and talk to Sparrow. That should give her some time to calm down."

"Okay. But just so you know, I'm going to warn her that you're planning to talk to her."

"Why on earth would you do that?" I ask.

"Because."

I concentrate on the gravel road, still muddy in patches after yesterday's rain, trying to summon the familiar calm that has always helped me through murder cases. That silence inside my head that made everyone talk about how detached I was. How I didn't care.

And yet, this new mess is my fault and mine alone. I knew who and what Sarah was and what she's capable of uncovering. And maybe I should ask myself honestly: why couldn't Janien confide in me? I would have supported her. Vonnie and Obie wouldn't have been able to touch her. And in time they would have come around...I think.

Sarah looks from the bristly veld to me. Her hands—constantly, restlessly tapping on her thighs—stop.

"That blood you found on Janien's wedding dress—you told me the police tested it for DNA?"

"Yes, but it wasn't much help, remember? The police database didn't deliver anything useful. We think the DNA belongs to a white man. You have no idea how hard Isak had to work to get an ancestry test done. And no one wanted to put their head on a block about the science of it either."

"Do the police have a good database?"

"We only recently started expanding it. We may have a big database like you see on *CSI* in a few years' time, but money's tight. The politics even worse."

I realize I'm saying "we."

Maybe I'll never stop.

Sarah looks surprised. "You watch *CSI*?"

"And *Law & Order* and *The Bridge*. *Bones* too."

"Don't you find the stories ridiculous?"

"Often, yes. The resolutions are silly and the timeline hopelessly too fast, but the idea—the science—is interesting. It shows you what's possible. Helps you realize there are new places, and new ways, to search."

"Okay then. So answer me this. Haven't the people of the district offered to let you...the police...test their DNA? Like on TV."

"What you're referring to were real police cases long before they got to TV. One of the most famous was a case in the Netherlands in 1999. A sixteen-year-old girl had been murdered. Marianne Vaatstra. All the men in the area eventually agreed to have their DNA tested in 2012. There were more than six thousand of them. It's hard to refuse when everyone around you is doing it. And why would you, unless you were guilty?"

"Then surely that would work here too?"

I shake my head. "There are too many men to test here, and too little money in the police budget. And Obie and Vonnie don't have the funds to help. Farming in this place is back-breaking work for very little income. And the people...well. They wouldn't necessarily cooperate. They want it to be someone who just passed through. And I imagine they wouldn't really trust the police with their DNA."

I struggle for a moment before I can admit to another truth: "And some people think like you do—that Janien commited suicide with someone's help. That she was bored and depressed. Why else would the whole thing be so strange and bloodless?"

"Get me a DNA sample from the wedding dress then."

"Why? What do you want to do with it?"

"Sparrow makes these really interesting art projects. She builds faces from random DNA she picks up in public spaces. I think she can use that sample and build a model that will give you an idea of the broad family features of the murderer. It looks almost like a mask. She has a few of them on display in her house. She's very good."

It's hard to disguise my disbelief. "That sounds pretty weird. Does it work?"

"She says so. Looks like it." Sarah shrugs. "It was just an idea." She stares out of the window again.

"Hang on. I'm not saying no."

"What are you saying, then?"

I clutch at the closest straw. "What would you do if that DNA proves it's Sparrow?"

"I don't have to do anything. That's your problem."

"You like her. The idea of her and Janien in this town…maybe you understand how isolated they felt…feel."

"What would you do if it turns out to be Obie? Vonnie?" she hits back.

I bite back an angry retort and retreat into silence. To the left, framed by the car window, a startled Karoo long-billed lark spreads its wings.

I pull the Corolla off the road. Take out my notebook and pen and start drawing, desperately seeking a moment of clarity.

I sketch a house with a front door.

Two windows.

"What are you doing?" asks Sarah

"I'm thinking. Maybe the DNA tests would be worth our while, like in the Vaatstra case. I can bluff. No one needs to know we don't have the money to test everyone. Isak could help. We put pressure on all the main suspects to give us their DNA. Stefan, Fanus, Henk."

"And then?"

"Then we see who refuses to take part."

Sarah considers the idea quietly. "Might work. But can I still get some of the blood to give to Sparrow?"

"That's the second thing." The house gets a neat fence. A cross-eyed dog. "Yes. Why don't we see what Sparrow can do?"

Isak Slingers hasn't changed much in three years. Stocky, short, shaved black hair and lively dark-brown eyes, his face still tight, his expression grimmer each time he sees me.

His clothes are the same too, in spite of the chilly air. Jeans and a white shirt so precisely ironed that its short sleeves steeple around his arms. Practical black lace-up shoes.

If I remember correctly, he's a weekend farmer with a few head of sheep, which he keeps on a piece of land some kilometers outside town.

"Jaap. Nice to see you again," he says, his Afrikaans as clipped and precise as always.

He's lying, and we both know it.

We shake hands at the gate of a white three-bedroom house on the outskirts of town, walk up the garden path and sit down on the stoep, underneath a rusted crucifix.

I try to remember his age. He was thirty back then, four years older than Janien.

His wife, Charmaine, comes out to say hello and then goes back inside to herd the kids into the bath. She brings coffee and homemade biscuits to the stoep. The late-afternoon sun is pooling at our feet. She kisses Isak on the cheek before she goes back into the house, her eyes flashing him something like a gentle warning.

I suspect she's reminding him to stay calm. I made him very angry the last time I was here. I implied he didn't know what the hell he was doing.

I point to the cross bolted to the stoep wall. "That's new."

"Charmaine wanted it up there. Something to do with her church group. I can't remember what exactly."

I fiddle with the red checkered table cloth. "I'm sorry about dropping in unannounced."

"Don't worry. I heard you were in town."

He drinks his coffee, waits for me to get to the point.

Suddenly I have no idea where to start.

"I wanted to apologize." The words come out.

His eyes register surprise momentarily, the chipped mug frozen in front of his mouth. The fingers of his left hand, with its matt silver wedding band, spread wide on his thigh.

"I said all the wrong things the last time I was here. Said things I didn't mean. I know how hard you've worked to solve Janien's murder."

He lowers the mug. "But?"

How does he know there's a but?

"It's an honest apology."

"Ja, and I hear you, but I'm not stupid."

I take out my notebook and pen, draw grass for the house I made earlier. Give the cross-eyed dog a collar.

"The DNA on the wedding dress," I said. "I may have a plan if you'll hear me out."

There's a low grumble at the back of Isak's throat.

"It's a good plan."

The hand on his leg becomes a fist. Then it's as if he wills it to relax. "You've got five minutes. Make it quick."

I explain about the DNA samples Sarah and I want to collect, but I keep quiet about Sparrow's masks. I first need Isak to agree to the most important part of the plan.

Isak drinks his coffee, ponders his answer for a long time.

My house gets two children, a sun, and some clouds.

"Every year, when you get into your car and go back to Pretoria, I still have to work with the people of this district. Every day, for every case, I have to talk to someone in this community and try to win their trust. And it's hard, even though I'm from here. Some people still have a problem with colored and black policemen. And now you want me to make it even harder for myself by forcing everyone to give DNA samples?"

"Not force. Ask. And then we see who says no."

"What happens if a lot of people refuse? If everyone starts to suspect everyone else? What happens when they finally find out the whole thing was a setup, that there are no real DNA tests? Because I promise you, the South African Police Service has neither the time nor the money to test the DNA of hundreds of people. People know that. It doesn't matter what happens on TV or what it says in the papers. We are not the Netherlands. There are too many murders here, and too little money."

"I can try to get together the money to test five of your main suspects."

What I'm offering him is huge. I know it's huge. A policeman would do a lot to get answers to the one big unsolved case that is likely to haunt him for the rest of his life.

"And where are you going to get the money?" Isak retorts. "Did you win the Lotto this weekend?"

"Doesn't matter. Finding the money is my problem, not yours."

"And what would a judge say about your clever plan?" He takes a biscuit from the tray and dips it in his coffee. Eats it in a single bite.

"I would be over the moon if this case got to court. It would be fantastic," I say.

"Okay, what if the right people don't want to give their DNA?" He looks at me pointedly. "How are you going to convince them to play along?"

"If that's the case I'll collect it myself. A glass here, a cup there."

"That'll be a problem in court and you know it. And Makeba won't like it either. He is likely to have you locked up."

Lieutenant-Colonel Jason Makeba is his boss.

"I'll cross that bridge when I come to it," I decide. "Isak, think about it. The DNA will give the investigation new momentum. Maybe it will even give you some new names to look at."

I give my house a chimney with smoke billowing from it. "You can blame me for being on your case about the murder. You can tell Makeba and everyone else that Vonnie and Obie want there to be an end to this mess and that they want to get on with their lives."

A hint of a smile creeps into Isak's eyes. "Vonnie's going to kill you. And you are right—she does want there to be an end to this mess, yet you carry on and on."

I look at him in surprise.

"Yes, Jaap. I still pop in there every now and then. I know Vonnie burned Janien's stuff yesterday. As I say, this is my community. I also grew up here. I'm only a few years older than Janien. Remember? I went to the same high school as Vonnie's kids."

I close the notebook. "What do you propose, then? That we just leave things as they are?"

He taps his left index finger on his mug while he thinks.

"Why don't you get the newspaper in town to help?" he finally proposes. "Let them ask people to give their DNA. After all, it was a journalist that kept the Vaatstra case alive. Using the newspaper will heighten the social pressure and take some of the heat off me and Vonnie and the family. And I think it's smarter to channel your money to the newspaper for the tests. But keep quiet about your involvement—for your own sake. Don't give me more work. I have enough as it is."

I nod slowly. Satisfied. Relieved. It's not quite a yes, but it's definitely not a no either.

"That could work. Thanks. It's a good idea."

He nods mutely, takes another biscuit. "Do you know that Vonnie and Henk's mother don't talk to each other anymore?"

"No."

"Exactly. You don't know anything. The shit is going to hit the fan with this plan of yours. Are you going to wait around to see what happens, or run back to Pretoria when things explode?"

He gets up when his daughter, probably about four or five, comes trotting out the front door, long yellow pajama pants dragging on the ground, her hair in two tiny ponytails. He picks her up, blows raspberries in her neck until she giggles and pushes him away.

"It tickles!"

"Have you eaten?"

"Ja. And I had a bath." She smiles at him. "Can we watch a movie? Mommy says I must ask you."

"Which one?"

"Not a scary one. The one with the witch." She makes claws with her hands.

"And that's not scary?"

"She's not scary. She's a good witch."

"Okay then. Watch your movie."

He puts her down and she runs back inside.

"You're going to pay for the police to do five quick private laboratory tests at the company of our choosing," he says when he sits down again. "And you're going to pay for the equipment we need to gather the DNA. We're going to have to take the DNA of about a hundred men, so that people believe our story. And yes, no one needs to know we're not going to test all the samples. Hopefully our man is among the five we do test. And if he's not, the newspaper will have to admit that their money ran out before we could test all the samples. I don't care how you get the *Courant* to play along. That's your problem. They'll have to drive this thing. From outside it will look like a nice example of the police and community working together to solve crime."

He points at me. "And then, when this is over, I don't ever want to see you in Carnarvon again. Come and visit Vonnie, but stay out of town. And don't call me or come around here again. As it is, I'm going to have to do some fancy footwork around Makeba to get him to play along. You'd better hope he thinks it's a good idea."

"He will if the newspaper pushes him into a corner. I hear he's angling for a promotion. Wants to go to the city."

"You're practically begging for trouble, Jaap. Pray you don't get caught out."

"What do you mean?"

"Exactly what I say. I can see you haven't thought this one through to the end."

I grit my teeth. I'm not here to fight. I simply can't afford to lose any more allies. "There's one more thing."

"What?"

"In the same way the DNA is able to tell that it's probably a white man, there are other leads we can get from it. Maggie, Fanus's daughter, would apparently be able to build a model of how the suspect would look—more or less."

"Sparrow?"

Is it just me who doesn't know about her nickname? "That's what I understand, yes."

"I remember a news report about an art project of hers. It was a few years ago, wasn't it? She won some big-deal prize. Can you trust her results?"

"You wouldn't be able to use it in court, but it could give us another idea of where to look."

"What does she need?"

"DNA from the wedding dress. Is there enough to give her some of it? The bloodstain was pretty big, wasn't it?"

"Depends. How much does she want?"

"I'm not sure."

"I'll have to think about it. And I'll have to find out from Forensics if I may actually do anything like that. I'll let you know."

I get up. That's enough begging for one day.

I finish my coffee and walk down the stairs, stop halfway and turn back toward Isak. "Who are you going to test first?"

He's at the front door, tray in hand. "Leon. Stefan. Henk."

He knows I don't like his answer.

"Why Leon?"

"You know very well. You made such a scene about us testing that DNA on the wedding dress. Said the results would show us if the blood on the dress belonged to anyone in Janien's family. But it didn't."

"I know. DNA shows family bonds. So?"

"But what if one of Vonnie and Obie's kids was adopted, meaning Leon."

I grow cold inside. "Who is talking such rubbish?"

"Says who?"

"What rumors have you been hearing all of a sudden? There have never been stories like that around town."

There's a shadow of a smile around Isak's mouth.

"Old Dominee Tiaan told me earlier this year that he once overheard Vonnie and Obie fighting, probably more than twenty years ago."

"They would never have a fight where anyone could hear them."

"You're right. It was early one Sunday. Dominee Tiaan was on his way to church. He was walking, as he always used to do, and there they were, two blocks from the church, in the car, arguing."

Damn it. That's what Isak meant when he said I hadn't thought this one through. "Why tell you? I thought dominees were supposed to be discreet."

"His head was surprisingly clear for a few days. His son called me to let me know he wanted to chat, so I went round immediately. Dominees, reverends, pastors—they know everything."

"What do you mean cleared?"

"He's got Alzheimer's, Jaap. Has had for ages. Since before Janien died."

"I didn't know."

"You've never really had much interest in anyone around here, except Janien."

He's probably right.

"Don't worry. Dominee Tiaan had himself banished to Cape Town, because he was afraid he would start giving away people's secrets. You know—the stories his parishioners had entrusted to him for years." Isak looks at me through narrow eyes. "He told me he couldn't figure out that morning which of the three kids had been adopted, just that Vonnie didn't want the child to know, and Obie did. This was years ago. They were still new in town."

I want to turn around and walk away. I'm angry with myself. Isak is right: I invited this trouble. All of it.

"What does Vonnie say?" I ask. "I expect you've spoken to her."

"She doesn't want to admit to anything. She just says all three kids are hers: Janien, Obie Junior, and Leon."

"Find the birth certificates then."

"I did."

"And?" I say it with so much confidence because I know what's on them. What I had put on there.

He doesn't answer me.

"Sounds to me like you have your answer."

"Jaap, you're a stubborn bastard, and you know bugger-all about team work, but you're not stupid. Why would Vonnie and Obie sit there having an argument about something that wasn't true?"

"Maybe Dominee Tiaan heard wrong."

"He was one hundred percent convinced of his story."

I ball my fists inside my pockets. "Are you going to tell anyone what he said?"

Is Isak laughing at me? Really?

"What can I say? I don't go spreading rumors unless I have reason to. I'm telling you, these are my people. Even old Prof. Sieberhagen, who took his kids out of that same high school when I got there because us colored folk just don't belong there. But this thing with Vonnie and Obie might come out if we test the DNA. Are you ready for that?"

No. *Not at all.* But my mouth seems to think it's in charge. "You can test Leon's DNA if you want to waste your time and my money. It won't be him."

On the gravel road on the way to the farm, I pull the car over and stare at the afternoon sun glinting from the tabletop hills.

Vonnie is going to be livid about the DNA tests. These tests…am I making the right decision? I never imagined the adoption would come out. All these years, no one suspecting anything.

Stubborn as hell and thick as mud. That's me. I always only saw Janien. Isak is right. I never thought about anyone else.

But I can't walk away now. I'll just have to make sure that Vonnie never finds out that this DNA story was my idea. She needs to believe the media is driving it, otherwise Isak's going to have another murder to investigate.

I watch the Corolla's clock jump over the 15:00 mark. I'm right. I know I'm right. It's not Leon. No turning back.

Where's my phone?

I call the regional newspaper's office to see if the editor is in. Luckily there's no deadline on Saturday, and I know he is always happy to run a fresh story on Janien's death.

Then I call Henk in Clarens. I want to drop by his place tomorrow. He agrees, though he's not keen.

"Can't you let Janien rest in peace, Jaap? How are we ever supposed to move on?"

"Who says you're supposed to move one?"

"Fuck it, man! I didn't kill her."

"I have a new lead. A good one."

"What lead?"

"That's what I want to talk to you about."

"So I must just drop everything and listen to what you have to say? Again? Just like last year? And the year before?"

"Please."

He sighs, long and exaggerated. "Bring warm clothes. It's snowing here.'

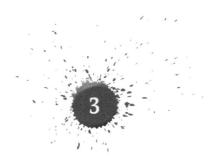

3

People who guess where Bells van Wyk's name comes from are usually right. It's the whisky—which he says he gave up five years ago, just before he started the *Cape Courant*, a regional newspaper covering the southern part of the Northern Cape.

He was the news editor at a national newspaper in Cape Town for thirteen years until the company asked him to resign. He says he never missed a story, but the personnel did, however, complain about some of his habits. The new journalists, fresh from varsity, weren't up to going drinking with him in the afternoons and then hammering out a quick story afterwards for the next morning's paper.

These millenials were too decent—too decent to write decent stories, he always said.

A month after Bells's last salary had been paid, he was sober, but it had been too late. The political editor had taken over the news desk until management could find someone more suitable for the job.

Bells looks seventy, but he's as old as I am. He ran the story of Janien's murder as long as he could. He always got the facts right and never went for the sensational angle. And he made Janien a human being, not just another victim, as so many other news outlets did.

The radio journalists were the worst. They reduced everything to thirty-second sound bites and Twitter spat. Apparently, the average person out there is unable to concentrate on anything for more than half a minute, and most of them don't actually want to know more.

Every six months, the *Cape Courant* places a story to say that Janien's murderer has not been apprehended yet.

I knock on the open door of the newspaper's office. Bells appears from the back, holding an empty kettle. He gestures toward his glass box in the corner.

"Go through. Sit."

A young woman in a brightly colored dress and with braids down to her waist is typing at one of two computers in the open-plan office. She looks at me with interest as I walk past. Why she's working on a Saturday, goodness knows. In fact, she looks like she should still be at school.

Or maybe I'm just getting old.

I walk into Bells's office and sit down on the single black plastic chair opposite his desk.

He walks in, closes his door, and squeezes past me to his seat.

The young woman is now staring openly.

Bells lifts his hands in the air and shows for her to carry on typing. He sits down, opens his bottom drawer and takes out a bottle of Bell's whisky and two glasses. Pours generous amounts of the light brown liquid.

"Whoa," I say when he hits three fingers.

He pushes the glass across the table. Winks at me, lifts his glass, and swallows loudly.

I take a sip. Pull my face. Bloody iced tea.

This on a day when I could do with the real stuff.

Bells laughs. The sound is surprisingly deep coming from such a lean, wiry frame. He wipes at his stubbled cheeks, gray and tired-looking from years of smoking and a diet of hamburgers and supermarket pies.

"I catch everyone out. And you'd be surprised how very few people argue when I start pouring." He slams his glass down on the desk, which looks like it's been through World War I. Fills it again.

"So. What can I do for you? Have you got a story for me?" He crosses his legs and watches me expectantly. "Is there news about Janien?"

I shake my head. "No. But there is something I want to discuss with you."

I explain my plan: that Isak and I want Bells to write a story asking for all the men in the area to give their DNA for a large-scale forensic test. The *Cape Courant* pushes the idea, allowing Isak and Makeba to reluctantly give in to media pressure. I will pay for the tests, but there is no need for anyone to know that.

"It would be great if the *Courant* could move on this quickly. Don't listen to Isak's time frames. I can't wait months for the bureaucracy to finally wake up," I add.

"So, you guys want to use me? You want to use me." Bells flicks an imaginary speck of dust from his khaki pants, adjusts the two copper bracelets around his left wrist.

No point in lying. "Yes. But I'll keep you updated on everything happening behind the scenes. And the investigation should give you a great run of stories."

I say nothing about the fact that not all the DNA samples are going to be tested. I'll come and explain later.

Or no, I'm really hoping the five suspects' tests deliver one positive result. That's all I need. And if they don't, I'll probably pay for all 100 tests to be done, even if it costs me my entire pension. I'd be lying to myself if I thought I was ever just going to let it go.

If this last hurrah gives us nothing, then I have no more ideas. Then everyone was probably right, and Janien was murdered by some junkie or truck driver passing through town.

"I don't like being used," Bells says.

"It's a good idea and you know it. And it's a solid story. We can say the paper's paying for the tests. Then the police can come in and say they support the idea and they're happy someone's helping. Everyone wins."

Bells rubs the stubble on his chin while he considers my offer.

"People are going to want to read these stories," I insist. "It worked in the Netherlands. A journalist was driving the story and they eventually found the murderer."

Bells nods slowly. "Okay. I hear you." He waves his hands around, pointing to the cubicle around us. Then outside, at the office with its water stain on the ceiling and the two dead pot plants. "Let's do it. If I don't start selling more ads soon, I'm going to have to close shop. And the SKA is coming and coming, but it's like it's never really arriving. And do you have any idea how expensive divorces are?" He folds his arms. "I'll do it, but you don't talk to anyone else. And you say nothing about the fact that you're paying. You let the *Courant* be the hero."

"I won't breathe a word. But you're going to have to talk to Isak about the other media. He is going to have to comment if they ask any questions."

"No." Bells points at me. "You must make sure he doesn't say too much." He taps his nose. "The Cape Town papers are going to come and sniff around here as soon as they pick up on it. And the *Volksblad* in the Free State. *Netwerk24*. *News24*. You're right. It's a good story: who gives DNA? Who doesn't?"

"Good. I'll try and twist Isak's arm."

"You better do more than that."

"I hear you."

He juts his chin in my direction. "How are things between the two of you?"

"Not too bad."

"But?"

"But nothing."

"Then why are you here on your own?"

"Isak doesn't need to be here too. But call him if you're worried."

"I will." Bells finishes his iced tea. "I don't want to piss him off. Anyway, not so much he never talks to the *Courant* again." He unscrews the Bell's bottle top again and pours some more tea. "So, be honest. How angry is he going to be if I hurry him and Makeba along?"

"He'll be okay. In any case, do you want to wait until next year for the story? It's been three years since Janien's death and we have a small window of opportunity right now. It's the municipal elections later this year, and don't you and the mayor play golf together? Put some pressure on him—tell them it's time for the police to solve Janien's case."

"I can probably go and find out what he has to say." Bells mulls over his options. "Maybe it'll also help if I offer to give my DNA first. Maybe I'll organize a nice photo op with Isak and the mayor. Do you have test kits?"

"The police do, but we're going to have to get more. I'll pay for those too—again off the record, please."

I take a sip of the tea. From the corner of my eye, I notice the young woman staring at us again.

Bells gestures for her to carry on with her work. "When do you want the first article? We don't have to wait for the press version, the *Courant* is online now too. Didn't want to, but apparently I can't stop progress."

"I'd rather wait for the print edition. The paper still comes out weekly, right? Can you place it this week? Just the first story, the idea. Then we see how people react. We might even start collecting some samples."

Bells nods his approval. Then he leans toward me, his eyes bright and alive in a way I haven't seen since Janien's death. I recognize that look. It's what starts to buzz inside cops the moment they are handed a big case. When they realize the hunt is on. It's the faint, consistent hum in the blood coursing through your body. The adrenalin. The expectation. The addiction.

He takes the last sip of tea and smacks his lips disappointedly, as though he wishes it was something stronger. "Let's get cracking then. I can't wait to see what happens."

4

It's late by the time I get back to *Lekkerkry*. The sun has already melted halfway into the horizon as I park next to the house. I get out of the Corolla and walk to the back door. A movement around the corner of the house catches my eye. It's Leon. He's leaning against the wall, smoking.

Probably doesn't want his mother to see.

He smiles when he spots me, a little sheepish. He's wearing a thin jersey and jeans. He must have decided to pop in for a quick cup of coffee before going home.

"Annemarie is just about as bad as Ma," he calls. "And I get that, she's pregnant, but Mom? You'd swear smoking is the devil itself."

I amble toward him, careful with my knee that starts to act up every night as the temperature drops.

Leon combs though his goatee with his fingers, then pushes the shaggy brown hair back off his face. Tucks his arm in around his body as defense against the evening chill.

I can't help but notice that he has picked up quite a few kilos since he got married.

"You started smoking when you were sixteen," I tell him. "Your mother knows that, so you may as well go sit on the stoep. In any case, your father also smokes."

"You're probably right. It's more in my head than anything. I suppose you're always six when it comes to your mother."

I stand next to him, shiver from the blustery wind pushing toward us from the plains. It's going to be icy cold tonight. The radio says minus one degree Celsius. I look at the man beside me, Janien's older brother. Wonder whether he knows what happened to his sister on the night of her death. Whether he knows that one of them is adopted.

What if the DNA shows what I refuse to believe? What if Isak is right? What if…

"Can you still not remember anything else about that night?"

My question surprises both of us.

Leon jerks his head toward the trees, where Sarah's KTM is parked, clenches his lips around the cigarette as he inhales deeply.

"How do you know that girl?" he tries to laugh. "She's quite pretty. I'm almost jealous."

"Leon, it's important."

He fusses with his hair again, avoiding my gaze. "If Ma hears… you know what she's like."

"I've always said I wouldn't say anything, that it's just between us, but I must know."

"It used to be so nice when you came to visit us. The cool detective uncle from the big city. Not anymore."

He draws on the cigarette again and blows out the smoke in a thin stream, motions toward the tree beside the house. "Oom, I told you, I smoked marijuana that night under Janien's tree—first and last time. Then I went to sleep. It made me feel fuzzy and stupid. I know nothing more," he says quietly.

He looks around to see if anyone can hear. "If the police or Ma find out…you promised me, Oom Jaap."

"I know."

Does he know that he and Janien both had secrets? That his parents have one too? What is Obie Junior's secret? He can't be the only one who doesn't have something to hide, who stands pure among the rest of us.

"Oom Jaap? Is that still okay? That you keep quiet?"

Leon's voice is strained and rising. He throws down the cigarette, crushes it with his heel and picks up the butt. Stuffs it into the coin pocket in his jeans, as he's always done, unwilling to litter or be the cause of a veld fire.

I wonder what Annemarie has to say about that when she does the laundry. What she has to say about everything. She likes Vonnie, and Vonnie likes her. She is calm and level-headed, and she knows how to work with Leon's insecurities. "I won't say anything," I promise him again.

I wonder whether I'll be able to keep my word this time. It suddenly feels as though everything's moving too fast. As though it's running away from me like a wild, frightened child I won't be able to catch in time.

5

We leave for Clarens a few hours later, the Milky Way a bright, silky ribbon in the sky. Sarah is driving. Within the first two hours, she finishes the contents of the picnic basket Vonnie packed for us, including the Flake chocolate that was clearly meant for me. Luckily for me she doesn't like biltong. Her phone rings once, but she ignores it, just keeps driving, one hand on the wheel, the other in her lap.

She turns the dial on the radio, looking for music, until she finds some late-night rock station. She listens to two songs by a rap group with the name Bittereinder, before she turns the volume down.

"Did you never suspect that Janien might be gay?" The window on her side is open a hand's width and a sharp wind is whipping into the car.

I open my eyes. I wasn't sleeping in any case. "I'll answer if you close that window."

She does as I ask.

Looks at me.

I stare at her hands. What's the point of gloves if the fingertips have been cut off?

"I did think she was different, yes, that her mother and father didn't quite understand her. But I didn't consider that she was gay, no."

The landscape speeds past in shades of gray and black. Farmhouses, birds' nests, dirt roads and wind pumps I know are there, but can't see. These are Sarah's optimal working hours and she shows no signs of fatigue. I look at my watch. By this time, I've usually watched two episodes of *Law & Order*, had a grappa and a coffee, and I'm heading to bed.

The routine of a man who's been divorced for a very long time.

Maybe it's a good thing that I'm out here working again. Maybe it'll finally spur me on to start doing the private detective work I've been threatening to do. You can only be pissed off about all the blood for so long. Work through the *Cook and Enjoy It* so many times. Learn how to make so many invisible furniture joints. Watch rugby and braai with your ex-colleagues—not one of them still married—so many times. Brood about the cases you didn't solve.

"Jaap?"

Sarah's voice brings me back, and I look at her questioningly.

"What do you think Vonnie would have done if she'd known?" she asks.

"To Janien?"

"Yes."

"Honestly?"

"Yes."

"What did your mother do? You did something she didn't like at all."

"You can't compare the two things."

"Why not?"

She stares at the road. The white and yellow road markings shooting by in the bright headlights. I look at the speedometer: 134 km/h. Didn't know the Corolla still had it in her.

"She was angry, to put it mildly," she says finally. "And very disappointed. And my dad...ja."

"If you could have avoided it all—all that disappointment—would you have done so?" I ask.

"Avoid what I actually did, or the fact that my parents found out?"

"That they found out. Let's say it's too late to change everything you are."

"Okay. Yes. I would have avoided it at all costs."

"Why?"

"Because we…because I…" Her words dry up.

"Because you love them? Maybe it was the same with Janien."

"That still doesn't answer my question," she retorts.

"Probably not."

She mutters something unintelligible.

We drive two, three kilometers before she speaks again: "You have a son, don't you?"

"Yes."

"Is he everything you wanted him to be?"

"Absolutely." My laugh sounds bitter, even to my own ears. "He's an actuary, been happily married for many, many years, and he and his lovely, clever wife have two lovely, clever daughters. Everything I always wanted for him."

"He's the one in Australia?" She cocks her head at me. "The one who never came to visit when you were in hospital last year?"

Her words sound like a clumsy trap, as though she's trying to say that she knows something about me too. Something I don't want other people to know. I don't answer. Instead, I dig my hands into the pockets of my jacket and shift around in my seat. Then I close my eyes, feigning sleep.

6

We drive into the small Free State town of Clarens just before breakfast. Nestled in the shadows of the Maluti mountains, the village is popular as a weekend breakaway, and even more so in the winter for its periodic snowfalls.

I have seen snow twice before in my life, but not like this. Dirty brown sludge lies ankle-deep on the town's few tarred roads, numerous haphazard car tracks betraying the fact that South Africans don't quite know how to navigate snowy conditions.

At least the sky retains some semblance of a fairy tale—dark blue with scraps of bright, white clouds streaking eastwards.

It's a beautiful day. And a bloody freezing one. The news on the radio reports unseasonally high snowfall from Matroosberg, in the Cape, all the way to Van Reenen's Pass, in KwaZulu-Natal. Trucks traveling on the pass, traversing the Drakensberg mountains, are stranded belly-deep in the white ice, their drivers waiting eagerly for the sun to come out.

A few sedans are also trapped—people with kids on the way to see the snow. A full-scale rescue mission is under way, if the newsreader is to be believed.

Sarah gets out of the car and puts on her leather jacket, zipping it up to her chin. She runs her fingers through her short, messy hair. Touches her earrings. Yawns. She must be tired, having driven all the way here. Maybe I wanted to punish her for mentioning my son. Maybe I was just too tired to offer to take the wheel.

I look to the sky again, wonder when last I saw a sunrise. Must be a year ago. The joy of being retired, I suppose. Right now, the sun is still low on the horizon, painting the surrounding sandstone mountains with a soft, yellow light. "It's beautiful."

Sarah points at the landscape. Then trudges around the car to the sidewalk, her boots seeking traction. She's holding her fine-boned hands out to the side as though she's expecting to slip.

She looks happy, the always present cynicism suddenly gone from her eyes. She also looks about four years old.

I smile. "Is this the first time you've seen snow?"

"No," she says quickly, frowning, as though she's embarrassed.

I let it go. I'm hungry. I remember seeing a café as we entered town. "Let's eat something, then I can go and chat to Henk."

After breakfast, we check into a nearby guesthouse. The woman behind the reception desk says we're lucky to find rooms. People are streaming in from Johannesburg and Pretoria to see the snow.

Sarah announces that she's going to sleep, so I put on my jacket and gloves and leave to find Henk. Down the road I spot a handful of muddy Gauteng province number plates already scrumming for parking in front of the Protea Hotel.

I navigate the route to Henk's gallery from memory. I walk up two streets, past Clarens's sandstone church and the garden square, turn left, then left again, to get to the Stoep Talk gallery.

Just like the last time I was here, the front porch is packed with old milk jugs, rusted street signs, pots full of herbs, and coffee tables made from old wine crates. The gallery itself is spacious; the sun is streaming in through wide skylights, lighting up the industrial space's exposed pipes and metal ventilation shafts.

A raw brick wall is densely hung with framed photographs, almost the same as in Janien's room. Opposite them, on a wall painted red, are some watercolor and oil paintings.

Henk is nowhere to be seen so I wander along the wall of paintings. Most of them are the familiar scenes of fall in the eastern Free State, the artists using mainly oranges, greens, and blues to paint the bright sky, grazing cows, cultivated fields, and cypress trees.

The photographs are more original. Black-and-white portraits of a female tractor driver in an apple orchard, a bearded young Harley rider, two grayhaired women in an open Ferrari, a toothless truck driver of well over seventy with thick glasses. At the bottom of each photograph, in small print it says: *Janien Steyn.*

Further down the gallery, where there is a little less light, I find more photos.

These ones are in color, more intimate. Shoes. Hands. The corner of a computer and the swell of a breast. An old woman with a tortoise on a leash. The signature belongs to Henk. They were all taken after Janien's death.

The last collection of photographs, also his, I recognize as the karretjiemense Janien had known.

In the first one, Tannie Queenie sits with her hands folded in her lap. Next to her, Oom Geel Koos laughs from somewhere deep inside. Then the next one, the two of them together, two profiles. Then just Tannie Queenie, with her thin legs, faded dress and dusty formal red shoes.

"Oom Obie said I could exhibit Janien's pictures."

I turn around. Henk is leaning against the nearest pillar, looking at me, his hands in his pockets. He looks different to the last time I saw him. Healthier, less tired. His light-brown hair is short on the sides, but thick on top and combed neatly to the left. A thick beard reaches to the first button on his light-blue shirt. He is wearing glasses with a clear plastic frame, and a black earring in his left ear.

He takes one hand out of his pocket and rubs his neck. Suddenly the tension he always carries around me returns.

"Morning, Henk."

I take off my gloves, put them in my jacket pockets, together with a pocketsized catalog of the photographs I pick up from a table nearby. I've always wanted to own one of Janien's photos. I don't know why I never asked to buy one when it might still have meant something to her.

I shake his hand, point at the photos. "Are they selling?"

"Those are prints, so they're not that expensive. And yes, people like them. They have a certain…"

"Compassion?" I venture when it looks like he's struggling to find the right word. For me, compassion has always been the central theme of Janien's photos.

"Yes. And before you ask, her parents get half of the profit."

"I'm sure they don't want it."

"Doesn't matter. It's the right thing to do." He makes for the front. "Come on."

At the door he grabs a jacket from behind the counter. "I have a few minutes before we open. Let's go and get some coffee. Then you can tell me about these so-called new leads of yours."

We walk to a nearby coffee roastery where the woman behind the counter greets Henk by name.

He chooses a table at the window, the slanting rays of the sun promising a degree of warmth.

The woman looks at me expectantly.

"Just a coffee, thanks." I look at the fresh scones on the counter, glance down at my stomach under the jacket, and decide to give in to the temptation. "And one of these with jam and cream, please. Extra cream, if you have."

Henk takes off his jacket, but not the brown cardigan underneath. He turns his chair to sit sideways at the table. Crosses his khaki-clad legs, ankle on knee, so that I can see the sole of one of his velskoene.

There are two things Henk and Stefan and a number of other men in the district have in common: size ten shoes and solemnly sworn alibis. Partying at the braai. Photos to prove it. People who say they were there.

All night? All six, seven hours of the party?

Of course, yes.

I remember Henk's impatience from the last time, so I make him wait. Most people with something to hide hate patient, pedantic conversations. Once they're in a corner, they just want to lie quickly and get it over and done with. Get out. Get away.

"Jaap…"

Wait, wait, I indicate, patting my pockets. "Where's my pen? And my notebook?"

He looks away, out the window, his chin resting on his fist, his jaw mincing the jammed-up words.

Janien always liked his mouth, she said. And that square jaw, before the beard, that practically had to be shaved twice a day.

I wonder if I can still trust that memory. Whether Janien told me and Vonnie all these things to convince us she liked men.

I inspect him again. The earring is new. And the hipster clothes. He looks like he belongs on the cover of a men's magazine.

"You're looking good," I say, as I flip open the notebook. I click the blue Bic pen to get the tip out, scribbling on the page to make sure it works.

Henk looks at me sharply. "Is that such a sin? I had to get on with my life, Jaap. I wish you would do the same."

"Everyone says I must, but Janien's murderer still sleeps in his own bed every night."

"There are lots of murders in this country. Every single day."

"Not like hers."

A waiter brings our order, what looks like filter coffee for me and an espresso for Henk. I push the notebook aside. Offer him half of the scone, but he shakes his head. I eat slowly, making him wait.

I finish my coffee.

Henk looks at his watch. Orders another espresso.

"So." I wipe my mouth and wave my thanks to the woman behind the counter. I pull the notebook closer, start drawing a tree like the ones outside. Tall and thin, stripped bare by winter.

"How did you react when you found out Janien was gay?" I ask.

Henk freezes. Puts his cup down. He parks the velskoene together on the floor and interlaces his fingers.

"What do you mean gay?"

"What I said: how did you react?"

"What makes you think I knew?" He blinks slowly, deliberately.

I weigh his reaction. Everything seems wrong. The sentence construction, the choice of words. It's as though he's working very hard to sound surprised.

"You, Janien, Stefan and Sparrow studied together. A year apart, but still. First BCom and then BA for you, BCom for Stefan, and art for the two women. You guys did everything together. Deep down, you had to have known she was gay."

"Where do you get this bullshit? Janien and I were getting married, Jaap."

"That doesn't mean much. People murder their partners every day."

"I don't know who's been whispering this crap in your ear, but they don't know the whole story. Janien messed around with women a little when she was younger. She was curious. About everything. You know that. But that changed after university. She grew up."

"No, things didn't change. I know they didn't." I start drawing a neighbor for my tree, a bigger, stronger one in the background. "Hence my question. How did you react when you found out?"

He sips on his espresso. "So you still think I killed her?"

"Yes."

I sit back in my chair. Give up on the trees and start a house. Foundations first, brick by brick. I watch him out of the corner of my eye.

"I didn't do anything to Janien, Jaap," he insists.

"Did you know about her relationship with S&M?"

Henk looks away, rubs his forehead. Blinks. Closes his eyes.

"Did you know S&M was Sparrow?"

Still he doesn't answer.

The round blue clock on the wall above his head ticks off the seconds audibly. The door to the coffee roastery opens and a couple walks in, hand in hand. A family of four follows in their wake.

"It's going to be a busy day," he says. "I have to go." He jumps up.

I get up too. Grin at him. "Isak Slingers will come and see you.

Do you remember him? From the police? Will you be here in the next few days?"

"Here? Why?" His hands are resting on the back of the chair. He pushes it in under the table.

"Do you really believe you don't have to answer, Henk? Silence confirms a lot more than it ever denies. That was one of the first things my father taught me, and he was a very good policeman."

Henk walks to the counter, takes out his wallet and pays the bill, says over this shoulder: "Let's go for a walk."

Not exactly what I expected, but I do as he says.

Outside the café the sidewalks are filling up with people. They're starting to pack in at the breakfast spots, mugs in hand. Children wearing bright gloves are clumsily rolling dirty snowballs. The sky is still as blue as it only ever gets in the Free State—so blue it feels as though you can dive in and swim to the other side.

We walk through the center of the village and up a slope to the edge of town.

Finally, Henk says: "I knew that Janien might have been gay, yes."

"Might have been?" Everyone says *might have been*, but I wonder.

"She wasn't certain. She didn't want to be gay, that I know for sure." He grimaces. "It was this terrible internal struggle. Her parents. Her faith, what she believed, what she felt. She couldn't understand why anyone had to be either the one thing or the other…it's Janien we're talking about, after all."

"When did you find out?"

"Four days before her death."

"Did she know that you knew?"

"She told me."

"Told you? And the wedding? It was supposed to happen the following weekend."

We turn right and walk up a gravel road. The snow is thicker here and almost pristine.

"She said she'd made a mistake and that she was sorry. She didn't know if she still wanted to get married." He shakes his head. "After almost two years of being engaged."

"Were you angry?"

He stops. Rubs his nose, red from the chill.

"Ja, I was. There's no point denying it. Janien was interesting and intelligent. She had this thing about her, this warmth. Some kind of wonderful allure. My parents didn't understand her. They thought she was too wild. What I couldn't get was that the sex was really good. I couldn't understand how she could suddenly say she was more interested in women."

"Did you know that she and Sparrow were seeing each other just before the wedding? That they'd dated before Janien got engaged to you?"

"Janien didn't say anything, but when I had time to sit down and think about it—really think about it—I remembered how the two of them had always looked at each other. I remembered once thinking that if Sparrow was a man, I'd have worried." He kicks at the snow. "Did Sparrow tell you?"

"Yes," I lie. "I got someone in who found some old messages on Janien's phone and computer."

"Do Janien's parents know?"

"No."

"She was scared of how they would react."

"I've come to realize that."

"And she was worried about your reaction too."

"Hmm."

I turn away for a second and rub my nose, my freezing cheeks. I wish I was wearing thicker socks. The cold is creeping up through my shoes and into my feet. Have I always been this sensitive to low temperatures, or does it get worse as you age?

I find my voice again. "Why was Janien worried about my reaction?"

"You were this famous detective. Right and wrong. Black and white."

"I believe the exact opposite. Everything is like water, gray and constantly moving. I wish it wasn't, but that's how it is."

"Three years ago too? And when Janien was at varsity?"

"Always."

"Pity she never knew that."

I dig my hands into my pockets. Stamp my feet on the frozen ground in an effort to regain some feeling in my toes. It's probably my own fault that Janien didn't feel she could trust me. But maybe Vonnie and Obie should also carry some of the blame. Sometimes you force some absurd morality on your children that you can never live up to yourself.

I turn around and start walking back. I don't want to talk about my relationship with Janien anymore.

"What did you do when Janien told you she was gay?" I ask. "You said you were angry. How angry?"

Henk turns his head furiously, bores his eyes into mine. "What do you want, Jaap? A number on a scale from one to ten? I was disappointed. And upset. About the money and the time we'd spent on that wedding. Try this on, get those shoes, buy that shirt. This photographer or that one? Roses pink, red, green or bronze? I told her to go and tell my parents herself. And tell her parents—tell everyone—the wedding was off."

"But that never happened."

He stops dead in his tracks. "You don't get it. After she told me, it was as though she suddenly had no idea what to do next. She was petrified. Overwhelmed. She kept going back and forth, until I told her on the day of the braai that I couldn't take it anymore. That I wanted to marry someone who was one hundred percent convinced they wanted me too."

"So you had a fight."

"An argument."

"Before the braai?"

"What did Sparrow tell you?"

"That you had a big fight," I lie again.

"Shit. Janien always told her everything." He looks to the sky. "So okay, yes, we probably did have a fight. Arguing with Janien was always messy."

"You told me and Isak three years ago that the two of you had gone for a drive, had a picnic in the veld that afternoon, and then you went back home to help your father with the braai. You had to go and chop wood, get ice, things like that. Janien wanted a quiet evening at home. *All was well.* Your words."

"We did go and have a picnic," Henk admits. "We had to talk, somewhere where no one would overhear us. I told Janien she had to sort her head out and stop messing me around. Stop messing everyone around. Afterwards, I dropped her at home, but then she called twenty minutes later and told me to come back, that she would meet me at *Lekkerkry's* farm gate. As you know."

I remember this part of his statement from back then. "And that was the last call she made from her phone. She didn't phone later to try and apologize again or anything like that?"

He colors slightly. "No. I met her and that was it."

"And why was your phone dead after that? Did you switch it off?"

It's always bothered me: that his phone was off the entire night of Janien's murder.

"No, I just left it to die. Maybe I didn't want to hear from Janien ever again. I wanted to drink and party. Just that. Drink and party with my mates before everything went to hell."

"What happened when you met Janien at the gate at *Lekkerkry*? You told Isak the two of you discussed some crisis about her dress."

He shrugged. "We spoke, yes, but obviously not about the dress. She wanted more time before she decided what to do. I told her she had to go and speak to my parents, or I would do it the next morning. Things had gone too far."

"An ultimatum, in other words."

"Wouldn't you have done the same?"

"Probably," I have to admit. "How angry were you when you left there?"

"You keep on and on about how angry I was!" he exploded. "Do you want to know whether I was angry enough to kill her? Think about how she was killed, Jaap. Everything was carefully planned and precisely calculated. It wasn't a crime of passion. It wasn't done in anger. And anger is exactly what I was feeling." He wipes his nose, sniffs. "My whole life was burning down around me."

"Your business shows that you are a pretty good planner."

"Jeez, Jaap. You don't get it, do you? I've always wondered whether I...maybe I was blind that day. Maybe I overlooked how desperate she was."

"What do you mean? Suicide?"

He looks me in the eye. "What was Janien's greatest weakness? Do you remember?"

"New shoes."

I'm being willful, and Henk knows it.

"She couldn't bear disappointing people, Jaap. She always wanted everyone to be happy. She continuously had to pour herself—her animated, eclectic self—into this acceptable little box. What if it had become too much? If she had wanted to make this huge statement about her true identity? Her true self?"

"The evidence shows someone else was involved."

"Maybe, yes. Maybe someone who helped her."

"Like you?"

"Fucking hell, Jaap! Are you deaf? Or just stupid? I loved Janien." We walk on.

"Why didn't you tell me or Isak about the argument?" I ask.

"I was scared. I thought I'd wait and see what happened, whether anyone picked up on the fact that we'd fought. But no one said a word. I knew how it would seem. How it seems now."

"You also never said a word about your suspicion about Sparrow and Janien."

"Same reason. And look, I was right. Here you are, accusing me of murder. And just to make things clear: Janien was uncertain about her feelings for me and for Sparrow. In fact, I don't even know exactly what was happening between her and Sparrow, no matter what you may suggest now. And you know Tannie Vonnie and Oom Obie. I wanted to protect Janien from them in spite of everything that happened. I know about being different, about having to pretend in order to fit in."

He rakes a frustrated hand through his beard. "It wasn't me, Jaap. I promise you that. I swear it. I loved Janien. Nothing she did could erase what I felt."

"Then why run away to Clarens if it wasn't your conscience chasing you?"

"I should never have gone to university. But my parents wanted me to finish my BA, at the very least. After graduation I sold my soul to the bank and opened Stoep Talk. I now send stock to about forty décor shops in the country, and I own another Stoep Talk, and a workshop making handwoven rugs in Dullstroom. I came to live here because I like the mountains and the fresh air. And it's not Carvarvon."

"Most importantly."

He gives a sideways smile. "Most importantly."

He wants to walk on, but I gesture for him to wait, watch him carefully while I talk.

"The local newspaper, the one in Carnarvon, wants all the men in town to give their DNA to be tested to see who left the blood on Janien's wedding dress. Would you be prepared to take part?"

He considers this for a moment, doesn't seem taken aback at all. "That's a good idea. Yes. Of course."

I feel a little disappointed. "Some people aren't all that keen."

He laughs, as if surprised. "You thought...Shit, Jaap, how many more times do you want me to tell you it wasn't me?"

"Okay. If it wasn't you and it wasn't suicide, who do you think killed Janien?"

"You asked me that back then too."

"And maybe your answer's different this time. Just look at what I learned today."

"Okay, maybe you're right. But we all know there is one answer you don't want to hear. Leon was at home with Janien when she was murdered, right? But he's your godchild and he would never do something like that. You've never wanted to consider him as a suspect."

"Why would Leon want to kill Janien?" I counter. "And why like that? She wasn't just murdered. She was exhibited. Like a painting or a sculpture. As though someone was angry with her for the life she'd chosen."

"That's why I say…" Henk balls his fists in frustration. "It's big. It's colorful. It's Janien. Leon would have got that. He would have helped."

"No. I refuse to believe that."

"Then why get stuck on me?"

"Sparrow has her doubts about you." Another lie.

"No. She may have told you about the fight, but she has zero doubts about me. I would have known, because we've stayed in touch over the years. I know she wonders about Leon. And not just whether he helped Janien commit suicide. About other, much worse things."

He says it quietly, convinced of the fact.

I don't want to ask. The conversation has slipped away from me.

I start walking, side-stepping a family wearing silly red beanies with bunny ears.

"Jaap."

I turn around.

"Test Leon's DNA and see what it says. Test mine too. I don't care, I'm not guilty. And then, when you're done, leave me alone. Every year, you come here and…I can't do this anymore."

Emotion glinting in his eyes, he takes out a pocketknife, opens the blade and folds his fist around it.

"Wait, Henk…"

He grabs my hand and holds it under his fist. He squeezes the blade until the blood drips into the palm of my hand.

"Here you go." His voice is pleading. "My DNA. Don't ever come here or call me again. I have nothing more to say to you. Janien wasn't sure about me, but I was sure about her. I loved her and I always will."

He lets go of my hand, turns around and walks away with long strides.

7

I buy earbuds, plastic bags, a cheap little cooler bag, ice bricks, and sticky tape at the pharmacy. I struggle clumsily to get my purchases into a shopping basket and pay using only one hand—the one that doesn't have Henk's blood in it. The cashier eyes my bloody fist suspiciously, but says nothing.

I leave the change on the counter and go to the Corolla. I take the cotton end of an earbud, carefully wipe the blood off my hand and stash it in a plastic bag inside the cooler.

It doesn't matter what Henk says, I still want his DNA tested. I know this sample hasn't been collected according to procedure and that it won't carry any weight in court, but at least it'll rule out one extra suspect.

Once I deliver Henk's DNA for testing, I'm moving on to Stefan. And then Sparrow. It's entirely possible that she paid someone to help her to get rid of Janien. Who knows, maybe she was angry because Janien was going to marry Henk.

People mostly commit murder for the same two reasons: sex and money.

And Isak can go ahead and test Leon. It will prove nothing.

That's four people. Who's going to be number five? Fanus?

Maybe I have to wait and see who refuses to give their DNA. Things could get interesting. It might be someone I haven't even thought of yet.

I drive to the guesthouse. Sarah is sitting in the sun on the stoep outside her room. She's working on her laptop and drinking rooibos tea. The pack of Marlboros, grubby by now, lies beside her, but I don't smell smoke.

I sit down next to her on a white, wire-work garden chair, just like the ones I used in my living room years ago—way back, when I had to give up most of the furniture in the divorce.

"Find anything?" I ask.

She looks up briefly. "No."

"Did you sleep all right?"

She leaves the laptop and sits back in her chair, light shining on the silver lenses of her sunglasses. She's wearing a tight-fitting pale-pink jersey. Pretty.

She lifts an eyebrow at the blood on my hand. "What have you been up to?"

I jam my fists into my pockets. "Nothing."

She points at the blue cooler bag at my feet. "Cops are terrible liars."

"Isn't that a good thing?"

She scoffs, takes off her sunglasses.

"Would you mind going to Gaborone alone?" I ask.

I'd carefully weighed my options as I sat in the car trying to preserve Henk's unexpected DNA sample. "We can stop in Bloemfontein and rent a car for you."

Suspicion flashes across her face. "What happened to your theory that I don't know how to deal with people?"

"I'm sure you'll be fine."

She gives me a look, nods in the direction of the bag. "What's in there, Jaap?"

"Blood."

She considers this for a moment. "Henk's DNA. How did you get it?"

"He gave it to me."

She picks up the cigarettes, turns the pack over and over.

"So whatever I'm going to be doing in Gaborone is not that important, because you think the answer lies in Henk's DNA."

I think about how little effort it took to get it.

"No." The sigh slips out unexpectedly. "That's the problem: it was too easy. I think I need to go back to Carnarvon and find someone who is unwilling to provide a DNA sample. I put pressure on Bells to hurry up and now I'm not even in town."

"Was Henk your first choice?"

"Yes, but now I'm not so sure anymore." Suddenly I want to leave immediately. "You'll be all right in Gaborone. You're just going to chat to Yolene Chen about Janien and that Skout app of theirs."

"Sure." She takes out a cigarette, pushes it back into the pack.

"Or maybe just phone Yolene?" I ask, guilty about dragging her to the Free State and then dropping her like this.

"It's not the same. Isn't that what you taught the rookie detectives? Before you retired? Go knock on doors, look people in the eye."

"How do you know that?"

"You keep your notes on your computer. In your email. It's not safe."

That pisses me off. "You hacked my private stuff? Sarah, I'm go—"

"Relax. That was last year. With Ranna and the work I had to do for her." Her eyes narrow. "In any case, you asked me earlier this week to poke around in other people's email, remember. Decide what's right and stick to it."

"Don't change the subject. Leave my computer and its contents alone. Do you hear me?"

She holds up her hands. "Whatever."

"Do you hear me?"

"Yes, yes. You can stop bitching now. Tell me about Isak Slingers. Which horse is he backing in this DNA race?"

I get up. I'm not in the mood for her now. It upset me that she read my private correspondence. "Which room is mine?"

"Isak first."

Bloody woman. "Leon."

"Why?"

"He was there. Proximity."

"And? That can't be the only reason. You're hiding something."

"What makes you think that?"

"I'm a quick learner." She leans forward and starts typing on the laptop again. "We can leave for Bloemfontein tomorrow morning," she says, without looking up. "You clearly need sleep and I like the snow."

She points to the row of rooms extending to the left. "Number four. The key is in the door."

Vonnie calls early the next morning. Sarah is in the Corolla, waiting while I finish up and pay the guesthouse bill.

I put the phone on silent and ignore the call. Put on my jacket and comb my hair. I look at the pale-blue eyes staring back at me in the mirror. The wiry eyebrows growing more unruly every year.

I remember that about my father. Everything about me is starting to look just like him.

The phone screen lights up again as Vonnie refuses to give up.

I know why she's calling. The newspaper report about the DNA project is probably out. Bells and the mayor must have finished their scheming.

Eventually my phone stops ringing. It beeps a message, only to start vibrating again.

Vonnie has always been stubborn.

"Aren't you going to answer?"

Sarah's voice gives me a start. She's standing at the bathroom door blowing into her cupped hands. It started snowing again in the night and it's still coming down.

I pick up the phone and put it in my pocket, grab my sports bag. "We better get going. The roads are going to be a nightmare."

SARAH

1

In stark contrast to Clarens, the capital of Botswana is hot and dry. Gaborone makes me long for the stinging cold of the Free State. Just like the Northern Cape, South Africa's northern neighbor is home to a desert—the Kalahari and its gently rolling landscape.

The address I found for Yolene Chen reveals a low white house with a black roof and black burglar bars, squatting behind a neat wire fence. The plot in the working-class neighborhood is bare and dusty, bedraggled bits of grass coming up here and there. A broad sidewalk runs in front of the garden gate.

Next to the house is a nursery, lush and green, the entrance an explosion of colors.

The Chens' front door stands open behind a sturdy black security gate. In the corner of the yard are two peach trees. A man is sitting in their shade, a black fedora pulled low over his forehead. I can't make out whether he's half-Chinese and therefore Yolene Chen's father. In fact, I don't know what any of the Chens look like since none of them are active on social media. The only photo of Yolene I could find was from when she was in primary school, and I'm one hundred percent sure she has changed a lot since then.

I'm starting to sweat in the hot sun, but I stay in the Mercedes-Benz I rented in Bloemfontein yesterday, pondering my next move. Should I go and wake the man or come back later?

Jaap was right about me and people. Why did I insist on coming here? Is this about my mother? About avoiding talking to her about my dad's death?

I look at my watch. Half past two, Tuesday 13 July. Maybe I should just go home. Go and have tea with my mother. Tell her I'm sorry.

I shake my head. Nope. Never gonna happen.

The Merc's door creaks loudly when I open it, but the man under the peach trees doesn't stir.

I take off the thin pink jersey I'm wearing, and run my fingers through my hair. I'm glad I put on my trainers this morning rather than the hot boots, even if they do make me feel really short.

I walk over and push open the garden gate.

Do I knock on the door, or wake the man?

I decide to walk to the front door. I slip my hand through the bars of the security gate and knock. The sound reverberates through the house. I peer inside, searching for any sign of life. Nothing.

I turn around, but the man is still sleeping.

An older woman, who has stopped on the sidewalk, catches my eye.

"You have to wake him!" she calls in English. She's wearing a neat green dress, tights and black court shoes.

"Excuse me?" I say, as though I didn't hear her.

I take a tentative step toward the garden gate. It's time to get out of here.

"Wake him." She points crossly at the man. "He sits there sleeping all day long."

I take a few more steps toward the Merc, stop in my tracks when she pushes open the gate and walks past me. She pokes his shoulder.

"Sam."

I try to stop her. "Wait, Ma'am…"

She shakes him. "Sam! You have a guest."

"Don't…it's okay…" I say.

The man coughs softly. He loosens his hands, which were folded over his stomach, and wipes at his chin. "I heard you the first time, Patricia."

He lifts the hat. "Afternoon."

He's older than I thought he'd be.

"I'm looking for Mr. Chen. Actually, I'm looking for Yolene Chen," I explain quickly.

The woman crosses her arms. "Well, which is it? Sam or Yolene?"

I look at the man. His brown eyes are slightly amused and untouched by sleep. He's probably been wide awake all this time, aware of my every move. He may well be Yolene's father. Or grandfather.

"Yolene," I say. "I'm looking for Yolene Chen."

The woman mutters, turns on her heels and walks back to the gate.

"Thank you, Patricia. See you tomorrow for coffee!" Sam calls after her. "And bring some of those homemade chocolate biscuits of yours, please."

"Thank you, Patricia. Ma'am," I echo uncomfortably.

She waves a fluttering hand at me. "Don't thank me. You've wasted your time coming here. You just don't know it yet."

Sam makes tea. Horribly sweet, hot, weak tea. I sit on the chair next to his under the peach trees and pretend to drink it.

His fedora rests on his knee. He holds the saucer in one hand, the cup in the other and drinks the tea as though it's cooldrink. He is almost as short as I am, but his hands are bigger, and his hair longer. It hangs down to his neck, a mix of gray and jet black. His jeans are ironed, his white shirt yellowed by age.

"Why do you want to see Yolene?" he asks.

"Are you her father?"

"Yes."

"Is she around?"

He shakes his head. "No."

It seems Patricia was right: I drove all this way for nothing. I should have called before I came, as Jaap suggested. Gaborone is a dead end. That'll teach me to try and run away.

"I'm sorry I bothered you." I get up, turn to put the cup down on the chair. Sam gestures for me to sit down again. "Were you and Yollie friends?"

I hesitate for a moment, then do as he says. "No."

He looks puzzled. "Then I don't understand. Why are you looking for her?"

"I wanted to know something about Janien Steyn, one of Yolene's friends from university."

He fingers the hat on his knee, coughs behind a calloused hand. "What do you want to know? Maybe I can help you. I knew Janien. She spent one or two of her varsity holidays here."

"It's about Skout. The app...the program your daughter and Janien developed."

He laughs and takes a sip of tea. I taste mine again, carefully. Still hot and horrible.

"I know what an app is, Ms. Fourie."

"Sarah."

"Do you want to buy it? Skout?"

"No."

"Really?"

"Yes."

He contemplates my answer. "Okay, then we can talk. What do you want to know?"

"Anything you can tell me."

"Well, all I know is that Yollie and Janien worked really hard on that app. When Janien came to visit they sat at the computer for days on end to try and finish it. And when she wasn't here, she and Yollie Skyped and FaceTimed at all hours. As far as I understand it, it was 70 percent done when Janien died. But Yollie carried on working, had meetings with people now and again, first one or two, then more, and then..."

He stops abruptly. Looks away, up into the peach trees.

I know I have to ask but I don't want to. Yolene probably found an angel investor and moved to Silicon Valley. Maybe she wants nothing more to do with her father.

I carry on sipping my tea, rather than interrogating him further.

Sam turns his cup around on its saucer, round and round, his eyes fixed on the white porcelain. "She's dead, Ms. Fourie," he says when he finally locks his gaze with mine again. "I'm sorry to have to tell you that my Yollie is dead."

Yolene Chen's room is blue. Like the sea and yesterday's Free State skies and my father's eyes. Her bedding, the chair at her desk, her walls. Her laptop is a silver fish flashing in and out of the water in the late afternoon sun.

Sam said I could have a look at Yolene's computer, but only if he could accompany me. Maybe he is worried that I'm going to steal Skout. He's had two offers for the app but he hasn't made a decision yet. One was a five-figure dollar offer, months ago, for what the buyer said was still only half an idea. The other was a local offer from a startup in Cape Town.

Sam doesn't want to sell. Maybe it's the last thing of Yolene's he can hold on to. I wouldn't want to let it go either, not at that price. With a bit of work, Skout would be worth far more than that.

And yet. If you know enough about the concept, surely you could create your own version of the app. Unless you think Yolene's family is going to make a big noise about you stealing her idea.

I told Sam about Jaap and about Janien's murder and that I'm helping the police, even if that is a bit of a lie, as Jaap is retired, but it made no difference. Sam doesn't trust me alone in his daughter's room.

He waits in the doorway as I search through Yolene's computer. The house smells of concrete, as though someone poured it this morning. Maybe a new floor or plaster for a new wall.

Sam's hovering is making me uncomfortable. I won't be able to sit here and work through Yolene's computer with him staring at me. In any case, it looks as though she maintained the same level of security Janien did. The two women protected Skout fiercely.

I decide to clone the hard drive, and put my equipment into my backpack.

I get up. "Done."

He doesn't move, just keeps staring at me. "You're the first person who hasn't asked."

Is it bad manners not to answer him? Probably. "Asked what?"

"How I, half-Chinese, ended up in Botswana." He frowns. "And how Yollie died."

Does this mean I have to ask? I hook the backpack over my shoulder.

"Come." He gestures for me to follow him.

I hesitate.

"Come on," he says again.

I walk behind him, trudging through the house with the threadbare carpet, past Yolene's graduation picture, Sam and an older woman by her side. The Chens must have saved every penny they had to put their daughter through university. Either that, or she had loads of student debt.

I realize that Yolene looks familiar. I'm sure she's one of the people in the photo I found in Janien's email last week.

We walk onto the stoep and down the stairs, past the peach trees, to a garden gate hidden by a giant hibiscus shrub. Sam pushes it open.

Suddenly we're in the nursery next door, green shade netting over our heads. Giant lilies that surely couldn't survive Gaborone's climate stand hip-high around us. White arum lilies.

We leave the dappled shade when we get to a neat patch of lawn, about four meters by four meters, surrounded by rose bushes.

It's pruning season, if I remember correctly from my own Ingrid Bergmans—middle of July—but someone's holding back. Red roses, maybe Oklahomas, wreathe the lawn in fragrant handfuls of blossoms, almost too many, at the wrong time.

A marble stone is laid into the grass, not much bigger than my two hands put together. I bend down and read the inscription: *Yolene Chen. Ours.* Just that. No dates to tie her to a time and place. Nothing that says she lived only then—from this day to that day—as though you can live forever when you belong to someone. My dad's gravestone has dates on it, I believe.

I step away. Sit down on a wooden bench placed between the roses, my backpack at my feet.

"I want to tell you what happened." Sam sits down next to me. "So that you will think very carefully about what you're going to do with Yollie's app."

I flinch. He must have realized what I did on his daughter's computer.

"Yollie came here in the evenings," he says. "She would sit here and read. She said it was the most beautiful garden in Gaborone. I retired from the diamond mines four years ago and started this nursery. My wife loves lilies, Yollie loved roses."

He smiles a little. "Then Yollie came and lay down here one evening, barefoot, in a sun dress."

He looks straight ahead and speaks as though he is speaking to himself. As though he is trying to convince himself that it really happened.

"She shot herself. Put the gun in her mouth and pulled the trigger."

Sam's wife is working late at the supermarket. He says she often takes extra shifts these days. I go to the kitchen to make tea, partly to regain some kind of equilibrium, and partly because I'm unwilling to drink Sam's attempt at tea again.

I carry the steaming mugs to the stoep where we sit and watch the evening settle down around us.

Patricia walks by again, maybe to make sure Sam is okay. She stays two doors down, he says.

He tells me how his father came from Hong Kong to Botswana

years ago, in search of space, freedom, and many children. How he met his wife and learned to speak English until he spoke it well enough to ask her to marry him.

Sam married a Batswana woman. After forty years on the mines, he retired, with a good pension and a persistent cough for all his effort. It was the dust, he says. All those years in the earth digging for shiny stones. Yolene was their late baby. Their happy accident.

"Was Yollie depressed?" I ask.

"No." Sam shakes his head. "She was a happy child. She was always laughing."

I think about Janien and the secret she carried around with her. "Was there nothing...could she have been hiding something? Something you knew nothing about?"

"That's a possibility, yes," he says, surprising me.

"Then how do you know she wasn't depressed?"

"I kept an eye on her. There are some things you have a better understanding of when you have children late in life. Her joy was deep. It was in her eyes. It wasn't shy or fleeting. It was a solid presence. And Yollie had plans. You don't commit suicide when you believe you're going to change the world, do you?"

"Yet she shot herself. Why? Was she frustrated about Skout? Maybe about having studied art, but then having to come and live at home again, without a job or money?"

"No," he says with quiet conviction. "She believed in Skout, that she was going places."

I leave it there, quietly try to find a new angle. What would Jaap ask Sam? What did the teaching notes on his computer say last year? Right now, I can't remember a thing.

Think.

"Did someone hang around here before she died?" I ask. "Someone who didn't belong? Did you see anyone who gave you reason to worry? Maybe someone argued with her? Followed her?"

He looks at me directly. "I also think someone shot her."

"That's not what I was saying."

"But you think it. Why would they? Because of Skout?"

"Maybe." Would Jaap have conceded that? Screw the cops. "Yes."

Just because Yolene's computer is here, it doesn't mean Skout hasn't been stolen. Look at what I did in the few minutes I spent in Yolene's room.

Sam smiles slightly. "Like I said, Yolene did have a few meetings about Skout shortly before her death."

"When was that?"

"Last winter."

"Who did she meet?"

"I don't know."

"I'll have a look on her laptop to see what I can find."

"Is that what you do? Talk to computers?"

"Yes."

He gets up. "There's more stuff that may help you. I'll go and get it. It might help you and the police."

I call Jaap before I leave for the hotel in town Sam recommended. The box beside me is full of Yolene's stuff. Papers and some photos—all things Sam felt he could let go or wanted to throw away anyway.

"Sarah. Are you all right?" Jaap sounds hassled.

"Yes. You?"

"Vonnie is giving me grief about this plan with the DNA. What about you? What have you found out?"

"Yolene Chen is dead."

"Dead?"

"Suicide."

"When?"

"After Janien. Last year."

"And they say it's suicide?"

"That's what the police think, but her father doesn't agree."

"And that app? Skout?"

"I cloned Yolene's hard drive. I'll see what I can find. I'm going to a hotel now to do some work and get a few hours' sleep."

He goes quiet. I know what he's thinking. What's the best lead at this stage of the investigation: Skout or the DNA?

"That's quite a coincidence," he says after a while. "Let me know what you find."

"I will," I say.

"And Sarah, be careful. If someone killed Janien and Yolene for Skout…I'm saying *if*…keep your eyes open. Especially if you now have the app. Come back to the farm as quickly as you can."

JAAP

1

By the time I get to *Lankdrink*, Isak Slingers has already arrived. He stretches as if straightening a kink in his back, then slams the door of his police-issue Nissan Almera shut.

He's going to be angry that I came, but I want to see Fanus and Stefan's faces when he asks them for their DNA.

I get out of the Corolla.

I was right about Isak.

"What are you doing here?" he asks.

"I was passing by."

"Bullshit."

"The DNA was my idea."

"You're looking for trouble, Jaap. Some people are very angry about your little DNA project."

"Mad at you?"

"At Bells, for now. But they'll get around to the two of us eventually. And don't think I'm going to protect you. The story broke on the weekend. I'm giving them until tomorrow. Maybe Thursday."

"Is everyone angry. Makeba too?"

"Makeba is furious because Bells went to the mayor. The two of them turned up to be tested at the station today, photographer in tow. I'm pretty sure it's you who fired Bells up to pull that stunt."

I say nothing.

He grimaces at my silence, starts toward the farmhouse.

"At least the various churches all think it's a good idea," he admits reluctantly as he walks up the stairs, knocks on the front door.

"They say the pure of heart have nothing to fear. They're urging all the men to go get tested. Hope you have money for that," he says with a certain amount of relish.

It's quiet inside the house and he knocks again.

Eventually we hear the sound of a walking stick in the passage.

Fanus opens the door. His ankle is still in a brace. He lifts his walking stick in Isak's direction. "What do you want?"

"Didn't Stefan tell you? I explained everything to him on the phone last night."

"Tell me what?"

"I'm here to collect DNA from the two of you," says Isak. "I understand Stefan is sick in bed, but I promise I'll be quick." He looks at me. "Jaap was just leaving."

Fanus narrows his eyes as he tugs at the sleeve of his green jersey. "What nonsense is this? What does Makeba have to say about this crap?"

"He says I must use the opportunity created by the *Courant* to collect and test DNA from everyone in the community. That the Janien Steyn case is still active."

I don't know if Isak is lying about Makeba, but it doesn't sound like it. "We've known about the newspaper's plans for a while now, Mr. Malan," Isak continues. "Bells came to talk to us some time back." Now he's definitely lying. "We serve the community and there is a lot of pressure to take the *Courant's* request seriously. I think in any case that the newspaper has a point, and it seems a number of people agree. No one can argue with the logic behind the project."

Fanus leans heavily on his walking stick. He looks old and tired today, as if something kept him up all night. His conscience?

Isak's eyes question why I'm still there, but I don't budge.

"Where else have you done these tests of yours already?" asks Fanus.

Isak moves back an inch, as if calculating the reach of the walking stick. "I only got the kits this morning."

"And you're starting here? On my farm?"

"I have to start somewhere, Mr. Malan. Let me take a DNA swab, then it's done. It'll eliminate you and Stefan from our investigation. And I assure you, I'm well trained in collecting DNA. It's a simple, painless procedure."

Fanus shuffles out onto the stoep.

Isak and I retreat a step or two.

Fanus balances himself and lifts his walking stick, taps me on the chest with it.

"This is your doing."

Tap. "Bringing the police here, as if we're common criminals. Hiding behind them."

Tap. Tap. "You fucking coward."

Tap.

I take a quick step back.

Fanus stumbles with the next tap he is about to deliver.

Isak catches his arm and steadies him.

"Get off me!" Fanus shakes off Isak's grip.

Fanus glares at me. "Leon killed Janien. It's always been Leon, but you've been protecting him every step of the way, and this asshole is too stupid to realize it." He points at Isak. "Don't think we don't know. Everyone knows. Everyone!"

Raw anger burns in my chest. "Just like everyone was at the braai? Every single man in the entire district?"

Fanus swings his walking stick wildly. It hits Isak on the arm.

"Wait now, Mr. Malan! Don't—"

"Get off my farm."

Isak puts up his hands. "We just want to—"

"Go. You're not getting anything from me or from Stefan." Fanus pushes the walking stick into my chest again, listing dangerously.

I grab the end and push it back. "If you have nothing to hide—"

"We were all at the braai!"

"And I'm saying, if everyone was at the braai, Janien would still be alive. Who says Stefan was there all the time? And you?"

Fanus bellows something incomprehensible. He wrenches the walking stick out of my hand and aims for my shoulder.

I block the blow with my forearm.

Isak grabs hold of the stick, tries to pull it from Fanus's grip.

Fanus lets go, limps forward and punches me in the face.

I duck so he's not quite on target, but still I stumble back a step or two, regain my balance and charge at him. I punch him in the stomach, winding him.

He falls backward, the plastic brace cracking.

I hear the sound of running feet. Stefan?

"Stop! What...Dad? What are you doing?" It's Sparrow. She bends over Fanus protectively, glaring at Isak and me as if we're schoolyard bullies.

Rage is bubbling inside my head and in my hands, red and hot.

"Dad?" She hooks her arms in under Fanus's shoulders and tries to help him up.

"Wait, let me," Isak offers.

"Leave me alone." Fanus slaps at the policeman's hands, then pushes Sparrow away. "Don't fucking touch me!"

Sparrow stands up straight, points to Isak and me. "You need to leave, please."

I wipe the blood dripping from my nose onto my chin. Fanus has a mean left hook.

"Where's Stefan?" I ask. "Surely he can decide for himself if he wants to do the DNA test?"

"Go!" Fanus roars. He's trying to find something to hold on to, a chair, anything, to pull himself up.

Sparrow shakes her head, her eyes urging me to listen. "Please, Jaap. You need to go. Now." She bends down again to try and help her father.

Isak tugs at my jacket, cocks his head toward the cars. "Come on."

We walk down the stairs, Isak touching his elbow gingerly.

He gets into the Nissan, says testily through the open window:

"You better stay home next time or I'll lock you up."

I don't argue as I wipe my nose with my sleeve. I look at the bright-red stains as the frosty morning slowly comes into focus again.

Isak doesn't start the car. He sits and stares at the Malan house in the rearview mirror. He smiles at me, a little reluctantly. "So that was interesting, huh?"

I swallow the bloody mucus in my throat. Cough. "Ja, it was, wasn't it?"

I remember the street from my previous visits, but I can't remember if this particular house was always blue. It's a quaint home, with a cozy stoep. Two well-worn easy chairs give the impression that its inhabitants sit here often, watching the Karoo sunset.

I ring the bell. There's music, but no one approaching to open up. I touch my bruised face. It still hurts, despite the ice pack I put on earlier. Fanus has a fist like a ten-pound hammer.

Isak promised he'd ask Fanus and Stefan for their DNA again, but then Leon has to follow suit. And I'm not allowed to be anywhere near when that happens.

I've given him Henk's DNA. He didn't seem too surprised that Henk provided a sample so easily, but frowned about the amount of blood in the bag, and the lack of scientific rigor in my collection method. I also provided my own DNA for elimination purposes.

I leave the bell and knock. Finally the music is turned down and a tallish figure in blue makes itself visible through the window.

The door opens.

I'm an uninvited guest. This much is clear from the look on the face of the woman before me. She's in her mid-thirties, and I would guess she spends a lot of time outdoors. The muddy brown construction boots make me think I know where: on the grounds around the SKA.

She must be Sparrow's tenant, if what Sarah told me is true.

"Evening," I say, carefully. "Sorry to arrive unannounced. I'm looking for Sparrow."

She just stands there, looking tired and miffed. Long brown hair down past her broad shoulders. Strong hands.

She crosses her arms and asks through the security gate: "Are you her father?"

"No."

Do I really look the same age as Fanus? Bloody hell, I need to stop with the chocolate and the biltong.

I touch my cheek self-consciously. "But I had a run-in with him earlier today. She probably told you."

"Oh. That makes you the difficult policeman then."

What can I say? "I suppose so."

She lifts her eyebrows, somewhat amused, then disappears for a second. She returns with the keys for the security gate, calls over her shoulder: "Sparrow, that cop is here for you!"

I follow the woman to the kitchen, where Sparrow is standing at the stove, cleaning it vigorously.

"Take a seat," the woman says before she retreats to the living room.

Sparrow makes us coffee, every movement curt and angry. She puts sugar in the cups, bangs the sugar pot's lid back on, slams the kettle down and stirs furiously. Practically drops the cup in my lap.

She sits down opposite me. A three-legged cat brushes up against her legs for attention. She ignores the animal.

"What do you want, Jaap? My DNA?"

I push the well-packaged scrap of wedding dress across the table toward her.

"No. I'm making a delivery. You can have this, if you'll do something for Isak in return."

"I don't have time for games. What is this?"

"Evidence. Don't you of all people want to solve her murder?"

She picks up her coffee cup. It looks as though she's just had a long soak in a hot bath. She is dressed in a blue tracksuit and thick socks, ready for a night in. As she runs a hand through her damp hair I catch the scent of green moss.

"I can't believe Sarah told you...seriously!" she hisses under her breath.

I hold up my hands. "She had to. Don't be cross with her. And don't worry. I'm not going to say anything."

Every word seems to deliver a blow to her elfin body.

"Only as long as it suits you, I imagine," she says.

"What do you mean?"

She looks away crossly. There's a vein pulsing in her pale neck.

"Okay then, Maggie...Sparrow. To be completely honest, yes, I won't say anything, as long as the DNA sample you give Isak tomorrow cannot be linked to the scene of Janien's murder."

She leans down and strokes the cat. "I thought you were only looking at men's DNA."

"Stefan won't give us his. Neither will your father."

She laughs bitterly. "Ah, but my DNA will show whether someone in my family was involved."

Sarah was right. Sparrow understands DNA.

"You want me to betray my family."

"No. I want you to show Janien one last act of kindness." I gesture toward the piece of wedding dress. "Two, in fact."

Sparrow stares at the plastic bag. "Is this what she was wearing...is this the..."

"Yes. This is the dress she was wearing when she was murdered. The one she had on when she was found on the pan." I watch Sparrow carefully as I speak. "Isak Slingers gave this piece of fabric to me."

"And what do you want me to do with it?"

"Sarah says you can use DNA to make some kind of likeness of the man who killed her. The one we believe spilled this blood on her."

Sparrow pushes a tired hand through her blonde hair. She pulls one leg up onto the chair and rests her forehead on her knee. The supple, easy movement reminds me of Janien.

She glances at me. "Where did you find Sarah?"

"Long story."

I push the scrap of fabric closer to her. I want to see again what I spotted in her eyes just now. The shock. The loss. I want to be sure of what I saw. That it wasn't regret for something she had done.

I sit silently. Sparrow is attractive in an unusual way, like those gymnasts you see on TV. Toned, strong-minded, focused. I can see why Janien would like her. She's careful, but not afraid. Sorted. Together. Aware.

"Why did Janien never tell me?" I blurt out the question I promised myself I wouldn't ask.

Sparrow lifts her eyes from the scrap of wedding dress, listens to someone—probably the brunette—walking across the wooden floor with long strides. The TV coming on. Sounds like Formula 1.

Is this how quickly she was able to replace Janien, in not even three years?

Or no, I remember, Janien replaced her. With Henk.

The green eyes appraise me frankly. Sparrow looks like I did, long ago, when I still cared whether people could handle the truth.

No, Ma'am, she didn't suffer. She really didn't.

I laugh. It happens before I can stop it. I laugh until I choke on my own emotion.

This is pretty shit, Janien. Thanks for nothing.

Sparrow doesn't say a word.

Eventually, I get a grip. "Sorry, but I just don't get it. How the hell did Isak and I miss something this big?"

Sparrow waits a beat or two. "You were too close. And Janien and I were really, really careful. No one knew. It helps that we've known one another since we were four and that everyone in town knew us that way. As us. The two of us."

"And this woman, is she…" I gesture toward the living room where the TV is droning in the background.

"Also a long story." Sparrow smiles, as though she's glad to get back at me. "But be careful not to make any assumptions."

I nod. "Tell me about the Janien I didn't know."

"Why? It's too late now."

"Please. I need to know who she really was."

"She wasn't different to the Janien you knew, just maybe more *her*. Freer, more spontaneous. Same wine, different vintage. Better vintage."

Sparrow unfurls her body, gets up and puts the kettle on for more coffee. I realize it's already dark outside, like a presence that's crept up on us.

"Towards the end," Sparrow grasps for the right words, "I got the idea Janien wanted everything to just stop for a while until she knew who she was and what she wanted to do with her life. Until she'd cleared her head."

"It must have been hard, knowing she was unsure about her love for you."

"It was." Sparrow takes two coffee cups from the cupboard. "Oom Jaap—"

"Just call me Jaap. Sarah does."

"Fine. Jaap." It's as though she's testing the sound of my name in her mouth. "Janien was…You don't forget your first love."

"Probably not, no."

She spoons instant coffee and sugar into the cups. "Who was the first woman you loved?"

I know she's looking for balance. She doesn't want to sit here bleeding while I get to reveal nothing about myself.

"She was sixteen," I say. "I was seventeen. We married when I was nineteen. It lasted just over twelve years."

"And you never wanted to marry again?"

I shake my head. "It's not for me. I get distracted. My work swallows…swallowed…me whole."

Sparrow's shoulders soften a little under the tracksuit top. I take the gap.

"Why did you never say anything during the investigation? You could have taken me aside, whispered the truth about you and Janien in my ear. I would have kept your secret."

"I was convinced it made no difference. I remain convinced it makes no difference. No one knew, so how could it drive anyone to kill her? And I wanted...I don't want to lose my job. What would I do? Go and live with my father, like Stefan, and work in the butchery until I'm old and gray? And Janien's parents...it was hard. And you—you weren't objective. Not one bit."

"Okay, I hear you," I admit reluctantly. "But you're aware that Henk knew."

This startles her. "Did Janien tell him?"

"Yes. A few days before the wedding, he says. Apparently she was thinking about canceling the whole thing."

"Because of us?" Something like hope creeps into Sparrow's voice.

"I don't know. Henk says she was unsure. Perhaps, as you said, she just wanted to put everything on ice until she knew where she was heading."

"I can't believe it. Henk must have been so angry."

"He said he'd actually known for a while. That if people saw the two of you together, they would know."

Sparrow shakes her head. "No, he wouldn't have. That's his ego talking. I also dated him for a while at varsity—before he showed an interest in Janien and before I'd made peace with my sexuality. Henk is intense—which is probably what attracted Janien to him. He's nice, yes, but make no mistake. He's driven. And very, very smart, in spite of those average marks. But he struggles to look beyond the things that interest him, the things he believes in."

"Maybe you're right. Maybe he was just pretending that he knew. Men don't like looking stupid," I say. "Did the two of you date for long?"

"No. I was never really interested. I have to admit, it was a bit odd when he suddenly asked Janien out, but maybe that had been his intention all along. It seems like it, anyway." She takes milk out of the fridge. "Is he...do you think he'll say anything? About me and Janien? Janien was petrified that her mother would find out."

"I don't think you have to worry. If he hasn't said anything by now, I doubt he ever will. All this time of not admitting to knowing about the two of you will make him look guilty. It may seem as if he's hiding something."

"I suppose so."

I shift uncomfortably in my chair. "I have to be honest, Sparrow. I still don't quite understand why you—you and Henk—are so hesitant about telling the truth. I think Vonnie would be fine, really."

"Back then too?"

"Ja, okay," I sigh. I rub my cheek as the dull pain picks up a notch. It's been a long day and I'm exhausted. "Maybe not."

The volume on the TV has suddenly grown louder. I listen to the sound of engines racing around a track. Round and round. I've never understood motorsport. I want to talk about something else, something lighter, something that would make Sparrow feel better, but it's impossible. "Who do you think killed Janien?"

She stirs the coffees. "I don't think you want to know."

I immediately know what she's going to say. What she meant when she said I wasn't being objective.

"Leon?"

She puts one of the cups down in front of me and sits down. "He was a little creepy, Oom Ja—, Jaap. Janien said she sometimes felt like he had this thing for her. Not brotherly, if you know what I mean?"

Really?

"So, you don't suspect Henk at all?" I ask.

"I suppose he could have done it," she concedes.

"Stefan?"

She doesn't seem offended that I named her brother.

"Stefan is a carbon copy of my father. He does exactly what Fanus Malan tells him to do."

Interesting answer. "Does that mean that you're afraid that it might be him?"

"No."

"So, you'll give your DNA to Isak?"

"I'll think about it."

"What about your father? Why do you think he's so reluctant to help with the investigation?"

She looks at me as though I ought to know better. "He doesn't like you. If it wasn't for your involvement, he probably would have persuaded everyone in town to line up at the police station and provide a DNA sample."

Probably true. "What about the DNA mask...would you be able to make one? Are you up for it?"

"Yes. I'll give it a try. Give me a week. But I'll have to go to Cape Town to do it. Luckily it's school holidays. It's time for a break anyway...maybe even a permanent one." She looks at me over the rim of her cup. "You do know that the mask will only give a broad indication of family traits, nothing more."

"It may be enough."

"It might be someone I know." She sounds worried.

"It might be Leon."

She shrugs and sighs. "Time to find out."

"Time to find out," I agree.

3

I sit and watch the farmhouse from inside the Corolla. From where I'm parked under the tree, next to Sarah's KTM, I can see Vonnie at the kitchen window, washing the dishes. Leon and Obie Junior are both here, their respective Toyota bakkies parked at the gate.

Vonnie invited her sons to dinner. I asked her to. But now I'm two hours late and she's not going to be impressed.

I can hear laughter, Obie's guffaws drowning out the rest of the men's voices. Obie is always in a good mood when Leon is here. Leon the jester.

Does Leon know about the adoption? Does it matter?

Each of the children would have inherited a third of everything when their parents died. Now it's half. It's not a lot, but it's more than it was.

Is that sufficient motive to kill your sister?

Or is there something else I'm not seeing? Another secret? Sparrow said Janien sometimes thought there was something creepy about Leon. That he felt more for her than he should have as a brother.

Janien didn't know Leon was adopted. None of them knew.

Maybe I've been blind, stubbornly so. But sometimes you try to save someone, try to save something of yourself.

Maybe it's time for me to wake up.

I get out of the car, stretch my stiff knee, and walk to the back door in the cold evening air.

Vonnie opens the door without saying hello. She probably saw me coming. Most of the supper dishes are already on the drying rack. The sound of animated conversation drifts in from the dining room.

I sit down without saying a word. She knows what it is I want to discuss with everyone. Bells' articles have made it clear.

"Leon wouldn't have done something like that," she says.

"I know."

"This DNA thing…It's you. I know it's you. You and Bells got on well after Janien died. I remember. And now he's supposedly first in line to give his DNA." Her eyes are unnaturally bright under the fluorescent light.

I nod.

"It's going to come out. It's all going to come out. And then what? What do I tell Obie Junior? And Leon? How do I explain that we never said anything?"

"It wasn't necessary for anyone to know. For everything that happened back then to follow Leon around forever. We all thought that—I did too. We wanted him to forget and get on with his life."

"Then why this mess with the DNA and the newspaper?"

"Because Janien also counts."

"I know that! But Leon is innocent."

"Then it won't matter."

She peels off her apron. "Why didn't he come to the braai that night? If only he'd come with us!"

"It's not going to be Leon's DNA on the dress," I say, trying to calm her panic. "I'm sure of it. As you say, it's not him."

"Are you going to ask him for his DNA tonight? Do you want the others' too?"

"No. Just Leon's. And only tomorrow. Isak…Isak's going to do it. I just wanted to warn them. That's why I wanted everyone here."

She leans against the sink as though it's keeping her upright. "I can't lose another child, Jaap. Nor a grandchild. Annemarie…her blood pressure is already too high. Please."

"I know, Vonnie. I know."

"Hello, Oom Jaap." Leon shakes my hand and sits down next to me at the kitchen table.

I put my cutlery down and push my empty plate away.

Isak called just as I drove away from Sparrow's house. So far, the only people who refuse to give DNA samples are Stefan, Fanus, a French astrophysicist, and the retired maths professor, Olaf Sieberhagen.

Leon looks around. "Where's Ma?"

"She went to bed."

Obie is smoking out on the stoep. Like Vonnie, he wants nothing to do with the DNA investigation.

I pick an apple out of the fruit bowl on the table, sit with it in my hand as though it's a crystal ball.

"Isak Slingers will be at your house tomorrow." I watch him closely, note the slight tremor of his jacket collar as he breathes. Evenly. Smoothly. "It's about Janien," I say. "The DNA article that was in the newspaper? Isak wants your DNA." His breath quickens for a moment, then returns to a steady, regular beat.

"It won't look good if you refuse, Leon."

"What's changed?" He leans back in the chair, his face unreadable, the always-friendly, glad-to-see-you expression gone. "Back then, nothing linked me to Janien's death. The blood on the wedding dress didn't belong to anyone in this family. The DNA was clear."

"Then you can give Isak your DNA without any worries."

"But why? What happened, Oom Jaap?"

"We want to know who murdered Janien. That's never changed."

Leon takes a cheap yellow cigarette lighter out of his shirt pocket. He makes it stand on the table, lifts it, and lets it swing upside down between his thumb and forefinger.

"Do you think I killed her?" he asks.

He has never asked me. Neither has Vonnie or Obie. Not once.

"No, I don't think you killed her."

"Really?"

"Really."

He pushes the lighter back into his shirt pocket. Then it's as though he remembers to smile, to be the gregarious farming equipment salesman again.

"I'll be ready for Isak, Oom." He gets up. "Don't worry." He shakes my hand. "I'm going to say goodnight to Ma and hit the road."

4

A phone rings loudly and insistently. Is it Obie's cellphone?

No. It's the landline.

I turn in bed, trying to drown out the noise by pushing a pillow over my head. Is no one going to answer?

Apparently not.

I get up, struggle down the passage to the living room in the dark, looking at the green numbers on my watch. 9.14 pm. Twenty minutes of sleep after Leon left.

Great.

I pick up the receiver. "*Lekkerkry*. Reyneke."

"Jaap Reyneke?"

The voice sounds hollow, faint and unnaturally deep, as though forced into the lower range.

"Yes?"

"Drop this DNA shit. You and the police and the newspaper."

"Who is this?"

"This is a warning. Next time, someone's going to get hurt."

"Wait…"

There's a click, then nothing.

I rush to my room, suddenly wide awake. I take out my notebook and write down the conversation word for word, followed by the date and time. Sarah might be able to trace it. Then I write down my observations. It was a man, trying to disguise his voice. I don't know whether he was young or old. Also, he doesn't have my cell number, or he would surely have used it.

I look at the words I wrote down.

Next time.

I call Isak, thinking of his wife and the cheerful little girl in his arms.

The phone rings and rings. I call again.

"Isak Slingers," he finally growls.

"Are you okay?"

"Jaap? What—"

"Are all of you okay? Someone just phoned and threatened me about the DNA. Said this time was a warning, but next time someone would get hurt."

Someone's calling Isak in the background. His wife. Then there's the far-off sound of frantic knocking.

"Jaap—"

"Go!" I say. "Go check if everything's okay. I need to get hold of Bells."

"And you guys? At *Lekkerkry?* Are you all right?"

"Yes. We're fine." I think.

I ring off, take my 9mm Parabellum out of the bedside table and creep to the window, the floor icy under my bare feet. I open the curtain slowly, just a bit, and peer out into the bright, starry night.

Nothing is stirring.

I turn around and walk to the kitchen, look out the window. The cold is starting to creep up my legs. It's easily below freezing out there and the farmhouse doesn't have indoor heating.

No one outside the kitchen window either.

"What's wrong?"

I jump back, pistol at the ready. It's Obie, in striped pajamas and wool slippers.

"Whoa," he says, his hands shooting into the air. "What are you doing? I thought I heard the phone ring."

"Where's Vonnie?"

"In bed. She takes a sleeping pill every now and then. What's going on?"

I tell him about the call. He leaves before I'm done talking and comes back with his hunting rifle, quiet and careful, the way people on South African farms have learned to move over generations of wars and farm attacks.

We stop at every window and look for something suspicious. For a shadow or vehicle that doesn't belong. We listen for voices carrying in the night air, for dogs barking. But there's nothing.

"We need to look outside." Obie gestures at the front door with the gun. "You said you called Isak?"

"Yes. And no, we're not going out. It just makes us easy targets."

I think about the call again. What did he mean by "this is a warning?"

Bells.

I need to get hold of Bells.

I call him on my cell. It rings once, then dies. I call again, peering out the kitchen window.

"Jaap!" Bells is wheezing. He sounds angry.

"What's wrong?"

"The office."

Something hisses and explodes in the background. "What's happening?"

"The office is—" The phone dies.

"Bells? Bells!"

"What's going on?" Obie comes closer, the .308 at his shoulder.

"It's Bells. I need to get to town."

5

Obie keeps watch at the farm while I race to town. Near the newspaper office, just off the main street, I spot a thin trail of smoke floating into the brightly lit night. Red and blue lights bounce off the surrounding buildings in a never-ending loop. I count one police van and a fire rescue truck. Two ambulances.

I get out of the Corolla and push my way through the curious onlookers. Dash through puddles of water to the *Courant's* office, the wind cutting through my jacket.

I peer through the broken window. No real damage, it seems. There are brown glass shards on the floor and the burned remains of a rag. A black streak runs all the way to Bells' glass cubicle.

I find Bells behind the building, talking animatedly to a young hulk of a constable. He cradles an overweight black Dachshund under his right arm.

"Jaap!" Bell calls when he sees me. He storms over, waving at the office. "Look what the fuckers have done!"

He smells of smoke and molten plastic. Like Obie, he's wearing flannel pajamas. Maybe that's how you know you're old: flannel PJs.

If that's the case, I'm still okay. "Are you hurt?" I ask.

He shakes his head. "No. Rambo..." He swallows visibly, angry and emotional. "Rambo warned me and Sly. We were watching a movie. My Wi-Fi is down at home and I can never fall asleep before midnight, so we came to the office. Sly is old, you know, so I just grabbed him and ran." He looks down at the shivering dog. "But Rambo's gone. He probably got a fright and ran away."

I think of Boris, my dog, who is lodging with my former commanding officer in Pretoria while I'm here. Bells is mad about his dogs. Minus wife and kids, they're all he has. A bit like me.

"I'll help look for him," I offer.

The young constable Bells was talking to comes over and taps him on the shoulder. I can't recall ever seeing him before, despite my yearly visits to the police station.

"Are you sure you're all right?" he asks.

"I'm fine, Jeffrey," says Bells. "Thanks. And thank you for playing fireman."

"Let me know if you have any more hassles. We'll come by tomorrow morning and have a look around. Sergeant Slingers called. He's going to check whether the guys who didn't want to give their DNA are all at home."

He says goodbye and leaves.

I look at Bells. "Did you see anything?"

"No. I was watching *The Martian*. Bloody good movie. Had me totally engrossed."

"What's the damage?"

"Our big-screen computer, the carpet, and the window. Whoever did it threw the bottle in through the burglar bars, so there wasn't much momentum. And, lucky for me, there wasn't a lot of petrol in it either. Stupid idiot. My dogs could make a better Molotov cocktail."

"I think it was intended as a warning."

I tell him about the phone call.

"Bullshit if they think we're going to stop!" he says angrily. "Watch me now. Just watch me now."

"And what if they try to silence you again?"

His eyes burn bright with rage. "Fuck 'em. I'm going to give this story light. That's what I've always done when people wanted me to shut up. From tomorrow this story is going mainstream. *Die Burger*, the *Volksblad*, *IOL*, *News24*, *eNCA*, you name it. If it's shit they're after, it's shit they're going to get."

SARAH

1

I order a pot of rooibos tea with fresh milk, a toasted ham and cheese sandwich, six Cokes and two packets of salt and vinegar chips just after I walk into my suite at the Peermont Mondior Hotel in Gaborone.

I drop my overnight bag next to the bed and put the box with Yolene's stuff on the bed. I empty my backpack. Eventually I find what I need—the email with the photograph of the group of friends I found on Janien's computer. I smooth out the creases in the paper.

It is Yolene in the photograph, just as I thought. Next to her is Janien, Sparrow, and an unknown man. I look at the word printed in the corner of the image: *Blink.*

The date on the email implies the photo was taken years ago, probably during Janien's final year at university.

There is a knock on the door. "Room service!"

I open the door and take the tray from the waiter, closing the door with my foot as I turn back. I put the tray on the bed and start eating the sandwich as I unpack the box Sam Chen gave me.

The contents seem mostly like mementos. There are three photos, two from varsity, I'm guessing, and one of Yolene next to an abstract painting. It must be hers. She beams as she stands in front of a canvas of about three meters by three meters. It's not to my taste, but I can see it's good. Shades of red that progressively draw your eye to the bottom right-hand corner, where it looks like a black hole is about to ferry you to another dimension.

Under the photographs I find orange sandals, a thin jersey, and a pile of documents. A lot of paper for someone who operated in the digital world.

I page through the stack. Old bank statements, electricity accounts, and two hand-written letters. Who still writes letters? Payslips from an expensive Johannesburg restaurant. Looks like Yolene worked there as a manager for eight months, until shortly before her death.

In one letter, written in black ink on thin light-blue paper, someone called Karl Ungerer asks Yolene whether he can visit her in Gaborone during the winter holidays. He might be able to organize an exhibition for her in Lusaka later in the year.

Google reveals that Ungerer is an art lecturer at Stellenbosch University, Chen's alma mater. His CV, filled with acronyms, is as long as my arm.

The second letter, also from Ungerer, asks how Yolene is doing after Janien's death, and whether Yolene has sold any of her new work. He tells her not to lose heart and arranges another meeting.

Aha. Ungerer makes a joke that email is probably too risky for discussing Skout. That explains the letters.

Maybe he wasn't joking, I consider. Maybe someone was indeed spying on Yolene to learn more about Skout. Or perhaps Ungerer thought that the effort of writing letters would impress her. His letters verge on intimate, considering they're from a lecturer writing to a former student.

Yolene's credit card statements reveal that she was down on her luck. She mostly lived in the red. Every now and then she bought something expensive at a boutique in Rosebank, at prices that seem well above what she should have been able to afford.

I page back. The restaurant she worked at is in Parktown. It's a fairly well-to-do suburb in Johannesburg, but I know all too well that no restaurant pays enough for boutique shopping.

I pour some more tea and stretch my stiff back, peer into the box. Almost done.

Right at the bottom, I find two printed emails about Skout. One says a venture capital company in Cape Town, ITFin, would consider financing the app in return for a 51 percent share. The correspondence, dated after Janien's death, is formal and official. It highlights a few legal aspects, asks what Yolene's intentions are for Skout, and whether she has a long-term development plan for her business beyond its launch—a Skout 2.0, so to speak.

The other email confirms receipt of her submission and asks where and when she and the directors of ITFin can meet. A meeting was arranged for July last year, here in Gaborone. The directors named on the letterhead seem to be related—both have the surname Visser.

An email two days later asks indignantly why she didn't show up for the meeting.

Hidden under the papers is Yolene's phone and a charger. I plug it in, wait a few minutes for it to come to life, and then hold the screen up to the light. The password uses touch tech: you swipe across the screen in a pattern to access the phone. Sometimes the user leaves a trace of the pattern, providing they don't touch the screen again after they've unlocked the phone.

Putting in the password was probably one of the last things Yolene did on her phone. Lying in a dusty box for a prolonged period of time, the phone now shows the outline of the oily residue of a finger swiping across the screen.

I guess the direction, get it wrong and try again.

Success. This is the first time it's been this easy to unlock a phone. Normally I have to spend a good amount of time hacking it.

I scroll through the messages and photos on the phone.

Almost four years ago, Janien, Yolene, and someone called Jack Fist shared a virtual Jack Daniel's, toasting one another. *Go Jane Stone!* writes Yolene in a WhatsApp group that has only the three of them as its members. Fist responds enthusiastically. *Go Jane!* Then he asks Janien when she's coming to Soweto again. He sounds a little in love.

I can't remember seeing this particular WhatsApp group on

Janien's phone. She must have deleted it. This conversation means, however, that Yolene and this Fist character knew about Janien's other identity and her more risqué website, *So What Now?* What else did they know?

Facebook reveals that Jack Fist is an attractive, compact black man with a strong jawline.

He looks familiar. I unfold Janien's photo again and compare it to the one on the Facebook page. It's the same guy. On Facebook, Fist is wearing a beanie and sunglasses, but that dimpled chin definitely belongs to the man in the photograph.

I yawn, glance at the clock. Half past twelve. Nowhere near bedtime. It must be all the driving that's made me so tired. And the roses. The rows and rows of red roses. That marble memorial.

No. No way. Don't go there.

I get up and rub my eyes. Would it be safe to go for a jog in Gaborone at night? My phone saves me from making a decision.

"Yes," I answer the late-night call.

"Sarah." It's Jaap.

"Did you find anything?" I hope he says yes. It would give me an excuse to leave, to get as far away as possible from the roses and from Sam Chen's eyes.

"No, but things are heating up. There's been a petrol bomb and a death threat."

"Whoa. You okay?" Jaap must have struck a nerve.

"Ja, I'm all right. The newspaper office less so, but at least no one's been hurt. What's happening on your side?"

"Not much."

"Did you find any sign that Yolene Chen didn't commit suicide?"

"Not yet. Looks like she was having a hard time finding work. And her paintings weren't selling. She waitressed for a long time, then managed a restaurant. But it seems more and more likely that Skout would have launched eventually."

I sink back down onto the bed. Look at the papers, the photo and the charging phone. Where to next? Karl Ungerer? ITFin? Skout?

Jack Fist? Or has Jaap been right the whole time in assuming that Skout has nothing to do with Janien's death? A petrol bomb is a pretty big statement.

"Maybe you should come back," says Jaap. "The DNA will probably solve the case, especially when you consider the people who are refusing to cooperate. And tonight's mess tells me that someone's getting nervous. Come and fetch your bike at the farm and go home. I'll pay you as soon as I can."

I know he doesn't have the money to pay my bill. He already had to fork out for a hundred DNA kits and five actual tests. There is R1,870 in his current account and a little more in an investment account, but not enough to pay my fee.

In any case, I'm not sure I'm ready to go home.

I get up and walk to the window, stare at the dark nothingness beyond Gaborone's shimmering skyline.

I don't have to stay here and neither do I have to go home, I realize. Jack Fist is smiling at me from the photo. Maybe he can tell me what happened. Why Yolene committed suicide if Skout was about to start making money. Why Janien insisted on keeping most of her life hidden. Maybe Janien had more secrets I don't know about.

"I don't want to go home yet," I decide. "I think there's one or two more people I should speak to."

"And who's that?" Jaap sounds wary.

"Not sure yet."

"What's your plan? Do you need help?"

"No."

"What are you up to, Sarah Fourie?"

"I'll let you know as soon as I know. You sound certain about the DNA, in any case."

"It's the only reason I'm not in Gaborone."

"So then it's fine, surely?" The lingering silence makes me wonder whether he's worried about me. "You did say the DNA should solve the case, right?"

He laughs a little uncomfortably. "Yes, it should."

"What's wrong then?"

"There's something else that might help."

"And what's that?"

He lets out a long breath. "Can you do me a favor? Since you're safely out of the country anyway?"

Now it's my turn to be wary. "What's going on, Jaap?"

"Don't sound like that."

"Jaap, what do you want?"

"Someone called me just before the petrol bomb. I want to know who."

"On your cell?"

"No, at the farm."

"Who would be that stupid?"

"That's what I want to know. Isak could probably track the person down, but it'll take a while. I want to know as soon as possible."

I remember what Jaap told me that night in my apartment in Pretoria: I wouldn't have to do anything unlawful. But here we are: breaking into Stefan Malan's email, which I haven't even looked at yet, and tracking down a telephone number. At least tracing S&M was my own decision.

"Jaap, you're looking for trouble. And once you start, it's hard to stop."

"Which is why it's a favor."

"Why don't you just wait for the police?"

"I'm tired of waiting. It's been three years."

"I'll think about it." I walk to the bed, pick up a Coke and crack it open. Massage my stiff neck and laugh. "Does this mean you're giving me permission to poke around in your electronic life too?"

"I thought you'd already done that?"

"Says who?"

"You."

"You're imagining things. I would never do something like that."

I order breakfast, arrange for a late checkout, and sit in bed with the computer open on my lap. I start by breaking into Stefan's email. Hopefully I'll manage, because the internet isn't vaguely as fast as it is at home in Pretoria.

Stefan, Fanus, and Sparrow all seem to use the same computer at *Lankdrink*. One of them is online this morning. The computer's history shows that someone regularly uses it for emails. Looks like Fanus and Stefan.

Stefan's login is his email address, and finding the password is easy. My software can guess 300 000 combinations per second. His password has eight characters: his name, the number 1, and an exclamation mark. How many times have I seen that before? Just one more unusual character would have made it so much harder.

I browse through his mail.

Interesting…Stefan tidied up his mail last night.

No, cleaned it out is a more accurate description. There's nothing. Every last personal email is gone.

I'll make time to find them later.

I start with my second search of the day. I have to discover who phoned Jaap to make the threat about the DNA tests. I let the computer do its work in the background while I try to find out more about Jack Fist, the thirty-six-year-old performance artist.

It seems Fist got involved in the art world a little later in life, after studying for a BSc at Wits. His last project, *Not so Instant. Gratification*, involved asking women to scream into takeaway coffee cups in a soundproof room while he videoed them. Then he pasted a picture of each woman on the cup and sold her scream like you sell takeaway coffee—but for much more money than Starbucks and Mugg & Bean would, of course.

There's an Americano for a Cape Town Muslim woman whose husband was killed in the September 11 attacks. A Tall Black for a woman raped by a gang in Sharpeville who now offers counseling to women in townships. A Skinny Cap for a biker woman from Vanderbijlpark who lost a leg in a road accident. Hot Choc for a fifteen-year-old Rosebank prostitute.

According to Fist, the project attempts to capture something of the soul of the women.

Fist, of course, is not his real name. Jack Fist, aka Brian Ndluli, was born in Soweto, Johannesburg's famous sprawling township and an area officially designated for black occupation during apartheid. His parents still live there, not far from Nelson Mandela's old house in Vilakazi Street.

I click back to Jaap's phone call search. Nothing yet, even though it was a landline call. I can't imagine who would be that stupid. Must be someone older, I'm sure. Someone who doesn't watch much television.

Back to Fist—, Ndluli.

My breakfast arrives. I slather butter and apricot jam on a slice of toast and drink another cup of tea. Why were the takeaway cups Fist's last exhibition?

I do a search for the name Brian Ndluli and finally find two newspaper articles. I almost choke on my tea. Jack Fist died in a car accident in Namibia, on the road between Walvis Bay and Swakopmund.

The accident, in another one of South Africa's northern neighbors, happened after Janien's death.

Coincidence? Or was knowing Janien simply a shitload of bad luck?

I again look at the photo of Janien and her friends.

Three out of four people in the picture are dead. Only one is still alive, a woman living with a three-legged cat in a blue house in Carnarvon: Sparrow.

JAAP

1

Janien, wrapped in a faded blue-and-pink beach towel, laughing. She is six, maybe five years old. I remember the Bela-Bela holiday where this photo was taken. I'd tagged along to the hot springs because I was single and it was Christmas, and Vonnie and Obie felt sorry for me.

I landed a few big cases soon after that December and got promoted. After that I came to visit less often.

Janien's graduation: proud, in a huddle with her mother, father, and Obie Junior. Leon couldn't be there. I can't remember why not.

I pour more coffee from the flask and page to the next page in the photo album. Janien having a wedding-dress fitting. The dress in which she died paired, in this picture, with a funky pair of shiny red high heels. She looks stiff and uncomfortable, but she's trying for a cheerful smile.

I put down the album, lean back against the side of the Corolla, and stare out over the pan and the tambotie tree. There's a gray-backed sparrow-lark that's come to rest on the fence on my left. It seems to be scouting for food. It gives a vigorous shake and a spray of fine droplets sift to the ground.

I don't get all this rain either, I want to tell him. The world has gone mad.

I pull my jacket's collar tighter around my neck, put the empty coffee cup down on the car's roof, and sink my chin onto my chest.

Janien. On her side. Half-submerged and frozen in the water. One eye in, one eye out. Aviator glasses.

Where did those glasses come from? Same question as three years ago and still no answer. Just like there's no answer to why the killer chose her. No, the why is becoming increasingly visible, thanks to Sarah. Janien was probably gay. She and Sparrow had been together again for a while, but not quite. Janien was bewildered, upset, uncertain. Depressed? Henk found out about Janien shortly before the wedding, which may never have happened had she not been murdered.

Henk must have been angry. And what about his parents? Did they know about the problems between him and Janien? Did he tell them?

And Stefan? Was he jealous, because he'd hoped to be the one who would marry Janien?

Or did Fanus and Janien have an affair, because why else would he refuse to give his DNA?

And Leon? What if it was Leon? I know I can no longer ignore that possibility. Sparrow said he'd acted creepy. Perhaps Leon had started to develop feelings for Janien?

And what about Sparrow? She could have paid someone to get rid of Janien. Maybe she was so angry and hurt that Janien had rejected her again that she wanted to make a big public statement.

Or what if there were people out to steal Skout? Who wanted to appropriate and commercialize the app Janien and Yolene Chen had developed?

Shit. Sarah has now provided more possible motives than I can deal with.

I pour some more coffee from the flask, blow on the sweet liquid. From the corner of my eye, I see movement. The sparrow-lark startles and flies away.

It's Obie approaching, a pipe in his mouth. Behind him, in the distance, a windmill grates rhythmically.

"Time for breakfast?" I call.

Obie keeps quiet until he gets to me. "Vonnie didn't prepare anything for you."

"She must be really angry."

"Even more so after last night's mess."

I try to gauge his feelings. "And you? How angry are you?"

His shoulders slump under the olive-green jacket. He leans against the car beside me, takes the pipe out of his mouth.

"I'm so tired, Jaap. Can't this thing just end? Every year you come here, make a nuisance of yourself, and then bugger off home. Vonnie and I live here. Our friends are here. We go to church here."

I take the gap. "Did you know that Dominee Tiaan knew about the adoption?"

He looks at me, annoyed. "No one knows, because that's what Vonnie wanted." He stands up straight. "Who told you that?"

"I might have to piss Vonnie off even more," I say, ignoring his question.

"You know they're taking Leon's DNA this morning."

"He's my son, Jaap. My oldest son. You brought him to us and we made him ours. He was Vonnie's saving grace when we were struggling to have children."

"Maybe it's time for him to know."

"And you think you're the one to tell him?" He jabs the pipe in my direction, pressing his body, used to manual labor, into my space.

You can't say "what if" to a father in a case like this. What if Leon murdered Janien? What if he was jealous? In love with her? You don't turn that rock over to see what comes scuttling out underneath, because chances are it's going to bite you on the heel.

"Maybe it would help him understand," I lie.

"Understand what? He's always fitted in. So perfectly, he may as well have come out of Vonnie's own body. Janien was the one we could never understand. All we could do was love her." The pipe waves fiercely in my direction. "You don't say a word. Do you hear me?"

He turns on his heel, walks away with long, angry strides.

"Did you know about her, Obie?" I call after him.

He stops. Turns around. "Know what about her?"

I can't say it. Suddenly I feel like Sparrow and Janien. Afraid to hurt, afraid to shock.

"Nothing."

"You don't say a thing to Leon," he warns again.

"I hear you."

"And you better stay away for a while. You need to give Vonnie some time to cool off."

"I'll find somewhere to stay in town tomorrow. Promise."

He stares at me. "You know, Jaap, you've got this compulsion to rescue people."

"I'm no—"

"No, don't argue. Just don't bring them here again. Not another Leon or a girl on a motorbike. You can't keep jerking everyone around."

He turns and starts to walk away again. Stops. This time he speaks without turning around. His voice is soft, wavering. I have to strain to hear what he is saying.

"And you are all wrong. We would have loved her no matter what."

I want to drive to town, get some scrambled eggs and toast at the hotel, drink a few cups of coffee, and think.

A compulsion to rescue people? What nonsense. I wish I could. Obie knows nothing. Not about the 1,533 corpses I've seen. Until I'd had enough. From road accidents to riots to six days dead in the living room, three shots to the chest. Entire families burned beyond recognition in their shacks.

Just over 1,300 of them have names. The rest are fingerprints, DNA samples, and computer reconstructions waiting for someone to say: I know who that is. It's my sister, my husband, my child.

No, that's wrong. I keep forgetting, because I want to forget. It was 1,533 until that last day.

Fourteen people dead in a taxi war. The youngest was three

months old. She'd been tied to her mother's back with a blanket and had caught an AK-47 bullet. There wasn't a scratch on her mother.

I left the crime scene with no explanation, got into my car and drove home. Put in my retirement papers the next day. Obie knows fuck-all.

Sarah calls as I ease into the Corolla.

"The call came from the Malan butchery." No hello.

I want to ask whether she's sure, but it sounds like there's more. "And?"

"Jack Fist is dead. Car accident."

I drop the car keys on my lap. Sit back. "What?"

"Something's not right, Jaap. Isn't that just one too many?"

She's right. It doesn't sound good. "Come back and show me what you have."

"Not yet. I want to know more about Fist. I just need to work out where to look first. Soweto, where his parents are, or Swakopmund, where he died."

"Swakop? As in Namibia?"

"Where else?"

"It's far to Swakop and you'd have to drive through the Namib desert. Go to Soweto."

"I could fly there."

"Why don't you hang on for a bit? I'll go and talk to Stefan to hear what he has to say. If the call came from the Malan butchery, it may just solve the case."

Sarah doesn't answer.

I hope I'm right. The butchery belongs to Fanus, but Stefan runs it. Sparrow also helps out every now and then, if I remember correctly.

"Maybe it's time to go back home and get on with your life," I say into the growing silence. "Your mother will be glad. I'll carry on looking. I'm sorry I dragged you al—"

"Don't pretend you know me," Sarah snaps. "That you know what I am and what I need."

Is everyone gunning for me today?

"No, I don't think that. Not at all. But I still don't like the fact that this Jack Fist is dead. It could be a coincidence, but maybe it's not. Don't rush into this on your own now."

"I'll be careful."

"No."

"I wasn't asking for your permission."

"For fuck's sake, Sarah! Why are you being so difficult today?"

Silence.

"Fine," I concede. "I have to be here today, because Isak is taking Leon's DNA and Leon and I need to talk. Let me know where you are and what you find out. Check in every two hours."

"Why? I'm not six years old."

"Will you just stop arguing? I'll call you later today. Let me know what you decide. I know someone in Swakopmund who can help."

2

Leon is not pleased about being alone in my company. Every now and then he glances at the front door as if he wants to run away, his foot tapping the floor nervously.

"Do you want to go have a smoke?" I ask.

We're in the living room of his three-bedroom house in town. His wife, Annemarie, is still at work, and Isak left fifteen minutes ago after coming to collect the DNA sample.

Well, he came for it, but left empty-handed.

Leon refused to cooperate. He insists that Janien's blood shows it's not family and that he is innocent.

Isak hasn't spoken to him about the adoption yet. He's likely to go over the birth records again first to be a hundred percent sure.

Does Leon realize that Isak's going to be here again tomorrow? And the day after that? That he is not going to give up?

We go outside.

I send Obie a text message as we walk. I tell him what I'm going to do and that it's in Leon's best interest. I guess I have about half an hour before Obie arrives.

Leon walks down the stoep stairs. He turns left to a sunny spot at the side of the house where he leans against the wall and lights a cigarette. Waits for me to start talking.

I move to stand next to him, back against the wall. "Why didn't you want to give your DNA to Isak?"

My phone vibrates in my pocket. I ignore it. What did Obie say this morning? *You don't say a thing to Leon. Do you hear me?*

"I told you: It's not me. It's clearly not family. Are they going to ask Dad too? And Mom? And Obie Junior?"

I close my eyes, feel the faint heat radiating from the wall. I look at the young man beside me staring at the coal of his cigarette. There's a shadow of a smile around his mouth, as if he escaped the noose today.

Is he hoping Vonnie and Obie will protect him the way they did when Janien died? They gave Isak hell to make him leave Leon alone, insisted there was no evidence against their son.

But the secrets we keep always catch up with us. They follow us with long, patient strides.

Did Janien know that her parents had secrets of their own? Driven by love, just as hers were, and then later by the fear of losing love. The fear of all the things that anger can destroy.

My phone vibrates again. Time is running out.

"Almost thirty years ago, when I was still in uniform, I walked into a house in Waverley, in Pretoria," I say. "I was young and fit, and I thought I knew it all. It was nine o'clock in the morning—I will never forget that."

If Leon knows what's coming, he doesn't let on. I wonder for the hundredth time whether he really doesn't remember anything from that day.

My phone rings again. I take it out of my pocket and switch it off.

"It was a yellow house with a green corrugated-iron roof. A little run down. The windows were dirty and the garden needed some work. On my way inside, I slid on something. It was blood from one of the German Shepherds that had been shot. There'd been three of them. One was eight weeks old."

"I don't have time for stories, Oom Jaap. I have to get to work." Leon throws the half-smoked cigarette down and grinds it under his heel. Shoots his body away from the wall.

I put up a hand to make him wait. "There was a family inside."

"Does Dad know you're here?"

"There were three people, all dead. The smell wormed into your nostrils, no matter how much Vicks you put on your top lip. The bodies had been there for three days before the cleaner came to work. She went to call the neighbors. It was hot. February. That dry Pretoria heat."

"I need to get to work," Leon says hurriedly. "Jan Kriel is waiting for his new tractor."

I place my hand on his arm. "Something tells me you know."

He doesn't move. Doesn't shake his head. Doesn't deny it.

"Do you remember?"

"No." He crosses his arms, looks past me toward the quiet street.

"The man in the house was in his twenties. His wife was younger. And she was beautiful. I remember that, as though it's somehow worse when a woman is beautiful. The house was full of photos of the kids, a girl and a boy, around three or four. The father had shot the little girl first. He'd used a homemade silencer. Then the boy, then his wife, then the dogs, and then himself. It took a long time for the woman to die. She'd crawled through the house, down the passage."

"Stop, please, Oom Jaap."

"Sh—"

"Don't."

"Why didn't you want to give Isak your DNA?"

"I didn't kill Janien. I loved her. She was my sister."

"Then you have nothing to hide."

"I know I don't have anything to hide, but everyone goes on and on at me!"

I look him in the eye, continue my story. "It took us more than an hour to figure out that the mother hadn't crawled to the front door to get help, but to the passage cupboard where her little boy was hiding. She must have realized he was still alive and wanted to help him."

"Oom Jaap. I swear…"

"When I opened the cupboard, there you were, hiding behind a box full of blankets. Your father's bullet had only just scraped your head. You'd sat there for three days before I found you. You hadn't eaten or drunk anything. You were almost dead. You wanted to shoot me. You aimed your hand at me as though it was a gun and said 'Pah.'"

Leon lights a new cigarette. He smokes with his back turned to me. When he finally starts to speak, his voice is soft.

"I get nauseous when I smell blood. And I have to go through all the cupboards every night before I go to sleep, sometimes three, four times in a row. And I have to do it without Annemarie noticing."

"Your father had to take all the cupboard doors down before you'd go into your bedroom."

"Who are we talking about now? The fucker who shot me or the people here?"

"The man who raised you. Obie. Your real father. Who loves you more than you can imagine." I shake my head. "How did you find out? Was it something someone did? Someone said?"

He turns back to me, dragging deeply on the cigarette. "I don't look like them. Or like you. And it always felt like I didn't quite fit in. It was as though I didn't think the same way you all did."

"Now you sound like Janien."

Leon laughs bitterly. "I felt something for her. I felt so guilty about that for such a long time." He jabs the cigarette at me. "And why is Obie Junior's name Obie, but I'm supposed to be the oldest? And why are there no baby photos of me with Dad and Mom, but there are loads of Janien and Obie Junior?"

"How did you finally find out the truth?"

"I paid an investigator to check whether my hunch was right. And it was. My parents were Petro and Wilhelm Oosthuisen, and I am Leon Reghardt."

"When did this happen?"

"Probably about three, four years ago."

Before Janien died. "Why didn't you say something?"

"Mom and Dad obviously didn't want to fess up all those years ago because they wanted to protect me. It was a nice thought, that someone cared enough about me to do that. But then Janien was murdered, and I realized what it would look like if it came out that I had been adopted. Of course the poor adopted child murdered his sister in a jealous rage."

He gives me a pleading look. "I don't want people to know, Oom Jaap. Please. Annemarie…I told her I needed to go and see someone because I struggle to sleep. Work stress, was how I explained it. I had to do something after Janien died, because the dreams wouldn't stop. Annemarie already looks at me as though she pities me. Ma never felt sorry for me, and I'm only now able to understand how much that means to me. I don't want it to change. If Annemarie had to know what the real problem was, it would kill me."

I think about the little boy who had no family left after his father murdered them all because he'd lost his job again. How Vonnie was visiting me that week, because she and Obie were forever fighting. He wanted her to give up on the idea of children, but she refused to give in.

Then Leon came along and then, a little while later, Janien and Obie Junior, as though everything fell into place as soon as Vonnie started to relax. And then Obie bought *Lekkerkry* and they started over in a town where no one knew them.

Vonnie made me and Obie swear that we would never say anything about Leon's past. He could keep his name, but he was not allowed to know where he'd come from or what had happened.

Leon crushes the cigarette under his shoe, bends down and picks up the butt.

I look at his boot. Wonder about the size-ten prints at the pan.

"Please, Oom Jaap. Just leave it. I would never have done anything to hurt Janien."

I hold my breath. "Then give me your DNA. Forget about Isak."

"Why? It wasn't me!"

I don't know what to say other than what I've been saying all along: "Then you have nothing to hide, do you?"

Vonnie is waiting on the stoep, arms folded. My suitcase, towel, clothes and shoes are all lying in a pile at the bottom of the steps.

I get out of the Corolla.

"You spoke to Leon."

"Did he call you?"

"Yes. He's heartbroken. How could you, Jaap? After all these years."

She juts her chin at my stuff on the lawn. "You'd better leave. I'd go all the way home, straight back to Pretoria if I were you."

We look at one another for a few seconds.

"Vonnie, it was time to tell him."

"It was not for you to decide."

"Leon was like my son too. It was just after my divorce. I'd lost my wife and my boy. Never saw them again for years."

"Don't fool yourself. He is my and Obie's son. And, just so you know, it wasn't me who dumped your suitcase there, it was Obie. You'd better get going before he gets back from Leon's place."

SARAH

1

The road to Swakopmund from the Walvis Bay airport is one of the most beautiful I've ever driven. It traces the coastline as it runs open and straight to town, the Namib desert on one side, the thundering, sky-blue sea on the other. Here and there, yellow sand from the dunes has sifted over the bleached tar. Double-story houses with panoramic windows, practically on the beach, dot the road.

I open the rental car's window wider, grateful to have survived the flight. I hate confined spaces almost as much as not being in control when any kind of movement is involved. The air outside smells and tastes of the ocean.

I ignore a group of fishermen packing up their chairs on the beach, waving to me.

My phone rings. I pull the Toyota Fortuner off the road and finally take the call.

"Hi, Mom."

"Your father didn't leave the Aston Martin to you."

She doesn't say hello. On the contrary, she sounds like I usually do—rushed and uncomfortable.

Then the words sink in. "What? Why not? It was our car! We bought her together. We fixed her together. And she's almost done. I've just got the plugs left to do. And I have to find a spare wheel."

"The car is Miekie's."

"Miekie?" My sister? "Why?"

"I didn't want to tell you over the phone, but now you refuse to come home and I have no other choice."

The accusation in her voice is unmistakable and I know I deserve it. If you're going to run away, the least you can do is admit to what you're doing.

"Okay. I hear you. I'll talk to Miekie. I'm sure she'll give me the Aston. Pa probably made a mistake…the last few days…he wasn't quite himself."

"He wasn't confused, Sarah. He made me promise that you wouldn't get the car and that you wouldn't fight with Miekie about it either, because he knew she would give it to you if you asked for it. You know she'll do anything for you."

"But why would he do such a thing? I don't get it?"

"Your father left something else for you. It's in a little box. I'll give it to you as soon as you get back."

"What is it?"

"I don't know. I didn't look. It's yours. It has nothing to do with me."

I feel like sobbing. I take the Marlboros out and get out of the Fortuner. I put a cigarette in my mouth and light it. To hell with Diederik Fourie and his emphysema.

I draw the smoke deep into my lungs and my head immediately starts to spin from the nicotine rush.

"When are you coming home, Sarah?" My mom's voice is gentler than I've ever heard it. "Life goes on, my child. I know this is the first time you've lost someone close to you, and that you're angry, but it happens to all of us. That's how things are. This is how things work and no one can change it. I wish I could make it better for you. And for myself."

Yes, I am angry. I'm angry with her husband. My father. Stupid bloody man. It's his fault. Why did he have to smoke so much?

I throw the cigarette down and grind it out with my toe. "I'll probably be back in Pretoria in about a week."

"Promise?" She knows to ask.

"Yes. Promise."

Jaap calls ten minutes later, just as I am approaching Swakopmund.

"Talk to Dorie. Chief Inspector Doris Engelbrecht. She's the station commander at Swakop. We met at an Interpol conference a few years ago."

"Dorie?"

"Ja, ja. We had a few glasses of wine together a long time ago. She's a lovely woman. Bakes chocolate cake like you wouldn't believe."

I'm not interested in chocolate cake. "Is she prepared to help?"

"She is, although she doesn't quite get what you're after. She says Fist's death was a car accident. But maybe she's up for a bit of excitement. Street children and house robberies are her biggest problems these days."

"I'll chat to her."

"Just be nice, please. I like Dorie. I'll text you the address where you can meet her."

"Okay, okay. But I'm calling her Doris, if you don't mind."

"With your people skills I'd suggest you go for Chief Inspector. But hey, that's just a suggestion."

Swakopmund has wide, sandy sidewalks and even wider streets, lined with palm trees. The houses are mostly indistinguishable from one another with their low walls and scraggly gardens.

The streets are teeming with pedestrians. Most are walking as though they know where they're headed, but the rest are ambling around in small groups, now and then posing for photos in front of one of the many old colonial buildings or coffee bars. The khaki pants and broad-brimmed hats tell me they're probably tourists.

If I remember correctly, Namibia—or South West Africa, as it was once known—was a German colony before it was handed over to be administered by South Africa during World War I. The country only gained independence in 1990, changing its name to Namibia.

I follow the directions Jaap texted me, the traffic thin despite what should be the afternoon rush hour.

I park the Fortuner in a street near the beach and walk to the town center, following the coordinates on my phone. The number of German bookshops and restaurants along the way surprises me.

Alte Bäckerei is long and narrow, with big windows in wooden frames that have been painted green. Inside, ceiling fans churn the hot air doggedly, but without much success. As soon as I open the door, I know why Chief Inspector Doris Engelbrecht chose this place. Suddenly the bustle of town is gone and the air smells of cinnamon buns and baked apples. It reminds me of Saturday mornings, when my mother would bake apple tart and I'd wake up to this same smell.

There's only one customer in the shop, a tall, largish woman in her fifties in a flowing green dress seated at a table in the corner. She looks up from her newspaper and stares at me over reading glasses looped around her neck with a string of colorful beads. Her eyes are a startling bright blue and she has wavy dark-blonde hair down to her shoulders.

"Sarah Fourie?"

"Ja?"

"Jaap said you were a wisp of a thing."

I shrug, nod.

She laughs. "Economical with words, right? He also told me not to mind your manners. Apparently there is a decent human being inside there somewhere."

I'm too tired to care what Jaap said. I walk across the black-and-white tiles and sit down opposite her. Then I shift my chair backward. It feels as though this woman's personal space is even bigger than mine.

Doris turns and calls toward the kitchen. "Make it two slices, Erik! This child needs to get some decent food into her body."

Doris scoops up the last bit of cream and apfelstrudel and gestures toward my half-eaten slice. "Finish up."

I push the plate away. "I've had enough."

I wave thank you to Erik, a bear of a man with hands bigger than my older brother's, before Doris says something about my manners again. You'd think I was six years old.

"Why did you come all the way here to talk about a car accident?" Doris asks. "And could we please call this guy Brian Ndluli? Which is his real name."

I can only think of him as Jack Fist. Fist with the strong jawline. Handsome Fist.

Sounds like a boxer. Or a Suzanne Vega song.

"I wonder...Jaap and I wonder whether his death really was an accident."

"What makes you think it wasn't?" Doris peers at me over her reading glasses.

I'm not sure how to explain my theory. "It could be that Fist's death is connected to Janien Steyn's murder."

"Jaap's stepdaughter? In what way? Can he really still not let go of that?"

I shrug. In some ways Jaap remains a mystery to me.

"I probably wouldn't be able to either," Doris admits. "Tell me first: how do you fit into all of this? Jaap didn't explain."

"I'm helping Jaap...he's paying me to help him. I'm good with computers."

"You're not..." A smile tugs at the corners of her mouth.

"Not what?"

She puts her two index fingers together.

What? Is the woman insane? "Are you mad? He's so...so..."

"Old?"

"No. So damn infuriating."

She tips her head back as she laughs and orders more coffee. I wait until it arrives.

"How did Fist die?" I ask.

"Like I said. Car accident." She picks up her fork and starts picking at the apfelstrudel on my plate.

I push the plate over to her.

I know about the accident from local newspaper reports. They were short, probably no more than two hundred words.

"I know that," I say. "I mean, how did he die?"

Doris frowns sharply and I realize how stupid my question must sound. But how do I ask what I really want to know?

"What's going on?" She looks at me with quizzical eyes. "Did I miss something? Let's leave the bullshit and do some straight talking here. Jaap calls, you show up, asking strange questions about a car accident. Something's up."

"I don't really know how to explain it."

"Try."

"Maybe I can do so after I've seen how and where he died. Can you show me?"

"I can tell you. Ndluli—Fist—was on his way to Walvis Bay. The East Wind had come and h—"

She sketches something like a wave in the air, but then drops her hands abruptly. I can see her curiosity getting the better of her, the same what-the-hell curiosity Jaap has.

She returns to picking at my apfelstrudel. "I'll take you to the accident site tomorrow," she says when the last piece of tart is gone. "I'll fetch you at six."

"In the evening?"

"No. It's best to go when it's cool. Don't be fooled by the fact that it's winter. It can get up to forty degrees Celsius on the sunny side of the dunes."

JAAP

1

"Goodbye, Ma'am. We'll refund you if those lamb chops aren't nice and tender."

Stefan, a red-and-white dishcloth over his shoulder, waves to an elderly woman as he closes the cash register. He looks surprised to see me.

"Oom Jaap."

"Morning, Stefan."

The butchery is empty. It's just the two of us out front, and someone in overalls in the back carving what looks like a sheep carcass.

Stefan stares at the shop entrance as though he's willing someone to walk through the door.

I do a quick scan of the ceiling. No security cameras. That probably would've been too easy, although I could do with easy right now.

I take out my notebook and open it, pretend I'm reading something. "Someone called me just before the petrol bomb went through the window at the newspaper offices. He threatened me. Said to drop the DNA drive. Funny thing is, the call came from here."

Stefan pulls the dishcloth off his shoulder and wipes his hands, starts to clean down the counter next to the till.

"Does my dad know you're here?" he says as he casts another hopeful glance toward the entrance.

"Are you going to spend the rest of your life hiding behind your father?"

He doesn't look up as he continues cleaning. "Where's Isak?" he asks. "Why isn't he with you?"

"Did you call and threaten me, Stefan? And then lob a petrol bomb through the *Courant's* window?"

"No." He sounds indignant. "What time was the phone call?"

"Just after nine."

"That's long after closing time."

"So you weren't here on Tuesday night?"

"No, I was here," he admits reluctantly. "But I was busy the whole night. The hunters and the farmers brought their venison in. I only went home after eleven." He motions toward the phone at the other end of the counter. "Anyone could have used it, and you know that. Pa has never minded if someone makes a quick call. It's the best way to sell biltong." He points at the packets of kudu and springbok biltong, neatly displayed next to the telephone.

It's bloody convenient, but he's right.

"Who brought their meat in?"

"A bunch of farmers and hunters. Like I said."

"Yes, but who exactly? Who was here?"

"The Van Stadens. The Botha brothers. Prof. Sieberhagen. Mullens, the professional hunter. And Jakob Drieriem. Those are the ones I remember."

"And your dad? And Sparrow? Were they here too?"

"Yes. They came and went. Everyone always helps where they can."

"Were they here around half past nine?"

"I don't know. I can't remember."

"And you say it wasn't you who called me at *Lekkerkry?*"

"I was busy at the back all evening. It's a lot of meat to weigh and process, and the Gauteng restaurants and grocery stores always want it yesterday."

The saw goes quiet and the red doors behind him swing open. A young man in blue overalls walks out.

Stefan looks relieved. "I have to get back to work. Sorry I couldn't be of more help."

"I hear you. Will you call me if you remember anything?"

"Of course."

He turns around and hurries through the doors to the back, fishing his phone out of his pocket as he disappears.

I walk to the Corolla to make a few phone calls, dying for a cup of tea, but unsure how welcome I am at any of Carnarvon's cafés.

It seems Professor Olaf Sieberhagen is in Cape Town and Mullens and the Botha brothers have gone off hunting again. It can't be Jakob Drieriem who made the call to *Lekkerkry*, as I would have recognized his voice and his Namakwaland accent. It's no use contacting Fanus, which leaves only the Van Stadens.

Henk's parents are what a kind, successful farmer would call unlucky. Henk's father seemingly made one wrong decision after the other—enough of them for his family to now have to bear the consequences. Cheaper but less dependable labor, nothing more than basic insurance. You name it. Save a few bucks here, just to lose a few thousand elsewhere.

The weather hasn't been good to Bart van Staden either. For some reason or another, perhaps a roll of the geological dice, his farm happens to be colder and drier than any of the others in the district. Sheep keel over easily from the cold if you're not careful. At least, that's what Obie tells me.

We're sitting on the stoep, making small talk. A mongrel, one of three in the yard, lies sleeping on my foot in the midday sun.

Truida brings us coffee and then disappears inside again, just like when Isak and I came to talk to them after Janien's death. She'd brought us coffee, answered two questions, and disappeared back to the kitchen. She and Mart, her unmarried sister, make clothing for extra money. Mart designed and made Janien's wedding dress, the one she was wearing when she died.

To my left, through the open front door in desperate need of a fresh coat of varnish, I can see bolts of bright fabric in the living room. There seems to be fewer of them than in previous years, but maybe that's just my imagination.

I remember what Bart and Truida told me and Isak that day. What was it? Thirty-six hours after Janien's murder? I was still bleary-eyed from the drive. They both swore that Henk had been here, at home, the whole night of the braai. The longest period they didn't see him for was the twenty minutes it took for him to go and chop more wood for the fires, which wasn't enough time to drive to *Lekkerkry* and kill Janien.

Vonnie says Truida is still bitter about the fact that there was no wedding. Says Bart was crazy about Janien.

Did the Van Stadens know what Henk knew about Janien? That Janien had doubts about her sexuality? Did they know that Henk and Janien had had a fight the afternoon before the braai? That the wedding would most likely have been called off anyway?

Henk says they didn't, but can I really take his word on that?

The Van Stadens spent a lot of money on the wedding—money they didn't have.

And what remains really strange is how everyone insists that everyone else was at that bloody braai. How everyone keeps willing it to be someone from outside Carnarvon who killed Janien.

Bart drinks his coffee without looking at me, gazing just past my head into the veld. His boots are caked with mud. He was busy somewhere on the farm when I got here. Truida had to send one of the workers to fetch him and it took a good twenty minutes before he arrived.

I finish my coffee. Decide it's time to jump right in. I've made so many enemies already I may as well add another name to the list.

"Why did you threaten me about this DNA business, Bart? A man called me from the Malan butchery just before the petrol bomb was tossed through the window at the *Courant*. Stefan says you were there on Tuesday night."

The surprise on Bart's face disappears as quickly as it arrived. "I didn't phone you."

I lean forward, put my cup down on the stoep wall. "Technology is wonderful these days. Think carefully before you answer."

"I don't have to. It wasn't me."

I look at the craggy face. The square jaw that Henk inherited, but which somehow seems too big on Bart. "Maybe it was Henk then. Is he around?"

"He's in the Free State."

"Has he been home recently?"

"No. And you would know that. You've just spoken to him in Clarens." He wags a finger at me. "Nice fishing expedition you're on, Jaap. Everyone knows there were lots of people at the butchery on Tuesday evening. Stefan gave us just one day to bring our meat, and it had to be done after hours. And the price he offers goes down every year. He's a bastard, just like his father." He leans forward angrily.

"Henk said he gave you his DNA, so fuck off now. Leave him alone. Leave us all alone."

"What are you so afraid of?"

He crosses his arms, then his legs. "Afraid? Of you? That'll be the day."

I think about the call again. The voice. Could it have been Bart on the phone? It's possible. But it could also have been Stefan. Or Mullens. Or someone else entirely.

I try again, as I do every year.

"What happened that night that you didn't tell the police?"

"Which night?"

"Don't play dumb. The night of the braai, when everyone was supposed to be here. When Henk went to chop wood. And I heard Stefan and Fanus arrived late. Half an hour or so? And someone said you went off to buy ice at the service station."

"I don't know what you're on about."

"Henk and Janien fought the afternoon before the braai. The wedding was probably going to be called off. Did you know that?"

Again, the brief surprise, then...fear?

"What do you know that you're not telling the police, Bart? Did Henk sneak away from the braai that night to go to *Lekkerkry*? Did he ever actually chop that wood he promised to? Are you protecting him? Or did you kill Janien because you were angry about spending all that money on the wedding? Because she was about to humiliate your son? Your family?"

He scrambles to his feet, his face an ugly red. "You need to leave."

"You're going to have to confess at some point."

"I've got nothing to say." He points at my bruised face. "Fuck off, before you get some more of that."

He walks into the house and slams the door behind him. I sit for a minute or so, perhaps out of spite, then get up and walk to the car. On the way to town I call Sparrow to hear when she was at the butchery on Tuesday evening. She doesn't answer her phone.

Another dead end, just like everything today. Just like everything the past three years.

I'm standing in Bells's kitchen, guzzling down All-Bran Flakes over the sink, when Leon calls. It's just like the old days, eating cereal for supper like this, except that my stomach could still handle the more fun brands back then.

"Hi, Oom Jaap," he says.

I say hello and wait for him to talk, but nothing happens. I start eating again.

Then I give in. "Are you okay?"

"I had a dream last night," he finally says.

"What about?"

"About how you found me in the cupboard. Was I wearing red Superman pajamas?"

I chew a little faster, swallow. "Do you remember that? The

psychologist we saw back then said you couldn't remember much. He said cupboards and guns would maybe always scare you, but that you probably wouldn't know why."

"I remember the shots. Eight shots."

"There were four of you and three dogs. Seven shots."

"Really?"

"The man who did it was a hunter. One-shot Bill. His name was Wilhelm." I refuse to say "your father." That man was a monster.

"I remember the name. Bill. Why do you think I remember that, Oom Jaap?"

"Lots of people called him that. And it was painted above the braai: *One-Shot Bill's House.*"

"Then why did he only wound me? Why fail so miserably at killing me?"

"I don't know. Maybe he'd begun to hesitate after your sister. And you and your mother probably ran for your lives. I prefer to think you were lucky. Your second life, here with Obie and Vonnie, was good...is good."

"They're good people."

"I'm sorry about yesterday. I could have handled it better."

He ignores my apology. "Why didn't you adopt me? Why did you give me to your sister?"

"I was already divorced and I wasn't the best father in the world. By then that was a well-proven fact. I worked all the time. I was never home. And Vonnie? She so badly wanted children she couldn't let you go, no matter how much the social workers pleaded with her."

"Did...do I have other family?"

"No."

I remember Vonnie's face the first time she saw Leon. My realization that he could save her, give her what she wanted most in life.

"You were so good for Vonnie and Obie. I've never regretted it. Not once."

"Never? Not even if I don't want to give you or Isak my DNA?"

I walk over to the window and watch Bells's sausage dogs sniff around the garden. Rambo is back. Someone found him on the street, half-frozen but healthy.

I dread asking the question, but I do it anyway. "Is there something you need to tell me, Leon?"

"Maybe." There is fear in his voice, thin and razor-sharp. "My nose bled that night, Oom Jaap. I'm worried…I think the blood on Janien's dress might be mine."

I want to swear, but catch the word in my mouth, brackish and bitter. "What happened?"

"It was late. Janien found me smoking a spliff. We fought, just like she used to when we were little. She was so angry about the weed. She accidentally knocked my nose with her elbow."

"Was she wearing her wedding dress?"

"I think so, yes. Don't know why."

I hold my hand over the phone and curse under my breath. "Why didn't you say?"

"I'm not stupid."

"But you are! Dammit, man!" Fucking stupid. "What happened then? Afterwards?"

"Janien said she would get rid of the weed in a place no one would find it, said I was stupid to smoke it at home, and that the stuff would make me even more stupid. She told me to shower and go to bed. You know she really hated drugs of any kind. She could be so liberal about some things and so closed-minded about other things. I could never really figure her out."

"And then?"

"I followed her outside. She went and threw my stash into the petrol tank of the old lorry in the shed. The Nissan Diesel. I went to sleep and when I woke up, she was dead. I swear it, Oom Jaap. I had nothing to do with her death. You have to believe me."

SARAH

Jeez, it's early. I open one eye and look at my phone's brightly lit screen. It tells me it's 5.30 am and that I need to get up right now if I want to be on time for Doris. It feels like I've only just fallen asleep.

Last night I again worked through the box of documents that Sam Chen gave me, as well as through Janien's computer data. I couldn't find any new leads. Janien had the early stages of Skout on her computer and Yolene had the more complete product. That doesn't help me at all, except if my plan was to secretly sell it.

At least I now know what the encrypted data was that Janien hid away on her hard drive and on the cloud.

The exact nature of ITFin's business, however, remains murky. The directors who expressed interest in Skout are from Stellenbosch. The company looks legit, although it's registered in the Bahamas. I called the number on the letterhead and an electronic voice informed me that office hours were eight to five.

One thing has become clear though: Stefan and Janien were emailing each other regularly before her death. Nothing serious, but Stefan lied to Jaap. The two of them had definitely kept in touch.

And I have to admit, Stefan sounds pretty unhappy about the fact that Janien was going to marry Henk. He asked her at least three times whether she thought she was doing the right thing.

I close my eyes and wake ten minutes later when the phone starts screaming at me again.

Dammit.

I get up, walk to the shower, and open the cold-water tap. I stay there until I start shivering, then open the hot-water tap. I dry myself quickly, gulp down a cup of rooibos tea and grab two individually wrapped rusks from the bedside table on my way out.

Reception is deserted. I bet Jaap instructed Doris to pick me up at 6 am. I'm sure nine would have been fine too. The heat can't possibly be that bad by then.

My watch shows it's 5.59 am.

Outside the hotel, the early morning sounds of the town are hushed, hidden under a cool blanket of mist.

Which way is the ocean? I close my eyes and listen. Definitely left. Which means the desert is on my right, which would be east.

I hear the throaty drone of a big, old engine before I see it, and step back off the road onto the sidewalk. Sounds like someone in a hurry.

A dirty green Land Cruiser from the Seventies comes around the corner and stops in front of the hotel. Through the open windows, I hear Brandy Clark singing something about a girl next door.

I zip up my jacket and pop the last bite of rusk into my mouth. I hoist myself into the off-roader, glad I've put on my trainers.

"Good morning, sunshine," Doris says cheerfully. Her cheeks are a healthy, glowing red and her eyes alert, as if she's been awake for ages. She's dressed in jeans and a navy-blue T-shirt one size too big for her.

"If you say so."

"There's coffee if you want." She points to a battered silver thermos at my feet.

I hate coffee, but maybe it's the kickstart I need this morning. "Would you like some?"

"Please."

I pour some of the hot liquid into two plastic cups and pass one to her. As we reach the outskirts of town, Doris slows down, like someone who knows the road but doesn't trust the mist. I wind the window down and smell the salty sea air. Mornings smell different to evenings, especially at the ocean. I've forgotten that.

Doris sips her coffee as she navigates the road. "You said Jaap is making use of your computer skills? What skills are these exactly?"

I finish my coffee, the caffeine an unfamiliar, muted buzz in my head. "What I'm more interested in is whether you and Jaap dated."

She lifts a lazy eyebrow, smiles. Doesn't answer.

"What was Jack Fist doing in Swakopmund?" I ask when the silence lingers.

"He won a holiday in some internet competition. One week here and one week in the Okavango."

"Just him?"

"Yes. His girlfriend could join him at half price, but she was writing exams. She was studying to become a pharmacist. Seems like they didn't have enough money for her to make the trip anyway. Fist was helping pay for his grandmother's funeral at that point."

"And the car? Was that part of the prize?"

"Yes. It was a rental, a silver sedan."

She holds her cup for more coffee, driving a little slower so I can pour.

We speed up again, overtaking two ancient bakkies with fishing rods tied to the roof. To our left a building appears, right up against the dunes. Looks like a place tourists can explore the desert from on quadbikes.

The sound of loud, excited voices briefly floats in through the open window and disappears again as Doris accelerates out from under the mist into a bright, blue-sky morning.

"Where does this road lead?" I ask. I've been trying to plot our course but the mist has made it hard for me to find my bearings.

"You came the same way yesterday. It goes to Walvis Bay. The mist is confusing. It messes with your orientation."

"Was Fist on this road when the accident happened?"

"Yes."

"Was he on his way to the airport?"

"No. Another part of his prize was a boat ride in Walvis to see the seal colony, with a tour into the dunes afterwards." She drinks the last of the coffee and gives me the cup to put away, glances at the odometer.

"It happened around here somewhere. Just over three kilometers past the quadbike place."

She slows down where the road makes a lazy S and turns onto the sandy ground. We travel through a gap in the cable fencing, which I assume is there to keep cars off the sand dunes. She drives past the first low dunes and parks the Land Rover on a firm patch of soil.

"Fist's car was found that way." She points at a dune marked by a dead tree at the bottom. "We'll have to walk. I'm not letting the tires down for this short distance."

I hop out of the Land Cruiser and follow Doris as she heads toward the dead tree, taking big, easy strides in her scuffed hiking boots. I immediately regret the Converse trainers as sand pours into the sides of my shoes with the first few steps.

"How did the accident happen?" I ask as I scramble to catch up to Doris.

She turns toward the road. "It looks like the car left the road and plowed through here, between the dunes, and then hit the tree stump. Your guy's foot must have been heavy on the accelerator."

I look back. There's a dune in the way of her theory.

"They move," says Doris cryptically. "The wind."

Ah. "Airbags?"

"The driver's airbag deployed, but it's not much help when a tree branch comes through the window and makes pudding of your head."

I consider the distance from the tree stump to the road. "You're right. He must've been in a hurry."

"My suspicion is that he veered off the road in the wind and sand. Visibility is pretty bad when the East Wind blows. Or perhaps he swung out for another vehicle. The cable along the road that's supposed to keep drivers out had been cut. Happens often." She points over her shoulder. "There's always some asshole with a quadbike insisting that the desert belongs to everyone and that he's allowed to come and play in it, despite this being a protected area."

I walk to the tree stump, lying on its back, its branches pointing at the sea like two outstretched arms. I turn around. Apart from the poles along the road and the rocks on the beach, there's nothing to see but sand.

"What exactly is this 'East Wind?'"

"The weather is usually extremely cold just before it hits, and wet, and then the East Wind comes in. I think it was a good eighteen knots that day. It chucks the sand you see here all over the place. Skews the odd lamppost and stop sign. You walk around in a kind of dust haze. About four years ago, the paint on one side of my car was practically stripped away when I drove home too fast. The sand almost works like sandpaper."

"Why would Fist drive in that?"

"Apparently it wasn't that bad when he started out. The closer he got to Walvis Bay, the worse it got. The people at his guesthouse warned him more than once, but he said he wasn't afraid of a bit of wind. And if the boats weren't going out, he at least wanted to go into the dunes, even if he had to do it on his own." She shrugs. "We often get them around here. The know-it-all tourist type."

I turn back to the tree stump and inspect it for anything that might look like blood, but there's nothing.

"When did you discover his body?"

"The next day only. No one saw the accident happen. No one else was crazy enough to be out in that weather."

"And his lights?"

"Lights?"

"Did no one see the lights from his vehicle from the road that night? If the battery lasted that long."

Doris gestures around her. "It's difficult for anyone to see what's going on back there. The dunes can be a pretty effective barrier."

She's right.

"So that's that," I say. "A car accident."

"Like I said." She jangles the Land Cruiser's keys as if she is in a hurry to get back to town.

I look at the dunes, the sky. "And there was nothing funny? Nothing that would make you think someone might have murdered him?"

"No. Why?" Doris tugs at the front of her T-shirt, looks at me suspiciously.

It's a feeling that's been eating at me for a while now, since I left the Chens' house. The people in Janien's photograph...something just doesn't feel right. I touch the tree stump, feel the clamminess from the morning dew and the mist, taste the ocean on my lips.

"I don't know. It's just something..."

I shouldn't have come here, I realize. And I shouldn't have gone to Gaborone either. I should have helped Jaap and left.

Doris is watching me, one hand resting on her hip. She turns her back to the sun, the morning rapidly becoming hotter. "Talk without thinking."

"What do you mean?"

"It's an old theory of mine. People supress their instincts. They don't trust them anymore, because it's all bright lights and big cities far away from nature. So tell me what you think. Don't censor yourself, just talk. What's bugging you?"

I take a deep breath. "There's just too much coincidence. One suicide, an accident, and a murder. Really? Three people in the same photograph? They all knew one another. And then there's the red. There's too much of it. Scarlet fabric and red roses. Or maybe that's my imagination. Who the hell knows."

"That doesn't make sense."

I groan inwardly. "You said it didn't have to—"

"Whoa, that's not it." She holds up her hands, turns back to the Land Cruiser. "Come. Let's have breakfast at Erik's. I need to show you something."

2

Jack Fist's eyes are closed, and his mouth is slack. A cracked pair of small, round silver-framed glasses is still in position on his nose, in spite of the fact that he'd been pummeled by an airbag and his head savaged by a dead tree.

He looks bigger than he did in Janien's photo. Well-toned biceps says he did some serious bulking up before he died. His clothes tell the same story. They look almost too small for him. In fact, he looks a bit ridiculous, like an adult wearing children's clothing.

Doris takes another bite of her scrambled egg and indicates with her fork that I should move on to the next photograph. It's one taken of the inside of the car.

It's a startling picture. Everything is red. The seats, the floor, the ceiling, Fist's lower body.

"What is this? Blood?" Can there be that much blood inside one person?

Doris shakes her head. She puts the glasses hanging from the beaded chain around her neck on her nose and takes the photo from my hands.

"It's red roof paint. Fist had a 20-liter drum on the backseat. It popped open during the accident and went everywhere. There was even some on the sand from when the door had opened a crack. The fishermen who found him took photos of the scene with their phones."

She takes a sip of coffee, her third cup since we sat down at the Alte Bäckerei.

"At first I thought the paint was a little odd, especially since he was a tourist, then I heard he was a performance artist. I assumed he had some crazy idea with the paint. A lot of these funny people get mightily upset when the seals in Walvis have to be culled, even though they deplete the fishing stock and then the fishermen are left without work and food. Anyway, there'd been talk about another cull at the time. The owners of the guesthouse where Fist stayed told us that the newspaper reports had upset him tremendously."

She wipes her chin, tucks blonde hair behind her ears. "His mother wasn't surprised about the paint either. She seemed almost embarrassed to talk about it, but apparently Fist had been arrested in New York two years before his death. Something to do with paint, the war in Syria, Times Square, and two half-naked women. She didn't get why the stuff going on in his own country didn't concern him more."

I stare at the photo, then try to pull all three scenes together in my mind's eye. Janien and her bicycle, red fabric laid out like a wedding train behind her. Yolene Chen, suicide among her father's red roses. Jack Fist, car accident with a drum of red paint spilled over everything. How could this possibly be a coincidence?

"When did Fist die?" I ask.

"July sometime, I think. Two, three years ago."

July.

"When exactly?" I take a napkin from the pile on the table and start writing. Janien died three years ago, in winter. Date? Yolene Chen, also in winter, one year ago. Date? Jack Fist, dead in July… two years ago?

Doris lifts her eyebrows when she sees my list. "I can't remember what the exact date was," she says. "I only grabbed the photographs out of the file yesterday. I didn't look at the paperwork."

She rummages in her bag for her phone and makes a call, asks someone to find the information.

"They'll let me know as soon as they can," she says, after she hangs up.

I google Yolene's death notice on my phone, text Sam Chen when I can't find anything. Then I look for the date of Janien's murder and write it down on the napkin. 20 July.

The phone pings. It's Sam texting me the answer to my question. Can't be.

I write it down.

Doris lifts a surprised eyebrow, but says nothing, orders a slice of apfelstrudel as though that will provide all the answers.

I can't even think about food anymore.

"Can't you call your people and hurry them up a little?" I say.

Doris pulls her coffee cup closer. "Be patient. They're on it."

Her phone rings just as the apple tart arrives. She looks at me for a long time when she's done talking.

She points at the dates I jotted down next to Yolene Chen and Janien Steyn's names. "Something's up. You need to talk to Jaap. Fist also died on the twentieth of July."

JAAP

The shed looks exactly the way it did three years ago when I first came searching for clues about Janien's death. Namaqua doves take flight as I push open the door, dry grass and dust sifting up with every step I take. The white building, housing mostly animal feed and sheep dip, is dusty, but neat and tidy, as always. Obie has a place for everything, but dust doesn't bother him.

He and Vonnie have gone into town to do grocery shopping and draw money for the week's wages, like they do every Thursday. I guess I have about an hour before they return.

The blue Nissan Diesel truck is parked at the back of the building, on the right. The lorry is old, forty years, I'd guess, and hasn't moved an inch in the past ten. Obie keeps it around to strip it for parts for his other vehicles.

I find the fuel tank, struggle to open it. I rub my hands together, grip the cap with both hands and try again. I can feel it budge, and pop it open. I peer into the dark cavity. I can't see anything. I look around, find a piece of galvanized wire in the corner, stowed under two new car batteries. I fashion a hook with a pair of pliers, stick it into the tank and sweep it along the bottom.

Nothing.

No…Wait. There's something to the right—hopefully something more than just the accumulated residue of a truck standing unused for years.

I take off my jacket, roll up my shirt sleeve, and try and reach deeper into the fuel tank.

Eventually the end of the wire hooks whatever it is, and holds. Slowly, carefully, I pull the wire out and catch the bag.

It's a Ziploc bag, like the kind my ex-wife used to pack my sandwiches for work. It's rolled up and haphazardly wrapped in black insulation tape. It looks like someone tried to tear the packet open on one side, but gave up. There's a dark spot on one corner. Looks like blood. Janien's blood?

No, Leon's. From his nosebleed. Supposedly.

I take a picture of the bag with my phone camera. Then I take a photo of the old truck and the wire. I pull on latex gloves, take out my pocketknife and cut the hole the wire hook made as I fished the bag out a little bigger.

It is weed, remarkably well preserved. I scratch around in it with the knife.

There's something in the dry leaves. I dig a bit more to reveal white powder in a tiny clear bag.

I touch the bag to test its consistency. Could it be Cat? The drug that amps up everything you feel to the extreme. Joy. Frustration.

Rage.

"Fuck it, boy," I swear under my breath.

Is it really Cat? Do I want to know? And why didn't Leon say anything about it?

I slip it back into the weed bag, take a closer look at the dark stain. It really does look like blood. I'll have to get it tested.

I place the weed bag into a larger plastic bag I brought along from Bells's kitchen and walk back to my car.

I know I should be happy that I found the bag right where Leon said it would be, but I'm not. The Cat opens up an entirely new possibility—that Leon was so out of his mind that he murdered his sister in an angry fit.

Maybe he doesn't even remember killing her. Or maybe he knows exactly what he's done.

"What are you doing?" Sarah asks, without saying hello.

"Waiting." I switch off the TV. Bells has all the sports channels, but there are only so many rugby games you can watch before it no longer matters who wins the next scrum.

"Waiting for what?" Her voice sounds far away.

"For the results of the DNA tests. It's going to take a few days for those I'm paying for. Weeks to collect all the samples." Something about her tone forces me to my feet. "Are you okay? What's wrong?"

"Janien's murder isn't what you think it is." The tension in her dark voice makes it even deeper than usual.

"What do you mean not what I think? Says who?"

"Me. And Doris. Janien was the first of three victims. Each of them was murdered on the twentieth of July. Each in a peculiar way involving something red, a year apart."

I sit down again. "What? Three people all on the twentieth?"

"Yes. Janien, Yolene Chen, and Jack Fist."

"How did you put all of this together?"

"I'll tell you later. I'm coming back to Carnarvon and then we need to decide what to do next. Doris says it might be a serial killer."

I'm struggling to digest this new information. After all the hassle with the DNA, Leon, Bells, and Vonnie. After everything. This? Now?

"Are you sure? Is Doris sure?"

"You can take a look yourself. I'm bringing you the info. I should be there by tomorrow. I wish I could fly, but I couldn't get a ticket."

"You hate flying," I say automatically.

"Yes, I do, but today is the fifteenth of July. And what if this guy wasn't planning on stopping at three?"

SARAH

1

"Finally. You're here. Come in," says Jaap as he opens the door.

I walk into his room at one of the guesthouses in Carnarvon. Dump my backpack next to the couch.

Jaap looks like he hasn't slept in days. His peppery beard is unshaven and his eyes bloodshot. He moves slowly, his bum knee an even bigger hindrance than before.

I scan the simply furnished room. "Why aren't you staying with that editor guy anymore? What's his name again?"

"Bells."

Jaap closes the door behind me. "His walls have ears. We're going to have to keep this story quiet until I understand what's going on. Three websites are already running with the DNA story. Luckily it's a busy news week, with the former president and his girlfriend on all the front pages."

He takes a tan folder off the coffee table and unlocks a glass door that leads to a courtyard. We sit down on hard concrete benches arranged in a circle around a matching table.

"Do you need an ashtray?" he asks.

"It was just the one, after Doris…No." I'm irritated that he can smell the smoke on me. Must be the jacket.

I open the box I brought from Swakopmund. "Here are some photos of the Yolene Chen murder scene if you want to look at them while I talk. Yolene's father emailed them through to Doris and she printed them for me."

"You said three murders. Who was the first?"

"Janien."

"Then?"

"Jack Fist. Brian Ndluli." I pass him the photos of the body in the car Doris gave me. "Doris thinks the East Wind…that's like a really ba—"

"I know what it is." He puts on his glasses.

"She thinks it might have interfered with the murderer's idea and that it somehow softened the impact of the scene. That it ended up being more sand than installation art. Landscape art. Whatever. I don't know the correct term."

Jaap peers at the photo. Then he fetches his notebook and opens it. It's full of silly drawings.

"Where are your notes?"

He looks at me as though he doesn't understand my question.

I point at the notebook. "I thought you take notes every time you use that thing."

"They're there, among the drawings." He gestures at the repeated patterns, circles, houses, and stick figures. "These just help me think."

He grins. "Come now. You smoke, sleep late, swear like a sailor, and don't know how to say hello or thank you. You win."

"You swear too. Don't think I don't hear you."

"You still win."

"Whatever…moving on." I point at the picture of Fist again. "He died two years ago, on 20 July. Janien died three years ago, same date, and Yolene died last year, also on July 20."

Jaap opens the folder with Janien's photographs. He takes one photo of each of the victims and arranges them in order of date of death in front of him, starting with Yolene Chen.

He gestures toward Yolene's grainy black-and-white picture. "She looks familiar. I wish I could see this in color."

"Where would you know her from?"

"Can't remember. It might come to me later. Tell me about the colors."

"The roses in the nursery where she was found were all in bloom. They're all bright red."

"And what was she wearing? What color?" He points at her dress.

"Red."

"Was it her dress? Did it belong to her?"

"I don't know." I make a note to ask Sam.

"And what does the police report say? Suicide?"

"Yes, but her father—Sam—disagrees."

"Parents seldom believe their children committed suicide. It's difficult to admit that you couldn't see what was going on inside their heads."

I think the same is true for godparents, but I don't say it out loud.

"What about Skout? The dating app?" he asks. "Do you still think it's relevant?"

"I don't know. It was obviously a possibility when only Yolene and Janien were in the picture, but Jack Fist? Nothing I have on him leads back to Skout—at least, nothing I can see. The three of them were friends, yes, but more than that? I don't know."

"Wait. Let's do this one at a time, before we get carried away. One person plus one person plus one person. Until you get the answer."

"I already know more than I ever wanted to know."

He turns toward me. "I'm sorry. And I really mean that. I didn't see this coming. If you want to go home, I understand. I can take this further. It's okay."

"No way." It's out before I can stop it.

"Think carefully."

"Nope. Not gonna happen."

I can't get Sam Chen out of my head. His text message to confirm his daughter's date of death. His voice on the cellphone speaker when Doris asked him to send us Yolene's photos. The marble stone between the roses. Yolene's blue room.

We need to find out what happened.

"It's okay, Jaap. I'm okay."

"All right. If you're sure."

"You just do your thing, and I'll do mine."

He smiles. That warm smile that radiates through his tired eyes and lights up his face, making him look younger. The charming one that turned Doris into Dorie, I'm sure.

"Sarah, you don't have to do this."

"Yolene Chen. Focus," I say quickly.

He shrugs and looks at the photos again. I tell him about the rose bushes and the nursery, the gravestone in the garden. He stops me when I tell him about the sundress.

"It was winter. What's winter like in Gaborone?"

I think of the night I was there, the morning. "Not unbearable, but chilly."

"Would she have worn a sundress in July?"

"Would it matter if you were about to commit suicide?"

His eyebrows lift. "But you and her father think someone murdered her."

I nod. "Okay, then the sundress is a bit strange, yes."

"What about the roses? The murderer had to have known about the roses, and that they're red when in bloom. He must have seen them, maybe he even visited."

"Yes, probably." Did Sam let the man in? Did Yolene know him? Did he come to visit? It's a strange thought, but not implausible.

"Also, how would the killer have convinced her to wear the sundress?" says Jaap.

He reaches for his notebook and starts drawing. First a circle, then a triangle above it. "Of course. M99. The same way Janien was killed. What do you think?"

"It's possible."

"I assume there were no blood tests done?"

"No. And she was cremated. No chance to try and trace it now."

"And Fist?" asks Jaap. "The murderer would also have had to put him in place, in a posed position. Send the car toward the tree without Fist's interference. Make sure the paint looks right. You need time for that, and a passive victim...or a corpse."

He draws a line through the triangle and looks up. "Dorie. If it was an accident, she would have drawn Fist's blood to establish alcohol levels. Call her and ask. We might just get lucky and get to test the blood for other substances too."

"Can M99 survive that long?"

"We'll find out, I suppose."

I eye him suspiciously. "Why don't you call Doris?"

"Because you know her now."

"Seems to me you know her better than I do. Far, far better."

"That was a long time ago," says Jaap.

"Did you guys date?"

"What's this nonsense?"

"Just asking. Chill. I'll call and find out."

I pick up the Fist photo again. "Doris says it looks like he lost control of his vehicle, left the road and crashed into the tree. The tree is about forty meters away from the road. Of course, the wind covered all the tracks within seconds. Even if she had wanted to investigate the case, there wasn't much to go on. The car door was ajar, maybe from the collision. Or maybe it was never closed properly in the first place. The sand got in everywhere. And it was a rental car, so there probably would have been a circus of fingerprints."

"Were there signs that Fist's or Yolene's wrists had been tied?"

"No. Doris says there were no obvious marks on Fist's body. Sam said the same about Yolene."

"It was the same with Janien. It could mean that the killer gave all of them the M99 before he started setting up his scene." He frowns. "Almost as though...It doesn't seem like it's about pain or sex...It's not about them necessarily. It's about him."

I don't know enough to make those kinds of assumptions. I'd rather stick to the tangible. "How do you think he delivers the M99? With a dart gun?"

"No, I think they trust him. He gets close to them and then he uses a syringe in a non-obvious place, like between the toes, or the back of the knee."

"Will Janien's...was she buried?"

He shakes his head. "Her ashes are in the sea at Pringle Bay. Thank goodness, otherwise I would have had to ask Vonnie to dig up her daughter."

He starts drawing again. "Why red? Why 20 July?"

"Don't know."

"Can you do a search to see if anything significant happened on 20 July to any of them? Anything that draws your attention, however small it may be. Something on their Facebook profiles. That Snapchat app. Weddings, funerals, birthdays. Doesn't matter."

"Will do."

I open my laptop and begin writing a to-do list: *Phone Sam and Doris. Search 20 July.* Then I take out the group photo from Janien's computer and give it to Jaap.

"What's also interesting is that three people in this photograph are dead. Sparrow is the only one still alive."

He studies the photograph of Sparrow and Janien with their arms around each other, Yolene next to them. Fist, glass in the air, like he's making a toast.

Everyone looks happy, young, carefree.

"Where did you find this?"

"Janien's computer."

It's as though a light goes on inside his head. "Of course! That's how I know her." He points to Yolene. "She was at Janien's funeral. I chatted to her briefly. I chatted to everyone there, in fact, looking for any kind of lead."

"What did she say? Did she talk about Skout?"

"No, otherwise Isak and I would have known about it. She just said she and Janien had worked together. And...ja."

"What?"

"She said she wasn't crazy about Henk and his family. Or Janien's...mine...either. It also looked to me as though she and Sparrow knew each other well, but they weren't necessarily the best of friends."

"Who did she think killed Janien?"

He takes off his reading glasses and folds them closed. "She thought it was suicide. She said Janien was deeply unhappy. I didn't believe her."

Not an unexpected theory, if you consider everything Janien confessed to Yolene in her emails.

"Was it a big funeral?" I ask. My father had a huge send-off. I never realized he had that many friends.

Jaap nods. "There were dozens of people from around here, but not many of Janien's friends. Vonnie wanted it over and done with as soon as possible. Janien's friends had a memorial service in Cape Town afterwards. I only heard about it later. I should have suspected then already that Janien had hidden a significant part of her life from us."

"Where did she live in Cape Town?"

"She was staying in the guest bedroom at some friends' house because her lease expired a few weeks before the wedding. They said she partied a lot and slept very little. Came home late almost every night."

"Did she also work from there?"

"No. Seems like she mostly worked at coffee shops." He pushes a hand through his hair. "Nothing in Cape Town looked suspect. Neither did anything on the *So What!* site. No one was angry or upset. And she was murdered here, on the farm. That has to mean something."

"You're probably right."

He returns his gaze to the photo of Janien and her friends. "I wish I'd known her better."

"Maybe you would have. Later. When she'd sorted out her life."

Jaap pinches the bridge of his nose, rests his head in his hand for a moment. "Three people dead, one left. Do you think it might have been Sparrow?"

"Maybe. Maybe someone's helping her. Or she's next."

"Do you have any idea who took this photo?"

"No."

He reads the single, faded word in the corner. "Blink," he says, pronouncing the word in Afrikaans, meaning "shiny."

"No," I say. "It's actually Blink. The English blink."

"What does it mean?"

"It's an art competition. I haven't had time to find out more. You can ask Sparrow. She'll probably also know who the photographer was." I nod toward my laptop. "I have enough work as it is."

He puts the photo to one side and looks at the images on the table again. Chen, Fist, and Janien. "Do these scenes not look like paintings to you? Art photos of some sort."

"Yes, I also thought so. I did a search of well-known paintings, but none of them match any of the murder scenes."

"That would have been too easy, I suppose." He sits back in his chair and closes his eyes for a moment. "This theory of yours, the timetable...it messes everything up. I wish I'd known about this before I saddled up this crazy DNA pony."

I take the Marlboros from my pocket. Put them back again.

"How many bridges?" I ask.

He looks at me as if I've been out in the desert sun too long. "What do you mean?"

"How many bridges have you burned? One is not too bad. Sometimes it's the only way to make sure the crazies don't know where you're heading—that's what my dad always used to say. Three is a bit more serious."

"How many have you burned in your life?"

I consider my answer. "One," I say. "The one that requires a clean police record when you apply for work. I used to wonder about the bridge to my family, but luckily it seems that one is intact." I hope that's still the case, anyway.

"And your friends?"

"I don't have many friends. And those I have, don't care."

Jaap counts on his fingers. "Vonnie and Obie. Leon. Isak. Stefan, Fanus, Henk. Henk's father."

He gives a lopsided grin. "What would your dad say about eight?"

"You don't want to know."

"Four-letter words?"

"Lots of them. Unless you're right, of course."

"What do you mean?"

"The DNA might actually belong to the murderer. That hasn't necessarily changed."

I leave Jaap with his photos and theories and go to reception to find out if there is any more room at the inn. I'm assigned a stand-alone cottage and I carry my stuff there. Then I hit the road to get a Coke and the cheesiest burger I can find.

Back in my room I call Doris once I've eaten. "Did you take a blood sample from Jack Fist after the accident? To see if he was drunk?"

An uncomfortable silence, followed by an exasperated sigh. "No."

"Why not?"

"Budget is always a problem, he was dead, and his mom didn't have any questions. And, like I said, he was a wild one. He'd been arrested for drunk driving twice before, in Durban and in Johannesburg. And he got off each time on some technicality or another regarding the equipment and/or the circumstances under which the police had taken his blood."

She says this as if we all know how the South African police screw up drunk-driving incidents. I tend to agree but I say nothing.

"Do you still have contact with Fist's mother?" I ask.

"No. I only met her once, when she came to collect the body and visit the accident scene. She was very upset. Her son was the first one in the Ndluli family to go to university. Why do you ask?"

I sigh audibly. "I suppose someone should talk to them."

"Shouldn't it rather be me?"

"Well, I certainly don't want to."

"You're not doing too badly. You followed the trail all the way to Swakop."

Doris hesitates. "Have you ever considered that? That he may be aware that you're chasing him down?"

"Him who?"

"The man who murdered these people. What if he knows about you and Jaap, that you're looking for him?"

I haven't thought about that. She's right. What are the chances he knows? Probably quite good.

"That's Jaap's problem," I decide.

But after I hang up, I make sure the room door is locked. Shit. That on top of everything else. Life back in Pretoria suddenly doesn't look so bad anymore, even though the Aston's gone.

The thought angers me again. What would my dad have left me in a little box?

Must be the Aston's keys. He always was a joker.

I call Sam Chen.

"How are you?" I ask, because that's what you're supposed to do, isn't it? Even when you don't really want to know the answer.

"Not good. Things were better before you started digging around. Now I'm beginning to wonder if it wouldn't have been better if Yollie had committed suicide. I'm worried she was terrified and hurt and I wasn't there to hold her hand. To stop this madman from going around killing people."

I can hear birds in the background. Sam must be in the garden, sitting under the peach trees. Then I hear the single, sharp sound of something toppling over.

"What are you doing?" I ask.

"That was the spade, sorry. I'm taking out the rose bushes."

"The red ones?"

"Yes."

I look at my watch. Friday 16 July, 3:42 in the afternoon. It feels like it should be much later. I'm tired. It's been a long drive from Swakop to Carnarvon.

"Why?" I ask.

"I am putting in white ones. Icebergs. After all your questions… about the colors…I just couldn't face them anymore." A sharp intake of breath. "But that's not why you're calling, is it?"

"No. I want to know about the dress Yollie wore when she died. Do you know it? Does your wife know it?"

"No. We spoke about it back then. It was new. We found the tillslip for it in the trash can in Yollie's room. Afterwards."

I immediately think of fingerprints. "Do you still have it?"

"No."

That would have been too easy, I suppose. "Do the shops in Gaborone sell summer dresses in winter?"

There's a moment of silence, then Sam says: "Maybe. There are shops here that sell anything. Especially the Chinese shops." He laughs a little, as though he finds it ironic.

"And the red? The kind of dress? Did Yolene often wear clothes like that? Colors like that?"

"I mostly remember jeans and T-shirts. Pink pajamas when she was four. The dress she wore at her graduation. The green shirt she had to wear for her job at the restaurant. That's it."

"And the gun she used?"

"What's with all these questions? Have you found the man who did this?"

I don't want to give him hope. "No, but we are getting closer."

"Who is it?"

"We don't know. We don't know anything for sure. We're still trying to puzzle all the pieces together."

I sink down onto the bed. How did Jaap make a career out of this? How did he deal with this much pain and grief?

"The gun?" I ask again.

"The gun was mine."

"Was it locked in a safe?"

Sam swallows audibly, then answers softly: "No."

JAAP

Trouble. Not the knee-deep-in-the-mud kind. No. The up-to-the-neck-choking-on-it kind.

I look at the photos again. Jack Fist, Janien, Yolene. All dead. And I know this thanks to Sarah. And let's not forget the very long list of people in Carnarvon who will never send me a Christmas card again.

Not bad for a few days' work. Well done, Reyneke.

But what does Sarah's new information mean? Is everyone I've been speaking to this week innocent? Stefan? Leon? Should I forget about the weed and the Cat? The DNA?

Probably not the DNA, no. Sarah's right. That could still belong to the killer. That hasn't changed.

I open the notebook. I have to work through this new information in a logical manner.

First fact. None of this feels like the work of a serial killer who randomly chooses a new victim every time. Janien, Fist, and Chen knew one another. The three of them also died on the same day of the year, so the date must have some meaning. Hopefully Sarah will find something that links the victims—something that points away from Leon.

Second fact. How did these people know each another? Was it through that art competition? Blink? If so, that might be where the motive for the murders lies. And, as Sarah suggested, Sparrow might be able to help, since she also entered Blink.

I call Sparrow. "Are you busy?"

"Yes. The DNA mask is almost complete."

I frown. "That was quick."

"I wanted to get it done. The stress is too much, Jaap. The entire town has gone mad about this DNA project of yours...You know my dad's going to kill you if you ever show up at the house again?"

I ignore the warning. I don't want to make promises I can't keep. "What does the mask look like? Is it someone we know?"

"I'm not sure yet. You're welcome to come and have a look, but you'll have to drive to Stellenbosch. The lab where I'm working is near the university."

I look at my watch. "How about tomorrow evening? Round six?"

"Sounds good. Just...please don't expect too much. I don't think it's going to give you the answers you want."

"Don't worry. Let's see what you come up with." I look at the series of photos in front of me again. "While I have you on the phone—can you help me with something else?"

"What?"

"Blink."

She thinks for a few moments. "The art competition?"

"Yes."

"What do you want to know?"

"I'm not sure," I answer honestly.

"Okay. I suppose we can chat tomorrow." She gives me the address of the private lab and rings off.

Back to the photos and my notebook.

Third fact. If the murders were carefully planned, then so were the victims' clothes, and the emphasis on the color red. The red fabric with Janien. Yolene's sundress, the roses. The red paint in Fist's car.

What was Fist wearing anyway?

I pick up the photo and look a little closer. Are those leather trousers? Looks like it. And black boots and a tight, white T-shirt. A chunky silver ring on each of his middle fingers.

I swallow my pride and call Doris.

"Twice in one month! Fancy that."

"Hello, Dorie."

"Be careful. I might get the wrong impression."

She's messing with me. Isn't she? "I…it's…"

"You never even said goodbye, Jaap."

"I went back to Pretoria that evening because the Church Street murderer had escaped. I'm sorry. I know it's a poor excuse."

"There's this technology called cellphones. They are pretty quick and easy to use. Thirty seconds. *Hello, I'm getting on an airplane. See you later.*"

"I'm really sorry." I don't know what else to say.

"Still the same old Jaap. Work before anything else. So, I assume you never married again? Or you're certainly not married anymore if you're talking to me at this hour."

She always was a straight shooter. "No. Never could face doing it again."

"And now? I doubt you're calling to invite me to dinner."

Strike three, but I'm not going to apologize again. "No, it's about Jack Fist."

"Work, in other words." She's laughing openly now.

I remember how those bright blue eyes could pin you down and make you squirm until you admitted the truth.

Maybe it was the eyes that made me run away, not the Church Street case. "Yes," I concede.

"What do you want to know?"

"Fist's clothes. The leather trousers. Do you think they were his? I have a feeling our man might dress his victims. Red dress. Red fabric. Bicycle. Aviator goggles. Small round glasses. It feels like he uses all kinds of props."

"Shit, Jaap, you and this Sarah chick are relentless. You make a pretty good team. Good old couldn't-hurt-a-fly Jaap and get-to-the-point Sarah. I get that it's important, but it was two years ago. How am I supposed to remember all these details about a strange man who drove into the dunes?"

"Were there footprints?"

"The East Wind had come in. You'll know how that is. You were in my bed once when it came up."

I ignore the intimate reference. "The paint? Was it bought locally?"

"Lots of places stock it."

"Did you work through the CCTV material?"

"The hardware stores'? Why would I? It was a motor-vehicle accident. If you didn't have the context I have now, it was just that—a road accident.'

I think back to what Sarah said—that Fist looked like a bodybuilder when he died, not like the slim young man in the picture on Janien's computer.

"The clothes Fist was found in."

"Back to that then. What about them?"

"Were they too small for him?"

Doris considers the question. "They were tight, yes. Very tight. The black leather pants made me think he was on his way to a rave and not about to get on a boat to go save the seals."

"Where were they made?"

"I don't know." Her voice is growing increasingly edgy.

"The tight pants mean the murderer might have known Fist, but that he hadn't seen him for a while," I try to explain. "Our guy took clothes along that were too small, because he didn't know that Fist had bulked up. Do you have any idea whether Fist complained at the guesthouse about someone following him or that he'd run into an old friend?"

"No. The owners said nothing, and I didn't ask."

"And the glasses? Were they a prop or real?"

"There was plain glass in the frames. No lenses."

That certainly supports my theory that the killer dresses his victims.

"Anything else, Colonel Reyneke?" Dorie asks.

"No. I'm sorry. I know we're asking you impossible questions."

A door opens in the background and I hear Dorie having a quick, muted conversation.

"Sorry about that. We had a big robbery here last night at a lodge." The door closes. "It's not about the questions, Jaap. It's more that I keep thinking there was something I didn't see. I feel like a stupid detective tannie who was too thick to notice what was happening on her watch."

"Don't worry. I also feel pretty stupid. I didn't manage to get anywhere with Janien's case until Sarah arrived." I can't stop the smile creeping up on me. "When last did someone call you tannie?"

"Last year. Snot-nosed kid at the ice-cream shop."

"And now?"

"What do you think? It's Chief Inspector Engelbrecht."

I laugh, ask: "Is there anyone in your life now? Are you happy?"

She answers without hesitation. "Maybe. I'm still deciding."

"I'm really sorry, Dorie. If I could do it over—do it better—I would."

"No. You would still have chosen work over me. And what's all this, 'I'm sorry' bull? You don't sound like yourself."

"Old age. It's a miserable bugger."

"You have a good twenty, thirty years left."

"Ex-cops rarely make eighty."

"I'm going to keel over at ninety-eight," she declares confidently. "I dreamed that one night. I'm going to close my eyes and not wake up again. Hopefully, I will have had a nice slice of Erik's apple tart the night before and a not-so-nice young man who kept me company. Anyone under fifty will do."

Another call comes in and I look at the screen. It's Henk.

"I have to take this call."

"Go. Keep me updated."

"I will."

"Hi, Henk," I say.

"Hello, Jaap." He sounds drunk. "Found anything yet?"

"No."

"And the DNA?"

"Nothing yet."

"Oh." He sounds disappointed. "You okay? I heard about the petrol bomb."

"I'm alive. As you can hear."

"Good. I hope you catch him."

"Me too. Goodnight, Henk. Go to sleep. And don't drive, please."

"Won't. Don't worry. Night."

SARAH

1

It's late morning when I pull up in the Toyota Fortuner I hired in Swakopmund. Jaap is at the gate, waiting for me, ready to put his bag in the car. The sky is bright and clear, the air crisp.

He tunes the radio to RSG as soon as he's seated. The forecast says its rainy and windy in Cape Town.

I open my window. "Where to first?"

He puts the heater on. "Coffee and breakfast," he says grumpily.

"What's going on with you?"

"Nothing." He gives me a sidelong glance. "Any news about 20 July and what it means?"

"It's Vonnie's birthday. I assume you'd totally forgotten about that."

Judging by his face, he had.

"Is that it?" he asks.

"Yeah. For now."

"And Jack Fist? Could you work out how Janien, Sparrow, and Yolene knew him?"

"It seems that they met at the Blink art competition. And before you ask, the competition's final judging was in May, not July."

"Tell me about Blink. And yes, before you ask, I did call Sparrow, but she was too busy to talk last night."

I accelerate as we leave Carnarvon behind us. "As far as I can tell, Blink is for art students. There's big prize money for the winner and almost nothing for the runner-up. It's usually won by someone from Stellenbosch University. As you know, the three women in the photo studied together at Stellenbosch, while Fist was at the University of Pretoria."

"Who sponsors the competition?"

"The prize money comes from someone's estate—an old-money family with a bunch of wine farms in the Boland. The mother, whose farm it was, dropped her two daughters from her will and left her money in a trust. That trust now sponsors the competition."

Jaap takes out his notebook and pen. "Who won the year Janien and her friends took part?"

"James Addison."

"Who's he?"

I'd also hoped it might be someone we knew. "Addison is a sculptor. He mostly makes these weird industrial things. The judges called his work 'boundary shifting, with astonishing insight into human vulnerability.'" I struggle to keep the mockery out of my voice.

Jaap jots down the name. "Where does he live? Can we go and speak to him?"

"I haven't tracked him down yet. It seems like he's constantly on the move. But we do have an appointment to see Janien's lecturer, who taught all of the women, at four o'clock. Karl Ungerer. He's at the Stellenbosch art department. He was also the convener of the judges for Blink. I want to talk to him about the letters he wrote Yolene. It seems he knew about Skout, so he must have known Janien and Yolene quite well. Sparrow too, probably."

"I remember you mentioned him."

I nod.

"How many Blink competitors were there?" Jaap asks.

"Finalists? Five. The four on the photo and Addison."

"Anything else? Anything new on Facebook? Emails? Another S&M hiding in Janien's closet? Something about Skout? Emails between Stefan and Janien?" Jaap's practically growling. "I don't want to be in the dark again."

"Relax, will you? Stefan and Janien were mailing each other

often, yes. He was lying to you. But it doesn't look like they were sleeping together. And yes, maybe he was trying to push her to look a little beyond Henk—at him, perhaps. I'm still working on it, but I can tell you from the emails between the two of them that the whole lot—Henk, Fist, Leon, Stefan, Yolene, Janien, and Sparrow—knew one another, but they weren't necessarily all friends."

"How did that happen?"

"Don't know. Maybe Janien introduced them all to one another. Fist, Yolene, and Addison were invited to the wedding, but they all turned down the invitation." I'm driving well over the speed limit now, but Jaap doesn't seem to mind. "Have you figured out who made the call from the butchery yet?"

"No. It seems like the whole town was there that night, except Henk and Leon. Henk was in Clarens and Leon at home."

"That's good news, isn't it? Then it couldn't have been Leon."

"I suppose so." Jaap puts away his notebook, leans back in his seat and closes his eyes. "It's good work, Sarah. Really good work."

It's quiet for a while, then he says: "I'm starting to worry about Sparrow. As you say, she's the only one in the photo who's still alive, and she was also a Blink finalist."

"Yes. She was the runner-up."

"Who came third?"

"Don't know. Maybe the professor can help."

"What's his name again?"

"Ungerer."

I close the window. How far is the closest rest stop so that Jaap can get some coffee and breakfast and chill out? Was it Doris who upset him this much?

"Did you talk to Doris?" I check. "What does she say about Fist?"

"I did." He rubs his palms over his eyes and suppresses a yawn. "It looks like our man dressed Fist, but that he probably misjudged his size. It seems to me as if he went to a lot of trouble with each murder to bring props and to dress his victims."

He counts on his fingers: "Bicycle, aviator goggles, round glasses, red fabric, red paint, Fist's leather outfit, and possibly also Yolene's sundress. It must be someone who has his own transport and a fair degree of money. He's a planner. Clever and patient. Very, very patient. He waits until 20 July ever year, not a day sooner. I'm also sure he knows his victims, so the props might have something to do with what he wants to say about himself in relation to them."

"I agree," I say.

"The murder scenes are like paintings," Jaap continues. "Or absurd, abstract photographs. Images. Works of art, in other words. He follows them, kills them, and dresses them. Perhaps he's trying to say he's better than they are. A better artist. And that they are nothing more than life-sized dolls he plays with."

I think again about my brief telephone conversation with Professor Ungerer yesterday to arrange the appointment. "Maybe it links directly to Blink then. James Addison is a sculptor, after all."

"He can't be bitter, surely. He won."

"Maybe he also had a thing for Janien."

"But then why kill Fist and Yolene?" Jaap shakes his head. "No, this is not about Janien. We have to find out why someone would want all three of these people dead."

I think of everyone in the photo. "Maybe the next murder will give us more information. If something happens to Sparrow...then ...ja."

"And what if she's the murderer and Addison is next? We better not reach that point, Sarah. We simply cannot allow that to happen." Jaap crosses his arms over his chest. "We have to work faster. The DNA on the dress could give us a new lead. And maybe Sparrow will give us a something fresh tonight that we can follow up."

"I hope so. But just out of curiosity, do you really think we can trust the DNA if the murderer is as clever as we think? What if that was planted too, like the paint and the bike? And if Sparrow is working with the killer...what if she is manipulating her DNA portrait?"

"Earlier you told me that the DNA is most likely still important."

"I know, but shouldn't I start thinking like you, Colonel Reyneke?"

He turns his head back toward the window, but I can still see his reflection. His smile is the warm one, the one I like.

"I also wonder about the DNA," he admits. "But what else do we have?"

He's right. It's Saturday, 17 July, and we are running out of time.

Professor Karl Ungerer is younger than I expected. Not that I know how old academics are, necessarily. I've never been to university.

Ungerer looks like he's just over forty. He is a tall man, with delicate hands and a neatly trimmed gray-brown beard. His hair is the same color, with a thinning fringe he flicks out of his eyes as he looks up when we knock on his office door.

He gets up from behind his desk and waves us inside. His jeans are worn, and the sleeves of his thin blue jersey are pushed up to his elbows. His fingernails are short and stippled with pink spots that look like paint. A stray drop of paint has also found its way onto his silver-framed glasses.

His office is big, the windows framing the huge oak trees lining the road we traveled on just a few minutes ago. I move a step closer to Ungerer's desk. Another. Spot the bright umbrellas bobbing and weaving as people move between the different buildings.

It's warm in his office in spite of the wind and rain outside.

Ungerer agreed to meet us on a Saturday morning, but not at his home. Perhaps he was painting there. Perhaps he has a family he doesn't want us to meet.

He shakes Jaap's hand briefly but lingers with mine. He looks at me the way men often look at me, as though they're wondering whether there's someone special in my life. Whether I'd sleep with them anyway. Whether I'd be exotic, different, adventurous in bed.

There's a silver ring on his left hand. He lets go of my hand and touches the ring self-consciously when he sees me looking at it.

He sweeps his fringe out of his eyes again. "Are you the people from the police?"

Jaap looks at me sharply, but I pretend not to notice.

"No," he says firmly, as though he wants to make sure we all understand one another. "I used to be in the police. We're doing a private investigation into the deaths of two of your former students. My apologies if we created the wrong impression."

"Private investigation? Someone has a lot of money." He looks at me, his eyes wandering up and down my body.

Jaap gives a slight smile—the thin one that fails to reach his eyes. "As I said, I'm sorry about that. But we'd still appreciate your help, if you don't mind."

Ungerer considers this for a moment, then finally nods his agreement. "Okay. Let's see what I can do."

He sits down behind his desk and gestures to the visitors' chairs on the other side. We take a seat.

"You're interested in Janien Steyn and Yolene Chen, I gather." His curiosity is palpable.

Jaap tries to sit up straight in the low brown chair next to mine. I can see he is not at all keen on having to look up at Ungerer.

"You remember them?" he asks.

Ungerer nods. "How could anyone forget those two? They were brilliant, especially Janien. She could put anyone at ease in front of her camera. She took perfect portraits. I still struggle to believe she lost Blink that year. And I certainly couldn't believe it when I later read that she'd been murdered. And Yollie's suicide? She's the last person I would have expected to do something like that."

He opens a drawer and extracts a pack of Dunhills, turns his head and smiles at me. "Sorry, but I really need one of these." He gets up and points at the window. "I'll stand over there, if that's okay."

He opens the window and a gust of cold air blows into the office.

The fresh, crisp smell of the wintry air is nothing compared to the wonderful aroma of the cigarette in his hand.

I breathe in the second-hand smoke in search of some satisfaction, the instant relaxation that usually flows from a hit of nicotine, but there's nothing. Nothing that can quiet the raging white noise in my head for a moment.

It's Jaap's fault. And Fist's fault. And Sam's. They turned up the bloody volume in my mind.

"Tell us about Janien," says Jaap.

I get up and show him that I'll wait for him outside.

Ungerer laughs as though he realizes why I'm leaving. As though he thinks he knows me.

"Have one," he says, holding out the Dunhills.

Jaap shakes his head and answers for me. "No, thank you."

Ungerer ignores him. "Have one. Really. I don't mind."

His smug smile makes me sit down again. I don't like this man. Not one bit.

I decide to get in a shot of my own. "Did you sleep with Janien?"

The question doesn't surprise him. "No."

"Yolene?"

"Only after she graduated."

So the rumor on Facebook was true. And it certainly explains the intimate tone of his letters.

Jaap looks at me in a way that makes it clear we're going to have a chat as soon as we leave here.

He takes out his notebook and starts doodling.

"And Jack Fist?" he asks. "Did you sleep with him?"

Ungerer draws the smoke in deeply and blows it toward me in a pointed way when he thinks Jaap's not watching. Invites me, with his eyes, to give in and have that cigarette with him.

I don't react.

"The Fist of Soweto?" says Ungerer. "Brian Ndluli? No, he wasn't interested."

"Were you interested?" Jaap draws a pistol.

"He was cute, but not quite my type, as it turns out. Too much of a drama queen."

I can't work out whether Ungerer is mocking us. "So you knew Fist too? And you know that he's dead?"

"I was a judge on the Blink panel. So yes, I know about Jack."

Jaap looks up from his notebook. "Isn't it strange that three Blink finalists from the same year are all dead?"

Ungerer flicks ash out of the window, takes another quick draw on the cigarette, then throws the butt out too. "Not really. People die all the time. And didn't they die after the competition? One murder, one suicide, and one accident—doesn't seem strange to me. Just shit luck."

My turn. "Did you know about Skout?"

Ungerer turns away to close the window. Answers with his back to us. "Yollie and Janien told me about it. I didn't think it could work, though." He's wearing a smile when he turns back to us, but it's fragile and false. "But then, I don't know much about IT."

"And yet you're a shareholder in a startup here in Stellenbosch. Cyber-Secure."

I sit back in my chair. I should probably have told Jaap about this first and not shown my hand so quickly, but this man is seriously rubbing me up the wrong way.

Jaap carries on drawing, but the pen is moving a little faster now. The pistol gets a trigger.

Ungerer feigns surprise. "That? I'm not really involved. Some students wanted to set up the company and they asked me if I could help them with a bit of seed funding. I have a five percent share and I don't exactly know what their plans are. My broker said it sounded like a good, low-risk investment, so I put in the money."

Jaap's pistol is complete. "Did Janien or Yolene ever ask you for funding?"

Ungerer sits down again, but his narrowed eyes are hinting that his patience is running out.

"After Janien's death, Yollie wanted to develop Skout on her own. She was tired of the bullshit and false promises of the big IT companies. She wanted to know whether I knew how she might get financing. I referred her to an investment company.'

My turn. "What's it called?"

"BIQ Financial Services."

I don't know the name. I'd hoped he would say ITFin, the company that was talking to Yolene about Skout shortly before her death.

"And? Did she get the money?" asks Jaap.

"I don't know. I didn't follow up with her."

Ungerer gets up, looks at his watch conspicuously. "You're going to have to excuse me. I have an appointment. Lunch with the ex."

"Sure." Jaap puts his notebook away and gets up. "Just one more question: James Addison, that year's Blink winner. Do you know where we might get hold of him?"

"As far as I know he's working on an exhibition in KwaZulu-Natal, at a place near Nottingham Road. In the Midlands." Ungerer rifles through the papers on his desk. "I received an invitation, but you're welcome to it. I don't have time to go. Addison's ego has overtaken his work in the last few years, in any case."

I step forward and take the white envelope from him.

Ungerer turns, puts on the black jacket and scarf that were over his chair. He shakes Jaap's hand, then mine, suddenly remembering to smile again.

He holds my hand a moment longer than necessary. "Let me know if there's anything else I can do to help."

"Will do," I say coldly.

We walk out with him. He locks the door, says goodbye, and strides down the passage.

Jaap and I follow in our own time.

I gratefully breathe in the fresh air, but it doesn't help. I'm dying for a cigarette. I take the Marlboros from by backpack. Put them back.

Open the invitation instead.

Jaap pushes his hands deep into his jacket pockets, scowls at the rain coming down with renewed vigor. "That was interesting. But you owe me an explanation about Yolene. A relationship with that idiot? And the IT company? Why didn't you say anything?"

I stop short.

Jaap turns around. "What's wrong?"

I look at the paper in my hand.

"Sarah? What's wrong?"

I pass the invitation to him.

He stares at it. "Surely it's a coincidence?"

"I don't think so."

The first solo exhibition in two years by talented young sculptor James Addison opens on Tuesday, 20 July.

3

The private laboratory where Sparrow is creating the DNA mask from the sample collected from Janien's wedding dress is not too far from Cyber-Secure, Ungerer's IT startup. I point out the small business to Jaap as we drive by the squat, nondescript structure, swerve to avoid hitting a woman and two Weimaraners, all of them in yellow rain jackets, jogging down the road.

My phone beeps. It's the verification from Gaborone I've been waiting for. "I have some bad news," I tell Jaap.

"What?"

"Leon was in Gaborone when Yolene died. Some or other agricultural conference."

"What? How do you know that?"

"His phone. Social media."

Jaap swears under his breath. "And Swakop? Was he in Swakop when Fist died?"

"Still looking."

"I was convinced the fact that he didn't make that phone call before the arson attack cleared him."

"Maybe someone just wanted to make a point about the DNA thing. Doesn't have to be the murderer who made the call, does it?"

"Guess not." He runs a tired hand through his hair, shakes his head. "What about the rest of them? Stefan? Henk? Did you trace their movements too?"

"It's not that easy to trace the Malans' phones. The phones Sparrow and Stefan use belong to Fanus's business, so I haven't been able to work out exactly where they were at the times of the murders. There are seven phones registered to the business and it seems that the family swap them among themselves. That's the only explanation I can think of because the GPS data is all over the place. I know someone was outside of South Africa when Yolene died, but I don't know who, or where they were. Leon made it easy. He posted a pic on Twitter. He stayed at the same hotel as I did in Gaborone so I recognized the background. I called yesterday to make sure the conference was held there and they've just confirmed."

"Shit. That's all I need right now."

I look at Jaap, notice the angry red hue that has crept from his neck onto his face.

"I don't get it." He turns in his seat to look at me. "Why would Leon want Jack Fist or Yolene Chen dead? Janien I might still understand. Sparrow said Leon was sort of in love with her...if you can believe her."

"Maybe he was jealous of them all? Maybe Yolene and Janien were more than friends. And I suspect Fist had a thing for Janien too."

"Does that mean Sparrow is next?"

"Maybe."

"No." He shakes his head, his mouth a taut line. "I can't believe it's Leon."

"The problem is that this case is much bigger than you right now. It doesn't matter what you think."

Thankfully, my phone's map app talks over Jaap's response, and I turn in at the building where Sparrow makes her DNA masks.

As I understand it, the laboratory she uses belongs to a listed company that specializes in medical research.

The guard at the gate says Sparrow is expecting us. I look on as Jaap writes his real name, surname, cell number, and ID number in the guard's register. Why he would just hand out his private details like that I don't know.

In the reception area Jaap reads through the list of names next to the elevator, looking for the DNA Dynamics lab. "There. Third floor."

I look up. The office block has a square atrium that tunnels all the way up to the top where rain is hammering down on the glass roof as though it's never going to stop.

The elevator slides open and Jaap steps aside for me to get in. I point at the stairs.

"I hate lifts. See you at the top."

He puts a hand on my arm. "Did you look everywhere when you did your phone traces?"

"What do you mean?"

"The woman who lives with Sparrow. Do you know anything about her?"

"Oh. She's got two doctorates, one of them from Germany. Astronomy, if I remember correctly. She's part of the SKA project. Jessica van Gaalen."

"And?"

"She earns good money and she's seven years older than Sparrow."

He lifts one eyebrow. *"And?"*

"I don't know if they're sleeping together, Jaap. There's only so much I can do."

"She looks strong. And she's tall, and she drives a bakkie."

"Almost everyone in Carnarvon drives a bakkie."

"Ja, probably."

The elevator doors start to close. Jaap presses the call button and they slide open again.

"Do you really suspect her, or do you think it's just too soon after Janien?" I ask.

"Isn't everlasting love supposed to last forever?"

I'm surprised. "Do you believe in that? You of all people?"

"I'm just wondering, that's all."

"You're asking the wrong person. I believe in the machine. People are fickle. You can't trust them," I say as I move toward the stairs. "And for the record, I don't think it's Van Gaalen. I think you're just looking for another reason why it can't be Leon."

He steps into the elevator without answering me.

Jaap is already at DNA Dynamics's front door when I exit the stairwell on the third floor.

I wait as he rings the bell beside the glass doors, then watch as Sparrow walks down a long hallway, wearing blue scrubs like a TV surgeon.

She stifles a yawn and presses a button under the reception desk.

Jaap opens the door and waves me through.

"Hi." Sparrow smiles at me. "I didn't think both of you were coming."

I shrug. "I'm curious, I suppose."

She shakes her head. "You expect too much. You've expected too much since the beginning. Come look."

We follow her down a sterile passage bathed in muted blue light, end up in a small sitting room decorated in earthy hues. On the coffee table, next to a stack of medical magazines, is the macabre, three-dimensional synthetic image of a face.

I lean down to the mask to take a closer look.

Jaap glances at it over my shoulder, mumbles something unintelligible, and sits down on one of the chairs.

I can feel the disappointment radiate off his body.

"May I...?" I ask.

Sparrow nods. "Of course."

I pick it up. It's remarkably true to life, except for the lifeless eyes.

"I did warn you," says Sparrow. "All my work does is to give a sense of the general family features, the greater genetic background, without being specific."

I hold the mask up. The youngish man with brown hair and eyes doesn't look familiar. It's a strong face, but not particularly attractive. It could be Stefan. Or Leon. A dozen men in Carnarvon.

It's quiet, I suddenly realize.

I look away from the mask. Jaap is staring down at his shoes, lost in thought.

"Jaap? Are you okay?" Sparrow kneels down beside him.

He gives her a defeated smile. "Sorry. I'm just tired. And you're right, maybe I was expecting too much. I wanted the mask to be the answer so this could all finally be over."

He's lying. I don't know how I know it, but I know. But what exactly is he lying about?

I look at Sparrow. "Let's go make him a cup of tea," I suggest.

Sparrow gives Jaap's leg a squeeze and gets up. "Okay. Three cups of tea coming up."

We walk to a small kitchen, hidden at the back of the reception area.

Under the bright fluorescent lighting, I can see that Sparrow is exhausted. She moves tentatively, like someone who has to concentrate not to bump into things. When last did she have a good night's rest? She looks like Jaap: dejected and tired to the bone.

"I'm sorry," she sighs. "I told Jaap not to expect too much." She runs her hands through her hair, fans it out across her shoulders. "But, to be honest, I think I also hoped the mask would solve the case. That I would finally know who killed Janien."

I put the kettle on and start searching for tea bags and cups.

Suddenly it feels to me as though Sparrow and I are forever standing around in kitchens waiting for the kettle to boil.

"Don't be sorry," I say. "I still think it's worth something. But I understand why you and Jaap are disappointed." I put three white cups down on the counter.

She waves away my sympathy. "We'll get over it."

"At least you must be glad the mask doesn't point directly to someone in your family?" I say.

"I am, but we're not in the clear yet. I gave my DNA to Isak as Jaap had asked. Isak was surprised, to say the least. He remembered how I always covered for Stefan at school. My brother wasn't exactly big on going to class. Anyway, I made Isak promise he'd keep quiet about the DNA. If my father had to find out...Anyway, I'm sure it's not Stefan or my dad."

I nod.

In spite of the news that Leon was in Gaborone when Yolene died, I still wonder whether Sparrow is not somehow involved. She and a partner...a man with brown hair and brown eyes. Someone like Stefan.

The mask doesn't really look like her brother, but she could have manipulated the image to suggest otherwise.

Maybe they did it because Sparrow was angry with Janien. And because Stefan didn't want Janien to marry Henk.

But what about Yolene and Jack Fist? How do they fit into the picture? That's the thing that doesn't make sense, as Jaap says. How all the victims tie together.

I take the group photograph out of my pocket. The one where Janien has her arm around Sparrow.

She gasps when she sees the photo, takes it from me. "Where did you get this?"

I pour the boiled water into the cups, spoon sugar in.

I turn around to the fridge for the milk, only to find Sparrow crying. She does it quietly, the same way she moved around her father's kitchen the first time I met her. Like she doesn't want anyone to notice.

"I'm sorry. I didn't mean to...sorry."

She shakes her head. "No, don't. The photo...This was during Blink. It was the best week of my life. It felt as though Janien had, for a moment, let go of her anxiety about who she was. Who we were. We were in a space where we could relax and be ourselves."

She points to Fist. "He was flirting with Janien, and the man who took the photo was a bit soft on me. It was so strange. The whole week was strange. We were all so different and yet so similar. We wanted to change the world. And for a split second it seemed everyone was listening. As if they understood what we had to say."

"Who took the picture?" I take the milk from the fridge.

"James Addison. He won the competition. The five of us were finalists."

I wonder how far I can push it. "And now it's just you and him left."

"You're right," she says, a little surprised. She brushes over the faces in the photograph with her fingertips. Then I see the realization dawn on her. "Just me and James left...what does that mean?"

"Don't know. What's he like?"

"Very private. He didn't hang out with us much, but he and I sometimes chatted. The rest of us would drink late into the night, but he wasn't interested."

"And his work? He's a sculptor, right?"

"He's good. There are very few people who can elicit such warmth from steel. His work is quite different to him. It's alive, upsetting, satirical, and yet empathic. It moves you."

"Can you think of any reason he might want the rest of you dead?"

"The rest of...Seriously?" Her green eyes look at me, turn a shade darker. "Has everyone been murdered? Jack Fist too? James said it was a car accident. And Yollie? I thought it was suicide!" Her hand flies to her mouth in shock. "It can't be true. I can't think of any reason James would want to murder all of them. Us. Are you sure?"

I ignore her question. "Anyone else perhaps? What about professor Karl Ungerer? Could he have done it?"

"Prof. Karl? From the university? Why would he want to do something like that?"

"He knows about Skout. And he was a judge for Blink that year, so he knows everyone."

"Yes...yes, of course."

"So? Is he capable of murder?"

"No. I don't think so. He's very arrogant, but he's not a murderer."

Sparrow goes up a notch in my estimation for seeing trough

Ungerer. "It sounds like you're not crazy about him."

"Not in the least. He has a habit of sleeping with his students... He and Yolene...I thought she was incredibly naive to fall for him."

I give her a cup of tea, take a sip of my own, put it down, and add more sugar. "Who else might want your friends dead?"

She looks at me, dazed. "I have no idea." She drinks the tea robotically, wipes her tear-stained cheeks. "Do you think it was me? I wouldn't...I could never do such a thing."

"No," I reassure her, even though I'm lying. "You're not strong enough. Someone had to carry Janien to that pan. That hasn't changed."

"I couldn't...I would never do anything to Janien..."

"I hear you. I do."

"But you don't believe me."

She frowns sharply when I don't answer.

"I should've expected something like this," she says. "We're talking about Jaap, after all. I should have known he wouldn't stop asking questions, not about me either. Janien always said he nagged her much more than her mother did."

"He can be quite stubborn."

"Quite?"

I give a half-smile. "Can I ask you something else?"

She shrugs. "I suppose so."

"Did everyone in this photo know about Skout?"

"Skout? I don't know. It was still far from finished, wasn't it?"

"I'm not sure. Did Yolene not send you updates? I mean, you did give her the fifty percent share you got from Janien, didn't you? Didn't she keep you in the loop out of some kind of courtesy?"

"We spoke now and then, but never about the app. Skout was never mine to begin with and I couldn't really help Yollie with the money to develop it."

"Sam Chen, Yolene's father, got two offers for Skout."

"And?"

"He's not interested."

She looks at the photo again. "Isn't there something similar on the market by now?"

"There is, but nothing identical, I think."

"So Skout still has value?" She looks surprised.

"I suppose so, yes."

"How much would it be worth?"

"A few million. More."

Sparrow wipes a wistful thumb over Janien's face on the picture. "She could have been rich."

"You could have been rich."

She puts the photo down on the counter and looks at me. "Who do you think killed her? Who do you think committed all these murders? You talk and talk, but you never really say much."

"Because I don't know what to say. I honestly have no idea who it might be. Neither does Jaap. We keep on digging, but we're not getting any solid leads. And that's the problem. It's like we can't move past square one. It's driving me nuts."

The traffic light turns green. I take a left toward the guesthouse, turning into Stellenbosch's main street. I guess I should be happy it's the winter holidays. I hear traffic in this part of town is normally terrible.

"What did you think of the mask?" I ask.

Jaap has stopped drawing in his notebook. Stopped taking notes. Stopped everything, it seems, except thinking and breathing. Something's bugging him, but I still can't figure out what.

"Brown hair, brown eyes. It could be a number of people," he says. "But maybe you were right earlier. Maybe the DNA was planted."

"Is that going to be your defense if it turns out to be Leon's DNA?"

"No." He looks at me, shakes his head. "But it's a realistic option, I have to say."

"I suppose." I wait for a break in the stream of traffic to pass a double-parked car. "Don't the police usually get a profiler in at this point?"

"Sometimes, but our time is limited. It's the seventeenth of July. We have two, three days if this guy sticks to his normal pattern. And what can a psychologist tell me that I don't already suspect?"

That's true.

I pull away when a Golf gives me a gap. I think about all the names associated with this case. The small window we have. "What's our next step?" I ask. "We can't look after all the people on your list—either as suspects or potential victims—until the twentieth. We're going to have to pick one or two of them and hope we've made the right decision."

"Picking the right people is not our only problem," says Jaap. "If the murderer decides to actively start courting the media or the police's attention, we may be in serious trouble. Janien's death was in the papers, but only for a few weeks. Yolene's death was supposedly suicide, and Fist's was a messy accident. What if the murderer is frustrated because no one is taking notice? You're the first person who has seen him, in a way. What if he goes for some big, grand statement? Something we're not able to predict?"

"I don't think he wants the attention," I say. "It's a complete coincidence that I was able to link the dates—it's three countries and three police forces. Maybe he sticks to one murder a year, on the twentieth of July, to make sure his work doesn't appear on the police's radar. It's like he's forcing himself to move slowly. Or maybe he's trying to get hold of Skout without anyone noticing. Maybe he's killing everyone who knows about the app."

"That would explain Fist's death," says Jaap, but without much conviction. "Is Skout still worth anything, by the way?"

"Sparrow was wondering if there wasn't already something similar on the market, but I'm not sure. I'll have to take a look. Maybe I should also try to find out whether she really did give her share of Skout away, or whether she sold it to Yolene. Janien gave it to Sparrow, but I only have Sparrow's word that she handed it over to Yolene. Someone paid for that house of hers. Maybe there's a money trail we're not seeing."

"Good point. Will you also see if you can figure out where everyone was during the murders? You say Leon was in Gaborone when Yolene died, but where were the others? I don't want the fourth murder to give us those answers."

"Why don't you talk to Isak? Maybe he can help you."

"He's fed up with me."

"Show him what we've got. See what he says."

"We've just started this DNA drive. I sold it to him as my last attempt at solving Janien's murder. I can't go and drag him into this mess now. All these murders? No way. Besides, it's going to take time to verify everything we've uncovered—time we don't have." He blows out a slow breath. "In any case, what would he be able to do? It's like you say: the list is too long. He'll just end up warning everyone that we think one of them is the killer. We'll cause large-scale panic in Carnarvon about a theory we can't prove."

"At least we'll be able to share the guilt then."

"That doesn't ever really happen," he says curtly. "Someone always gets the blame. Usually the person who deserves it least. You should know that by now."

JAAP

1

Sarah says she's tired from all the driving and disappears to her room immediately after we've checked in and eaten dinner around the corner from the guesthouse.

Finally I'm alone. I open the beer I brought with me from the restaurant and switch the TV to one of the sports channels. Supper was pizza. Quick, painless, and one of Sarah's favorites.

That woman is so much more than I thought. She's definitely more than that computer of hers. Wide awake, intelligent, and not half as bad with people as she imagines.

I throw away the empty can, turn the rugby game down on TV, take a deep breath, and call Isak.

"Evening."

"Jaap."

"How is it going over there? Has everything settled down after the petrol bomb?"

"More or less, but the town's split in two. Those who are giving their DNA suspect those who don't want to. Everyone's talking crime statistics versus right to privacy. It's a good thing you're gone. Vonnie's having a hard time, though. The whole world's media is now officially here. And you know what's worse than the newspapers? Journalists wanting to send out a fresh Tweet every few minutes."

"How many people refused to give their DNA?"

"Stefan, Fanus, Henk's brothers, and his father. And Prof. Sieberhagen. Says it's a violation of his rights. He's talking about approaching the Constitutional Court. The Frenchman at the SKA project changed tack and promised to cooperate.'

"And Leon?"

"I got his eventually. Obie brought him in for a cheek swab."

"Test it first. Immediately. I want it tomorrow."

"It's at the laboratory already. We should get the results soon." He sounds amazed. "What's gotten into you? What's changed all of a sudden?"

Everything, but I can't tell him that. "I just want to erase any uncertainty you may have about Leon so that you can start looking at Stefan. The call about the petrol bomb came from the butchery."

"How do you know that?"

Crap. You're getting old, Reyneke. "I asked around."

"It's that woman you brought here, isn't it? The one on the bike with the computer."

"I told you. I asked around."

Isak is quiet for a long while. Probably decides to leave it there. "There were dozens of people at the butchery that night. I was there too. As were Fanus and Henk's father."

"Did you see anyone at the phone?"

"A few people. You know Fanus doesn't mind people using his landline, as long as they buy biltong."

"Then go and chat to all of them. And I'll wait to hear from you about the results of Leon's DNA."

I put the phone down before he gets fired up about me telling him what to do. I turn up the TV volume and watch the struggling Bulls drift across the rugby field after another failed lineout.

After a while, I switch the TV off and reach for my phone again, stare at the photo I took this afternoon of the mask Sparrow made.

I still can't believe it.

I remember the face, although it isn't quite the same.

The man was lying on his side in the main bedroom. On the tired double bed with its dirty, bloodied sheets. Head shot. Under the chin, through the palate and out the back.

It was years ago, but I will never forget that face.

Leon's father.

The DNA in the blood on Janien's wedding dress belongs to Leon, and he knows it. He's known it all along.

Nosebleed?

Why does that suddenly sound like complete bullshit?

2

The guesthouse manager deposits our breakfasts on the table with a practiced smile and hurries back to the kitchen.

Sarah douses her eggs in Tabasco sauce. "Did you figure out what our next move should be?" she asks, glancing at her watch.

I know she's looking at the date, not the time, just as I've been doing since last night. Like you could change it by staring at it.

It's Sunday, 18 July.

"What do you think?" She digs into her food with gusto. "Is James Addison or Sparrow next on the killer's list? Or Ungerer? Or is one of them the murderer?" She points her knife at me. "And are you going to talk to Isak? I think you should. I don't care what you say, we can't play with people's lives like this."

"I called him last night."

She doesn't need to know what about. I supress a yawn. I didn't sleep well. Leon's father haunted my dreams.

"What does he say?" she asks.

"What can he say? We don't know enough to make a move."

"Ja, I suppose."

She butters a slice of white toast. I look at it longingly as I taste my bland oatmeal.

"We're going to have to split up," she suggests. "Or we have to take Sparrow with us to the Midlands for Addison's exhibition. Forget about Ungerer. If he's next in line, the killer would be doing us a favor."

"I don't like either of those options."

"Then lock Sparrow up until the twenty-first. Isak should at least be able to do that."

"Sparrow would never allow that. And in any case, if the killer has such strong feelings about the twentieth, he'll make a plan. Maybe he already has."

That gives me an idea. I should call Annemarie and find out what appointments Leon has for the twentieth. She'll be keeping track of her husband with the baby's due date so close.

I leave my breakfast, lie to Sarah and say I'm going to the bathroom.

I walk into the guesthouse, down the cool passage toward the courtyard with the grapevine-covered trellis.

Annemarie answers on the third ring. "Hello, Oom Jaap. This is a surprise."

"How's the baby? Have you decided on a name yet?"

"We're both fine, thanks. We're going to call him Oberhardt, after Leon's father. I can't believe he'll be here in less than a month." She sounds tired, but proud. "Are you looking for Leon?"

"No. I wanted to talk to you. I would like to take you and Leon out for dinner. The night after tomorrow? To apologize."

"He said you'd had a fight, but he didn't say what about." Her voice has increased in pitch, concern at its edges. "Does it have something to do with the *Courant's* DNA drive? Because he's given a sample to Sergeant Slingers now."

"No," I try to calm her. I remember Vonnie saying that she was struggling with high blood pressure with the pregnancy. I am not going to add to her worries. "It was just family stuff. Nothing serious."

She laughs, relieved. "You lot don't often fight. Definitely less than my family."

If she only knew what has happened in the last few days. "Is Leon looking after you?"

"Yes, thanks. He treats me like a queen. I just wish he'd stop smoking."

"And otherwise? How are things with the two of you?"

"All good, Oom Jaap. No complaints."

She goes quiet suddenly, as though she doesn't want to talk about Leon behind his back. "Let me call up his diary so we can make a date. We share one on our phones. Hang on."

She's back after a minute or two. "He's at a wine show this week. It says here he's leaving for Stellenbosch this afternoon. He always says business is good at these sorts of things. Happy farmers spend money."

Stellenbosch. I force myself to ask: "And next week?"

"We have Wednesday open?"

"Wonderful. See you then."

I say goodbye, keeping my voice light and friendly.

Fuck, fuck, fuck.

I stuff the phone into in my jacket pocket, walk back to the dining room, and sit down. Sarah is drinking a pot of rooibos tea. I order more coffee.

Leon is on his way to Stellenbosch. Sparrow is in Stellenbosch. That's all I know. Make a plan, Reyneke.

"I was thinking about what you said about our next move." I clear my throat, try to speak with conviction. "I think I'll stay here and keep an eye on Sparrow, then you can go and see James Addison. That's to say, if you don't want to go home." I look at her hopefully.

She puts down the cup. "And why would I do that?"

"Okay. Go to the Midlands then. Sparrow said Jack Fist was into Janien, right, but Addison wasn't interested?"

"That's how it sounded to me, yes." She butters what must be a third slice of toast. "So you think the murders all link back to Janien?"

"That's my suspicion. Fist and Yolene were both close to Janien, and Sparrow, of course. Not Addison. I'll call Ungerer and warn him, tell him to stick to his plan and stay away from the Midlands. Just to make sure you and he are both okay."

I fold the napkin that's been on my lap and put it down next to my plate. "But get out of KwaZulu-Natal tomorrow, do you hear me? Don't be there on the twentieth. I'll give you a number to call as soon as you get there. Colonel Ben Brandt. He'll be able to help you."

I suspect I know what's going to happen on the twentieth, but I still have to make sure Sarah doesn't walk slap-bang into trouble.

"Maybe Sparrow and I will go to Pretoria, to my place. I'll look after her there." I lie to her for the second time this morning.

Sarah tugs on the silver earrings, looks at me through narrowed eyes. "What are you up to, Jaap? Are you going to do something stupid, like set a trap or something? If you are, you better get Isak to help you. You're no longer in the police, and you're not exactly a spring chicken either."

"Well, thanks for the compliment. But okay, if it'll make you feel better, I'll phone Isak and tell him to come with me." Another lie.

"And if it's Sparrow? If you're looking after the murderer?"

"Then that's fine too. Then we're keeping someone else from being killed. I know what I'm doing, even if you think I'm over the hill and completely senile."

I don't say that Sparrow and I are going to stay right here and wait for Leon to show up. No. That I hope the DNA results will ensure that we can lock him up tomorrow already. If Sarah finds out what I'm up to, she'll insist on staying, and that's not safe.

And if—big if—the DNA test says it's not Leon, then I'll follow Sarah to KwaZulu-Natal. And I'll take Sparrow with me, so that I can keep an eye on her and on James Addison. If I have the results by tomorrow morning, I can be there by tomorrow evening, the nineteenth of July.

Sarah pours more tea. "What do I do once I'm in the Midlands? Do I warn Addison that someone might want to murder him, or do I see whether it's him?"

That's a damn good question.

"Why don't you rather just go home?"

She laughs. "Forget it."

"Sarah…"

"No way."

Leon is in Stellenbosch. Sparrow is in Stellenbosch, I tell myself. That's all you need to know.

"Fine. Warn Addison and get out of there. But do not, under any circumstances, talk to him on your own. And be careful. I'll make sure Colonel Brandt attends the exhibition so that you can be back in Pretoria by the twentieth. You can go and fetch your bike from *Lekkerkry* some other time."

"Don't worry. Nothing's going to happen to me."

"Sarah. Please. You have to make sure you're not anywhere near Addison on the twentieth." Just in case.

"Okay, okay. Chill."

I drink the last of my coffee, feel it burning all the way down into my stomach, just like last night's pizza. I'll need to stop and buy some antacid.

Sarah fills her teacup. "What happens when I'm back in Pretoria? Do I come and find you and Sparrow?"

"No, definitely not. I'll phone you and let you know what happened on the twentieth."

She narrows her eyes again. "You're hiding something."

"Nonsense."

"I know you're up to something, Jaap. I'm not stupid."

"You know everything, it seems. Good for you."

Sarah runs a frustrated hand through her hair. "What the hell is going on? I don't think you spoke to Isak, otherwise he'd have been here by now. Why won't you talk to the police?"

Because I don't want them around when I confront Leon when he comes to Stellenbosch. Because cops get nervous and sometimes they shoot before they ask questions. Because I'll talk to Leon until he listens to me and gives himself up.

But I don't say that.

"Because we're useless. See…I've started thinking just like you."

"Very funny, old man." She gets up and walks to the door.

Just before she walks out of the dining room, I hear her boots turn on the tiles. "Just don't do anything stupid, Jaap." She zips up her leather jacket. "I spoke to Sam last night. He says Yolene and Sparrow had a terrible fight about Skout. Sparrow didn't just hand it over to her. I know we're not sure whether Skout still matters, but be careful around Sparrow. Sam says she fights dirty when she believes something belongs to her."

I knock on Sarah's door when I reckon she's done packing and will be too rushed to argue.

"Here." I hold the butt of the .38 revolver out to her. "Can you shoot?"

She looks at the weapon, then at me. "Yes."

"Take it. In case. It's not loaded. You can do that yourself."

"And you?"

"I have a pistol. This is my second weapon."

"Your backup?"

"Yes. I believe in having a Plan B. Which is why you're here."

I want to laugh, to affirm that I'm joking, but I realize it's the truth. Apart from her computer skills, Sarah is here to help me uncover my blind spots.

Maybe I already knew that when I showed up on her doorstep in Pretoria. Knew that regret and love can sometimes turn you into an unseeing fool.

"You better hope I never have to use it." She reluctantly takes the revolver and the rounds I offer with my other hand.

"You won't." I check my pocket. "And here's Colonel Ben Brandt's number. Call him when you get there."

"Okay."

"Call him."

"I said okay."

SARAH

1

"Hi, Mom."

"Sarah? What's wrong?"

"Nothing. I'm just phoning to find out how you are."

I recognize the sound of the oven opening, the ancient hinges squeaking like since I was little.

"That's it? Are you sure you're okay?"

I don't know why I made the call either, but then I realize it's because I miss her. "What are you baking?"

I swerve to the left to avoid a car changing lanes blindly.

"Ginger biscuits for the church fair."

"Sounds nice. Save some for me. Looks like I'll be home by next weekend."

"Sarah? Are you…is everything all right?"

I'm driving to the airport to go and interview someone who might be a serial killer's next victim, or the serial killer himself. But you can't tell your mother stuff like that.

"Everything's fine."

"Sure?"

"Yes. Promise. I'm just calling, you know, to see how you are doing. Like I said."

"Ah, okay." Relief creeps into her voice. "Next weekend is perfect. Miekie will be here. She's taking a break from gymnastics till August. She has a groin injury. Then you guys can talk about the car."

"I know. She texted me. I said we'll chat about it when I get there."

"She's ecstatic about the Aston. I sometimes think she never got to see enough of your father. The gymnastics has kept her so busy. She's always off somewhere competing. And she still has school. When she's not training, she's studying. The car is something of his …something to remind her of him as she grows older."

"We'll go and have one of those Frappuccino things she likes so much."

"Ask her about her new boyfriend. She won't tell me anything."

"I will." The road signs on the N2 show I'm approaching the airport. "I have to go now. I'm flying to Durban."

"Durban?"

"Yes, work. With the police. Remember?" I don't want her to think I'm doing something illegal again.

"I'm glad. That's good."

I wonder if she believes me.

"See you next week?" she says, her voice a mix of hope and doubt.

"See you then."

"I'll save some biscuits for you. Look after yourself."

"I will. Bye, Ma."

2

It's almost as cold in the KwaZulu-Natal Midlands as it was in the Free State, but there's a difference. It's greener and wetter, with mist blanketing the gently rolling hills. From the N3 highway, I turn onto the R103, which winds along a railway track past farm buildings, trees, and lush fields where cows huddle together for warmth on this chilly Sunday. It's late afternoon, and the sun still hasn't made an appearance.

I turn left onto a muddy dirt road and drive through a set of heavy black gates. Steel letters in an old-fashioned typeface tell me I've arrived at Faure Manor Studio & Art Gallery.

Whoever owns this place keeps it well maintained. The gravel road is neat and clean, with just a few dead leaves scattered here and there. The lawn is neatly edged, and the grass cut short.

A lane of trees, their white branches stripped bare, takes me past a handful of black horses in paddocks, playfully biting one another's backs. I open the window wider and breathe in the fresh air.

The flight was particularly bad, especially the landing. I felt like a pea in a washing machine. The gray suit next to me seemed worried I was going to puke.

Three workers in overalls and gumboots wave as I drive past. Thirty meters on, the road circles back around a fountain. To the right are the arched double doors of an imposing stone house.

I sit for a moment and inhale the smell of wet grass and damp gravel, feel the chill pricking at my face and fingertips. Listen to the silence of the mist.

It's different to the silence of the desert. Every sound is muted, blanketed, its origin unclear. With sand, it's more like every sound haphazardly scatters in the hot sun until it evaporates and disappears.

I get out of the Merc, zip up my leather jacket, and take a scarf and gloves out of my overnight bag in the boot.

No one emerges from the house to greet me. Why would they? I haven't booked a room, nor have I let anyone know I'm coming to see James Addison.

A sign pointing to the right says *reception*, so I turn left, curious about Faure Manor Studio.

A tennis court appears immediately ahead of me, with what looks like stables and a cowshed further down the road. I step onto the lawn in front of the house. It stretches from the three-story stone building to a handful of pine trees about eighty or ninety meters away. The open space is dominated by five steel structures, each about three meters high. One of them immediately grabs my attention—a figure that is half-buck, half-woman, running with a knife in her hand.

Is she fleeing or attacking?

I walk closer. The bottom half of the figure is made of brown scrap metal, while the woman's torso has been cast from steel. Here and there, gears and bearings are visible inside her chest, her heart an old fan belt.

She rears up on her hooves, her face a study of tension and excitement.

No, joy. Liberation, almost.

The work's title is *Escape*.

I touch her flank. The steel is cold and clammy under my fingers, but it's almost as though I can hear her breathing.

"Beautiful," I murmur.

"Are you one of James's friends?"

I turn around, startled.

The plump woman standing there is in her fifties, with her

gray-brown hair hanging loose around her shoulders. The fine pearls of dew in her hair say she's already walked quite a distance this afternoon. The mud-spattered corduroy trousers and hiking boots tell the same story.

Two English Springer Spaniels mill around her legs, sniffing the ground before warily moving on to my trainers.

It all feels like a scene out of a British tourism brochure, but then she breaks the spell and speaks Afrikaans, although slowly, as if she hasn't spoken it for a long time.

She must have heard me commenting on *Escape*.

"Where are my manners. Hello. I'm Magrit."

"Sarah, hello," I say. I bend down and greet the dogs.

She has a delicate smile. "So? Are you friends with James? You look like someone he would know."

She cocks her head slightly, as though she's evaluating me, and suddenly she seems familiar to me. As though she's someone I might have seen on TV—except I don't watch television.

"I don't know him," I admit. "I'm here for the exhibition." Which is the truth, I suppose.

I turn back to the buck-woman. I have no idea how much the sculpture costs, but she needs to be in my garden in Pretoria. Every ton of her. "I want to buy her."

Magrit's green eyes gain an almost friendly warmth. "The exhibition only opens the day after tomorrow, but I'm sure we can make a plan."

"It's quite a strange day for an art show, isn't it? In the middle of the week? I was wondering why it's on a Tuesday."

"It's what James wanted. 'If people are serious about my art, they'll show up,' he said. He regularly sabotages himself like that. And the irony remains. No one wants to be commercial, but everyone wants their art to sell. And make no mistake, he'll blame me if the sales aren't good."

She gestures for me to follow her to the house. "Did you drive far?"

"I flew in from Cape Town."

"Just for the exhibition? I don't remember your name. Why aren't you on my guest list?"

"I don't really do guest lists. And I wanted a proper viewing before there were too many people around. Is that a problem?"

"Not at all. Come inside. Let's go and have some tea."

"Is James around?"

She stops, but the dogs run ahead through the open back door of the house. "He's probably in the barn, working on *Irony*."

"Irony?"

"She's the last sculpture in the series, the one he simply can't get right—he says. She's made of aluminum and steel salvaged from an airplane crash. *Escape*, the one you like, is made from old car parts. The bottom half is pure Mustang. All James's art is made of recycled materials."

I smile involuntarily. That's why I like the buck-woman. I probably smelled petrol on her.

"I'm actually also here to talk to James, if I may," I say. "I want to commission a sculpture."

Magrit holds the back door open for me. We hang our jackets in a small alcove dirtied by muddy footprints. I take off my gloves, watch as she kicks off her shoes.

The warm house smells of freshly baked bread.

"James isn't really a talker. And he can be prickly before an exhibition," she warns me.

She blows into her hands with the same sense of familiarity as before.

"Are you related to James?"

She laughs. A clear, bubbling sound. "No. This is my guesthouse and gallery. I'm only managing James's exhibition. His work needs a lot of space to come into its own, and he hates the cities and their pretentious galleries—again, his words, not mine. It also helps that I have an industrial oven. I even vacated my studio for him and his hundreds of sketches. I'm a painter. Portraits, mostly."

I follow her down a passage into the kitchen, where two women are kneading dough for bread. In the oven I can see four loaves on the rise, with another two cooling down beside it. She invites me to sit at a six-seater table.

"Are you going to stay?" she asks."Or are you just buying and leaving?" There is a keen interest in her gaze. "And, if I may ask, are you buying for someone else or for yourself?"

I'm not surprised by her question. I know most people imagine me too young to have money of my own. Magrit's probably wondering whether my rich sugar daddy is going to show up in his Ferrari waving his wallet around tomorrow.

"I'm buying for myself. I'm in IT."

The two-letter acronym usually answers most questions when it comes to money. The unknown virtual world few people understand, but which almost everyone believes generates vast wealth.

"I see," she nods. "Would you like something to drink?"

"Rooibos tea. Please." I look over her shoulder at one of the ciabattas, fresh from the oven. "Any chance I could have a slice of bread as well?"

"Sure. Would you mind eating in the kitchen?"

"Not at all."

She speaks rapid-fire isiZulu to the women, then joins me at the table.

"How many guests are you expecting for the opening?" I ask.

"James wanted to keep it small. Around thirty or forty people? A few collectors. Corporate buyers. Two journalists. I didn't waste time with people who don't have money to buy James's work. He is not cheap. Half the people are staying here and the other half at the hotel down the road. I have two rooms available, if you are interested."

"I'll take one, if I may, but I'll probably only stay one night."

She laughs. "I assume we don't have to negotiate the price for *Escape*?"

"No need."

One of the women puts a plate down in front of me with two slices of bread, butter, strawberry jam that looks homemade, and goat's-milk cheese. Magrit gestures for me to start eating.

I butter the warm bread and put some jam and cheese on it. Delicious, I signal to the woman as she returns to place two teacups on the table.

"So, where did you hear about James?" Magrit asks.

"Professor Karl Ungerer told me about his work," I say. "He said James was very talented. And now that I'm here, I have to agree."

Magrit's mouth tightens a little when she hears Ungerer's name.

"You don't like him?" I put sugar in my tea. "Don't worry. Neither do I."

"Well, he's probably tried to get you into bed already. It's all the same to him. Married, male, female, young, old."

"He tried, yes," I sip the tea, sigh with a deep satisfaction. "How do you and James know each other?"

"Through mutual friends. The world is a small place." She drinks from her own cup. "I'll go and get your room sorted. It's on the top floor. I hope that's okay."

"That's perfect. I'll come and settle the bill in a while."

I butter the second slice of bread. "I really would like to meet James before I leave. It would be nice to put a face to the creator of *Escape*. I'm sorry I can't stay for the exhibition."

"I'll go around to the barn and find out if he's in a generous mood. You may just be lucky, who knows."

3

It's dusk when I wake from my afternoon nap. I slept like a dream on a bed big enough for four people.

Magrit's left a note under the door to say James has agreed to see me, as long as we can meet before eight o'clock. Like me, he seems to prefer working at night.

I haven't called Colonel Ben Brandt yet, as Jaap suggested, and I'm not going to either. I'm guessing the two missed calls from an unknown number on my phone belong to him.

I delete the call record. I'm leaving tomorrow, so they can all just stop hassling me. If I were them, I'd be worried about what I am planning next. I want to know what Jaap is up to and, in order to do that, I need to trace his phone. He's lying about something. I just know it. I also want to keep tabs on Leon, Sparrow, Stefan, and Karl Ungerer's phones, so that I know exactly where everyone is on the twentieth of July.

There's no way I'm going to leave this all to chance.

I shower and dress quickly.

I shiver as I exit the front door of the Faure Manor House. I pull my jacket close around me as I head to the large industrial building the receptionist pointed out to me.

I hear noises as I approach—loud, rhythmic and continuous. Metal on metal. Then I smell it: sweat. Not old sweat, but wet-on-the-skin testosterone salt.

I stop at the wooden sliding door. A man of about thirty is hammering a thin, red-hot piece of metal into shape. Behind him an industrial oven casts a warm orange glow. I watch as he attempts to bend the steel into an arch, sweet-talking the metal to yield to his touch.

The scene is like something out of the Middle Ages. James Addison is of average height, but he has an unusually well-developed upper body.

"Are you Sarah Fourie?" he asks between blows.

How did he know I was here?

I wait for the heavy hammer to lift again. "Yes."

He glances up. His eyes are brown, his dark-blond hair a thick, sweaty mass touching his shoulders. The sleeves of the blue overalls are cut short like the legs, which reach just above the knee. On his feet are black steel-capped boots.

"You're going to buy *Escape*. You have lots of money."

"Relative to?"

He doesn't answer, just keeps on hammering.

I wait patiently for him to finish. Five, ten minutes, then he gestures with his head that I must follow him. We walk to the corner of the barn, past a motorbike hidden under a tarp, where the figure of a woman is crawling out of the tail of an old Cessna. The plane is covered in black news headlines. The woman's face still needs to take shape, but I can see she is angry. Wild, turned-steel hair curls out of her head.

Must be *Irony*.

Looks like metamorphosis is Addison's thing.

"The truth," he explains unexpectedly. "It always grounds us, rather than liberating us. It's the lies we tell ourselves about ourselves that move us forward, not the truth. Who we think we are is more important than who we really are."

Interesting. Not sure I agree, though.

"I have to leave tomorrow," I say. "Can I do an electronic transfer tonight?"

He nods.

"Delivery?"

"After the exhibition."

He looks at the bent piece of metal in his hand, then at the sculpture. He doesn't look pleased.

How should I warn him about the twentieth? Sparrow was right, Addison doesn't look like the social type. But he certainly looks like a man who could easily have carried Janien to that frozen pan in the Karoo. Who might think her murder has some or other deeper, esoteric value. Same for Fist and Yolene.

I look over my shoulder. The doors to the building are still open.

"Did you know Janien Steyn?" I ask.

Addison freezes, says nothing, just stares at me.

"And Jack Fist?"

He narrows his eyes.

"Yolene Chen?"

"Who are you?"

"Sarah Fourie."

"Never heard of you."

"But you knew all those people."

"Knew?"

"They're all dead."

He looks surprised, but then grabs at another emotion. Anger. Why is anger always the easier one to grasp? We all seem to shelve it at exactly eye-level.

"Who are you?" he repeats.

He steps forward threateningly, the piece of metal in his hand suddenly a weapon.

Where's Magrit? Too late now. I should have listened to Jaap and not spoken to the man on my own. And why did I leave the damn revolver in the room?

I refuse to step back, to show any fear or discomfort. James Addison is big, but I'm fast.

"I'm helping the police with a murder investigation," I say.

"So you're not really interested in my work?"

"On the contrary. I like it very much. It's...it says something I can't express myself. Something about me. Something deep inside."

He considers this a moment, then lowers the piece of metal. "Really?"

"Yes."

I'm equally surprised. Where did that answer come from? Worse yet, it's the truth.

I wish the bloody man would put on more clothes.

Addison might have lowered his weapon, but the distrust remains. "Which murder investigation are you helping the police with? Janien's?"

I don't want to talk here. Not with the two of us alone in a building where no one will hear me scream.

"Meet me for dinner," I say. "In the dining room, seven o'clock. Then we can talk. I'll be quick. I promise."

He thinks about it, then nods slowly.

I get out of there. Jog back to the house through the light rain and mist, past the sculptures that loom up out of the dark like grotesque fairy-tale figures. I take the stairs up to my room and close the bedroom door behind me. Make sure it's locked.

That could have gone better, but at least I now have a better grip on who James Addison is.

Now for step two.

I open my laptop and put traces on the phones I want to track. Watch as they all appear on my screen.

It seems Jaap and Sparrow are both still in Stellenbosch. I knew he was lying about going to Pretoria.

Leon is on the road. Two people from the Malan business too. Looks like Stefan and Fanus. Fancy that. They all appear to be heading to Cape Town. Or Stellenbosch—it's the same road from Carnarvon.

Ungerer's phone is off. Probably entertaining one of his students.

Time for step three.

I kickstart the new software I rushed to finish last night after months of work.

LittleRedRidingHood goes into the virtual "wilderness" and collects all the information on a specific person. From Instagram photos people take and geolocate—foolishly indicating exactly where they are—to Facebook, Twitter, Snapchat, WhatsApp, bank accounts, other accounts, email, loyalty programs, memberships of organizations, hotel and Airbnb records, competitions they've entered, everything on Google—you name it.

If people only knew how important data was, they wouldn't give out their personal details everywhere they went.

I didn't tell Jaap about the program because clearly not all the information is gathered in a strictly legal way. That's also why I won't be able to use it for the corporate projects I earn most of my money from these days.

James Addison will be LittleRedRidingHood's first proper test.

I take a shower while I run the software. When I'm done, the program has transformed the information into a digestible format. Facts appear in black, statistical assumptions in yellow, and exceptions and anomalies in blue. The information that wasn't harvested legally, like bank statements, is marked in red. It's pretty much the same information I would have gathered anyway, but it's much quicker and packaged in a far more accessible way.

LittleRedRidingHood announces, in blue, that Addison doesn't have a Facebook profile.

A photo on Instagram of a new sculpture in what must be his garage is marked in yellow. Geotagging reveals he lives in Bellville, near Cape Town. He lives in a rented house with the number 67 clearly visible in the photograph. His utilities account confirms his address, in black.

He is unmarried and childless. He also doesn't seem to have a girlfriend or a boyfriend. None of his photos or WhatsApp messages uses keywords like "our," or pet names like "babe" or "angel." No late-night check-ins or early-morning hellos. No long phone calls. This information also appears in yellow. His email confirms there are no love letters.

His mother is still alive. He facetimes her once a week for about an hour. She lives in the Cape coastal town of Knysna with a man James seldom refers to. He probably doesn't like him. Same with his brother, whom he last spoke to six months ago, in a bust-up that seems to have had something to do with a conversation in which James was told to get a real job.

An app that logs exercise times shows he's a cyclist, a good one, and that he regularly rides sixty or seventy kilometers at a time, mostly along the same route, and mostly on his own. His times have improved radically over the past four months, since he got back from London.

He saves about R98 a month through membership of a big chain store's loyalty program. The program that collects information for targeted marketing, among other things, shows that he often buys spaghetti and mince. He uses Mitchum, shaves with old-fashioned razors, takes too many Panados, braais often and uses a lot of body lotion.

James also likes beer. Amstel. Lots and lots of it, it seems.

He buys a pack of condoms about once a month, which seems to reveal something about no-strings-attached sex, or perhaps sex with someone who is married or in a relationship.

What Addison doesn't buy reveals just as much about him.

It says in yellow that he doesn't like chicken, cocktails, salads or eating at restaurants, as he never spends money on any of these things.

It's also clear that he was supposed to have renewed his driver's license by now. He has no criminal record.

He has sold photographs, as a freelance photographer, to two magazines. His credit card is deep in the red. Most purchases are for food and coffee. Looks like he needs my money.

He pays cash for a light antidepressant. His medical purchases indicate that he has high cholesterol. He has no medical or life insurance.

Looking at his financial history, it seems he spent the prize money he received for winning Blink within months. It looks like he blew it all overseas, or perhaps he put it away somewhere I haven't yet been able to reach.

His electricity bill is sky-high, probably because he needs so much electricity to render his sculptures.

He buys steel from a scrapyard that was raided by the police last year, according to an article in *Die Burger* newspaper. He has coffee at Java City in Muizenberg, where he sometimes goes surfing.

Twice with Jack Fist, according to Instagram.

I open the photo. Fist is laughing, and James is standing to the side watching him, his eyes hidden behind sunglasses. I wonder who took the picture.

Addison mostly buys Americanos at Java City. Tall, strong, black coffee, as he says in a single cheerful WhatsApp to his mother. A photo of his hand holding the coffee cup shows burns on two of his fingers.

He's obsessive about the news, reading everything he can online. But he doesn't watch TV at all, he noted in an interview two years ago, and he has zero interest in politics.

He has had three solo exhibitions to date. The last one, in Cape Town, made headlines when a mining magnate acquired four of his sculptures for his private collection at a hefty price. Addison's happiness is clear in the photographs. The deep joy of having finally made it. The relief of earning some real money that would cover more than the rent. Yet, there is also a glint of anger that it only happened now, after so many years of nothing but bread and water.

4

I spot James Addison as he comes to a standstill at the entrance to the dining room. He surveys the room through narrowed eyes, then makes his way toward my corner table.

His black shirt and jeans are creased, and he's wearing the same big black boots from before. He somehow looks smaller in clothes that cover his arms and legs.

He sits down, starts fidgeting with the edge of the white table-cloth. He's showered, and I miss the smell from earlier. Every woman has her own thing about men. I dislike suits and ties. Too civilized. I like it when the varnish has rubbed off a little and you can see what lies beneath the polished surface.

Magrit, wearing a flowing black dress, is standing near the fire-place, talking to a guest. She tries not to look at James and me, but I can sense that her ears are tuned in to our conversation.

Maybe James told her what happened in the barn, or maybe she's simply looking after her artist. The exhibition is tomorrow, and *Irony's* wings are still clipped.

A waiter asks us what we'd like to drink. Addison orders an Amstel and a lasagne. I order a Johnnie Black.

"Tell me about this murder investigation of yours." He sounds impatient and irritable, as though he's here against his will, held hostage by his curiosity.

I nod. "Three people who took part in the Blink competition with you are dead. It's just you and Sparrow—Maggie Malan—left."

He picks up his knife, stares at his reflection in the silver blade.

"I didn't know Yolene Chen died."

"Everyone thinks it was suicide, but there's something that makes us question that assumption."

"Us? You and the police?"

I nod.

"What?"

I don't want to tell him yet. Who knows how he will react? "Tell me about Blink," I ask instead. "You walked away as the big winner. Was anyone jealous? Jealous of any of the other finalists? Did anyone threaten you in any way?"

"So you think that either Sparrow or I are next?"

Can't he just answer my questions? "Maybe."

"Why?"

I shake my head, unwilling to lose control of the conversation. "Blink. Do you know of any—"

"You show up here uninvited, throw money at my ego, and talk about a murder investigation. Who the hell are you?"

The couple at the table closest to ours snap their heads in our direction, then quickly look down at their dinner again.

Magrit is staring openly.

"Okay. If you really want to know. I want to prevent someone from killing you on the twentieth of July," I say quietly.

His face betrays his disbelief.

"Janien, Fist, and Yolene were all killed on the twentieth. Each of them a year apart," I explain.

He stays quiet for a long time, but then gives me a slow, mocking smile. "Ah. You're here because you want to see whether I'm the murderer."

"No," I lie. "If that was the case, the police would have been here too."

He doesn't believe me. "Don't worry. I won't be able to murder anyone on the twentieth. I'll be right here, surrounded by people the whole damn night. And Sparrow said she can't come, so she's safe from whatever I may be planning."

"Couldn't come or didn't want to come?"

He shrugs. "Who cares? Whenever I think I finally get her, she pulls back into her safe little bubble."

I consider his answer. "Why is your opening night on the twentieth? I mean, did you pick the date specifically, or did it just work out that way?"

He picks up the knife again, points it at me. "Why not the twentieth?"

I close my eyes for a second. I wish I was back on the KTM. I should have driven to Cairo when I saw Jaap at my gate.

"It's interesting that you, of all people, are helping the police. Sarah Fourie. Convicted hacker." He laughs at my surprise. "You're not the only one who knows how to use a computer."

He must have searched far and wide for that little nugget of information. I have managed to erase most of my existence from the internet.

Addison crosses his arms, the shirt straining over his biceps. "You'll know by now that I'm not very active on the net. I don't trust it. I don't trust you."

I nod gratefully at the waiter delivering my whisky, take an eager sip. It burns into the fist in my stomach but does nothing to relieve the tension.

"That's what you think." I finally find my voice again. "You're actually very active."

"I'm not even on Facebook...Whatever. Forget it."

He pushes aside the frosted glass the waiter brought, picks up his beer, and gets up.

"You don't have to trust me, James. I don't care. But just know that you've been warned. Your exhibition is on the twentieth of July, the same date three other Blink contestants died. Watch yourself—for your own sake. And if the police arrive here, don't chase them away. That would just be stupid." I empty the glass and get up too. My work here is done.

Addison makes for the door, turns back.

"Sarah," he calls back to me. "Talk to Maggie...to Magrit." He points to the older woman still standing at the fireside. "I don't have time for this. I have to finish *Irony*. The twentieth is pure coincidence, believe me. Magrit will be able to tell you about Blink and about all of us. She's Sparrow's mom."

Sparrow's mother? I glance briefly at Magrit. He's right. I should have realized that earlier. That's why she looks so familiar.

I walk over to her. She gestures for me to follow her to an open table near the fireplace, the curiosity plain on her face. We sit down. I watch her in the light of the flickering flames. She's a little taller and a little rounder than her daughter, but she has the same full bottom lip as Sparrow. The same green eyes.

"Are you and James okay?" she asks. "Is he unwilling to part with *Escape*?"

"No, it's not that."

Curiosity gets the better of her. "I overheard something about Blink. And Sparrow? My apologies. I didn't mean to eavesdrop."

It's the same nonsense as with Addison. What am I supposed to say? Hey, your daughter might be murdered on the twentieth, or, shit, we're not sure, but your daughter might be a serial killer?

No, I decide. Jaap is with Sparrow, so she's in good hands. I don't have to reveal anything about our investigation. Jaap can come and tell Magrit Malan the truth himself if he wants to do so.

"James said you would be able to tell me more about Blink," I say. The words sound false, even to my own ears. "That competition he won? Your daughter was also a contestant, as I understand it. She was a finalist, right?"

Magrit nods. "Yes, Sparrow...my daughter...took part in the competition. But that was quite a number of years ago."

"And James won?"

"Yes. Why are you asking?"

"What about your daughter? I understand there's considerable prize money involved. If she'd won, she could have used it to establish herself as an artist, especially with your contacts."

Magrit frowns at my question. "It is what it is. James won. Art competitions, much like any other competition, are about much more than deciding whose work is the best. There's a lot of politics involved." She adjusts the knife and the fork in front of her. "And winning a competition doesn't guarantee success. James threw his prize money away. He lazed about overseas for a year hoping some-one would spot him and give him a free pass to the top. I tried to tell him to use the momentum created by Blink, but he didn't want to listen."

There's a note of bitterness in her voice.

"How is he doing now?" I ask. "I mean, he's here, under your wing? Has he learned his lesson?"

She laughs. "I don't know about that. But I know he's doing well. I'm sure he'll sell most of his work on Tuesday. Apart from the one you bought, of course. It's good money. He'll be able to live off it for quite a while."

"And Sparrow?"

"She teaches. She's happy," she says curtly.

Magrit sounds unwilling to talk about her daughter, so I change tack. "What happened to the other Blink contestants? The year James won? Do you know?"

"Why are you so interested in Blink? That was years ago."

"I'm curious whether I might like the other contestants' work too."

Magrit gets up, adds some logs to the fire and sits down again. "I can't help you there. I don't know where they all are."

"What about Janien Steyn? I heard she was pretty good."

It's as though a curtain comes down in Magrit's eyes.

Sparrow told me her mother knew she was gay. Does that mean she knows about Janien too? About her daughter and Janien?

"You said Professor Karl Ungerer told you about the exhibition?" Magrit asks.

"Yes."

"Did he also tell you about Janien?"

What is she referring to? The murder, Skout, or Janien's relationship with Sparrow?

"Yes."

Magrit is smart enough not to fall for half an answer.

"What are you actually doing here, Sarah? Something doesn't feel right. Something…I can't put my finger on it. You turn up here with an invitation from Professor Ungerer. Spend money like a millionaire. Who are you exactly?"

"Someone interested in James's work. Really." It's not a lie.

We look at one another for a long time. In the distance, I hear rain approaching. Seconds later, it starts pelting down on the roof.

What's the temperature out there? Minus two? Minus three?

I think about Sparrow and her teaching job. The unhappiness that weighed down her every word when she spoke about her nine to five.

I try again. "Did James win outright? Was it a close call? Was Sparrow unhappy that she was the runner-up?"

Magrit pushes her chair back and gets up. "I hope you sleep well, Sarah. Remember to switch off the heater before you get into bed. I usually remind all my guests. Accidents happen so easily. We can chat some more tomorrow."

She says goodnight to each of the guests as she leaves the room, not once looking in my direction.

I'm sure she's going to call Sparrow, and then it's game over for me. There's no way her daughter won't tell her what Jaap and I are up to. I'll have to pack my bags as soon as I can tomorrow morning, before Magrit Malan tells me to leave.

Jaap calls just as I close my laptop and get into bed. "Why are you still awake?" The alarm clock next to the bed shows it's 3 am.

"I can't sleep," he says.

"Where are you?"

"In Stellenbosch. Is Addison still there?" He sounds tired and stressed.

"Yes. Where else would he be? Are you okay?"

"Yup. Except that you haven't called Colonel Brandt yet. He wants to know when he needs to be there. He sounds busy."

"Sorry."

"He's called you three times already."

"My phone is probably off."

"Sarah…"

"I'll call him tomorrow. Promise."

I hear the TV in the background. Sounds like some rugby-game recap.

"What do we do if nothing happens, Jaap? If Sparrow and James are both still alive on the twenty-first? If the murders have nothing to do with Blink? Where do we go looking then?"

"Then we give everything we have to Isak and start again at the beginning. Me, not you. You go home."

"So Isak still doesn't know? I thought you'd spoken to him."

"I'll call him if you'll call Brandt."

That'll be the bloody day.

"Remember, Sarah, you have to leave later today," says Jaap. "It's the nineteenth. Warn Addison and go to Pretoria. That's your only job. I'll meet you there, just give me a day or two."

"Why can't I come to Stellenbosch tomorrow, to you and Sparrow?"

"You've already helped more than I could have hoped for. See you in Pretoria."

JAAP

1

Leon Reghardt Steyn.

How long have I been lying to myself? Like those people who continue to believe that their children will be found alive. That their husbands aren't cheating on them. That their wives would never hire someone to kill them.

Did the violence take hold of Leon on that day his father shot and killed everyone around him? Or was it there, in his blood, long before that? Father and son, cut from the same cloth.

Is he really the one who killed all these people, his sister included? Did none of the love Obie and Vonnie gave him make any difference? None of the lessons from Sunday-school? None of the playing in the dusty Karoo veld from sunrise to sunset, until all three children were so dirty Vonnie had to hose them down before they could come inside the house?

Nothing?

And why? Because of Janien? Because he felt something for her? Because he was jealous?

I take out the Parabellum. The weapon is old and somewhat worn, but trustworthy. Just like me.

I make sure it's loaded and put it away again in the bedside table. Stare at the passage light bleeding under the door, watching for any dark shadows that might break it up.

Sparrow took over Sarah's room in the guesthouse, the one in the corner that doesn't have a door to the outside. Anyone who wants to get to her room has to come past me.

I had quite a fight on my hands to get her to sleep here. I even drove with her to the flat of the IT lecturer where she was staying to pack a suitcase. I lied and said I had one or two things I still needed to discuss with her, and that it would be easier if she stayed here.

I suppose in the end she was just too curious to say no.

Isak has promised me he will know by tomorrow whose DNA was on the wedding dress.

It's 3.30 am.

The morning of the nineteenth of July.

The time isn't right yet, but it will be. Soon.

"I need to go to work." Sparrow butters her toast with short, sharp jabs.

"No."

"Jaap, I can't sit here all day. I want to go to the lab. I have an idea for an art project."

There's an eager glint in Sparrow's eye, something that's making her shine like a woman who has rediscovered what makes her happy. She is wearing the same kinds of clothes as always—a colorful dress and black boots—yet she seems transformed.

"Let's first talk here, where no one can hear us." We were the last guests to show up for breakfast and have the dining room to ourselves.

She leans back in her chair, her breakfast forgotten. The morning is cold, but at least the rain from earlier has subsided. The distant, ragged Drakenstein mountains, framed by the dining-room windows, are a hazy blue.

"You need to eat. You and Sarah both. You are both so skinny."

"What's going on, Jaap?"

"Eat first."

She throws her napkin down on the table and gets up so suddenly, her chair falls over backward. "I've had enough. The DNA, all of these bullshit stories, your and Sarah's nonsense!"

"Wait, Sparrow. Please."

"What's going on, Jaap? And stop lying. You wanted me to sleep here last night, saying you want to talk to me, but then you don't have anything to say. It's all just lies, one after the other."

"The twentieth."

"What about it? That's tomorrow."

"Janien, Jack Fist, and Yolene Chen. They all died on the twentieth of July."

The color drains from her face. "What?"

"Every year on the twentieth."

She sinks down into the chair next to me. Looks at me, bewildered. "The twentieth...Sarah said that everyone was murdered, but she never said anything about the date."

"She should have shut up about the murders too," I grumble.

The realization dawns in her eyes. "You think I'm next. That's why you needed me to sleep here last night."

I nod.

Then another thought hits her. "Or...wait...you think it's me?"

Again, I curse. Sarah has given Sparrow too much information.

"That would be difficult," I hurry to explain. "You're not strong enough. Someone had to carry Janien to the pan."

"You and Sarah both say that, but I can see what you're thinking—that I might have had help."

I shrug. "I don't think so, no."

She sneers at me.

"Okay. I suppose it's a possibility."

She stares out of the window. "Why the twentieth?" she finally asks with a moody scowl.

"I don't know. It must mean something to the killer. Does it mean anything to you?"

"No. Not off the top of my head." She shakes her head, gives a bitter laugh. "So what was your plan? Do we just wait around here until the day is over?"

I look on while the grimace fades as yet another truth reveals itself. "Wait a minute. Am I bait, Jaap?"

"No. Not at all." It's not a complete lie, is it? "I hope to get the DNA results from Janien's wedding dress in a little while. Isak and I asked for it to be compared with an initial five samples from the DNA drive in Carnarvon. An expensive private laboratory in Cape Town is doing the tests, so things should go quite quickly. Fanus and Stefan didn't want to give theirs, but you provided yours. Once we have the results, I'll know how to move forward. Who to trust."

I cover her right hand with mine. "Please just let me stay with you until then. I need to make sure you're going to be okay. Your mother would never forgive me if something happened to you."

"I can't just hang around here forever. I have a job interview in the North West tomorrow. Near Vryburg. At a new private school. It's time I left Carnarvon."

"I'll know by tomorrow."

"And if it doesn't happen?"

"I'll have the results. I promise."

She looks at me through narrowed eyes. "You'd better, Jaap. I'm tired of hiding. I can teach art at this new school. Art to high-school kids. I fly tomorrow morning at seven."

"Tomorrow morning is fine. I'll even drive you to the airport myself. Please, just wait until then."

She thinks for a while. "Okay. I suppose I can do that. But only till tomorrow and then I'm leaving. Not one second longer."

"No, no. Also no," Sparrow says as she scrolls through her iPhone.

I drink my fourth cup of coffee for the day. We've been at the DNA laboratory where Sparrow made the mask all morning, and now we're sitting in a café wasting time. The large-screen TV is set to *eNCA*. It shows a tropical storm racing across the Mozambique channel.

"Why the twentieth?" Sparrow mumbles for about the third time since we sat down. She shakes her head, types on her phone again.

"What are you doing?" I ask.

"I'm googling the twentieth."

"And?"

"It's the 201st day of the year. It's Gisele Bündchen's birthday."

"Who's that?"

"Model."

"Who else?"

"Carlos Santana and Natalie Wood."

"I like Santana," I say. "He makes good music. Natalie was beautiful. My father was crazy about her movies."

"John Sterling. Writer." She swipes up. "Max Liebermann. Painter. Emperor Toba of Japan and Marconi both died on the twentieth of July. I don't think that means anything, but who knows. Ah. That's interesting. Robert Smithson also died on the twentieth. He was a very good land artist. My favorite." Swipe. "No, no. No."

I say nothing about the fact that the twentieth is also Vonnie's birthday. When is Isak going to call with those damn test results?

I summon the waiter over and ask for more coffee.

"Anything else?" I ask Sparrow.

"Nothing," she sighs, frustrated. "Blink was in May, so it can't be that...Let's see. Hitler survived an assassination attempt. Emil Zátopek won the 10 km race at the Olympic Games." She looks up. "It's impossible. It's like looking for a needle in a haystack. You could go mad looking for an answer."

Her phone rings. She looks at the screen. "It's my mom. Twice in one day. Sarah must be stirring like crazy." She gets up. "Back in a sec." She weaves between the tables and stands outside on the sidewalk, arms folded to keep herself warm.

I wonder again about the coincidence of James Addison's exhibition being at Magrit Malan's gallery. What could it mean? Does it mean anything at all?

I feel the vibration through the table before I hear my own phone's ringing.

It's Isak.

"Hello, Jaap."

I look at my watch. It's one o'clock already.

Wait. One o'clock.

Dammit! I never checked whether Sarah left the Midlands today. But she's not stupid. She's probably in Pretoria by now.

"How are you doing, Jaap?" Isak asks, his voice uncharacteristically soft and patient. "Everything okay?"

Then I know. I know what it is that he's about to say. I've used exactly the same tone many times before when I've had to give someone bad news.

"Let me guess. It's Leon's DNA," I say.

"Yes."

I close my eyes, block out the town and all its noise. "He says his nose bled that night. That he and Janien fought." I don't want to bring up the Cat right now. The marijuana wouldn't matter. That has largely been legalized over the last few years.

"And you didn't think to tell me?" Isak doesn't sound surprised or angry.

"Actually, it doesn't matter. Do you know where he is? He's not at home and Vonnie doesn't want to say anything. She just said I should talk to you."

"Did you tell them? How are they doing?"

"Of course I told them." He sighs. "Jaap, it's time."

He's right. It's time. It's the nineteenth of July, even though he knows nothing about that. Not yet.

"Ask Annemarie," I say. "She'll know exactly where he is, but as far as I understand it, he's in Stellenbosch somewhere."

"Thank you."

"Isak…" My voice is as patient as his was. "You need to bring him in today. Not tomorrow. Today. I'll get someone to trace his phone if you're struggling."

"That shouldn't be necessary." He gives a slight laugh. "You can let the redhead rest."

I stick to the soft, defeated tone, add a tinge of sadness. "Can I be there when you arrest him?"

"Why?"

"I don't want him to get hurt."

"Let me think about it."

"Please, Isak."

"Let's first figure out where he is. Why don't you get him a good lawyer in the meantime?"

"No. Once you've got him, I'm done."

And I know that's the truth. This one is for the woman on the bicycle. The one with the aviator goggles and the wedding dress and the dreams. I owe her that.

Vonnie can help Leon if that's what she wants to do.

2

The café in Stellenbosch fills up as the clock hands inch along. People sit wrapped up in scarves and coats, warming their hands on big steaming mugs of soup and hot chocolate. It's late afternoon and the sun's warmth is waning.

I have to stay with Sparrow, take her to her friend's flat and make sure she's safe while she packs for tomorrow's trip to the North West, just until Isak has Leon in custody. But I'm unwilling to move. It's as if doing so will be to admit that it's all over for the little boy I tried to save more than twenty-five years ago.

Sarah wasn't surprised when I told her about Leon and the DNA. She is finally on her way to Pretoria, she says. James Addison is difficult and moody, and the police can look after him.

"Jaap? Are you okay?" Sparrow leans across the table and puts her hand on my arm. "I'm sorry," she says again. "Leon...who would have guessed?"

"You. Isak. Half the town. Your father."

I order more coffee, glance at her. "I'm just going to finish this, then we can leave so that you can pack. What time is your flight to Joburg again?"

"Seven. I have a lift to the airport. Why don't you sleep in? Sounds like you need it."

"This friend you've been staying with...who is he?" I probably should have asked this when she first spoke about him.

"He was a student here and now he's lecturing in IT or something. I'm never quite sure what exactly."

"Have you known him long?"

"A while." She's picking at a stray thread on her jersey. "You don't have to worry. He never crossed paths with Janien or anyone from Blink."

"Okay." That's a relief.

She tucks her hair behind her ears, fiddles with a bulky silver ring. "Tell me how you found out about Jack Fist and Yollie. That they were murdered. You're not saying much about what's been happening. Neither is Sarah."

"Sarah was the one who uncovered it."

"Are you guys good friends?"

I think about it. "No. It's more of an employer–employee relationship. Just don't ask me which of us is which, though."

I take out my notebook. Start drawing. I really don't want to talk about myself. We'll just end up at Leon again.

"Tell me about that artist who died on the twentieth…Smithson," I ask. "Is that his name? Robert?"

The coffee arrives and I drink it quickly, feel the acid push up in my throat almost immediately. I'm going to be up all night with regrets and heartburn by the looks of it.

"Why do you like his work?" I ask. "You seem to be into all this DNA stuff. Not anything to do with land art."

"That doesn't matter. Smithson's still brilliant. He had a different way of thinking, as far back as the Seventies. He built a rock spiral in a salt lake in Utah. It was original. Grand. You had to see if from the air to truly appreciate it. And he didn't need paint or brushes to do what he did. He used what was around him."

Her eyes light up like they did earlier. "He believed in the concept of entropy, the second law of thermodynamics. All systems become exhausted and eventually give in. Everything returns to dust, from stones to shopping centers. He died in an airplane accident in 1973. He was 35. Imagine what he could have done had he lived longer."

It's all a little beyond me. Where are the days when art was a pretty picture? Or a symphony. Now art is the incomprehensible.

"What happ—" My phone rings.

"Jaap?" The echo of Isak's voice tells me he's talking on speaker-phone. "Leon is at Asara, the wine estate. We're on our way there. Are you coming?"

I look at my watch. I know Asara. I drove past it on the way from the airport. I'd guess it's about a fifteen-minute drive, if there are no roadworks and the traffic's easy.

I glance across the table. What do I do with Sparrow, though? What if it's all a ruse and Leon's not at Asara, but around here somewhere?

"Are you sure he's there, Isak?"

"I contacted his boss. She's in the same restaurant. She says he's there, right next to her."

"How did you explain the situation to her?"

"I said we needed to speak to him urgently."

I hold the cellphone to my chest and ask Sparrow: "Can I drop you somewhere quickly? Somewhere safe? Not at the lab. The lec-turer. Will he look after you?"

"Is this about Leon?"

"Yes. As soon as we have him, it'll all be over. Until then..."

She nods.

"I'm on my way," I tell Isak.

"Good." He sounds pleased. "As I said, he's in the restaurant, and there are lots of people around. Perhaps you can go in and get him to leave with you quietly. He'll come if you ask."

"Okay. I suppose I can do that."

"Great. See you in twenty minutes."

I'm at the Asara wine farm within twenty-one minutes. It's dusk when I drive through the gate, the vineyards sloping up on my left. When I open the window the early evening smells of fermentation and mold. Must be all the rain.

I drive to where Isak and two uniformed officers are waiting under a pair of leafless trees in the corner of the parking lot. I spot their blue-and-white police ride hidden behind an empty tour bus as I get out of the car.

I walk to the men.

No. One uniform is a woman, about thirty-five years old.

The uniformed man looks nervous. Must be a rookie. I register his smooth cheeks, the anxious glint in his eyes, the way his highly polished shoes shine in the parking lot lights and his perfectly ironed shirt sleeves.

What unnerves me the most is the fact that he keeps on touching his side-arm, like someone not quite used to its bulk and weight.

"Where's Leon?" I ask.

"In there." Isak motions toward the building with its panoramic windows, bright lights, and corrugated red roof. "They're on dessert now." He gestures toward the uniforms. "Blom, Jansen."

Jansen is the young man, Blom the woman.

"We have to hurry," says Isak. "Leon's boss doesn't believe my story. I'm scared Leon will try to flee if she tells him about my call earlier." He looks at me, eyebrows lifting in a question mark. "Can you get him out of there without causing a scene?"

I release a slow breath. "I can try. Wait for me near the entrance. And please try and look less obvious."

The woman at reception is friendly and immediately points me to the right party.

Leon's table of twelve is in the corner of the restaurant filled to capacity despite it being a weeknight. I can instantly see that Leon has had too much to drink—he's tilting his head to the side as he speaks, something I remember from when he was a teenager and he and Obie Junior had stolen two six-packs of beer out of the fridge.

The older woman next to him must be his manager. She has two large gold rings on fine-boned, fidgety fingers that keep on squeezing and releasing the napkin on the table in front of her. She looks alarmed when she sees me.

I nod slowly, trying to put her at ease.

Leon looks up, smiles, his eyes struggling to focus for a moment.

"This is a surprise! What are you doing here, Oom Jaap?" He gets up. "Come. Sit. Join us. I'm sure Audrey wouldn't mind." He points to his boss. "Audrey, this is my uncle, all the way from Pretoria."

I smile too, tell the story I made up on the way here in an attempt to spare him in front of his colleagues. "Your mother is trying to get hold of you. It's urgent."

He makes a quick step to the left, away from the table. "Is she all right?"

I nod. "Yes. But something's happened. Let's talk outside."

He considers this for a second or two, then grabs his jacket from the back of his chair. He turns toward the table. "Sorry. See you guys in a while. Leave me some malva pudding, hey."

"Of course. I hope it's not serious." Audrey sounds like she means it.

Leon walks out beside me. He's pulling on his jacket, turning the collar up. "What's wrong? Is Ma all right?"

"Yes, don't worry."

We walk toward the exit. I refuse to think of Leon all those years ago, hiding in the cupboard in his Superman suit, shooting at me with a determined finger. Focus on Janien instead. The macabre scene, the surprise on her face.

Aviator glasses. Wedding dress. Shoes. Bicycle. Red. Rain.

Wait…

I slow down.

Something's trying to surface, something important.

Almost at the front door.

"Oom Jaap, what's wrong? Is my ma hurt? Is it her heart?"

Jansen, the young uniform, reaches out and grabs Leon's arm as soon as we exit the restaurant.

I jump to the side.

Stupid bloody constable is too eager.

Leon gets a fright, shakes Jansen off and stops. He stares at me, at the uniforms, at Isak.

"What's this? Oom Jaap?"

I try to calm him down. "Hang on now, Leon. Let me explain."

He steps back, as if seeking the shelter of the restaurant.

Jansen moves forward.

"Back down, Jansen, dammit," Isak barks.

But it's too late. Jansen lunges at Leon again. He clings to his wrist, this time with a grip that turns his knuckles white.

Leon jerks his arm in an attempt to release Jansen's hold. He staggers and falls back. The smaller, lighter man lands on top of him.

"Leon. Wait!" I storm toward the pair, but Isak is quicker. He pulls Jansen up and aside, swearing, his eyes nailed on Leon.

Leon's up in a flash, Jansen's pistol in his hand.

He shuffles two, three steps away from us, a look of betrayal on his face.

The young constable rolls over onto his back, looking dismayed. He jumps up.

"Stay, Jansen!" Isak orders him. He's reaching for his weapon. Blom's is already out.

Jansen looks stunned. I can't believe what's happened either.

"Drop your weapons and put your hands up." Leon's voice is steady. The booze is gone, dissolved in adrenalin. "Stop fucking around. Put your hands up!"

I raise hands, but know the two police officers won't comply. "Leon, Isak just wants to talk to you. Don't make things worse than they already are."

"You lied about Ma. I can't believe it! You came to get me so they could arrest me?"

"The DNA on Janien's dress is yours. Isak just wants to know how that happened."

"I told you it was mine. Janien and I wrestled. She was trying on her wedding dress and she smelled the marijuana. I told you!"

"And the other stuff? The Cat? I searched the truck's fuel tank and found it."

"What other stuff?"

"Don't pretend you don't know. It was all in the diesel tank, as you said it would be—in a small black package."

"No! Janien said she tore everything open and dumped it in there. There shouldn't be..." It sounds like he's on the verge of tears. "Why did you have to go and look? Couldn't you just leave it? Couldn't you just trust me for once?"

"How angry were you with Janien that night, Leon? How scared were you that she would tell your mother?" I dread asking the next question. "How much did you feel for her? Really feel for her? Enough to kill her when she rejected you? To kill anyone else who might have felt something for her?"

"I promise...I didn't murder her." He steps back, glancing over his shoulder.

I inch forward.

Isak does the same, showing Jansen to stay put. Blom's movements to the left are that of a seasoned cop as she tries to circle around Leon with careful, small steps.

"Leon, I can see you're angry with Jaap," Isak tries to appease him. "Forget about him. Talk to me. Tell me what's going on. I'm sure we can work something out."

Leon moves backward again. Stops. Points the gun at me. "Does everyone in town know that you're here? Do my parents know?"

He blinks tiredly. Beside me, I sense Isak is aiming to go right, Blom still inching left.

"And Annemarie?" he asks. "She can't...not now...the baby. His name is Oberhardt."

"I know. I spoke to her. Leon, it's all okay." I look him in the eye. "Please. Isak really just wants to talk to you."

"I'm not my father."

"I know."

"I'm not!"

He pulls the trigger. The bullet hits Blom.

Isak jumps to assist her as she goes down.

It doesn't matter what people say about policewomen, that

they're just as good as their male colleagues—most men are just hard-wired to help when a woman is wounded, even if she is in uniform.

Jansen grabs the weapon out of Blom's hand and fires it into the air. "Stop!"

Leon turns, runs. Down the path, around the corner of the restaurant. Jansen chases after him.

I take out my phone. Call an ambulance. Pray Leon can run like the wind. That Jansen can't shoot for shit.

I pocket the phone to find Isak watching me. "You and I need to talk." His voice is sour with anger.

I nod.

"Leon shot a police officer." He motions toward Blom, who is lying on the ground, clutching her arm, groaning. "That says something. He's guilty. And you know it."

Behind us, the restaurant's doors open. People come rushing out, inquisitive, jittery.

"Blom would've been dead if Leon had wanted her dead," I say. It's the only defense I can muster. "I can promise you that. Leon can kill a springbok at fifty feet. He's been hunting with his father since he was fourteen."

I call Sparrow on my way back to Stellenbosch.

She doesn't answer. I call again.

Finally, she picks up her phone. "Jaap? Hello."

"Where are you?"

"Where you left me. Packing." Someone's talking in the background. A deep, hurried voice.

"Can that friend of yours take you to the airport tomorrow?" I ask. "I think it's going to be a long night."

"I'm sure he can. What happened?"

"Nothing. But stay in the flat. Lock the doors and don't go to the airport on your own tomorrow. Promise?"

"Okay. I promise. But why? What happened with Leon? Do you have him?"

"No. He got away."

She laughs in disbelief. "And now? What happens now?"

I don't answer. "Please make sure that friend of yours looks after you properly. That's all. I'll try to arrange security for you." I wonder who in Stellenbosch might be able to help me. I scroll through the names of a few ex-cops in my head, but can't come up with anyone who owes me a favor.

"Jaap, that doesn't sound good. What are you going to do now?" Sparrow insists.

"Drive around and look for Leon. He'll need clothes, a car, money. I don't think he's going to waste his time on you. If he had a plan to harm you, it's probably out the window now."

"Are you sure?"

"No. But you know who he is. What he looks like. You know not to open the door to him."

I end the call, stop at the side of the road and take out my notebook, gather all the papers and notes on the backseat. I drive to a nearby restaurant, order a coffee and a home-made chicken pie, and read through all of it again. Maybe Leon at some point mentioned a name I can't recall right now. Someone he trusted and who might help him with money and transport.

Maybe Sarah can tell me as soon as he uses any of his credit cards.

I have to find him before some eager cop puts a bullet in his back.

My phone rings. Speak of the devil.

It's clear, from Sarah's voice, that there's trouble. But her words are lost in the din of voices around me. I get up and move outside.

"What? Say that again?" I look at my watch. It's 9.32 pm. "You are where? You stayed in the Midlands? Why? Dammit, Sarah!"

"Don't be so upset," she says. "I moved my flight after you told me that Leon's DNA is a match. By the way, his phone says he's in Stellenbosch with you."

"Where exactly in Stellenbosch?"

"Well, it's off now, but the two of you were practically on top of one another a while ago."

How the hell does she know that? Is she tracking my phone?

"Why are you asking?" she says. "What's going on?"

"Leon got away."

She stays quiet for long. Too long.

"What's wrong?"

"Jaap...?"

"Talk Sarah. I'm tired."

"James Addison is gone."

"What do you mean gone?"

"Disappeared. No trace. No communication. Gone."

SARAH

1

"Sarah? It's me. Are you awake?" The knock at the door is hesitant and even softer than the voice.

"Yes, come in." I close the laptop. I'm busy collating all the information I have on Magrit. So far there's nothing that worries me, but I still don't think she should know what I'm up to.

I am, in any case, unsure what exactly I'm looking for, or why. I know now that it was Leon's DNA on the wedding dress. And I'm pretty sure that's what Jaap has been hiding from me since we saw the DNA mask Sparrow made.

The case should be solved, done and dusted, but still there's something niggling at the back of my mind.

After Jaap told me the result of the DNA tests, I went for a scenic drive through the hills of the Midlands and then came back to the guesthouse to pack. But the temptation to run LittleRedRidingHood on a few more people proved too much.

Next thing I knew, my plane had long since put the Drakensberg behind it.

The door to my room swings open, but Magrit remains in the passage with its thick green carpet, wringing her hands. She looks at me as though she's not sure that she's in the right place, glances at her watch.

I look at mine. It's 9.27 at night, 19 July. Jaap's going to flip. I was supposed to have been in Pretoria ages ago.

"He's gone," she finally announces.

I get up from the desk. "Who?"

"James." She sounds perplexed. "We were supposed to meet at eight to talk about the program for the opening. He has to deliver a short speech. He didn't want to, so I wanted to try to convince him…he's gone."

"Define gone."

"He's not in his room or in the dining room. Neither is he in the barn." She frowns. "And the barn is messier than I'm used to. I think there's blood on the floor."

"Maybe he injured himself and went to an emergency room?"

"James is very professional when it comes to his diary. When he says eight o'clock, it's eight o'clock. He's fanatical about time. He would have called if he was going to miss our appointment."

I weigh up our options. It could be coincidental, but then again, we're stuck in the middle of a set of rather extraordinary circumstances. I decide to call Jaap, just so that he knows what's happening. Then I'll take the revolver and go out with Magrit to look for Addison.

No. I'll go with one of her farm workers. Preferably the biggest, scariest one on her payroll.

"I'm sorry to bug you." Magrit's hands unknot themselves and become fists she pushes into the pockets of her long black cardigan. "But you spoke about Blink. My daughter, Sparrow…I phoned her. Something didn't feel right, ever since you arrived here yesterday. Earlier she didn't want to say much, just that I could trust you. Now she says you—you and Jaap Reyneke—know who killed Janien? That you're not necessarily here to see James's exhibition."

I don't know what to say. What would Jaap say? I'd better call him quickly.

"I think we're getting ahead of ourselves," I say, trying to calm her. "Maybe James forgot about your appointment. Let's go and look for him. I just need to call someone, then I'll be down."

Faure Manor House's foreman turns out to be a giant of a Zulu man by the name of Sibusiso Ngubane, or, as everyone calls him, S'bu.

The search party for Addison is assembling in the kitchen and I watch S'bu in awe as we hurriedly put on rain gear. He has the calm confidence typical of big men who know that no one is likely to mess with them. He's wearing a yellow rain suit and white gumboots up to his knees. He is also carrying a powerful flashlight, a first-aid backpack and a shotgun, and I have no arguments against any of them. I hope that anyone lingering on the farm who doesn't belong here sees the outsized bright yellow suit and runs away.

"Did Magrit tell you what happened?" I ask him.

"Yes. James Addison is gone. You and I are going to look for him, from here to the gate, and she and Patrick will move from the house to the other side of the cowshed."

Patrick is a wiry man with a cowboy's gait and distant stare. S'bu's righthand man, if I understand correctly.

Magrit walks in the back door. She has a shotgun of her own in one hand and green gumboots like the pair she's wearing in the other. "Size five?"

"Yes."

"Then you better put these on. When it's this wet, you're likely to lose your shoes in the mud."

I take off my shoes, put the boots on, zip up my red rain jacket and pull the hood over my head. I feel, against my back, the weight of the revolver. I want to laugh at how ridiculous we all appear, but temper the emotion. It feels a tad too close to hysteria.

I gesture at the two shotguns. "How many of these things do you have?"

"Four," says Magrit. "We have lots of rats. They often migrate from the farms to our property. S'bu, let me know on the radio as soon as you find anything."

The big man nods.

"Are you sure James isn't around here somewhere?" I ask again. "Have you searched the whole house?"

"Except for the guests' rooms, yes."

"What if he's in someone's bed?"

"All he's focused on since he's been here is his work. I wonder whether he even remembers how to talk to women."

"But he liked Sparrow," I say, suddenly remembering what her daughter told me in Stellenbosch.

She looks at me, frowning. "Lots of men like Sparrow. She's small and delicate, something they imagine they can look after and protect. Maybe even control. But you know she's gay, don't you?"

"I know about Janien, yes."

"Does Janien's death have something to do with James? Is this about Blink?" Magrit's voice is tight, high. "Do I need to be worried about my guests? About Sparrow? She didn't want to say much, because she never wants me to fuss, but I know something's going on, something bigger than Janien."

I think of Addison. How long has he been gone? Long enough to get to the Cape? To Stellenbosch? Does his disappearance mean that Sparrow is in danger? What if he boarded a flight this afternoon, returning in time for the exhibition's opening tomorrow?

Shit. I better call Jaap again. I take my phone out of my bag and gesture to Magrit that she and Patrick must start the search.

She doesn't move, just stands there as though she's waiting for an answer.

"Your guests and Sparrow are safe," I assure her. "Jaap is looking after your daughter."

"And James?"

"I don't know. But we're going to look for him now, aren't we?" I point to the shotgun. "Just don't shoot at us, please. And don't touch anything if you find him...anyone. Anything." Man, I suck at this.

"What do you mean? Touch anything? Do I need to call the police, Sarah?"

"It's no use calling the cops. James is a grown man and he hasn't been missing long enough for them to do anything about it." I wave her out the door. "We need to go. We're wasting time."

As soon as she and Patrick have disappeared into the night, I call Jaap for the second time that night. "Do you still have Sparrow?"

"She's at the flat of a lecturer friend of hers. I'm looking for Leon."

"What if Sparrow's friend is James Addison?"

"She would have said."

That's probably true.

"What's up?" he asks.

"What if Addison is in Stellenbosch? The last time anyone saw him was at breakfast. He could easily be in the Cape by now."

The silence drags on for a moment too long.

"Fuck," he says. "Fuck, fuck, fuck."

"Are you okay?"

"Yes. No."

"Are you sure Sparrow is okay? Are you one hundred percent sure she is there, in Stellenbosch?" I ask again.

"She was at her friend's apartment busy packing, the last time we spoke. She's flying tomorrow morning. I went and dropped her off before this mess with Leon."

"Is she still there?" My suspicions turn a hundred and eighty degrees. "What if her flight was tonight? To here?"

"Wait. What do you mean? First you suspect Addison and now it's Sparrow?"

"I don't know what to think. We know it's Leon's DNA on the dress, but what if we were wrong about him? What if it really was a nosebleed?"

He says nothing.

"Jaap?"

"I'll go check in on Sparrow. You stay in your room and lock the door. Don't go anywhere. I'll call you as soon as I've located Sparrow. And please phone Ben Brandt. He can go and look for Addison. He should have been there ages ago."

I touch the revolver, lie: "I'll call him. Promise. And Ungerer? Have you got in touch with him?"

"No. He's not answering his phone."

"I traced his cell earlier. It's off, just like's Leon's, but maybe you should keep trying anyway."

JAAP

1

"Come on, pick up the phone!"

I end the call. It's no use. Ungerer's cellphone is dead as a door-nail. It's after eleven on a Monday night and I would probably also turn off my phone if I was going to sleep.

Or doing something I really shouldn't be doing.

I shift in my seat, my knee in pain after the many hours spent behind the Corolla's wheel. I again look through the car window at the block of flats where I dropped Sparrow this afternoon. Just about all the windows are dark.

Now what, Reyneke? Ungerer is not answering his phone, and neither is Sparrow. And you're no longer convinced she is where she promised she'd be.

I make sure the Parabellum is loaded and get out of the car. The night smells of the rain from earlier. Above me, stars litter the blackened sky. The moon is a sickle, narrow and pale yellow behind occasional wisps of cloud.

I am so sick of this incessant rain. I miss Pretoria and its pleasant, sunny winter days.

It's about fifteen meters up the path to the entrance of the block of flats. The intercom sits white against the brown wall, its screen an orange beacon.

Sparrow is visiting at number five. The building has three stories. Nine apartments. I didn't get to meet Sparrow's friend when I dropped her off this afternoon. He was still on his way home when I walked up with her to make sure she locked herself in properly.

If she's gone, if someone took her—if Leon took her—it's my fault. And ditto if she and James Addison are working together. Or if she murdered Addison...or plans to murder him.

I press the bell for number five, listen to the ring on the other side.

No one answers. I press the bell for number four. Someone picks up, curses, and cuts me off.

Number three. No answer.

I push against the wooden doors that lead into the entrance hall. Locked.

I peer through the windows. No one there.

I press number two.

"Yes?" says a cheerful female voice.

"Police," I say with all the authority I can muster.

"Police? Ha-ha. That's a new one." She sounds as though she's drunk too much coffee. Probably pulling an all-nighter.

"Is there an—"

She cuts me off. Shit. Must everyone here be a savvy, street-smart South African tonight?

I press the bell for number one. Maybe it's the caretaker's flat.

No one answers.

I walk back a few steps to see whether anyone is around, and then check the doors again, pushing harder this time.

There's a lock in the middle holding the doors together. I push near the copper doorknob, putting my weight behind it. The doors move ever so slightly.

I try again, putting all those Flake chocolates and the biltong to good use.

"Come on..."

More weight, and finally I feel the doors swing open.

There's no one inside the foyer. No security cameras that I can see. And I don't seem to have set off any alarms.

I close the doors and quickly head up the stairs, gritting my teeth as my knee protests against the sudden momentum.

Apartment number five looks dark and abandoned. I knock. Nothing stirs.

Perhaps Sparrow went back to the guesthouse?

I call her, but yet again there is no answer.

I leave a voice message. "It's Jaap. Call me as soon as you can."

I turn around and head toward the stairs. Then I hear the door opening behind me and turn back quickly.

"Hello!" I call out, just as it closes again. "Whoa! Wait. Please!"

The door swings open and a stocky man steps into the hallway.

He looks me up and down, and then seems to decide that I'm not a threat.

"I'm looking for Maggie Malan...Sparrow."

"It's the middle of the night." The man rubs his balding head with its stringy blond hair, then tugs at his washed-out T-shirt before he crosses his arms as if looking for some protection from the chilly air.

He's at least twice as old as Sparrow.

"Who are you?" he asks.

"Jaap Reyneke."

"The policeman? Sparrow told me about you."

"Where is she? Can I talk to her? It's urgent."

"She's gone. She decided to drive to Vryburg. She was worried that you'd find some new reason to keep her here. I lent her my car. That Beetle of hers has had it."

"Drove to Vryburg? But she was supposed to fly there tomorrow."

"She was very upset. What can I say?" The man shrugs.

"Was she alone?"

"I think so. Ja."

"When did she leave?"

"About an hour or two after you dropped her off. I'm not sure."

I turn and walk down the stairs.

Now what? Do I wait for Sarah to call and tell me whether Magrit's men have located Addison?

I should be able to get a flight to Durban tomorrow morning.

Maybe I can even catch one directly to Pietermaritzburg and then drive to the Midlands. I could be there by seven or eight.

Or do I drive to Vryburg?

Or do I carry on looking for Leon?

"Hey!" calls the man. "Wait!"

I stop at the top of the stairs and turn around. "Yes?"

"Do I need to be worried? Sparrow said something about a murder?"

"No. Go back to sleep."

He's the last person who needs to be worried. No such mercy for the rest of us.

SARAH

1

The mist is so thick you could kick holes in it. How do you find someone in this mess, and in the dark, to boot?

The only sound I hear is the faint, rhythmic squeak of S'bu's rubber boots. I know he has the shotgun at the ready in his hands, so I make sure to stay behind him.

"Can you see anything?" I whisper.

He stops. Looks left, right. "No. Nothing."

I can only just make out the pale, naked tree trunks on either side of us. The stone manor house is behind us, its warm yellow lights shrouded in mist.

Since we've set out, we've walked across the lawn, past two paddocks, and up the road I drove in on yesterday. I would guess that it's probably about another four or five hundred meters to the gate.

A horse whinnies restlessly, followed by another's nervous neigh. No point trying to find what's making them uneasy with my flashlight, as the beam simply reflects off the mist.

I think of the previous murders. Two women and one man, all possibly injected with M99, strong enough to fell a rhinoceros, the bodies arranged as though they were portraits or sculptures.

I ask S'bu for the two-way radio.

"Magrit?"

"Yes?" She's breathing heavily.

"You okay?"

"Yes. I just haven't climbed the hill behind the house so quickly for a long time."

"See anything?"

"No. This mist is not helping."

How should I frame my question? And how far will the sound of my voice carry? What if someone hears me—the wrong someone?

"What's up?" asks Magrit.

"If you wanted to kill someone…No, if you wanted to make a painting with a real person. If you had red fabric and red paint and you wanted to do something striking with it, something that would attract attention, where on the farm would you do that?"

"Why are you asking?"

"Think of Janien's murder, think of Blink, the people who took part. Think of yourself—you're a painter, right? An artist. What would you do? Where would you do it?"

She lets out a slow breath. "The entrance hall? The open space with the lead windows…" I can almost hear her imagination churning. "With the double doors that look out onto the fountain outside it would be quite spectacular."

"What if you had to do it away from the house? If you had to work where no one would see you, but where you could still make a statement?"

"You're scaring me, Sarah."

"We can't afford to be scared now. We have to find James."

It's quiet while she thinks.

"The barn. It's high and open, with lots of natural light…but obviously not tonight. The windows have wooden frames that are painted green and are flaking, a natural frame." A sharp intake of breath. "Or the lane of trees on the way in. The grass, the white fences of the paddocks, the silver bark of the trees. That would work."

I look over my shoulder. The barn is too far, so is the house, but S'bu and I are in the lane already. I look at the trees on either side of me. The gravel. The ghostly outline of the white fencing.

I hear the horses whinnying again, hooves milling restlessly.

I take out the revolver. "Go to the barn," I tell Magrit. "S'bu and I are in the lane."

"I was in the barn this afternoon."

"Doesn't matter. Go check again."

I turn down the volume on the radio and hand it back to S'bu, indicate to him to walk up the left side of the road, near the fence, away from the noisy gravel, closer to the solid ground under the trees. I put my finger over my lips to show him we need to be quiet. Then I switch off the flashlight and start walking up the right side of the road, using the grass to absorb the sound of my footsteps.

Ahead, near the gate, the mist thins slightly, and visibility improves to about five meters.

I almost slip on the dead leaves underfoot, the ground wet and muddy. As I try to regain my balance, my left foot sinks away. I stop and pull it out slowly.

Freeze.

What was that sound? A rope?

Yes. A rope being pulled tight.

I search for the vague outlines of S'bu's body. He lifts the shotgun and looks at me, motions with his head: do we go on or do we turn around?

It's too late now. Way too late. It's been too late since Pretoria.

We move forward.

One step.

Another.

The next tree.

We stop. Listen.

This is a bad silence. It's loaded. Heavy. Dead. A silence like The End. A silence I remember from my dad and the hospital. The noise, the machines, the gasping, then nothing. Just like that. All of a sudden. The body robbed of everything that makes a difference.

The road swings left.

How far are we from the gate? A hundred meters?

I want to warn S'bu to be careful, but realize he knows it already. His white boots move gingerly, slowly, from one tree to the next. I follow his example.

Next tree.

Next one.

I jump when the grass behind me rustles, press my back against the tree trunk. The mist hides whatever it was from sight. Then I feel something strange under my hands. Where there should be bark there's...fabric?

I stand back slightly and switch on the flashlight behind the cover of my hand. It's red fabric, wrapped around the tree.

I touch it again. It's wet from the mist.

Red, like the veil Janien wore. The paint in Jack Fist's car. The rose bushes in a half-moon around Yolene Chen. Her red dress.

I tap the revolver against the trunk to draw S'bu's attention, to show him the red fabric around the trunk.

S'bu stares at me, his hands a question mark in the thin light of my flashlight.

Ahead of us, someone coughs.

How far away was that? Thirty meters? Forty?

What do we do now? I curse silently. I should have called Colonel Brandt. And where the hell is Jaap when you need him?

I take a deep breath, lift the revolver and fire a shot in the air.

Another.

If the threat of violence can save someone's life, why not? I'm not about to plunge into the mist to confront a man who has committed three murders.

The shots linger, as though the mist clings to the sound itself.

Then a car starts up. It's an old bakkie, I imagine. Diesel.

I start running to the gate, hear S'bu doing the same behind me.

We turn the corner, the gate in front of us. Red brake lights flicker in the mist next to the road.

The license plate! I point the flashlight. Can't see through the mist. Can't shoot. What if it's someone innocent?

The white Nissan pulls away. Swings sharply to the left. Skids in the mud.

I run, the revolver ready, adrenalin like needles in my hands.

The back of the bakkie hits a tree as the driver tries to speed away. Comes to a standstill.

"Stop!" I scream.

S'bu stops. Lifts the shotgun. Fires. The sound drills through my brain.

I see a dark figure in the cabin.

The ignition turns. The engine struggles.

"Stop!" I keep the flashlight trained on the driver as we run closer again.

S'bu shoots again. Pock marks appear on the tailgate. The right brake light shatters.

"Stop, S'bu!" I shout. There's no license plate, I realize.

I run the way I run in Pretoria at night, a full-on sprint until my lungs burn.

Ten steps. Nine. Eight.

Who's in the bakkie? Addison? Sparrow? Leon?

The engine roars. The wheels spin in the mud. Four steps. Three.

The bakkie jerks forward and kicks into life, belting down the drive toward the gate.

"No, no, no!"

I come to a standstill, hands on my knees, gulping down air. I watch as S'bu reloads before he shoots again. But it's useless. The mist swallows the single brake light, then the engine's diesel roar.

S'bu takes out the radio and calls Magrit. They probably heard the shots anyway.

My watch says it's 00.35 am. The morning of the twentieth of July.

I put the revolver away and turn around, stare at the white wall of mist that refuses to yield.

I walk to the closest tree and touch the naked trunk.

Next one. Also just bark.

Next one. Cloth.

Next one. Cloth.

I walk back to the first wrapped tree, and then to the tree opposite it. It's also wrapped. I stand in the middle of the road, at the start of the row of red trees on either side of me.

What was the driver of the bakkie doing? Did we interrupt him? Were we in time?

I take a deep breath, fed-up and angry. There's an unexpected coppery smell of blood in my mouth.

I look around in vain. What is the mist hiding?

I hear voices approaching, quick footsteps on the gravel.

"Sarah? S'bu?" It's Magrit.

"Here!" calls S'bu.

I wipe a hand across my face and neck, everything clammy from the mist. It dawns on me how cold it is. It must be below freezing.

The shaking starts in my legs and bears upwards, but I catch it in my stomach. Hold it there. Not now. Focus. Silence the fear. All the things that might have happened.

Magrit appears out of the mist, mud up to her thighs. She looks worn out, her face exhausted. "What happened? We heard shots."

She walks up to me. Holds her flashlight up as she approaches. Jerks back. Points to my shoulder.

I look down. My jacket has three dark drops on it.

Four.

Five.

I scurry back. Look up. Duck the next drop. It rolls down my neck instead.

James Addison hangs above me, his arms spread wide, as if cru-cified, his face white and grim.

2

"Leave it," the forensics technician snaps at me.

I pull my hand away from the red rain jacket on the kitchen table and cross my arms again.

"The jacket is evidence. I have to take it with me."

"It's my jacket." I give the burly policeman in his blue overalls a hard stare. "What about my neck where the blood dripped? Do you want to take that too?"

"Miss Fourie." The tech lets out a long and irritated sigh. "I'm just doing my job."

I push the jacket across the table. "Take it. Are we done now? You've photographed me, scraped my fingernails, taken a sample from the blood on my neck. For fuck's sake, can I just go and shower now?"

My breathing is becoming more rapid. I was fairly calm until the blue lights started arriving. Then it all started feeling exceedingly familiar. I remember the day the cops came for me at home. The astonishment on my mom's face, then the shock and the anger. The call to my dad. The sound the very first time the cell door slammed shut behind me.

"We need your shirt too," says the policeman, whose name somehow slipped past me. "I'll send a female constable to accompany you to your room. Only then, when Captain Naidoo is happy with your statement, you can go and shower."

"He's already spoken to me. We've gone over the whole story four times. Over and over. And, yes, wait, over and over again. I'm innocent. I'm the one who called you, remember?" I get up and start taking off my T-shirt.

"What…wait," the technician protests, "there's a female constable who can go with you so you can undress in your room."

I throw the shirt on the table. Lock eyes with the cop. I refuse to look down in case I spot more blood on my body.

The policeman's mouth is hanging open.

"And now? Can I go and shower now?"

Magrit walks in. "Sarah? What's going on?"

My arms remain stiffly by my side. I don't want these strangers to touch me again. My personal space has already been invaded too many times tonight. "Nothing. Apparently, everyone's just doing their job."

"You can't stand here like that." She looks sharply at me, then at the technician. "Can she go and put on something warm?"

"Of course." He bags the shirt, takes two or three photos of what I assume is blood evidence on my body.

I remain there as though I suddenly can't move. As if I'm incapable of putting one foot in front of the other.

I'm aware of Magrit shaking her head at the policeman who is slowly packing up his kit. She asks impatiently: "Do you want more coffee when you're done?"

"No thank you, ma'am, but more of those rusks would be great."

She takes out a tin next to the pantry and passes it to him, turns to me when he's left.

"Would you like some tea? I'll bring it to your room. Go and have a shower and change into something warm. Off you go, before you catch a cold."

I stand there, rooted to the ground.

"When is Jaap coming?" she asks. "You can't talk to him looking like that."

I close my eyes, open them. Regain some focus. I look at my watch. "He's landed. He'll probably be here in an hour or so." I jut my chin in the general direction of the gate.

"His friend Colonel Brandt is here. He's talking to the police team."

Magrit takes my wrists in her hands and starts rubbing the skin in small circles, coaxing some warmth into my body. "Go on now. Go take a nice, warm shower. You'll feel better once you're out of those clothes."

"I will." As soon as I can move.

Why didn't I call Brandt? Make sure Addison was safe?

Magrit's hands stop. "Is there something you want to talk about, Sarah?"

"No."

"Okay then. Is there anything I can help with? Anything that will help me understand what happened tonight?"

Nope. Not going to go there either. I'd rather be interrogated by the police. I don't want to talk to this woman about her daughter.

"Can Jaap talk to you later?" I ask.

She looks unwilling to say yes, but her good manners win.

"Sure. But please just tell me one thing. Is my daughter safe? Yesterday you spoke about James and Blink, and Sparrow was the runner-up in that competition. I need to know. Please?"

Shit, what can I say? Addison is out of the picture, which quite likely makes Sparrow the killer. It couldn't have been Leon. I can't imagine he could have made it from Stellenbosch to here in time, not with the police looking for him.

I shiver from the chill creeping into my body. "Have you called Sparrow?"

"About ten times already."

"And?"

"Voicemail."

I shrug. "Then you know as much as I do."

In the room, I take off my socks and peel off my jeans and underwear. Walk past the mirror without looking.

I climb into the shower and turn on the hot water. I can feel the tension vibrating in my hands as I grip the taps. A buzzing starts up in my ears, growing louder and louder, like cicadas on a hot bushveld afternoon in February, shrill and insistent. I close my eyes, trying to shut out the noise. I lean forward, putting my head under the stream.

My knees buckle and I sink down to the floor. I sit like that while the water steams up the room and washes James Addison from my skin, wishing desperately there was a similar remedy for the images in my head.

JAAP

1

I turn my collar up against the wind sweeping down the road in the direction of Faure Manor House. Another province and yet another freezing morning. At least it's not raining.

I gesture a silent apology to Sarah as I listen to Isak blowing off steam on the phone.

"I don't know why Leon ran away if he's innocent, Isak." There's a rock-hard ball of tension in the pit of my stomach. "All I'm saying is, don't shoot. Addison's murder is just like Janien's, which means Leon is innocent. The DNA…maybe his nose did bleed, as he says."

"He could have committed all the murders. This new one included."

"How? He couldn't have made it to KwaZulu-Natal in time. You were on the lookout at all the airports, and even that would be a stretch."

"Earlier you were certain it was Leon who killed Janien. Now you're telling me about a James Addison who was murdered just like Janien somewhere in the KZN countryside, and you suddenly want me to believe that Leon had nothing to do with it."

"Yes. I made a mistake."

"Says who?"

"It was me who told you to test Leon's DNA first."

"Which I would have done in any case."

"Forget about the DNA. For heaven's sake, Isak! Listen to what I'm telling you about James Addison."

"Yes, now we're talking about a serial killer who's killed a number of people, but it's not Leon. Sounds very convenient, if you ask me."

"It's the truth. Addison's death confirms it's not Leon. I'm telling you."

"How sure are you that these murders are all linked? This whole case has been riddled with lies and mistakes from the very beginning."

"Maybe that's true, yes, but they weren't all mine."

He keeps quiet.

I take a deep breath as I try to ease the rising anger in my chest. "Don't shoot, Isak. That's all I'm asking you. Don't drive Leon into a corner where he does something stupid. I think he's frightened... was frightened. That's all. Afraid that Vonnie and Obie would find out about the Cat. That they would think he'd murdered Janien. That he would lose his parents for a second time. It was sheer, raw panic, that's all."

"Well, I still believe he killed Janien. Plus, he shot a policewoman."

"He only wounded her. On purpose, so that he could get away. Think whatever you want, just don't hurt him, please."

Isak swears. I don't think I've ever heard him swear before. I remember the crucifix on the wall of his stoep, his wife's soft eyes warning him to play nice.

"Jaap...I can't believe...Okay. I'll see what I can do. But you know it's no longer just up to me. It's become a high-profile case, because of you and Bells and your damn DNA tests. The entire Western Cape police force is looking for Leon. In fact, it might soon be the whole country's police force. If Leon calls you...you'd better let me know."

"I will. Just keep your promise."

I hang up before we start arguing like children about promises we never made. I turn back to Sarah, waiting for me with uncharacteristic patience. "Sorry."

"It's okay. No news about Leon?"

"No." I put the phone away. "Where were we?"

"You were asking me where I was standing when I found Addison. James."

"Good. Tell me again, please."

She points to the trees alongside the gravel road between the white fencing.

"No. Don't show me like that," I say softly, gently. I can see last night stripped something from her. Something I know she'll never get back. "Naidoo might see. I'm comforting you, not questioning you. I don't want him thinking that we're standing here making sure our stories match."

I step closer and carefully put my arm around her shoulders. I can feel her tense up, but somehow she tolerates the gesture.

She examines the trees again, as though she's looking for traces of James Addison.

She won't find any. Naidoo said the body was on its way to the pathologist. Brandt has also left. He made sure Sarah was safe and then waited for me to arrive before he packed up his Jeep. He says I owe him a case of KWV brandy.

That'll be the day. Why wait for Sarah to contact him before showing up here? I told him to come and help her.

I watch as Naidoo rounds up some of his people to do another grid search from the house to the gate. We spoke briefly when I arrived, and I can see he doesn't trust the peace. Doesn't trust me.

He is especially suspicious of my relationship with Sarah—an ex-cop and an ex-con. I know he's going to get stuck into that when he does his formal interview with me later today.

The members of his team who are not working outside are searching the barn and Addison's room. It's an unusual murder and it's going to draw attention. I wouldn't be surprised if some shrewd journalist started drawing parallels between Addison's murder and Janien's death.

It's precisely the blatant, open way in which Addison was murdered that concerns me. The killer is no longer being careful. It's as though he wants people to notice him. As if he believes it's time for everyone to know who he is. To hang Addison like that, strung up across a road before the opening of his exhibition—it's audacious. It's big. It says look at me. Look at what I'm doing.

"Where was Addison when you first saw him?" I ask Sarah.

"Above me." Her expression is an odd combination of anger and vulnerability. "He was hanging above me. His wrists were tied with rope."

"What kind of rope?"

"Climbing rope. Red and white, not very thick, but strong."

I glance at the road from the corner of my eye. Notice Naidoo staring at us. He seems like a thorough detective, and his people respect him. That's always a good sign.

He said he'd already phoned Doris, so at least he knows I'm not sucking the whole twentieth-of-July connection out of my thumb.

The only problem is that it's going to be time-consuming for him to check my facts formally. Three countries, and then two provinces in one of those countries. By the time everyone starts cooperating, it's going to be the twentieth of July next year.

I give Naidoo a small wave and turn my attention back to Sarah. "How did Addison look?"

Sarah steps away from me. She wraps her arms around her upper body. "His arms were spread out, each wrist tied to a tree by a rope. S'bu and I brought him down because he was still bleeding. We hoped he would still be alive."

"Spread out?"

"Yes, like in my children's Bible. Like he was crucified? The ropes were hitched over trees and tied to the fences on either side of the road."

"That requires some muscle. Can't be Sparrow. Sparrow and someone else, maybe?"

"Stefan could have helped her," she says. "Don't forget, that phone call came from the butchery."

"What can you tell from the phones?"

"I traced all the Malan business phones. Two are off, including

Sparrow's, three are in or around Carnarvon, and two are in the Western Cape. I called the one there, which I thought was Stefan's, but Fanus answered. Leon's is also dead, but that's not surprising, given the circumstances. Ungerer's phone has been switched off since last night. I don't know what the hell he's up to."

I take out my notebook and add Ungerer to my to-do list. "I'll try to find out where he is." I tap the pen against the paper. "Tell me about Addison's wounds."

Sarah looks toward the house, at her rental car parked near the front door. It's as if she wants to jump in it and get away from here as fast as possible.

"Sarah?" I say when she doesn't answer.

Her eyes return to me reluctantly. "Somebody cut his throat. I know what it looks like. From jail. He must have died just before we got there. His body was still warm."

"Did you see any needle wounds? M99?"

"It was too dark. And the blood...I was standing in it."

"I'm sorry..."

"Don't."

"Okay. The red fabric stuck to the tree trunks?"

"It was wound around the trees," she corrects me. "And I think it was nailed into place. That's how it looked when Naidoo was talking to me. One of his people tugged at it until it came loose."

"Wearing gloves, I hope."

"No."

"Stupid."

"Don't worry. He had a major fit about it."

I manage a half-smile as I rub my eyes. I'm tired. So tired, and yet I can't sleep. Something's bugging me. Something that remains out of reach. It's been like that since just before Leon ran away. Bicycle. Shoes. Crucifixion. Red dress. Red paint.

The countrywide weather report on *eNCA* in the café in Stellenbosch with Sparrow. It's as if I can sense that all these elements are linked, I just don't know how.

"What about the bakkie?" I ask. "Could you make out anything on the vehicle that could help us?"

"It was a white bakkie. Nissan Hardbody. Diesel. Single cab. No number plates."

"And the people inside?"

"Man. Singular."

"Big? Small?"

"Bit taller than you, if I had to guess. But he was sitting, so it's hard to say. And the mist was thick."

"Age?"

"Can't say." She sweeps her hair back with her hands tucked into fingerless black gloves.

"How do you imagine he got onto the property?"

"Magrit says the gate is locked each night with a chain. She says it was cut."

I nod. "You've been here a few days now. Did you see anything funny? Notice someone who didn't belong?"

"No." She bites her bottom lip. "Did I miss something, Jaap? Should I have done a better job of warning James?"

"No, no," I rush to say. "I'm pissed off that you didn't call Brandt when you arrived and that he didn't get here earlier, but I can't imagine anyone else handling the situation better than you and Magrit did. This is my mess, not yours. First, I refused to consider Leon a suspect because of something that happened a long, long time ago. Then I thought the DNA would give me all the answers, and then that was a dead end as well. I never, from the very beginning, looked widely enough. This one, I'm afraid, is on me."

2

I remember Magrit. She was with Fanus for six or seven years before she divorced him. She said she could no longer live that isolated, on a farm in the middle of nowhere, away from everything and everyone that had made her happy in Durban.

The open plains were too much for her. The arid land. Fanus's rigidity. His womanizing. And you can probably only paint Karoo clouds that many times, before one canvas starts looking like the next and you have to start wondering where the hell your husband is so late at night.

The courts granted Fanus care of the children. He got a pricey lawyer, who maintained that Magrit was emotionally unstable and not a good caregiver. That she was on strong antidepressants. That she hated routine—and children needed routine, not so?

Magrit spots me the minute she steps out of the front door.

"Jaap! My goodness. I can hardly believe it." She gives me a quick hug, her lips grazing my cheek.

"Hello, Magrit."

We're standing in front of the Faure Manor House, at an angle where I can still keep an eye on Naidoo and his team as they keep on working the crime scene. When I look to my right, I can see the barn where Addison was apparently surprised by his attacker.

"So, Sarah works for you," says Magrit. "How did that happen?"

"I think she'd prefer to say that she's helping me."

Magrit gives a little laugh. "She was very competent yesterday evening. She tried to revive James and then called the police."

"I'm glad. She's very together, more than she knows."

Magrit fiddles with the bright-green scarf around her neck. "She won't say much about what you two are up to, but it's not hard to put two and two together. Did Sarah come here because of Janien and James? Because they…" She feels around for the right words. "Because it's all the same?"

"Yes."

Should I put my cards on the table? Probably, especially since Sparrow may be involved.

"We started getting worried about the Blink competitors a few days ago," I say. "Jack Fist and Yolene Chen are also dead."

Magrit's hand flutters to her throat, grabbing hold of the string of silver beads around her neck as if it's choking her. "I can't get hold of Sparrow."

"She's on her way to the North West. An interview at some school in Vryburg."

"I know. But why isn't she answering her phone?"

"She seemed very focused on this interview," I explain. "And I suspect I made her nervous. She wanted to get away from me and Leon before I sabotaged this opportunity for her."

I take off my jacket and roll up my shirt sleeves. The late morning sun is wonderfully warm. Even my knee is starting to feel better.

Magrit tugs at the beads, worry still etched on her face.

"I'm one hundred percent certain Sparrow is okay," I try to reassure her. "And in any case, the murders all happen on the twentieth of July and this year's one is done."

"But what about next year?"

"Hopefully by then the case will be solved."

She nods. Keeps on fidgeting with the beads. I watch as her worry gears up into anger. "Why are you only telling me about Sparrow now? Sarah should have mentioned this the moment she got here."

"I spent the whole of yesterday with Sparrow to keep an eye on her. She only left for Vryburg last night. You really don't have to be worried."

She looks away, blinks back tears.

I put my arm around her shoulders and pull her closer. Unlike with Sarah, there's no resistance. "I'm sorry. Sorry about James. All of this."

"You really could have told me, you know. Both of you."

"You're right. We probably could have. Sarah did try to warn James."

"He wouldn't have listened." She turns away, wipes her cheeks.

"And now Sparrow is the only Blink finalist left."

She looks at me. "What does that mean?"

This time I'm fully prepared to lie. "I don't know. I'm not allowed to touch the case anymore. You'll have to ask Captain Naidoo."

3

"Four people. Four years. Four artists, each of them active in a different field. Each of them murdered on 20 July."

I look up from my notebook. Sarah is typing something on an invisible keyboard on her legs again.

"All of them know one another," I continue. "Two are sleeping together—that we know of. Four towns, three countries. Red is a common theme, but each of the bodies is positioned differently. It's not about sex, nor is it about money—as far as we can tell. Which means it must be revenge. Or power. That's all that's left. Or some kind of compulsion. Something up here that's come unhinged." I tap my forehead.

We're in Sarah's room, looking at the photos of Yolene, Janien, Fist, and Addison she's stuck up on the wall. She snapped the shot of Addison's body with her phone before the police arrived and printed it out in Magrit's office.

We're staring at the images, desperately searching for something that will help solve the case.

The same words keep on cycling through my head. Wedding shoes. Bicycle. Red. That *eNCA* weather report that day in the café in Stellenbosch. I keep going back there and I don't know why. Perhaps I should try to get some sleep. Maybe the answer will surface once I've rested.

Sarah stops the air typing. "I don't know about that. Who would want revenge, and why?" She takes a cigarette from the pack next to her and spins it between her fingers.

Round and round and round.

"What about Sparrow?" I offer. "And Ungerer is also a possibility."

"At least revenge means it can't be Leon," she says. "He's not close enough to half these people."

"True."

"Have you had any updates about him?"

"Apparently a farmer and his wife spotted him near Kuruman. At least, they think it's him."

"Wouldn't you rather be there, just in case something bad happens?"

"Vonnie and Obie are on their way. Isak called to let them know what's going on."

"Are you sure?" she asks.

"Ja. In any case, you said you'll tell me if Leon uses his phone or bank cards."

"Okay then." She looks at the photos again. "Tell me why Sparrow would want these people dead?"

"Because she should have won Blink."

"And Ungerer?"

"He thinks he's a better artist, but instead he has been demoted to being a lecturer."

Sarah draws a big question mark on a clean sheet of paper and sticks it up next to the photos. "Maybe it's someone completely unknown who imagines that they should have won Blink."

I groan in annoyance. That's the last thing we need.

"What about Skout?" I ask. "Have we dropped all our theories about the app?"

"I'm not quite sure. As far as I can see, Addison didn't know anything about Skout. If Sparrow was the one in the tree, it might be a different matter." She tosses the cigarette into the bin. "I'll dig around and see what I can find. Maybe there's something I'm missing. I really think you should go to Kuruman. Go and help Leon. He may need it."

"I don't think I'd be welcome."

"Sometimes that doesn't matter."

I look at my watch. It's 11.40 in the morning. If I leave now, I could be there by this evening. Maybe stop some trigger-happy cop from killing Leon.

"Go," says Sarah.

"I can't leave you alone. Not again."

"You can. It's over."

"What if it's not?"

"Bullshit. Go."

I get up. "I'll think about it."

I sit down again.

Shoes. *eNCA*. Wedding dress.

No. Wait...

eNCA.

That's right. I jump up.

Sarah looks at me as though I'm a few sandwiches short of a picnic. "What's wrong?"

"Our man plans very, very well, right?"

"Yes. So?"

"So what do we think about the locations of the killings? Are they a coincidence? Why Gaborone? Swakopmund? Carnarvon? Here?"

She frowns. "What do you mean? That's where his victims visited and worked."

"And our guy—or woman—followed them there? Here?"

"Yes."

"Fist was on holiday and James had his exhibition here. Janien was at home for her wedding. And Yolene?" I ask.

Sarah thinks quickly. "She worked in a restaurant in Joburg and went home for a visit, to take a break and work on Skout."

"Nothing more? Was there nothing compelling her to be in Gaborone on the twentieth of July?"

"Someone wanted to see her about Skout, but not on the twentieth. The day before."

"Close enough. Who?"

"ITFin."

"Who's this ITFin?"

"Not any company we know." Sarah gets up and takes off her jacket. Underneath the black leather she is wearing a tight, bright-green T-shirt. "Why are you suddenly curious about where the murders happened?"

"Because everything matters to the killer. So why wouldn't location matter too?"

I take out my notebook again. Begin drawing while I think. The Western Cape. KwaZulu-Natal.

"How did Fist get to Swakopmund?" I ask. "Who sponsored the competition?"

"I don't know."

I get up. "See if you can find out. I'm going to get something quickly."

"What about Kuruman?" she calls after me.

I don't answer. What can I say? I can go and look for Leon or I can hand Isak the real killer.

I call Isak while I walk to the kitchen. No answer. I try Vonnie's number. She picks up straight away.

"I'm sorry I'm not there for your birthday."

"I don't care about my birthday. How could you, Jaap?"

I step around a middle-aged man wheeling his suitcase to the front door, his anxious face betraying that he's eager to leave Faure Manor House.

"The DNA sai—"

"I don't care about the DNA. Leon grew up in our home. He's one of us. I know he would never kill anyone. I know that! Why don't you?" She is crying.

"I'm sorry."

"If something happens to him…it'll be on your conscience and yours alone."

Obie starts talking in the background, his voice angry and low, and Vonnie ends the call.

I slip the phone back in my pocket as I walk into the kitchen. Two women baking bread tell me that Magrit is in the garden.

I walk out the back door and into the bright sunlight. Magrit's sitting on a garden bench knitting, a straw hat casting a shadow across her face.

I walk over and sit down next to her. "I didn't know you knitted."

"It keeps my hands busy when I'm worried."

"Have you heard anything from Sparrow yet? Did she arrive safely in Vryburg?"

"Why should I tell you?"

"Magrit, I..." I sigh morosely. "I don't know."

"She got there some time this morning." Magrit puts down the needles and olive-green wool. "She drove through the night. She was never anywhere near here."

"I am glad to hear that."

"Really?"

"Yes."

"Wasn't she your most likely suspect?" There is distinct sarcasm in her voice.

"I'm not that sure anymore," I'm forced to admit.

Magrit looks relieved at first, but then her curiosity takes over. "Why? What happened?"

"Do you have a map of Southern Africa? I'll show you."

4

Sarah doesn't look up from her computer when Magrit and I walk into the room. She carries on working, her fingers like those of a concert pianist. There's a cup of steaming tea next to her laptop, along with a half-eaten tube of salt-and-vinegar chips.

Magrit gets a jolt when she sees the photographs on the wall. She raises her hand quickly to her mouth the way women often do when they're shocked, as though to keep themselves from making a sound. As if they imagine doing so would somehow offend someone.

She walks past Sarah and stares at the images of Yolene and Fist's bodies. She steps forward and touches Janien's crime-scene photo as though she can't believe what she's seeing. "They're like James...like last night. All of them."

I nod. "Exactly."

"What are you guys doing here?" Sarah snaps. "I'm trying to work." She swivels the chair around, one hand on the armrest, the other scrubbing through her already messy hair.

"We'll be two minutes." I take the map of Southern Africa from Magrit and roll it open on the bed. "We need something...string or something. And sticky tape," I ask her.

"I'll go and get some," Magrit says and exits the room.

"What's going on, Jaap?" asks Sarah.

"A suspicion. Just be patient. It's not all that clear in my head yet."

She takes a sip of tea, looks at me with a strange glint in her eyes. I know that look. "Have you found something?" I ask.

"Maybe. ITFin sponsored the competition that sent Fist to Swakop. That's what it says in his email."

"The same company that wanted to meet Yolene in Gaborone about Skout?"

"Yes. Their CEO had ostensibly been on holiday in Zambia and wanted to stop there on his way home."

I consider her answer. The nature of competitions. "How would ITFin have known that Fist would enter their competition?"

"He didn't need to. ITFin said he was client number 12 345 at a coffee shop in Muizenberg, near the beach where he often surfed. The coffee shop has confirmed that ITFin approached them with the idea for the competition. And, what's more, ITFin installed the electric counter that selected the winner."

I sink down on Sarah's unmade bed. "What is this ITFin exactly?"

"I'm still trying to figure that out. All I know is what the letter-head says. Two J. Vissers are the sole directors. There's a telephone number in Johannesburg that no one's answering. I have a postal address, a website that gives just about zero information, and a business bank-account number overseas. No cell numbers to trace. ITFin also doesn't seem to pay tax in South Africa, so I can't track them down that way either."

"And James Addison? Does he have any link to ITFin?"

"Don't know yet. But I might be looking in the wrong place. Perhaps they worked through Magrit?"

"What's the bet they sponsored his exhibition?" I say. "Or they promised to buy some artwork or something if he held it on the twentieth of July."

"There's nothing about ITFin on the invitation, but you could be right." She pushes herself up from the chair, looks at the map on the bed. "That's me. Now what the hell are you up to?"

The information about ITFin has further crystalized my theory. The where is important—in fact, perhaps even more important than the how.

"Come look," I say with more confidence than I felt minutes ago.

I straighten the covers on her bed, walk to the windows to open the curtains so the afternoon sun falls on the white duvet. Sarah blinks a few times against the sudden brightness and I notice for the first time how tired she looks. I wonder when last she slept. It's 12.23 pm. If we were still on the farm, she'd only be getting up round about now.

There's a quick knock on the door and Magrit walks in.

I want to laugh. In her hands, of all things, is half a ball of left-over red wool.

I take out my pocketknife and cut two lengths of about forty centimeters each.

Sarah steps closer—closer than I'm used to—her hands on her hips, guarding her space. Magrit waits at the foot of the bed.

I put one end of the wool on Swakopmund and the other where we are now and stick it down with tape.

The second piece of string stretches from Carnarvon to Gaborone.

I can't believe it. I was right.

Thank you, *eNCA*. The weather report that day in Stellenbosch showed a map of Southern Africa and the image somehow stuck in my mind.

Sarah twigs first. "It's a cross." She looks at it in disbelief. "How did you know that?"

I don't answer. I should have thought of this earlier.

Magrit stares mutely at the red lines.

"What do you think it means?" I ask her. "You know art. You've owned a gallery in Cape Town and in Durban. And you worked on the art scene in New York." I motion toward the photos against the wall and then the map. "What does it mean that someone kills four people in this way, every time on the twentieth of July? People who knew one another and who were all finalists in a hot-shot national art competition."

Magrit shakes her head. "You should have told me this a long time ago, Jaap. Sparrow is the only Blink finalist left. She could have been the one hanging from those trees!"

"But she isn't. I looked after her all day yesterday."

"And you spoke to her this morning, so she's safe," snaps Sarah.

"But last night she wasn't," Magrit insists.

"Jaap was there. So quit worrying about her. We have more important things to focus on right now."

"Hang on now. Just take a deep breath." I motion for Sarah to keep quiet. "Magrit, I made sure Sparrow was safe before I even knew what was going on."

"Were you looking after her, or watching her?" Magrit laughs bitterly.

I put my hand on her arm. "We never really considered Sparrow to be the killer. It takes enormous strength to hoist a dead body into a tree. And Sarah saw a man in the bakkie last night." I say nothing about the fact that her daughter might have had an accomplice. "If we all work together we may be able to catch this guy. Then Sparrow will be safe next year."

"Us? You, Sarah, and me? I want the police involved, not just the two of you. You knew about all of this and look what happened. James died last night."

I ignore the accusation. She's right and I'll have to live with it, but right now this cross is more important. "I'll tell Isak and Naidoo about the map. You can too. I don't care. Just help me here first, please." I'm struggling to stay patient. "What do you think this means? This cross? These murder scenes?"

She looks at me, Sarah, and then walks over to the photos. She closes her eyes for such a long time I start wondering whether she's praying. Then she inspects each photograph closely.

"It's a cross, so it might be referencing the Christian idiom. It's a little old-fashioned, pretty obvious and a little dumb—religion is an easy and lazy target when it comes to art these days. As an urbanized society we have become mostly secular, no matter what we may think. We are materialistic and cynical, geared toward the immediate, not the immortal, the life hereafter. What's clever about this is that you have to see it on a map, from above. As though it tells a single story. As though each individual piece forms part of a greater work of art. Like land art that you can really only appreciate when you're standing at the right angle."

I hold up my hand. "Wait. Say that again."

"Each individual piece…"

"No. Land art?"

"Yes. Sometimes also known as environmental art."

"Like Robert Smith." Another piece falls into place.

Magrit looks surprised. "You mean Robert Smithson? Yes. Sparrow is a big fan of his. I first told her about him when she was five years old, and she couldn't stop asking questions about him."

"She told me about Smithson. He died on the twentieth of July, not so? What about Karl Ungerer? Does he like Smithson? Does he perhaps have an obsession with him?"

Magrit shrugs. "The date might be pure coincidence. It might have nothing at all to do with Smithson. Land art is gaining popularity worldwide. Even South Africa has produced one or two big names. People like Strijdom van der Merwe and Hannelie Coetzee."

"Take us through the cross again," says Sarah, speaking up for the first time. "What you said about religion."

Magrit gives a rapid-fire explanation: "We no longer live in a state ruled by Christianity, a government that forces its version of it on us for its own ends, like it did under apartheid. You know, in order for us not to question it. These days, now and again, a corrupt politician will still play the Jesus card if he thinks it'll keep him out of jail, but our constitution puts all religions on a par. Christianity no longer dominates politics and society. Trying to say something with a cross these days is passe. It's a simplistic idiom, an outdated rebellion. Couples live together before they get married, children are born out of wedlock. The rules have changed."

"Got it. Been there, got the T-shirt, moving on," says Sarah. "So it's no longer relevant to comment about religion."

"Yes. Especially not about Christianity. Islam is a different matter. It may become increasingly relevant as it spreads." Magrit points to the red cross. "So, this is not particularly clever or original. Unless the person doing it is very religious and it has particular meaning for him."

The knot in the pit of my stomach pulls tighter. Just what we need—some fanatic going around killing people.

Magrit looks at the photos again. "Two of the scenes suggest movement: a car, a bike. The red could be blood. Hate or rage. Or love. Especially if the murderer is working with obvious themes." She gently touches Janien's and then James's photos. "These two are special. They're more...they're bigger."

"More personal, maybe?" I ask.

"Yes. More challenging. More powerful and more shocking."

I say nothing about Swakopmund and the East Wind and the assumption of suicide which probably weakened the impact of the other two scenes. "Anything else?"

Magrit stares at the pictures. "Maybe. Give me a minute to think."

My phone rings. It's Isak.

I turn away, muting the conversation with a cupped hand. "Any news? Is it Leon? Do you have him?"

"No. He's already left the bar where he apparently ate something in a big rush. He also made a call on their landline. Did he phone you?"

"No."

The silence suggests he doesn't believe me.

"Isak, he didn't phone me."

"Fine. We'll carry on with the search. Bye." He sounds seriously pissed off.

"Wait. Can you please do me a favor?"

A moment of silence. "What?"

"We need to know who isn't in Carnarvon. Who was away last night? Think of Stefan, Fanus...especially those people who didn't want to give their DNA."

"So you still think the murderer lives in Carnarvon?"

"It's worth checking, isn't it?"

"I'll phone around, but I can give you a few names right now. Leon, Vonnie, and Obie weren't there. And Prof. Sieberhagen is in Bloemfontein for a conference. Fanus was at a specialist in Cape Town for his ankle and Stefan drove him there. And Sparrow isn't here, as you already know." He snorts. "Oh yes, and me."

He rings off without saying goodbye.

So, Stefan and Fanus weren't in town. Interesting.

Wait...I lean down toward the map again.

"Was that Isak?" asks Sarah.

No. It must be a mistake.

It has to be.

But it's not.

I follow the piece of red wool from Nottingham Road in the KwaZulu-Natal Midlands to Swakopmund, Namibia, stopping half-way.

Exactly where the two lines cross, small, but there, is a black dot marking the town of Vryburg.

SARAH

1

I will Sparrow to answer her phone, but it just keeps ringing.

"No luck," I tell Jaap. I throw my phone down on the desk.

Magrit is on the bed, crying, her face pale with worry.

I turn to her. "Give me your phone. Perhaps she just doesn't want to take my call."

She hands it to me.

Sparrow still doesn't pick up the call.

I shake my head, handing the phone back to Magrit. I look at my watch. It's just past one in the afternoon. Why isn't she answering? From what I can see on my computer, she's still in Vryburg and not back on the road. Her phone isn't switched off, she's just not taking any calls.

The phone I now suspect is Stefan's shows he's in Cape Town. Ungerer's phone is still off. Maybe it was stolen. Maybe he knows not to give away his position.

"Would it be possible for the killer to commit two murders in one day?" I ask Jaap.

He dips his head toward Magrit, his eyes flashing me a warning.

I point at my watch. We don't have time to spare her feelings.

I kneel down in front of the older woman. "Is there a motorbike in the barn, Magrit? Where James was working, under a tarp? I thought I saw one there earlier."

She nods, Jaap's handkerchief pressed to her mouth.

"Does it still run?"

"I...I think so. Why?"

"Get someone to fill it up. Use the petrol in your car if you have to."

She sniffs. "Why?"

"It's the quickest way to get to Vryburg. I can track Sparrow's phone. I'll find her."

"How would you...really?"

"Yes. But we can't waste time. Every second counts."

She stuffs the hanky into the sleeve of her cardigan and gets up. "You have to help her. Please. If anything happens to her...if this man..."

"I'll do my best, but we have to move."

She rushes out of the room, her face twisted in fear.

Jaap hurries to the door as if he remembered something. Opens it. "Magrit!"

I watch as she turns around at the top of the stairs.

"Did anyone sponsor James's exhibition?" I hear Jaap ask.

"Why does that matter now?"

"It's important for us to know, for Sparrow's sake."

"I received an anonymous donation. The man said he was a great admirer of James's work and that it was about time he exhibited again. It happened last year some time."

"Did this guy specify any date for the exhibition?"

"He asked for the second half of July, because he said he'd be abroad till then."

"Did he phone you?"

"Once. The rest of the time we communicated via email. The money was in my account before we even settled the deal."

"Who made the payment?"

"A Juan Visser. James said Visser bought some of his work two or three years ago, but he'd never met him. He said he'd heard the man was a recluse."

"Thanks, Magrit."

I hear her footsteps retreating down the stairs, light and quick.

Jaap walks back into the room. "You heard?"

"Yes. Juan Visser…it must be one of the ITFin Vissers."

"I'd guess so," he says. "I'll give the lead to Naidoo and Isak. Let's see what they come up with."

I open my backpack. Throw in my wallet, some underwear.

Jaap looks at me as though I'm mad. "You're not going to Vryburg on your own."

"The bike is the fastest way to get to Vryburg. There are no flights there. You and Brandt can follow in the car."

He shakes his head. "Brandt left ages ago. We'll take your rental Merc. It's too dangerous for you to go off on this wild goose chase alone."

"You should have thought of that earlier."

"I fucking know!" He looks at me with a mix of anger and regret.

I carry on packing my backpack. T-shirt. Laptop. I should have charged it. Revolver. Phone.

I slip on my jacket.

Jaap puts his hand on my shoulder. "Sarah. Just stop and think for a moment."

"What about?"

"What if Sparrow is luring us there? What if she's the killer?"

"And if it isn't her? Are you going to be the one to look Magrit in the eye and tell her her daughter is dead? Because there's no way I'm doing it."

He looks at his watch. "It's a nine-hour drive, maybe more." He gives a slow nod, blows out a slow breath. "Okay. Go. I'll be right behind you."

"Talk to Naidoo. Ask him to drive with you."

"I doubt he will. He's very skeptical about Addison's death."

"Then ask Magrit if S'bu can come with you. He's the foreman who helped me. He's calm and he's good with a shotgun."

"You know she's going to call Naidoo the minute we leave here, right?"

"Doesn't matter. The more police, the better." I can't be bothered with the irony of it all right now. "Hell, you can even ask the

Vryburg police to help. Tell them I'm on my way. They can go and look for Sparrow at whatever guesthouse or hotel she's staying at and hopefully prove all this panic pointless."

I want to take my backpack, but Jaap grabs my hand. His eyes have turned a dark, serious blue. "Just promise me you won't do anything stupid. Track Sparrow down and let me know where she is. Leave the rest to me."

"I'll do my best."

"Sarah. Please. I mean it. If something happens to you...your mother will never forgive me."

2

The motorbike is a Honda Fireblade, CBR1000RR. It's a monster of a machine and I'm going to have to know what I'm doing not to be thrown off. It belonged to Magrit's fiancé. When he died of a stroke two years ago, she parked it in the barn and never looked at it again.

It's freezing on the bike, but at least I haven't run into any rain yet. I ride as fast I can. There are too many manned speed traps on the N3 highway during the day to go faster than 140, 150 km/h and getting myself locked up is not going to help anyone.

I stop in Harrismith, down two Cokes and go to the toilet. Jaap says he and S'bu are on their way. He says Magrit hasn't yet managed to find out where Sparrow is staying in Vryburg. I tell him that I hope to get a location on her when I trace her phone again.

I stop whenever I need to fill up the bike. I turn off toward Senekal as the sun starts to set. Potholes become a problem, especially near Bloemhof. I ride as close as I can to the faded white line in the middle of the road in attempt not to lose too much time.

I stop just after Bloemhof. Stretch my legs and light a cigarette.

"Hi, Dad," I say to the night sky. "I'll try to stop smoking again tomorrow. Promise."

I flex my hands, tell myself the slight tremor is due to the cold, not the speed and the fact that I've almost fallen twice. The frigid air burns my ears and nose. I press my chin into my scarf, throw away the half-smoked Marlboro, and call Jaap. He says they're a little bit more than an hour behind me.

I call Sparrow. Her phone rings, goes to voicemail.

I call again. "Come on, answer."

The phone rings and rings.

I take out my laptop and trace the phone's location again. It's painfully slow, connectivity a trickle in this part of the world. Just as the screen lights up with a possible location, the phone is switched off.

"Wait...No! Don't...Shit."

I slam the laptop shut and get back onto the Honda. I'm too close to Vryburg to give up now.

An hour and a half later, just before ten, I enter the North West town. A bright, pale moon hangs over the small, sleepy settlement.

Immediately I'm faced with the next problem. Where do I start looking for Sparrow?

I ride through the streets. It takes just a few minutes to travel from one end of town to the other. I turn around and ride back through, hoping that I'm not attracting too much attention. The Honda and its roaring engine were made to show off.

At the Caltex gas station, an attendant watches me warily as I pass for the third time. I turn around, pull in at one of the fuel pumps and ask him to fill up.

"I'm looking for someone," I say while he pumps the gas. "It's an emergency. He drives an old white Nissan bakkie."

"Lots of white bakkies come through here," says the attendant. He sniffs, wipes his mouth with the back of his hand. He's probably in his twenties, with a nose that's been broken more than once.

"He has a short blonde woman with him. And the back of the bakkie is full of small dents at the back."

He releases the nozzle from the bike's fuel tank. "I remember a bakkie like that, but not a woman. Did it have Northern Cape plates?"

"Maybe." That probably rules Ungerer out. "What did the man look like?"

"White. Brown hair. Young."

Can't be Fanus then either.

"Where did he drive to?"

"Why do you want to know?"

"It's my sister. She's in trouble. This guy…he's bad news."

He nods as if he knows all about bad news.

I open my purse, flash the cash inside.

He eyes the bunch of pink fifties inside. Then turns and shows me that the bakkie left Vryburg the same way I entered town.

"What's on that road?" I ask.

"Farms. A school. That new private boarding school."

"Thanks." I pay for the petrol and give him R200 for his help.

I follow his directions out of town, park next to the road, at the last row of houses, and swing the backpack off my shoulder. Maybe I can try and trace Sparrow's phone again.

I open my laptop, phone Jaap while I wait.

"Where are you?" I ask.

"Another twenty kays. You?"

"Next to the road, just outside town. Near the school." The laptop lights up, a clear target in the pitch dark of the freezing night. "I'm trying to get a lock on Sparrow's phone again."

I stretch the tired muscles in my neck, open and close my hands. I'm going to be stiff from all this high-speed riding tomorrow.

"Magrit spoke to Naidoo once we left," says Jaap. "He's pissed off with us, to put it mildly. And she finally managed to find out where Sparrow is staying. It's a guesthouse just outside town. She checked with the owners, but apparently Sparrow never arrived."

"What time did she call?"

"A few hours ago. Six o'clock or so."

A gleam in the veld to my left draws my attention. "What the…?" A soft orange light is flickering in the distance.

I look at my watch. It's 11.01 pm.

"Sarah? Are you still there?" says Jaap.

"Must be a veld fire."

"What are you on about? Sarah?" I can hear the muffled sounds of Jaap and S'bu talking. Then he asks: "Where exactly are you?"

I explain while I keep staring at the light in the distance.

It's not a veld fire, I decide. It's something burning in one place. And as far as I can see, it's near the school where Sparrow is probably scheduled to have her interview tomorrow.

My laptop flashes a warning that my battery is almost flat, followed by an answer to my search.

"Sarah…What's going on?"

"Sparrow's phone is still dead."

Jaap swears. "Stay where you are. We're coming. We can start looking at the school and work our way back to the guesthouse. What's the school's name?"

"North West Academy of Excellence."

I hang up, type in the name. It's a small private school for Grades 8 to 12. Financed by Excellence Holdings, a smallish, JSE-listed company. I search some more. Sport. Academics. Educational philosophy. Sponsors.

Sponsors?

Surely not.

I open the tab.

Close my eyes for a second.

One of the school's sponsors is ITFin. They're donating sixty iPads and free afternoon classes in innovation and art as part of a three-year program.

Who the hell is this ITFin? And does it confirm that Sparrow was lured here as well? That she is not the killer?

Wait.

Something Magrit said suddenly jogs my memory. A Juan Visser sent her an email about sponsoring James Addison's exhibition. Could he be one of the two Vissers listed as the company's directors? Maybe I can find that out some other way.

The screen fades a little and warns me I have seven percent power left. The weak signal isn't helping either, every search running like cold syrup.

What's going to be quicker? Combing through Sparrow's email for details on the interview, or searching Magrit's inbox for info about the exhibition?

Sparrow's it is, I decide. I've spent some time inside her computer before and know my way around.

I work quickly, the laptop's battery indicator turning red.

Six percent power, and the last five percent means nothing anyway.

"Come on, come on!"

The machine warns me that it's about to go to sleep.

"No, no...five seconds...just five seconds!"

I get the IP address for the user that sent her the email inviting her to the interview, trace the location as best I can.

The laptop dies.

I slam it shut. Did I really see the name of the town correctly before the screen went black?

I put the computer away and fire up the Honda. Look again at the light in the distance. Must I wait for Jaap, or go?

I check my watch, then turn left toward the faint orange glow.

JAAP

1

Traveling gives you time to think, especially when you don't have to do the actual work of getting from A to B. That's why I don't care when Sarah takes the wheel. Or S'bu. Both of them are good drivers and they mostly keep quiet while they're doing it.

I drove the last two hours while S'bu slept and then handed him control of Magrit's Audi again.

I take out my notebook and switch on my phone's flashlight.

"Is this okay?" I ask S'bu. I don't want to wreck his night vision. He nods.

I page through my notes. I now know why *eNCA's* weather map got stuck in my head, but something is still bugging me.

I turn to a clean page and write the words: *Shoes. Red. Photos. ITFin and its directors, the Vissers.*

Shoes. Vissers.

Wait…isn't that someone's maiden surname? But whose?

I flip through my notes again. Nothing. Maybe I'll remember later.

I look at the words again.

Shoes. Vissers. Photos.

Shoes…that's it. Shoes that looked out of place. I take a bunch of papers from my jacket's inside pocket and page through the till slips and coffee-bar bills to the folded catalog from Henk's gallery. I find it on the third page: a photo of deep-red high-heel shoes with laces, kinky and modern.

Suddenly the Vissers make sense too. The call from the butchery.

I was right. My instinct has been right the whole time.

I call Vonnie.

She answers immediately. "Jaap. Do you have news about Leon?"

"No. Sorry." I soften my tone, bite back the impatience. "Vonnie, what happened to Janien's wedding shoes? Do you know? Can you remember?"

"What? Leon is out there somewhere and you want to know about Janien's shoes?"

"Yes. I can't explain right now but it may help him. Please."

I can hear the sheets rustle as she gets out of bed, Obie stirring next to her. She must have decided against her usual sleeping pill. Probably afraid she might miss any news about Leon.

A few muted footsteps. Then: "I wanted to burn them too, just like everything else, but they were gone."

"Did you ever see the shoes again after Janien…after her body was found?"

"No."

"They were a deep red, right? With laces?"

"Yes. I could only just convince Janien to wear a white dress. The red shoes were a compromise." She pauses. "Now I wouldn't care if she wanted to wear black from head to toe."

"I'm sure she knows that."

"I hope so. I hope she knows that I love her so much that it still makes my heart hurt like it did the day she was born and I first looked into her eyes."

A sharp intake of breath, a muffled cry, and then Vonnie ends the call.

I stare at the catalog in my hand. At the red shoes Tannie Queenie is wearing in one of Henk's photographs, the old woman proud, her back straight, and her eyes open and clear as the Karoo itself.

SARAH

1

I don't know much about small towns, but I'm sure a fire would attract attention, especially in a farming community in an area as dry as this one. No winter rains for the North West, only mild to warm days and often freezing nights. From what I've seen in the Honda's headlights the grass on the side of the road is a soft, brittle yellow, and I'm sure that extends well into the surrounding veld.

I turn off the Vryburg main road and follow a narrow, tarred road to the North West Academy of Excellence. Something tells me not to park near the school. I leave the bike about two hundred meters from the main gate, and call Jaap while I jog closer.

His cell is busy. I leave a message telling him where I am.

I take the revolver out of my backpack, make sure it's not cocked and tuck it into my left boot.

The school's newly painted blue gates are as high as the crown of my head, but there are toeholds and I can easily climb over.

I listen for footsteps, but it's dead quiet, except for what sounds like wood breaking and snapping as it burns.

Directly in front of me are two square, double-story buildings. To the right there is a soccer field and netball courts. The flickering flames I saw from the road are coming from between the two buildings.

I advance slowly to the building on the left; the darker one provides more hiding place.

The wind turns slightly and the smell of petrol reaches my nose. I look around to see where it's coming from. There's a big pile of wood not too far behind me. How did I miss it on my way in? It must be petrol that's making it gleam like that.

What the hell is going on? I peer around the corner of the building. There's a concrete square between the buildings. In the middle of it is a single young tree and what looks like a pyre.

No. Two pyres, with a stake planted in the middle of the second one. The first one is already burning high and bright.

The second pyre chills me to the bone. Sparrow. Tied to the stake, surrounded by a circle of wood.

She is wearing a blood-red dress, a cheap one that reveals more than it conceals, at both the neckline and the hem.

The weirdest thing though is the wings—white wings, with feathers, soaring probably two meters above each shoulder, like she's some kind of scarlet angel.

A light flashes once, somewhere on the right. Then twice more in quick succession.

I duck back behind the building, peer around the corner again.

Someone's taking photographs.

Is it him?

It is. He turns. I've never personally met Henk van Staden, but the emails on Sparrow's computer inviting her to the interview at the school were sent from Clarens, so I know it must be him. Plus, the Facebook photos I saw of him confirm his identity, even though he's shaved his beard.

He puts the camera down on the open back of a bakkie. Looks like the same Nissan bakkie I saw last night at Faure Manor House. He picks up an armful of wood and walks over to Sparrow, where he adds it to the logs around her feet. He does this five times, until the pile reaches up to her knees.

"Henk, please," Sparrow pleads. "Talk to me." Her body is shaking. The fear has worn her voice thin, making it shriller than I remember. "I'm sorry. Please. Just...please."

"No, no, no." He holds up a hand. "Shut up. You're ruining the photo."

He picks the camera up again. It flashes.

"Smile! I can't send the pictures to the papers with your face looking like that. You're the grand finale. The pinnacle of so many years' work. The point of it all."

Sparrow's arms wrestle with the black cable ties Henk has used to tie her to the stake. She spits something incomprehensible at him.

He laughs, looks at his watch.

I look at mine. It's 11:20. There are forty minutes left of the twentieth of July.

Henk takes something out of his pocket. Clicks it twice, three times, until a flame appears.

A lighter.

I retreat from the corner of the building, into the darkness, dig my phone out of my pocket and call Jaap. Still no answer. Where the hell is the bloody cop when you need him?

I leave another message. "The school," I whisper. "Come quickly. It's Henk."

I kill the call and return to my vantage point.

"Sparrow, the witch," says Henk, mockingly. "Sparrow, the angel. Your heart full of lies and deceit, just like every other woman's. I'm calling this one *Two Face*. It's the best one so far."

Sparrow frantically looks around for a way out. Again she pulls at the cable ties around her wrists, her ankles. For the first time I notice the rusted chain around her middle, shackling her to the pole.

"Did you take photos of everyone?" Her words are fast, raw.

"Yes."

"Janien too?"

"Yes. But she was dead already. They all were. You're different. You're special. But you know that already."

"Did you hurt her?"

Just as I wonder whether I should take out the revolver, my phone starts ringing.

Shit. I fumble for the device. Why didn't I put the fucking thing on silent?

Henk looks my way. Did he hear it?

"Who's there?" he calls. He inches closer to Sparrow, lighter in his hand. "Come out! If you don't, it's bye-bye birdie. Don't test me."

"Help!" Sparrow screams. She's still fighting against her ties, sobbing in frustration. "Help me, please!"

"The light, Jaap," I whisper hurriedly into the phone. "Follow the light. Keep your phone on."

I put my phone in my back pocket, the bright screen facing outwards in case my butt accidently ends the call. Then I stand frozen, wondering how to win time for Jaap to get here.

"Come out!" Henk shouts. "Jaap? Is that you?"

Sparrow starts sobbing.

I walk out from the shadows with hesitant strides. "No, but he's on his way."

Henk looks surprised, then angry. "Who the fuck are you?"

"I work with Jaap."

I approach him with slow, careful steps. Stop about six meters away from them. I can feel the heat of the fire from here.

Sparrow looks at me as if she's praying that the cavalry is right behind me.

You and me both, I think silently.

"Where's Jaap?" asks Henk. He peers past me into the dark night.

I don't answer. From here I can see that Sparrow's arms have started bleeding from her struggle with the cable ties.

Henk steps closer to Sparrow, his eyes locked on me. "Answer me! Where is he?" He pushes the lighter into her neck.

She freezes. For two, three seconds there's just the panicked heaving of her chest, her breath—fine, white, fragile—in the air.

"It's beautiful," I say.

Henk frowns.

"The cross. Gaborone, Swakopmund, the Midlands, Carnarvon, here. It's extraordinary."

Think, Sarah, I tell myself. You need bigger, better words.

"Each scene, so perfectly planned and so beautifully executed." I clear my throat. "They're all so striking. The red everywhere. Truly original."

Henk remains frozen, as though he doesn't know what to do. Clearly I wasn't part of his planning.

As I stand there, a single thought shoots up from my consciousness. Everything that has happened in the past few days—the past three years—suddenly comes together in my head, forming a clear picture: this is who Henk van Staden is. He is exactly as Sparrow described him. A deliberate, meticulous man. Someone who plans. Measures. Considers and reconsiders.

A businessman, not a bloody artist.

I take a breath. "ITFin? Is that your company? You had to find a way to get Jack Fist to Swakopmund. To get Sparrow to come here."

"Maggie." He says it softly. Firmly. "Her name is Maggie."

"I'm sorry. Maggie."

I can't believe this is why we're all here...because of Maggie. Sparrow. The woman Henk dated before Janien. The woman he really wanted. Sparrow, who said no, because, unlike Janien, she realized she wasn't into men.

"Maggie didn't ever really see you, did she?" I guess.

He doesn't look keen to talk. Instead he fidgets nervously with the lighter, his eyes locked on the darkness behind me.

How does he want to kill Sparrow? Light the fire he built around her without using M99 first, taking photos of his final artwork as Sparrow burns to death screaming?

"Henk?" Sparrow's hands stop their struggle. "I'm sorry," she pleads softly. "I'm really sorry. I'm so very, very sorry. If I had known..."

I nod at her, urging her to keep on talking till Jaap gets here.

"Henk. We could try again. I'm willing to try again. Aren't you?"

"Shut up!" He turns away from her and looks at me. "Where is Jaap?" He spits out the words.

"It was stupid of me. It was all a mistake. Janien too," Sparrow says in rapid-fire mode. "I'm sorry, Henk, I'm sorry!"

"Sorry?" He snaps his head back toward her, his voice like a whip. "You wanted nothing to do with me, because I supposedly didn't get you! Because you wanted someone who was like you, not someone who understood numbers better than Smithson and Kentridge. And then Janien was just like you, and so was everyone else at fucking Blink, all of them apparently better than me. All of them telling Janien to leave me. That she would be happier without me. That it's the right thing to do. The right thing? None of you knew what the hell that even looks like. Yolene fucked around with Ungerer, and he's married with two kids. And Addison drank like a fucking fish. Janien told me everything. Told me about you and her, and I could see it had all started with you. That you were the original sin. The fucking two-faced liar who corrupted my fiancée."

"I didn't realize, Henk. If I'd known...if I'd seen things more clearly...seen you for who you really are, I wouldn't have made those mistakes!"

"It all started with you. And it'll end with you." He lifts the lighter.

I step forward. "No! Just hang on a second. Henk!"

His thumb works the lighter.

Nothing happens.

He smacks it against the palm of his hand in an attempt to get it working.

He tries again. Laughs when the tiny yellow flame pops up.

Dies.

"Shit." He holds the lighter in front of Sparrow's face. Against her cheek.

I realize her hair looks wet. Petrol?

"Wait," I plead as I inch closer. "Just wait a bit now, Henk. Please."

Henk grabs Sparrow's chin in his hand and turns her head so that she's looking at him. "And of all the worst things Janien could possibly have done, she leaves Skout to you. That fucking whore.

Can you believe it? I help pay her bills, help her to set up *So What!* and that's how she repays me...she gives you her half of Skout.'

"You can have it," says Sparrow, crying. "What else do you want? I'll give it to you. Anything you want! Anything!"

"It's too late now." His thumb slides down on the wheel of the lighter again.

Sparrow tries to turn her face away, her entire body wrestling with the chain, the cables.

I bend down, my hand blindly seeking the butt of the revolver in my boot.

"Hey! What are you doing...stop!" Henk shouts at me.

Stupid mistake. Of course he would see me. Stupid, stupid mistake.

But it's too late now.

My hand locks around the revolver and pulls it free.

"I'm going to kill her!" The lighter spits a spark.

"Henk. Please." Sparrow's voice has become a desperate whisper.

"You don't want to do this," I call loudly and clearly. "Not like this. No one is going to know what you've done here. Only me, and that means nothing."

"They will know. The photos—everyone's photos—Janien, Fist, all of them. They'll all be online tomorrow. Didn't you know? I am about to be *So What Now?'s* latest, greatest artist.'

I aim for his forehead.

I don't want to shoot. Realize I can't shoot. Sparrow is in the way. And what if everything goes up in flames as soon as I pull the trigger?

JAAP

1

S'bu is driving as though the four horsemen of the apocalypse are breathing down his neck. He turns into the road that leads to the school, almost losing control of the car as he corners at speed.

I keep my own phone pressed against my ear, only vaguely hearing Sarah's voice as she talks to Henk. I call the police helpline using Sbu's phone, but 10111 is engaged. Then I type Isak's number on Sbu's phone and give it to him, telling him to explain to the detective what's going on when he answers.

I press my own phone tighter against my ear, but still I can't make out what Henk is up to.

It had to have been Bart van Staden, Henk's father, who called me from the butchery that night. Henk must have disappeared for quite a while during that pre-wedding braai, longer than the twenty minutes his parents had provided as his alibi.

And the Vissers of ITFin...Visser is Truida van Staden's maiden name. Henk's mother. How she fits into all of this, heaven knows, but I'm going to find out.

Next to me S'bu shakes his head, indicates to me that Isak isn't answering his phone.

A clusterfuck. That's what this is. One spectacular fuck-up.

S'bu slams on the brakes. The Audi's headlights illuminate the red Honda in front of us, then a set of blue school gates behind it.

"Stay here," I tell him.

"No. I'm coming with you." The giant man gets out of the car and takes his shotgun out from behind his seat.

I look at him over the Audi's hood. I'll be happy if he comes with me, but I also don't want him to get hurt. "You sure? Things could get rough out there."

"Yes. It's Mrs. Malan's daughter."

"Then I really hope you don't have any family."

"Three sons." He cocks the gun.

I shake my head. "Well then I bloody well hope you know what you're doing."

We rush to the gate. I motion to the right.

"Go around the school and see if you can find another gate. I'll try and talk to Henk and play for time. Maybe I can keep him busy so that you can grab Sparrow and make a run for it."

I rattle the lock on the thick chain woven through the steel, flex my leg to test my knee's stability. S'bu must have a sixth sense, because he puts the gun down and links his fingers together, making a step for me.

"Thanks." I climb over the gate and jump down the other side.

My knee collapses as I hit the ground.

I roll. Get up with difficulty. When I turn around, S'bu's gone.

I take out my pistol and jog as quickly as I can to the building nearest me. Glance around the corner. Take in the scene.

Sarah has her revolver trained on Henk, who has Sparrow in a tight grip, standing in the middle of what looks like a funeral pyre, another fire roaring nearby. And why the hell are there white wings strapped to Sparrow's back? They must be almost two meters long.

"Drop it!" I can hear Henk call. "I'm not going to say it again."

"Let Sparrow go," hisses Sarah.

I move a few steps forward, careful to remain in the shadows.

From here I can see that Henk is holding what looks like a lighter against Sparrow's neck. The smell of petrol is thick in the air.

She'll go up like a paper doll, especially with those wings on her back.

Henk is striking the lighter but it's not taking. It seems to be the only thing that's keeping Sparrow alive.

"I'm going to finish this!" he shouts. "I have to finish it. Everyone must see. After today, everyone will know."

"Know what?" Sarah asks sharply. I can hear the tension in her voice. The anger.

"Know that you're better than Jack Fist?" she continues. "Better than Addison? Sparrow? That she was too stupid to be with you? That Skout should have been yours? What the hell is wrong with you? Why did you have to kill four people to say that? Why not bitch on Facebook, like normal people?"

I limp forward, take a deep breath and step out of the shadows. "Henk! Let Sparrow go. Then you and I can talk."

I lift my pistol.

Henk turns on his heel. "So, you've finally arrived."

Sparrow looks at me, her eye wide and hopeful. Sarah doesn't turn around. It's as though she knew the whole time that I was standing behind her.

Henk tries the lighter again.

A spark, but no flame.

I move forward swiftly, quietly, ignoring the sharp pain in my knee.

"I don't want to talk, Jaap," he says. "I'm sick of talking. Especially to you."

Twenty steps between me and Henk.

I narrow the distance some more.

Eighteen.

Sarah is dead ahead of me on my left, motionless.

"Stand still, old man," says Henk. "I don't have time for your bullshit."

He looks at his watch.

I glance at mine—11:47. Maybe there's nothing wrong with the lighter. Maybe he's just playing with us, waiting for something. Midnight? A minute before midnight? It's possible. Henk planned every one of these murders down to the last detail.

I take another step toward him.

"Stop right there! I will kill her, Jaap." His thumb rests on the wheel of the lighter.

Now that I'm closer, I can see how he holds the Bic away from Sparrow's skin every time he flicks it, his other hand guarding her against the sparks.

He is definitely waiting for something. The right time?

He better hope he doesn't get caught up in his own plan. Petrol's not something to play with.

I spot S'bu only because I know where to look. He stands tight up against the building behind Henk and Sparrow, his shotgun aimed at Henk.

I indicate to him with a vague, quick gesture to shoot up into the air. Then rub my hand over my hair.

He gives me a thumbs up.

"Henk," I call. "The police are on their way. You won't get away with this and you know it."

I nod to S'bu.

Now!

He pulls the trigger.

The shot echoes around the buildings.

Henk falls to his knees. The lighter falls into the wood pile at his feet.

Sparrow sinks down the pole.

S'bu storms toward her.

I do the same, the pain like a thousand needles in my knee.

Henk roars as he frantically searches for the lighter in the flickering light of the fire behind him.

S'bu is struggling to free Sparrow from the chain holding her to the pole. Then he tries to lift it out of the ground so that she can slip the chain out from under it.

Sarah shoots. She aims high above the wood pile, over Henk's head, away from the petrol.

Henk sinks to his knees, but keeps digging around for the Bic. When he sees S'bu trying to help Sparrow, he lunges at the shotgun.

S'bu jerks it out of his hand. Hits him with the butt.

Blood blooms on Henk's face.

I run around them, looking to see if I can spot the lighter in the pile of wood at Sparrow's feet.

There it is.

I dive into the logs to reach it. Something in my knee twists, explodes in painful shards that cut into muscle and bone.

Henk pushes S'bu away and jumps on my back. My knee gives in, flattening me onto the concrete. He tries to grab my pistol, bites into my arm digging for the lighter.

"Ow!" I roll out from under him. Aim the Parabellum at his head.

But it's still too dangerous to shoot, so I use the gun to hit him in the face.

Blood splatters onto my neck, into my mouth.

"Jaap!"

Who's that calling? Sarah? No, it's S'bu. He has Sparrow over his shoulder and he's running toward the gate.

"No! Come back!" Henk is crawling toward them.

I want to stand up, but my knee gives way.

Henk spits blood. He gets up, jumps over the ring of wood and runs to the fire behind us. Comes back with a burning log.

I lift my pistol, fire once, but miss.

Henk holds the log to the wood pile near me. Flames leap up instantaneously.

"Burn, Jaap Reyneke. Fucking burn in hell!"

He runs with the log to another pile of wood, one at the far end of the buildings. One I didn't see before. It blazes up immediately, the flames running out in a straight line toward town.

I dive over the burning wood. Fall. Roll up on to my knee, my ears and hands red-hot. I roll in the sand, this way, that way. Lift my pistol, shooting blindly at the figure with the flaming torch disappearing in a haze of smoke and dust.

"Jaap!"

It's Sarah, running up from the gate.

What the hell?

"Stay away," I shout. "Go back. Get the bike and go get help."

"Sparrow is safe. She's at the car with Sbu. Come on. Leave Henk!"

Behind her another line starts to burn, this time in the opposite direction, away from town.

I stare in astonishment. The night is lighting up, bright as day.

The veld takes flame, the dry trees.

Henk appears from around the building behind us. "Come, Jaap! Come, old man, come and get me!"

He turns right with his burning log.

I struggle to get up. Push Sarah aside. Shoot.

Again.

Another line lights up, east, away from the gate.

Wind directions. That's what he's doing. Or is it another cross? I count three points rushing out toward the horizon.

"Jaap, shit. Come on! Please!" Sarah hooks her body in under my arm. "Leave him! We have Sparrow. We need to go. Who knows what else Henk had planned for today?"

I give in, and we hobble toward the gate.

"Where are you, Maggie? Hey? Are you watching?" Henk jams his torch into a pile of wood near the gate. It lights up immediately, flames leaping into the air. "Fuck Smithson. Fuck all of you who thought you were better than me!"

A new, fourth, fire line jumps over the gate toward the Honda and the Audi.

"Maggie!" he bellows. "Can you see?"

But she's gone.

"Maggie!"

Henk turns around, bewildered. Runs toward us, his shirt suddenly aflame.

Sarah lifts her weapon.

"Sarah, no!" I shout.

She mustn't kill anyone. She's not even supposed to be here.

She's supposed to be in Pretoria, at home with her mom and her computers.

I stumble in front of her. Crouch, dust in my throat, my hands on fire.

Aim.

Pray.

Shoot.

Henk stops. Sinks to his knees.

Keels over backward.

There are flames all around me. Four fire lines haring into the night.

Far worse is the smell of burning flesh.

Sarah is pulling at my arm, trying to help me to my feet.

"Next time I tell you to leave, you leave," I yell at her.

"Fuck that. You would never leave me, would you?" she snaps, but there's relief in her voice. "Henk? Is he…? Should we…?"

"I will."

I use her arm to pull myself upright.

Henk is rolling in the sand, the sound coming from his throat like that of a dying animal. Then he goes quiet.

I look at my watch. It's 11.59 pm, the twentieth of July.

I wake up in Vryburg's most expensive guesthouse. I feel like the old man I am. I struggle upright in the bed with its crisp white sheets and review the damage. My knee is buggered. It's swollen and blue, a creaky hinge that refuses to move. When I force it, even an inch, it hurts like hell.

The doctor in the emergency room said I needed to see an orthopedic surgeon. Sounds like it's going to cost a fortune. I'm sure some ice packs would do the job just as well—that and a handful of Myprodols.

My back is stiff, but a warm bath will fix that. Somewhat less easy to doctor at home will be the burns on my right leg, right ear, and both hands.

Sarah somehow escaped injury. She drove back to Pretoria in a hired car yesterday, just like that, without collecting her bike from *Lekkerkry*.

I want to leave for Kuruman as soon as the police are done with me. I may as well go and keep Vonnie and Obie company, although I don't see the point in hanging around there in the hope that Leon will somehow magically reappear.

But who knows, miracles are always possible, especially since all the news outlets are now carrying the story of Henk's death. Maybe Leon will read of it and realize he's in the clear.

Sparrow's wrists are badly cut, but luckily the wounds are not too deep. She says Henk surprised her when she arrived at the deserted school for the interview. She's in the hospital here in Vryburg, with a madly worried Jessica van Gaalen by her side. Sparrow was a little surprised about the sudden appearance of her roommate. Me, not so much.

Magrit is there too. She sent S'bu back with the Audi, the bike on a rented trailer, and said I could borrow her car to drive to Kuruman.

I limp to the bathroom, go through the cumbersome process of trying to pee with burned hands and a useless knee.

I flush the toilet and peer at myself in the mirror. Still as handsome as ever.

I put toothpaste on my toothbrush, which is another difficult process. I drop the toothbrush in the sink when the phone rings. It's Isak.

"Bart van Staden admits that he and his wife lied," he announces. "Henk was away from the party for much longer than twenty minutes. Bart thought Henk went to get a grip on himself because he was sick and tired of Obie and Vonnie—apparently he never really liked them. He spoke to Henk the next morning when he heard about Janien, but Henk swore high and low that he'd just gone to fetch more wood."

"And Bart believed him?"

"Bart says he was sure that Leon killed Janien, but I'm not convinced. He must have been worried, otherwise he wouldn't have called you and thrown that petrol bomb through the window at the *Courant*."

"Why didn't anyone at the party notice Henk was gone?" I ask. "I still don't get that."

"*Lekkerkry* is nearby. And Bart says Henk was gone for just under an hour. And by then, most of the people there were a bit drunk. It was a huge party, remember. It would have been impossible to keep track of any one person."

"Where's Bart now?"

"Under arrest. I don't even know whether he can afford bail. He and Truida needed Henk to make ends meet. He sent them money every month. Paid a heck of a lot of bills for them."

"And ITFin?"

"The company belongs to Henk, but he made his mother and her brother directors."

"Her brother? Isn't he in a home?"

"Yes. It was all just for show. Henk told Truida it provided some or other tax benefit for his business. He also admitted to her that he had to create ITFin to buy Skout from Yolene without her knowing that the interest in the app came from him. Yolene didn't like him at all, remember. Truida didn't mind. She was convinced that Skout belonged to Henk, that it should have been his reward for helping Janien and Yolene with the money to develop it."

I hear papers being shifted around, feel the question hanging in the air.

"So that's it," I venture when he keeps quiet. "Case closed."

He doesn't answer.

"What's up, Isak?"

"When did you know it was a series of murders and not just Janien? Was it before James Addison's death?"

"No. I got stuck on Janien and the DNA drive," I admit. "By the time I realized what was going on, it was too late."

"That redhead is quite something."

"I'll pass on the compliment."

"I hear she's been in prison. Cybertheft. Hacking."

I can't decide whether he's warning me, or surprised that I'm prepared to work with someone like that.

"She's brilliant," I defend her. "And she doesn't do that anymore."

"Then how did you know that call before the petrol bomb came from the butchery?"

"Didn't you tell me?"

"No, I...never mind." The sound of shuffling papers again. "Jaap?"

"Ja?"

"One last thing. Stay out of my town for a while, will you?"

"I will. Promise." And I think I mean it.

I'm sitting in a Wimpy restaurant, on my way to Kuruman, when Isak calls again.

His voice is dark.

"What's wrong?"

"Leon's been shot."

I put my coffee down and get up, wave to a waiter to bring me the bill.

"Where?"

"Other side of Kuruman. Vonnie and Obie are almost there."

"I thought you sent word that he's innocent?"

"It's near the border. Sometimes news takes longer to filter through to that part of the world. And Leon was aggressive. He stole a car when he saw the police and sped off. They caught up with him ten kays later. I can tell you now, he shoots much better than he drives."

3

Obie looks up as I walk into the waiting room of the Kuruman hospital, carrying yet another round of coffees. I hand him one of the flimsy paper cups.

"The doctor was here. Looks like Leon's going to be okay," he says. "It's just a shoulder wound. And he's a bit dehydrated."

"Thank goodness." I look at him. "What about Annemarie? I hear she's gone into early labor while you're all here."

"Yes, her mom let us know, but we can't be there right now."

I suppress a yawn. It's quite a distance to Kuruman, especially when you have to navigate a potholed road with burned hands. "Why don't you go and make sure she's okay? Go check up on your grandson. I'll take Vonnie back to the farm when we're done here."

"You sound like Leon. Annemarie will be fine." Obie tastes his coffee, pulls his face in disgust.

"Yes, I'm sure she will be, but she needs her family around her right now, and I think Leon would prefer it if at least one of you was with her."

He considers this.

"It's your grandson, Obie. Go. Vonnie will survive. So will Leon. You heard it with your own ears."

"Vonnie is very angry with you."

"I know."

"That's exactly it. You always know. And you and Vonnie always know better than everyone else. You're like two peas in a pod."

I don't argue.

"It wasn't your place to tell Leon about the adoption."

"I do—"

Obie lifts his hand to shut me up. "But we shouldn't have kept it quiet for so long either. Leon should have known a long time ago."

He puts the coffee down, gets up, and puts his coat on. "Thank you for Henk. I'd started to wonder whether it would make any difference to know who killed Janien. But it does. It matters a lot."

I nod.

"By the way. You'd better apologize to Vonnie," he says.

"I have."

"You don't know your sister very well if you think once is enough. This mess with Leon...he shot that policewoman. That's on you."

"I know. I'm sorry."

His face softens a little. "Maybe it's on all of us. And Leon needs to take some responsibility too." He gives a smile, a small wave. "But for now, I still prefer to blame you."

Vonnie doesn't say a word until we're almost at the farm. Leon is still in hospital, but she wanted to come back quickly to see little Oberhardt before returning to Kuruman for Leon's first court appearance.

"Jaap...this thing...I'm going to need time." She says as she stares at her hands.

"I understand."

"Next Christmas." Her voice is tight. "Come and visit us next Christmas."

I nod. "Okay."

She takes a deep breath and looks out of the window at the sun setting over the Karoo in every possible shade of orange. "And if anything happens to me before then..." She trails off with a little smile.

I smile with her. "I hear you."

That's exactly what our policeman father used to say when he was cross with us and had to leave for his shift.

If something happens to me before then, before I get back, remember that I still love you. Even if you are bloody naughty.

I take the final turn to *Lekkerkry*, fish the last Flake chocolate out of the shopping bag in the car door, pass it to Vonnie and ask for half.

SARAH

1

My mother slips quietly into my room just before noon. I know, be-cause I've been struggling to sleep since what happened in Vryburg.

I haven't told anyone about Henk and Sparrow and the fire. I figure it will get better with time. If that little bit of cliched first aid works for dead fathers, it should work for dead criminals.

"Ma?" I say.

"Sarah? You're awake?"

"Yeah."

"Good. I have something for you." She opens the curtains and sits down on the bed next to me.

I blink against the sudden light flooding the room. "What is it?"

She hands me a jewelry box. It is black and has a dark-blue rib-bon—my favorite color—wrapped around it.

"I don't know," she says. She tucks her graying hair behind her ears. She smells of lemons, sugar, and flour. "It's yours."

"Does Miekie even like the Aston?" I can't help but still be peeved about losing the sports car to my little sister.

"She's crazy about it. She wants to know when you can start teaching her to drive."

"That's about as scary as her starting to date."

I yawn. Study my mom as she sits motionless.

"Are you okay?" I ask her.

She shrugs, folds her hands into her lap. "I think so. Ja."

I wonder if I can believe her. I watch her surreptitiously, look-ing for a familiar gesture. Something I can grab hold of to be sure.

Some point of contact. Jaap says I'm not as bad with people as I think, but I'm not so sure.

"I'm sorry," I venture. "I'm sorry I ran away. That I wasn't here for you."

She moves one hand closer to mine where it lies on the bed, then stops, as though she's unsure how I'll react to her touch.

I reach out and give her fingers a squeeze. "Tell Miekie to be ready for her first lesson on Sunday."

"Have lunch with us then. Geo will be here. He misses you. We all miss you."

"That'll be nice."

She points at the box. "Open it. It's been long enough."

I tug at the ribbon and lift the lid.

My mother gets up, although I'm sure she's dying to know what's inside. "Lunch is in a bit," she says before closing the door.

I don't answer. Just lie there staring at the contents of the little black box.

I unfold the tiny scrap of paper inside. Read the single-sentence letter in my dad's almost illegible handwriting, and laugh.

And then, finally, I cry.

Where the hell is Jaap?

I knock on the door of his townhouse in Centurion. He's here. His phone says he's here. So does the blaring TV and that furious barking from inside.

"Jaap!"

Eventually I hear a voice. Good thing, because the gray-haired tannie next door looks like she's about to drop her little garden fork and call the police.

The door swings open and Boris the Labrador runs out to greet me.

"Why are you shouting?" Jaap has the remote control in his hand. It's Saturday afternoon, rugby time, and he's wearing a light-blue rugby jersey.

"Are the Bulls winning?" I ask.

He mumbles something, spots the cooler bag at my feet.

"Aren't you going to invite me in?" I ask.

"Only if there's beer in that bag."

"Among other things," I lie.

He waves me inside, limps to the easy chair, and lowers himself into its worn upholstery. "Lock the door behind you, will you?"

I fight the urge to give him hell about the crutches gathering dust in the garage. If he wants to suffer, then he must suffer.

"Why aren't you watching the game with your cop buddies?"

"I'm not in the mood for them today."

I carry the cooler bag to the open-plan kitchen. The counter is spotless and the oven off. "What happened to the whole cooking thing?"

"I'm at soufflés in *Cook and Enjoy It*. Who the hell can make soufflés?" He looks at me suspiciously. "What's going on?"

I take the chocolate cake out of the cooler bag and a candle out of my pocket, planting it in the icing. Wave him over.

"You have to come and blow out the candle."

"What the…? Have you been snooping around my stuff again?"

I light the pink candle. I couldn't resist the color when I had to choose one from my mother's selection this morning. "Happy birthday, grumpy old man."

He groans as he gets up. "I don't want to have birthdays anymore."

"Sixty is not so bad."

"Only people who are twenty-five ever say that."

"How do you know how old I am?"

"Do you really think you're the only one who knows how to dig up information on people?"

I look at him pointedly.

"Okay, okay. I looked in your wallet while you were sleeping in Clarens. And I read your file—what's left of it. Good old-fashioned police work."

He turns down the volume on the TV.

"Hurry up." I cup a hand around the flame. There's a draught from the back door. "Did Doris get hold of you? She says you owe her a visit. And soon. She says Swakop is lovely at this time of year."

He grunts something I can't make out, limps closer, bends down, and blows out the candle. "Did you bake it?"

"My mom helped. But I reckon you better taste it before you dish out any compliments."

I give him a knife from the cooler.

He takes it. Stops. "And that?" He points at my right ear.

I touch the single little silver ring. There are still six in my left ear, one for each member of my family, but now there's one in the other ear too.

"It's a gift. From my father."

"Just the one?"

"Yes."

"It's a rather strange gift," he says.

I watch as he cuts the first slice of cake and lifts it in the air.

I lean forward to inspect the texture. Better than expected. Not as light as my mother's, but pretty good for a first time.

"Sarah? The earring? Did your dad say why?" He juts his chin in my direction.

Always the detective. "Apparently it's for balance."

"Huh?"

"That's what he wrote."

And *Love, always, Dad.* But Jaap doesn't need to know that.

ACKNOWLEDGMENTS

This book was partially inspired by the DNA artwork of Heather Dewey-Hagborg, and the investigation into the murder of Marianne Vaatstra, in the Netherlands.

I would also like to express my gratitude to the former Gauteng Deputy Provincial Commissioner of Detective Services, Crime Intelligence, and Visible Policing, Major General Bushie Engelbrecht, as well as retired Brigadier John Lambert, from Forensic Services, for their very kind assistance in writing this book.

ABOUT IRMA VENTER

Irma Venter is a journalist and thriller writer. She loves traveling, Labradors, good coffee, excellent whisky, and expensive chocolate—not necessarily in that order. She writes books about strong women, interesting men, and that fascinating space between right and wrong.

www.ingramcontent.com/pod-product-compliance
Lightning Source LLC
Chambersburg PA
CBHW031815210425
25265CB00008B/4